Instant silence and the tableau froze in front of him.

The children were seated cross-legged on the floor, their faces rosy in the dying rays of sunlight. The baby lolled in the crook of Beth's chubby arm; she was holding his hands to show him how to clap the complex rhythms of the dance.

Mistress Taverner and her grandmother were standing in the centre of the room. Nona so short and stocky, with her tiny, wrinkled face: Doll all height and austere beauty. Both were breathing rapidly, and their cheeks were flushed. For a brief moment, as the door opened and their movement stopped, Josiah glimpsed the pleasure on his wife's face, and her happiness cut him to the heart more cruelly than the look of anger which swiftly replaced it. Never once had he seen her happy in his presence.

The Puritan's Wife

Joanna Hines

CORONET BOOKS
Hodder and Stoughton

First published in Great Britain in 1996
by Hodder and Stoughton
First published in paperback in 1997
by Hodder and Stoughton
A division of Hodder Headline PLC
A Coronet paperback

10 9 8 7 6 5 4 3 2

British Library Cataloguing in Publication Data

Hines, Joanna
The Puritan's Wife
1. English fiction - 20th century
I. Title
823. 9'14 [F]

ISBN 0 340 65367 1

Printed and bound in Great Britain by
Cox & Wyman Ltd, Reading, Berkshire

Hodder and Stoughton
A division of Hodder Headline PLC
338 Euston Road
London NW1 3BH

**For my son
Peter**

Chapter 1

❧

On a morning crisp with winter sunshine, the Taverner family were, unusually, all gathered in the winter parlour of the Priory House while Thomas the painter put the finishing touches to the portrait he had been working on since the beginning of the year. The windows were feathered with frost, a slow fire wheezed in the grate, the children scratched and fidgeted.

This last sitting was, strictly speaking, unnecessary. Thomas had brought them together just one more time for his own curiosity: he wanted to see if he could at last fathom the riddle of this apparently commonplace, yet most unusual, family.

Nothing in his patron's appearance hinted at a mystery. On several occasions Thomas had had to suppress a temptation towards caricature: just a touch more fullness in the lips or a slight exaggeration of the deep-set, watchful eyes and he would have created a cruel satire on the pitfalls of greed and complacency. But Josiah Taverner did not inspire levity. Although of medium height, he exuded an aura of slow power, almost of menace, with his suspicious eyes and his massive, fleshy jaw. His head, slightly too large for his body, was topped with thinning, cinnamon-coloured hair. He appeared oblivious to anything but profit and self-advancement, his body was grown heavy and sluggish with success.

Thomas shifted his attention, with some relief, to the representation of the merchant's wife. He had spent twice as long on his efforts to represent Mistress Taverner, recalling her many times for sittings. Partly because he appreciated objects of beauty, and the mistress of the house was beyond doubt a pleasure to behold; but he was also driven by a desire to pin

1

down the elusive quality which made her more than just another handsome woman.

Though handsome she undoubtedly was. She had the dark good looks of her Spanish origins: black hair drawn back from a high forehead, finely arched eyebrows, and those quite remarkable eyes . . . bewitching eyes, Thomas had thought when he contemplated her first. He knew she had been only fifteen when she first came to Tilsbury with her husband, and even now she could be no more than twenty-seven or eight. Various rumours were current locally to explain why a Protestant mercenary had returned from the German wars with a Spanish-born wife who was hardly out of childhood, but he had found none convincing.

If her past was a mystery, then so too were her thoughts. Once, when she had been sitting for her portrait and staring at nothing in particular, Thomas had observed that her eyes were brimming with tears.

'Is there something wrong, Mistress Taverner?'

She had turned to him with genuine surprise. 'No. Why?' A single tear rolled down her cheek.

'But you are weeping.'

She shrugged her shoulders. 'Maybe the smell of your paints troubles my eyes.'

'What were you thinking of?'

'Nothing. My mind was quite empty.'

Thomas had gradually realised that his subject's innermost thoughts were hidden even from herself. Sometimes, especially when she was with her children, he could see on her features the fifteen-year-old girl who had had to begin a new life in a strange town in a foreign land. At other times he thought from her expression that she had never yet been young.

Pale sunlight was filtering through the windows; the children shifted impatiently from one foot to the other. It was a shame, Thomas mused, that the older two resembled their father so closely. That same fuzz of cinnamon hair, the unprepossessing, almost frog-like features. Their fair chubbiness was charming now but would soon slide into corpulence. Only the younger boy, Philip, had inherited his mother's looks; with his black hair and eyes, and a bantam's fierce pride, he was the pampered plaything of his older brother and sister and the bane of his mother's life. Of the baby, scarcely six months and stiffly cocooned like a little silk worm in his swaddling bands, it was too soon to tell.

Thomas sighed. He had grown fond of this winter parlour where his paints and easel had been placed for the past two months. Like the rest of the Priory House it was sparsely furnished but its oak-panelled walls and handsome fireplace needed little adornment. On a chilly March morning like this there were the clean smells of wood smoke, beeswax and fresh rushes. But no matter how seductive the charms of this house, he could no longer spin out the commission. His work was done and in a day or two he must quit this tranquil town in the valley and seek employment elsewhere.

He dipped his brush in a shining blob of dark paint and, very carefully, began to write his signature just below Mistress Taverner's slippered foot. '*Thomas* ...' he wrote carefully. Usually the single word was sufficient: he stripped his name, like his possessions, down to a minimum to suit his itinerant life – but after a moment's hesitation he added a second word, '*Talpa*'. Thomas the Mole. He had never assumed such a title before, and hoped never to have reason to do so again; but he felt the need to record for posterity his unorthodox employment during his weeks at the Priory House.

He glanced for the last time at the family group assembled before him. Master Taverner was, if anything, more puffed up than ever: like those of some squat and greedy bullfrog his jowls seemed to be expanding to trumpet his success. His wife in contrast remained remote and austere, seemingly unaware of the lavish array of jewellery her husband had insisted she wear. As always, her thoughts were unreadable.

The children's thoughts were only too evident. Every variety of boredom was displayed on their faces. Harry, the eldest, leaned forward and whispered something in his little brother's ear. Philip's black eyes were instantly bright with the prospect of mischief.

Out loud, for the benefit of the adults, Harry offered the bribe. 'Not long now, Pip. You may have first ride on Bonnet after.'

Philip jigged up and down with excitement. 'Bull's pizzle!' he exclaimed, 'Bull's pizzle, izzle, izzle, izzle, izzle!'

Harry and Beth dissolved into giggles. Pip, who had no idea what he was saying except that it was deliciously shocking, was thrilled. Master Taverner merely frowned. His wife said, 'Really, Pip,' and tapped her son lightly on the top of his head, but her smile showed that she had been as bored as the children. From the first, Thomas had realised that the Taverners were

3

startlingly indulgent parents. The affection that neither showed for the other was lavished on their happy little family.

Thomas took pity on them all. 'There,' he said, ''Tis done.'

Harry, Beth and Philip at once exploded into a whirl of skipping and stretching and whooping until Mistress Taverner, who had handed the still-sleeping baby over to her grandmother, stopped their exuberance with a firm dismissal. The stairway echoed with their footsteps, upstairs a door slammed shut, and then there was silence.

Master Taverner rose from his high-backed chair and came over to appraise the finished work, examining it with that ponderous way of his that Thomas had found so irritating. 'Well,' he said, 'You've wasted no time, I like that.'

Thomas realised he must expect no praise for the beauty of his achievement from his patron. He glanced towards Mistress Taverner, who had moved to stand at a little distance from her husband. To his surprise she was gazing at her painted image as if at an enemy. He wondered briefly if she might be disappointed at the way he had represented her, but no, it could not be that. Although he had failed to capture the layers of expression he had glimpsed from time to time, her beauty was displayed for all to see.

'It displeases you, Mistress Taverner?'

She turned to him suddenly, with that dipping gesture of her head, as though seeking to free herself from the necklace at her throat, and her expression changed completely. Unlike her husband, she at once recognised his need to hear his achievement praised before parting from it for ever.

'You should be proud of your skill, Thomas,' she told him, before adding in that low, slightly accented voice she had, 'You are a lucky man, Thomas. You will leave something behind you in this world when you go.'

There was a hint of regret in her words, but before Thomas had a chance to wonder at them, she had swept from the room on a rustle of silk skirts.

Josiah Taverner had been nodding his approval as his wife spoke, and his smile was now a fraction more satisfied than before. Thomas realised that his patron was that rare thing, an older man with a young and beautiful wife, who, far from being threatened by other men's interest, actually revelled in their envy. He must have no doubts about her loyalty. A lucky man indeed.

4

Thomas would have been astonished had he witnessed Mistress Taverner's actions on leaving the winter parlour. Ignoring Mabs from the kitchen, who was coming to her with a question about dinner, she almost ran up the wide stairs and across the landing into her bedchamber, flinging the door shut behind her. Gasping for air, she struggled with the catch on the necklace that had lain around her throat all morning, tugged at the rings on her fingers, the bracelets that had adorned her wrists. Why should jewellery be fashioned to resemble items of restraint? Chains and manacles and the harness of dumb animals. Decorations for a toy, a doll. It was Josiah who had insisted she display his wealth, plunder brought back from his years as a mercenary in the European wars. Perhaps it was only fitting that his booty should be displayed on the person of his wife, most exotic of all his trophies.

She bundled the treasures into a little casket that stood on an oaken chest, turned the key in the lock and went to stand at the window, leaning her forehead against the cool glass and gazing down into the wide street below. Gradually her breathing grew easier, the tide of frenzy receded. The agitation Thomas had observed on her face had settled into a hopeless desperation.

She avoided looking at the portrait after that. She loathed it, loathed it for that self-same permanence that was so prized by her husband.

Ever since her arrival in this tranquil valley she had seen herself as a temporary exile from the land of her birth. Like the migrant birds she would fly south again one day. But the portrait told a different story. The woman who sat in the centre of that formal family group was rooted in this soil for ever more. With her English husband and her English clothes and her English children, the actor had become the part she played.

It was late afternoon by the time Thomas was ready to leave. He had few possessions and he dawdled only because he was in no hurry to confront the outside world again. He was half hoping that Master Taverner – or, more probably, his wife – would offer him lodging for one more night. Getting about the country had been hazardous at the best of times; after more than two years of civil war it was now downright dangerous.

He found Mistress Taverner coming out of her stillroom. She locked the door behind her and then turned to him with a smile. 'Are you leaving us, Thomas? Where will you go now?'

'To the King's court at Oxford, perhaps. Or to Bristol. I have no desire to travel far.'

'But you have no fixed plans?'

'I'm better off without them,' he said ruefully, 'I'll spend this evening at The Lion, and if I'm lucky I'll find someone to travel with me. I don't relish going alone.'

'I wish we could offer you further work here. But our portraits are all done.'

Thomas said tentatively, 'I could always paint your grandmother.'

'Nona?' Mistress Taverner was startled by the suggestion. 'Why would anyone want a picture of an ugly old woman?' Her expression softened as she thought she understood him. 'For a moment, Thomas, I thought you were serious. What an idea! And Nona would hate it. She'd believe you wanted to steal away her spirit.'

Thomas pretended to share her amusement, although his suggestion had in fact been far from frivolous. The face of the old grandmother, so wizened and ruthlessly intelligent, had fascinated him from the beginning. He had even amused himself with a few preliminary sketches. Now he was intrigued by the notion that the crone would regard a portrait as a threat. Among some of the more superstitious inhabitants of Tilsbury, he knew, Mistress Taverner's unusual grandmother was credited with supernatural powers, and her stillroom cures were highly prized. Some people claimed she could see into the future, or locate missing objects. Even Master Taverner seemed to view her with a certain wary respect. Only his wife was apparently dismissive. The two women bickered constantly, but there was an unmistakable closeness between them. Thomas found it all most perplexing.

Doors banging at the back of the house, shouts and footsteps on the stairs signalled the children's return from their afternoon outing. The old woman was fussing round them like a little black hen as the groom transferred them to her care, and the children gave shrill and conflicting accounts of their adventures.

Mistress Taverner was listening to the rumpus. 'I must go,' she said, 'I hear the baby waking.' She raised her hand, and Thomas noticed that she held a small flask; its label read only, '*For Thomas*'. 'Here, I have prepared this for you, in case the fever ever returns. But remember, this is for your benefit alone. It would not work so well for anyone else.'

Thomas was touched. He had fallen ill during February and Mistress Taverner had nursed him carefully. 'Now I know I shall be safe. And may you, Mistress Taverner, and your fine home, be for ever unaffected by this wretched war.'

'Unaffected?' Her dark eyebrows were raised in mock disbelief. 'Two of our best servants have been lured off into the fighting already, and we ourselves have been taxed half out of existence.'

Thomas thought of the busy kitchen and the well-stocked cellar, the regular meal times and the placid, unchanging pattern of her family's days. He said, 'But your home has been spared, even so. There have been no soldiers here yet.'

'I should think not.' Mistress Taverner dismissed the notion briskly, 'Nor will there ever be. Didn't you know? My grandmother cast a spell on this house years ago. Any soldier who tries to enter will be instantly deprived of all his strength. Have no worries on our account, Thomas.'

As he bid her farewell, Thomas considered it possible that Mistress Taverner herself half-believed in the myth of her family's invulnerability. He remembered the devastation and suffering he had seen last year in other homes and towns not so very far from here, and he offered a silent prayer that time would prove her right.

Josiah Taverner was to be found in the small room to the side of the house from which he conducted his business affairs. Thomas had only entered this room once before, on the day of his arrival in mid January. He had not liked it then and he did not like it now. Whereas the rest of the house was elegant and airy, this back office was gloomy and cluttered with papers and boxes. In this room it was wealth, grabbing it and holding on to it and adding to it, that was all important.

And now Josiah Taverner was sitting behind his crowded desk and patting his round stomach thoughtfully and talking about money. Not a word about the merits of the painting, only the various methods by which the bill might be paid. Thomas listened courteously, but soon he began to be depressed by the sensation that he was being made a party to the other man's obsession. He had to fight down a sudden urge to distance himself from this transaction by refusing any payment at all. But such high-handedness was a luxury he could not afford. He was scarcely in a position to venture into the world with only

7

Mistress Taverner's fever syrup to maintain him.

He realised the man was offering to give him a bond redeemable at the house of one John Rolfe, a London business acquaintance.

'You may have it in coin if you prefer,' said Master Taverner, reasonably enough, 'But in my opinion it is a mistake to carry money at a time like this. The roads are crawling with cut-throats.'

'I was not planning to go so far as London.'

'London is safe enough once you're there. For the present. I heard there's a couple of Welshmen come to The Lion today who are headed that way. They'd doubtless be glad of a third.'

'Then I bow to your judgement.'

Josiah Taverner nodded. He signed and sealed the document he had already prepared, and handed it across the wide table.

'And now, as for that other matter. I have given this some thought. Your payment is not so much for the work itself, which was negligible, as for your discretion. Secrecy is all.'

'I know that, Master Taverner. And I gave you my word.'

'Yes, yes, yes. But promises have an unfortunate habit of being broken.'

'I shall ignore that insult, sir, which I have done nothing to deserve.'

'Once this confounded war is done, the secrecy will be irrelevant. I propose giving you a further draft which will be redeemable only after the cessation of hostilities and only if you have kept your side of the bargain.'

Thomas felt a flash of rage. 'Strange, Master Taverner, that you never thought to mention this caveat when I agreed to do your secret work.'

'I will increase your fee because of the delay in payment. More than that, I will not do.'

'Very well.' Thomas was sick at heart. Always the creation of a work of art ended with this sordid haggling. 'The painter will take his fee now. Thomas Talpa, the mole, must bide his time.'

He watched as Master Taverner drew up a second document for the London merchant. As had happened from time to time over the past couple of months, Thomas felt an unexpected surge of pity for the man. He had the churlishness of someone who has never learned the trick of being liked. Thomas thought he understood at least a part of his cynicism. Like himself, Master Taverner had apparently been reared in the Catholic

8

faith. Both men had abjured the religion of their families. Thomas had found a substitute of a kind in the creation of physical beauty. He guessed that for Josiah Taverner the accumulation of wealth and power was now his only true Gospel. He disliked him, he felt sorry for him, and he was heartily glad to be leaving him.

It was only as the heavy door swung shut behind him, that he heard the sound of singing begin in an upstairs room.

Josiah had heard the singing too. As soon as he was sure the painter had gone, he stood up and went to the door of his room, pushing it open gently. The sound was louder. For some moments he remained without moving, his large head slightly to one side. There was a rhythmic, irregular clapping, the stamp and beat of feet. And there was the song itself: a song both harsh and yet melodic, a song that many might have called discordant, but which contained within it a haunting beauty. A song that had no more business in this quiet valley in the midst of England than did a bird of paradise.

The voices of the two women moved from unison to harmony and then back to unison as they repeated the familiar undulating phrases. Its cadences were filled with both triumph and yearning. A defiant, pagan song it seemed to Master Taverner as it echoed through his respectable merchant's house.

Though he heard it seldom enough, the strange music had been a part of his life ever since his wife and her grandmother came here. In theory, of course, Josiah disapproved, but he made no effort to silence the women. Now he found his mouth was suddenly dry. And then, although he knew it was futile, he could not resist the urge to tread softly up the wide flight of stairs and across the landing. He stopped outside the door of the first floor chamber which Nona shared with Philip and the baby.

Here he stopped. His heartbeat seemed to be keeping time with the clap of hands and stamp of feet. He would have put his eye to the crack around the door, but he had tried that in the past and he knew it was futile. For years he had been reduced to skulking and spying in his own home. He despised himself for his weakness, hated the women for reducing him to this beggarly state. He pressed his palms against the smooth oak of the door and closed his eyes. He would have been praying, had he thought there was any point to it. Such a haunting, hypnotic song: it could drain the heart from a man and leave him with nothing but madness.

The singing and the stamping and the clapping wove their disjointed rhythms through every nerve in his body until he could endure it no longer; he turned the handle and the wide door swung open.

Instant silence and the tableau froze in front of him.

The children were seated cross-legged on the floor, their faces rosy in the dying rays of sunlight. The baby lolled in the crook of Beth's chubby arm; she was holding his hands to show him how to clap the complex rhythms of the dance.

Mistress Taverner and her grandmother were standing in the centre of the room. Nona so short and stocky, with her tiny, wrinkled face: Doll all height and austere beauty. Both were breathing rapidly, and their cheeks were flushed. For a brief moment, as the door opened and their movement stopped, Josiah glimpsed the pleasure on his wife's face, and her happiness cut him to the heart more cruelly than the look of anger which swiftly replaced it. Never once had he seen her happy in his presence.

For a few moments all was fixed and still, and the silence was so intense that Beth almost imagined she could hear the dust motes dancing on the pink sunbeams, then there was a loud clatter of pots from the kitchen below and the spell was broken. All at once his wife smiled and took a step towards him.

Josiah said, 'Don't stop on my account, Doll dear,' though knowing all the time it was useless, 'I have no wish to spoil your entertainment. Carry on, carry on.'

He could not prevent himself from adding to his humiliation by grinning oafishly all the while.

'Tst,' she dismissed his plea with a wave of her hand. 'It was just a piece of womanish nonsense. You have far better ways to spend your time.'

'But I would—'

'Besides,' she interrupted him, 'We've finished.'

Harry and Beth, looking from one parent to the other, were aware of the struggle taking place beneath the smiles. Beth was suddenly miserable, without knowing why, and Harry felt that he had been caught in an act of unintended betrayal. As he was nearly eleven, he did not know if he still wanted to be included among the women and children of the household, even if it meant forfeiting the rare enchantment of the dance. But Philip, too wrapped up in the music's lingering spell to notice anything else, began singing to himself in childish imitation of the women's voices, and drumming his fists against the floor boards. His mother whirled about and tapped him on the head.

'That's enough, now, Philip. It's finished.'

'But—'

She snapped her fingers and glared at him. His protests died. The children scrambled to their feet.

Harry, tucking his thumbs into his belt, went to stand beside his father. 'It was nothing much, Father,' he said, in his grown-up little-boy's voice. 'Just something to amuse Pip and the baby, really.'

Josiah did not even look at him. 'Go on downstairs, Harry. Take the others with you.'

Harry hesitated. His mother was regarding them coldly, her eyebrows raised in a manner that appeared almost contemptuous. Beth had gathered up Pip and the baby and was preparing to leave the room. Suddenly Harry feared to leave the adults alone.

'Go on, boy. Time to prepare for evening prayers.' His father spoke more harshly.

Dragging his feet, Harry left the room, followed by the other children, and the door closed behind them.

In the west-facing bedroom, no one spoke. Doll Taverner remained motionless; the old woman waited impassively as Josiah struggled to control his emotions.

Years ago, when young Harry himself had been no more than a baby, Josiah had tried to bribe his young wife to dance for him. He was ashamed to think how he had humbled himself, the treasures he had been prepared to offer her. But she had refused, had wrapped herself around in silence, apparently compliant and yet utterly unreachable. Later she had told him that in the country of her birth such dancing was only for the eyes of women and young children. He was not sure that he believed her. Sometimes he thought that if, just once, he could watch her while she danced, then the hold she had over him would be broken.

And today, of all days, he had reason to wish to be free of that spell.

'Dance for me, Doll.'

Her eyebrows lifted a fraction higher. 'Why waste time asking? You know I will not.'

'I could command you.'

'Do as you wish. I will not dance.'

'I can force you.'

'Never.'

She was not defying him, so much as stating a simple fact. That was what Josiah found impossible to endure.

He never knew what he had been intending to do, only that the frustration boiling inside him was suddenly unbearable. He picked up the nearest object to hand, a tapestry-backed chair, and took a step towards her.

'Dance, when I tell you.'

Doll lifted her chin a fraction higher and stood her ground. 'The dance is over, Josiah.'

'No! This time you will—'

He did not finish. The old woman had slid between them. Her head was tilted back, her eyes were half-closed so only the whites were showing, and she was muttering feverishly, repeating the words that Josiah had heard from time to time over the years, but had never properly understood.

'Be quiet, stop I tell you, stop!' but now his fury was impotent. The chair dropped from his hand and he raised an arm to shield his face from the old woman's unseeing eyes. He was gasping for breath.

'Damn you, make her stop!' He sank down on the chair, clutching at his chest, his fingers scrabbling to undo the buttons of his doublet, which was suddenly grown too tight.

He never saw the little smile that flitted across Doll's face before she came and knelt beside him.

'Here, let me. You should not excite yourself, my dear.' He attempted to push her away, but found he had not the strength.

Nona, an ordinary little old woman once again, had fetched him a glass of water from the jug in the corner of the room. Gradually Josiah recovered his breath and his composure. As soon as he was strong enough, he brushed aside his wife's offers of help and hurried down the stairs to the large hall where the household was waiting for him to guide them in their evening prayers. Because he had been frightened and ashamed, Josiah was unsparing in his religious zeal that evening. The sound of his own deep voice, more confident and louder than all the rest, was reassuring to him.

But even so he could never forget that the wife who followed him into the room, the demure young woman who sat next to him in her dark dress with the plain white collar and appeared faultless in her show of piety, was as elusive as quicksilver, nor that he became a grotesque buffoon in the face of her infinite indifference.

Chapter 2

~

It was late, the house had lapsed into silence, and Doll herself was nearly asleep when her husband came to his bed. She knew as soon as he came in, knew almost from the sound of his footsteps on the stair, what was on his mind. At once she was wide awake, and tense, cursing herself for not having read the signs earlier in the day. Her distress at the portrait must have made her careless or she would have seen how Josiah reacted when she was talking to Thomas in the winter parlour. Instead she had sought solace in the luxury of dancing, and that too had been a mistake; she should have waited until Josiah was absent from the house. The sound of their music always excited him. But his attentions had been so rare since her last churching that she had grown lax: she could have slipped a few drops of herb grace in his evening drink; she could have made sure she was occupied with the baby. Sometimes it was enough simply to feign sleep. Now it was too late.

He was undressing by the warmth of the fire and humming cheerfully: he always hummed when his mind was set on nocturnal satisfactions. Doll closed her eyes so as not to see his naked body, round and pink and bristling with hairs like a pig before slaughter, then forced herself to open them again.

Now he was dressed in his nightshirt, and smiling. Doll looked away, avoiding his eyes. Josiah noticed her gesture, and he recognised also the disgust that had prompted it. With a sudden impulse towards cruelty he advanced towards the bed and announced, as if the news was so trivial it had slipped his notice earlier, 'There will be soldiers here soon, Doll.'

15

'Soldiers?' All at once her breathing had grown constricted. 'Surely you're mistaken.'

The four-poster bed heaved and creaked as he climbed in and pulled the covers over him. He had heard the panic in her voice and he smiled as he turned to face her.

'It's definite, my dear. A company of men are to be garrisoned here by the end of the week. Perhaps even tomorrow. The quartermaster was making arrangements for their lodgings at The Lion this afternoon.'

'But why here?'

'There are soldiers everywhere now, Doll.' He noticed she was trembling under her white cotton shift. He placed his hand over her breast and squeezed it, as if testing for ripeness.

For once his wife hardly noticed. 'They'll not come to this house,' she declared.

'They'll go where they please,' he said, then spat on his palm and moistened himself in readiness.

The news that a company of soldiers was at this very moment preparing to invade her peaceful town, perhaps even the safety of her home, was so shocking that for once Doll forgot herself. She sat bolt upright in the bed and thrust her husband away.

'I'll never allow it!' she insisted.

'You've no choice, Doll,' said Josiah, using his greater weight to push her back against the pillows.

For a moment he thought she might resist him, a thing she had never done before. Long ago the newly wed Mistress Taverner had resolved always to allow her husband his rights, just as she had vowed to herself that he would never see her dance. And she was a woman who never swerved from a decision once made. But this news of the soldiers' coming had undermined even her self-control. She gasped and began to turn away. Swiftly Josiah rolled on top of her. He felt a kick of excitement as she began to arch her body to repulse him. After his humiliation that afternoon, he welcomed the chance to assert his superior power. But his arousal was quickly disappointed as his wife subsided into her customary apathy.

'Don't fuss over what cannot be changed,' he growled, but whether it was the coming of the soldiers or his own urgent needs that he referred to, was not clear. It had become irrelevant, now, anyway. He knew his wife no longer heard him. Doll, he called her, and a doll she might have been at these brief moments of intimacy when she lay beneath him as wooden as a child's plaything, utterly divorced from what was being done to her body. Thus had their four children been conceived.

He was right. She did not hear his words, though she was aware that he had spoken. Usually during these despised interludes she was careful to fix her thoughts on some distant image – the pattern of light falling through the vines on the courtyard where she had played as a child, or the words of a song – but on this occasion the prospect of soldiers had driven all else from her mind.

Beyond the noise of Josiah's grunting breath, she could already hear the roar of cannon and the rattle of musket shot. She could hear the triumph of the soldiers as they swept onwards like an evil flood, could hear the shrieks of old men, women and children being cut down with sword and pike and dagger as their world exploded in terror and fire and soon would be gone for ever. And the screaming inside her head was so loud that she barely noticed when Josiah had finished and capsized beside her in the big soft bed.

Still she did not move. After a while he patted her side. 'Never mind, Doll,' he said.

He should have been used to it by now, her deathly stillness and the face covered in tears. Sometimes it troubled him; tonight he felt that there had been some kind of reckoning, that justice had been done.

When the silence grew oppressive he said, 'Time for prayers, then.'

Only when Josiah had settled himself on his knees beside the bed did his wife unclench her fists and begin to make a few small movements. Then she also left the bed, but not for prayers. She carried the single candle that still burned on the little table and retreated behind the screen that hid the wash basin and pitcher. The warmth of the evening fire was fading and she shivered as she wiped herself clean with the towel and splashed lavender-scented water on her legs and stomach and neck.

Josiah was back in bed, and his small eyes scanned her as she moved with impersonal dignity to join him. As usual their coupling had left a sour taste in his mouth, a wordless shame and irritation. He blamed her for this feeling, and began to be angry again, but then he glimpsed the misery in her eyes as she reached over to snuff the candle, and he said with a gruff effort at kindness, 'No need to fret over the soldiers, Doll. These ones

17

will be different. Englishmen don't make war on women and children.'

Doll threw him a bitter smile. 'They are happy to slaughter their fellow countrymen. Soldiers are the same the world over.'

'You'll be safe here.'

But it did not feel safe, not any more. As she was falling asleep she had a sudden sensation that she was sliding towards the edge of a precipice. Panic jolted her awake again just before she reached the brink, but it was a long time before she was able to master her fear: the darkness that seethed at the base of her fall was made up of all the demons of war.

Sheep bleating in the frosty air, the chink of bridles, and the tramp and shuffle of tired feet. They had journeyed all night through an open, airy country: leisurely hills, high-spreading trees and slow, spacious rivers. The spring equinox was not far off, but there were as yet few signs of the changing season. In Cornwall by now the hedgerows would already be dappled with primroses: here in the heart of England the ground was hard, trees were black outlines against the dawn and spring remained a long world away.

Captain Stephen Sutton slid from his horse to walk beside his men, as he had done from time to time throughout this night of steady marching. The gesture encouraged the soldiers, rested his weary mare Breda and, for a short time at least, alleviated his stiffness and helped to keep him from falling asleep. For some while their pace had been slowing. Pikes and muskets and packs made intolerably heavy by exhaustion: the rancid smell of bodies that have been wrapped in the same clothing far too long. The men stumbled and cursed in their thin leather footwear. The road was so rutted and the ruts so hard with cold that there was no rhythm to their walk. Concentrate on placing your feet. One foot in front of another, like sleepwalkers, now and for hours past.

Grey light rimming the far horizon. The waking song of birds.

At the edge of the escarpment, the guide paused for Stephen to catch up. Yonder, the man gestured with a sweep of his arm. That is your town.

Stephen looked. He blinked.

The town of Tilsbury appeared, when he looked down on it for the first time that early March morning, to be a magical place that rose ethereal from a sea of vapour. Overnight mist had blotted out the river and all the lower ground of the valley. A few high points only were visible: rooftops, the uppermost branches of trees, church spire and market cross, all floating gossamer fine on their shimmering cushion of white.

The march began its slow descent, and Stephen remounted. He felt as if he was riding through a world of vapours, a world as vague and inconsequential as a dream. Steam rose from the shoulders of his horse. When men spoke to one another in the shuffling column that followed him, their breath formed a visible cloud. Fog trailed through the hollows of the far hillside.

The morning star faded as the sky above them grew bright. And then suddenly the summit of the far hill was drenched with pink, the sun rose up behind them and the frosted branches of the trees sparkled and glittered in the dawn light.

An enchanted valley, it seemed to Stephen then, and that in itself was a cause for wonder, since he had thought himself too numbed by war for enchantment.

He had returned to Oxford two days before from a secret mission to be told he must set off at once with a body of men to garrison Tilsbury. Throughout that night he had journeyed with the fevered persistence of a man past all exhaustion. Sleeping and waking had become blurred, and from time to time he had fallen into the illusion that it was still the year 1643 and he was marching east with Sir Bevil Grenvile's army once again. Dreaming while he went, he thought he heard the songs of his fellow Cornishmen as they sang their way across half of southern England to the legendary victories that had cost them so dear. Stephen had never believed in ghosts, yet he could have sworn that his brother Nicolas had been riding with him in the starlight, and that the others had been beside him too, Grenvile and Trevanion and Godolphin, and all that band of family and friends and neighbours who had been butchered in their glorious but desperate campaigns. And now the dawn had come and his ghostly companions had proved as fleeting as the mist, and he picked up the threads of the present with weary resignation.

His hour had not yet come.

The Cornish army, best and most loyal of King Charles's forces at the beginning of this war, had been shattered by the victories of 1643. A remnant struggled on, but now they were led by second-rate men and their devotion was being frittered away in the siege of Plymouth. Driven to near despair by their incompetence and petty squabbles, Stephen had attached himself to Lord Hopton and had been based in Oxford through the winter. He would continue to serve the King faithfully until either this war or his own life was over, but his enthusiasm for the task was gone; in its place was only a stubborn determination not to give up what had been begun with such optimism. At least with these men there were no Cornish voices to remind him of the proud army which existed no longer.

The column made its way steadily down the hill. Slowly the mist was dissolving in the morning warmth, at every moment new objects were revealed before them: sunlight glinting against an upstairs window, an orchard wall, the roof of a barn. There was no wind, and the smoke that rose from a few chimneys was straight as a pikestaff. From the outlying farms came the sound of early morning cock-crow. Somewhere a dog began to bark. Stephen thought of warm firesides and kitchens smelling of baking. Beeswax and clean linen.

Major Darbier rode up beside him.

'Tilsbury, eh?'

Stephen nodded.

'Hardly more than a village,' grumbled the major.

The knowledge that they were approaching their destination had spread like a whisper through the column of men. Stephen could sense how their exhaustion lifted a fraction, to be replaced by a glimmer of expectation. And he himself was not immune.

He almost smiled. An enchanted town, slumbering in its feather bed of mist in this sun-warmed, frosty valley. Despite the weariness aching in every bone, Stephen felt a tingle of something unfamiliar, something that might perhaps have been a relation of a long forgotten hope. Tilsbury looked to be a place serene, untouched by war. Even, perhaps, a place of new beginnings.

It was only when they had nearly reached the end of their long descent that he saw the woman.

She was standing beside the road. Her fur-trimmed cloak showed her at once to be a person of some wealth. Stephen wondered briefly what a woman of quality was doing abroad and alone at an hour of the day that was normally the preserve of dairymaids and country women on their way to market.

But as he drew closer his speculations were swept aside. He saw the look in her dark eyes: some mixture of hate and terror that was more potent than either. He shivered.

She was standing immobile as a column of black marble. Her gaze travelled slowly along the line of men and horses and wagons that straggled down the hillside, and then returned to the guide and the two officers at the head of the line. Stephen could have sworn she was cursing them, that she was in fact a dark-robed sentinel placed there by the townsfolk to ill-wish the hated intruders. She lowered her lids, half-closing her eyes, and her head tilted back slightly.

Major Paul Darbier drew in his breath. 'Now there's a fine-looking woman,' he said. 'Tilsbury might not be such a bad billet after all.'

Though she was much too far away to distinguish his words, the woman made a sudden movement when Darbier spoke, like someone awaking from a trance. She slipped the hood of her cloak over her head and turned away, going back towards the town by a narrow path through the woods while the soldiers continued by the broad road.

The guide made a salty comment. Then, 'Foreign looking, though,' he added more thoughtfully.

'Welsh probably,' said Darbier. 'I like a dark-haired Celt myself. Plenty of energy.'

They laughed, and Stephen laughed with them. Yet, light-headed with lack of sleep as he was, he felt a twinge of disappointment that the other two men had seen her as well. He had almost been hoping that the unknown woman was one of those mythical apparitions visible only to a favoured few.

He was mocking himself for his fanciful thoughts, when Major Darbier rode up alongside him. 'Cheer up,' said the young major, and even at this early hour of the day, his smile was infectious and hard to ignore. 'We'll ferret out a local beauty for you as well, Stephen, never fear.'

They rode on together amicably, with the morning sunshine warming their faces, and all around them birds were singing in the frost-bright trees.

Chapter 3

❧

Mistress Taverner had retreated to her stillroom. With its high, north-facing windows, it was one of the coldest rooms in the house, except when the furnace under the still was burning – but today she was too distracted to notice heat or cold.

She had returned home after dawn just in time to watch from an upstairs window as the soldiers marched through the early sunshine into the waking town. The two young officers rode at the head of the column. The one with dark curling hair was mounted on a splendid coal-black gelding, and he looked about him cheerfully, relishing the impression his cavalier finery must be making on this rustic audience. His companion rode a bay mare, strong but not showy. Soberly dressed in buff coat and breeches, he had the economy of movement of a hardened campaigner, and he examined the town and its situation only for its strategic weaknesses and strengths.

The soldiers who followed were a raggedy-looking bunch. They numbered about sixty, some with pikes, a few had muskets, but most appeared to have no weapons of any kind. About two dozen were mounted on weary horses. To a man they were dirty and unkempt and looked as though they had not had a proper meal since Christmas. Like the other good wives of Tilsbury, Mistress Taverner's heart sank as she thought of the provisions that would be necessary to keep such a hungry crew fed and clothed. Unlike the others, however, Mistress Taverner was in a fury.

Unreasonably, as she moved among the jars and pots in the stillroom, her rage was directed not against the soldiers themselves, but against her husband. Josiah Taverner had betrayed her. He had reneged on the bargain they had struck nearly fifteen years ago. When Nona had advised her granddaughter to throw in her lot with the young English mercenary, it was because he had told them warfare was unknown in his country. He had described a land of plenty where men went about their work untroubled by marauding armies, and where women and children could walk and live in safety. Until then she had not believed such a place still existed this side of Paradise.

Even after their hasty marriage, she had found it hard to trust in the vision he had promised. It was only after they had come to Tilsbury, and she had learned to accept the placid rhythms of the little market town, that she gradually began to believe in her good fortune. By the time her little Beth was born, Doll had been able to watch over her daughter's cradle and know that this girl child would never be exposed to the horror of lawless armies.

Her fragile optimism had proved to be folly after all. Nearly three years ago King Charles declared war on his subjects – or else his subjects rose in rebellion against him depending on whose propaganda you listened to. Doll had little interest in the rights or wrongs of the situation. In her opinion all fighting men were equally to blame. If pressed, she would probably have said her sympathies lay with the King: tradition and order were what she valued, and besides, the Parliament's adherents regarded all Catholics as disciples of the Antichrist. Doll had abandoned the religion of her childhood when she married her Protestant soldier, but she could not forget that Popery had been her family's faith. In those far-off days when she still had a family. She suspected her husband favoured the defeat of King Charles, or at least a conclusion to the war that would effectively curb his powers. So far he had succeeded in declaring for neither one side or the other. When she had questioned him on the subject he had declared that his only aim was to preserve his family and fortune from harm. She felt comforted by his lack of idealism, as though his neutrality would somehow shelter them from this murderous war. But that too had been a lie.

She took some cloves from a jar and emptied them into the mortar. The baby had been begun teething and her supply of oil of cloves was getting low. She set the mortar on the slate work top and began pounding the cloves to a powder. Their scent rose, spicy and astringent, in the cold air.

She worked the pestle angrily. Usually her stillroom was a sanctuary, and soothing. No one ever entered this cool, vaulted room except her and Nona. This was a place of healing, with ointments and medicines that offered hope of protection against the random hazards of life: remedies for every ailment from green sickness or dog bite to the fevers that sometimes follow childbirth or the ache of a broken heart. And this also was a place of danger. Along the very highest shelf were ranged several small bottles whose secret contents were indicated only by a sign. Doll knew the substance of most of them; there remained one or two that were a mystery to everyone but Nona. (As she worked, Doll wondered what quantity of herb grace would be needed to dampen the lusts of all the soldiers now polluting her town.) In this room, if nowhere else, the women enjoyed at least an illusion of control.

But this morning, as Doll ground the cloves, not even her meticulous rows of creams and powders and elixirs had the power to reassure her.

Soldiers had brought their own particular poison to her home. Her fragile security was crumbling to dust.

Josiah had woken her an hour before dawn. She was startled to see that he was fully dressed and held her warmest cloak over his arm.

'Get up, Doll. Get dressed. We have work to do.' He silenced her questions with a curt, 'Hurry, we must be done before anyone wakes.'

While she was pulling on her clothes he busied himself with sorting through the items in the casket containing her jewellery. She noticed that he had removed some of the smaller pieces and was putting them in a pouch which hung from his belt. In their place he had set one or two valuables of his own, including a precious watch studded with tiny emeralds.

When she was dressed she asked again, 'What are you doing?'

'Being a good steward of the wealth Our Lord has seen fit to bless me with. I have given plenty already in taxes and loans because of this unnatural war. I do not intend to give more in plunder.'

'Plunder?'

'Soldiers are coming to Tilsbury, Doll. I told you that last night.'

'But you said Englishmen were different . . . that they would not—'

'Different in degree, only. There is little danger of the kind of atrocities that have ruined Germany and Ireland. But all men are hungry for gain. Free from the constraints of peace, they help themselves to what they find.'

No one knew that better than Josiah, thought his wife bitterly: the young English mercenary who set off for the wars with nothing, and returned a rich man.

'This is my wealth, Doll. I do not intend them to find it.'

'So where will you hide it?'

'Here.'

As Josiah pressed his hand against the oaken panelling to the side of the fireplace, Doll exclaimed, 'Surely you do not mean to use the priest's hole? Everyone knows about that. The children always played hide-and-seek there until you stopped them. There's not a less secret corner in the whole of Tilsbury. I can easily find you a better hiding place than that!'

Stung by the scorn in her voice, Josiah said angrily, 'Do you imagine I had not thought of that? Why do you suppose I forbade the children to play there any more? Go on, then, tell me what everyone knows about our famous priest's hole.'

'Really, Josiah, this is a waste of time, it's been common knowledge ever since that wretched Jesuit was caught. Even Pip can tell you where it is, how far down it goes—'

'And how far is that?'

'One or two steps only, you know I've never gone inside. But this is the first place anyone would look.'

'After the Jesuit priest was apprehended the stairway to the tunnel was blocked off, yes. But what no one else knows is that I have reopened it.'

'How?'

'That painter fellow, Thomas. I could not have a local man do it, he would be sure to talk. But Thomas should spend the rest of this war in London. He has no reason to blab. So now we have the priest's hole which everyone knows of, a small space, not much bigger than a cupboard. But beyond that lies the escape route to the ruins which all believe derelict.'

'As usual, husband, you have thought of everything.'

'Naturally. But on this occasion I am obliged to share my wisdom with you. If anything happens to me while Tilsbury is threatened, then you must know where my children's wealth is hid.'

'Very well, then, now I know. I do not see that I had to get dressed in the middle of the night simply to be told where you intend placing the casket.'

'Not me, wife. We shall do this together.'

She stared at him.

Josiah smiled and pushed open the panel which led into the priest's hole.

'Come,' he said.

She did not move. Then she whispered, 'You surely do not expect me to go in there? You know I cannot abide small places.'

'You will do as you are bid, Doll.' He lifted her cloak and placed it about her shoulders. 'It will be cold in the tunnel.'

'I will not go with you. It would kill me.'

Even in the candleshine her face was ghostly pale. Josiah was unmoved.

'This is no time for petty fears, Doll. Here, you must carry the casket.' He thrust it roughly against her chest. 'Follow me.'

'No—'

He caught hold of her wrist. 'Must I make you go first?'

She shook her head.

'Very well then. Hurry.'

Still grasping her wrist, Josiah stepped into the priest's hole. Narrow steps built into the side wall of the house led downwards, as was well known. After two steps, as she knew from the children's reports, the priest's hole ended in a blank wall. But no more. As she began to descend into the airless dark, Doll felt panic rise up from the pit of her stomach and burst against her lips. Don't scream, she told herself, don't cry out. Her lungs felt as though they were collapsing in on themselves. Already she was covered in a cold gloss of perspiration and the hand that held the casket was slippery and unsure.

Now they had reached the base of the stair. The floor of the tunnel was rough and stony underfoot, and led steeply downwards.

Ahead of her was Josiah's bulk, almost blocking out the light from the lantern. He had to crouch most of the time. The Catholic priests for whom this secret route was built must have been slighter men. He could stick fast in this place, thought Doll, one could die down here and never be found. The walls and ceiling were hands pressed against her skull. Smaller and smaller. . . .

Josiah had halted. He is unable to go on, she thought, the

tunnel leads nowhere. We must turn about. He cannot pass me. I will have to lead, but I cannot do it. I cannot breathe. I am dying here.

He was talking.

'Stop staring like a simpleton, Doll. Give me the casket. Here, look, take note of where I set it.' He laid it in an alcove which had been fashioned in the wall at about the height of his knee. 'See,' he said, 'they may raze our home to the ground but they will never discover this.'

She could not reply. Why was he taking so long? The candle flame dipped and guttered in the stale air. If it goes out, she thought, the darkness will never end. No longer bothering to hold her by the wrist, Josiah went on swiftly. Suddenly terrified that he meant to trap her down here with his hidden treasures, Doll stumbled to keep up. Now her face was level with his belt as the path began to climb again. There was a taste of clean air and ahead of them a fragment of mist-pale night. As Doll surfaced from the tunnel her claustrophobia broke out in a sob of sheer terror. Gasping for the pure air, she staggered a few paces before collapsing against an ice cold stone. Above her head she saw stars and mist, rafters open to the sky and the jagged outline of the ruined priory tower.

Josiah was speaking, but his words were a meaningless babble.

Slowly she raised herself on one arm and brushed her hair back from her face. Every muscle in her body was aching from the earlier effort of self-control.

'Did you hear what I was telling you, Doll? Do you understand how this entrance is kept hidden?'

She shook her head.

Josiah crouched down beside her. He held the lantern up to her face. Those dark eyes huge with child-like terror moved him to compassion as they had done on the day he saw her first.

'My poor Doll,' he said gruffly, 'I know how you fear these narrow places. Here—'

He offered her his arm, but she pushed him away and struggled to her feet unaided. She would not allow him the satisfaction of comforting her when he had been responsible for her torture. She listened impassively while he showed her how the two stones could be rolled back into place, disguising the entrance to the tunnel as just another pile of fallen masonry.

At last she found her voice. 'Should you not extinguish the

lantern? It is nearly dawn and someone might see us.'

'So much the better.' He raised the lantern and swung it to and fro. 'You know how this place is feared. Elfin lights bobbing in the darkness will increase the rumours. It's high time the Grey Lady was seen again by some poor fool. Now, we must return to the house before it gets light.'

This time she did not even bother to protest. She could not have re-entered the tunnel even if she had wanted to. And Josiah must have accepted this, because he said, 'Replace the stones after me in the manner I have showed you. Do not linger. People will assume you've been out on one of your early morning walks. A pity we did not think to bring a basket.'

It was incredible to her that Josiah, still holding his flickering lantern, stepped quite cheerfully into the tunnel. Even the sight of someone else being swallowed by the earth's mouth caused her to break out in a cold sweat all over again.

The pale flame vanished in the endless black of the tunnel. Above ground, the mist was paling with the coming of the dawn. She looked about her. She had hardly ever set foot inside the Old Priory before, though it adjoined their own property – and certainly never at night. Most of the townspeople gave the place a wide berth, even in daytime, so great was their superstitious fear of the place. Although it had been derelict for a hundred years, the ruin retained a kind of beauty. The stone walls were still largely intact, a roosting place for birds and the scuffling bats. Grudgingly she had to acknowledge her husband's foresight in reopening the forgotten tunnel.

Somewhere in the clear air above her an early blackbird began to sing. She felt a fierce urge not to return straight away to her home, but to find a place apart and open, somewhere she could pacify the demons which had sprung into life when Josiah spoke of the soldiers, and which had been increased tenfold by her horror of the underground passage.

Leaving the ruined priory she began to walk away from the town. The air was chill against her face. She took a short cut through the woods and joined the Oxford road at a little distance above Tilsbury. She had emerged into bright sunshine. The thick covering of mist, seen from above, was transformed, no longer sinister, but a thing of beauty. Dawn light was flooding the valley. Gradually she forgot the cold, her horror of small spaces, her suspicions and her fears.

She drew in a deep breath and turned her face to the sun. All will be well, she told herself. Josiah has arranged for our safety, mine and my children's. This English war will not harm us.

She stood very still. The sound was so faint that at first she thought she might be imagining it. She remained quite still, waiting for the sound to go away. But instead it was coming closer. Marching feet, horses' hoofbeats, the rumble of heavy wagons.

She heard them not with her ears only, but with her whole body. A remembered horror she was powerless to withstand. Mistress Taverner, respected wife and mother in the small town of Tilsbury for over a decade, felt that she was a child again.

And her world was about to end for the second time.

Alone in her stillroom, she bit her knuckles and fought down the scream. A cry of terror and hate and rage that had been forever silenced long years before. She looked down at the bowl she had been holding. Without noticing what she was doing she had ground sufficient cloves to soothe a dozen teething babies.

The church clock struck the hour. This was her usual time to collect Beth for their morning walk into the centre of town. Together they exchanged the news of the day with their neighbours, and purchased eggs and other items from Goody Tucket or Dame Fryer who traded under the market cross.

But today was different. Today the town would be awash with soldiers. Doll cursed every soldier in the world to hell and jammed the mortar down on the slate shelf with such fury that it smashed into a thousand pieces. Shards of pottery and clove dust were everywhere.

Tears of vexation sprang to her eyes. Mistress Taverner, whose stoicism was legendary among the local midwives, blinked back the unaccustomed tears and deftly swept up the broken mortar. No paltry band of riff raff was going to get the better of her.

Locking the stillroom door behind her, she went to the screens passage which ran down the centre of the house between the winter parlour and the dining hall. There she put on her cloak and called up the stairs to Beth, who had been waiting on the landing.

'Oh good,' Beth raced down the stairs to join her mother, 'I was so afraid we wouldn't go.'

'Why ever not?'

'Because of the soldiers.'

'Soldiers? And what have they to do with anything? They're nothing but a nuisance, like rats in a barn. No need to bother about *them*.'

This outing with her mother was always one of the best parts of Beth's day. She was not an especially bright child, and she found her morning lessons irksome. Nor was she good with a needle, though Mabs in the kitchen said she had the makings of an excellent cook. All through the hours when she was bent over her horn book, or when she fought with her sampler until linen and thread had turned the same sweaty and unappealing shade of grey, she envied almost every other child in the town, whose mothers were not so strict about lessons. But most of all she envied Jinny Crew.

Jinny lived with her mother and a heap of little brothers in a collapsing cottage just across the wide street from the Priory House. Goody Crew took in washing and never had time enough for anything else, certainly not for lessons. The children were tipped into the street almost before they were awake, and there they stayed, playing and squabbling and observing the life of the town until it was dark and they stumbled into bed. During the endless hours of morning study, Beth thought it must be delicious to be free to wander the streets, to come and go as she pleased and never to bother with the time of day until darkness fell.

But as soon as Beth stepped out through the front door with her mother and walked down their wide front path between beds of lavender, rosemary and thyme to the gate, she would not have traded places with anyone else in the world. Certainly not with poor Jinny Crew, who watched with awe as the beautiful Mistress Taverner and her daughter swept down the main street towards the market cross.

Beth knew her mother was beautiful, just as she knew that she herself was not. Neither fact was troubling to her at all. She had her father's love and her brother Harry's friendship. Since she was seldom any trouble and not prone to putting on airs, she was popular with the servants. She was well contented with her particular share of good things and, once lessons were over for the day, not at all given to brooding over what can never be changed.

Above all she was proud of her mother. Harry, she knew, was sometimes embarrassed by Mistress Taverner's oddness: by

31

the fact that, unlike all the other good wives and ladies of the town she had not been born within a ten-mile radius of Tilsbury, but no one else had a mother with quite that proud tilt to her head, nor one who walked through the town with the arching stride of a queen. Nor did they perform strange dances in secret with their grandmother, nor defy their husband with cold smiles, nor produce bottles from their stillroom with no descriptions on them, only signs. When she walked beside her mother, Beth felt she was no longer just a plain little person with commonplace features and rusty-coloured curls, clumsy fingers and a brain that tended to fog over when faced with a difficult question. She was transformed into the proudest of proud shadows.

Good at lessons Beth was not, but she was acutely sensitive to the moods of others. On this particular morning, no sooner had she breathed in the crisp sunny air, than she realised her mother was distressed. It was nothing that was said: as usual, they spoke little. But Beth's chubby hand was gripped with a particular tightness, her mother's head was held just a little higher, and there was a tension that made the child both eager and apprehensive.

Little Jinny Crew, stamping on the ruts in the road to break the ice, watched Mistress Taverner stride past with her fur-trimmed cloak and her daughter with her scrubbed and cared-for clothes, and she envied the other child with all her heart.

The town was in chaos. The main street, with its market cross and public buildings was exceptionally wide, but in spite of this their way was almost completely blocked by the sudden influx of wagons, horses and men. Outside The Lion the billeting officer, a tall thin man with a beaky nose and a nervous tic in the region of his left eye, together with the quartermaster, who was as brown and short and round as one of his own barrels, were engaged in a ferocious argument over the relative merits of their separate lists. The battle had raged between them for the best part of the morning and showed no signs of ending. All around them were the soldiers. Most had discarded their packs and lounged in the sunshine with their tankards of ale and a few hunks of bread; some had fallen asleep where they sat. And as several had already eased off their leather shoes, the air was pungent with the smell of well-marched feet. The local people watched them with curiosity and dread, and gave them a wide berth. Sir Diggory Page, Justice of the Peace and leading dignitary in the area, rode in from his home which lay a couple of miles away. He joined the quartermaster and the billeting officer, bringing their argument to a temporary halt. Sir Diggory was a grey-haired gentleman, and very conscious of his dignity.

'Where is your commanding officer?' he demanded, 'Your officers must lodge with me. They'll be sure of every comfort at Furleys.'

The tall thin billeting officer squinted at his list in despair. The quartermaster, who was making a mental note to ride out to Furleys that very afternoon and see what 'comforts' could be of use to the soldiers, merely nodded.

Major Paul Darbier and Captain Stephen Sutton were relaxing on a bench in front of The Lion and listening with half an ear to the discussions of the three men.

'Damned dismal hole, this,' reflected Darbier. 'We'll have to find a way to liven it up, the Lord only knows how.'

'We've done that already,' said Stephen, looking at the crowd of poorly dressed children who were gaping at them from a safe distance.

Darbier eyed them irritably. 'Have they never seen soldiers before?'

'Probably not.'

'Damn their insolence. I'll give them something to gawp about.' And he roared at the children, who scurried away in terror.

Stephen observed his superior officer carefully. 'Our orders are to convince the local people of the justice of His Majesty's cause, not to alienate them.'

'My dear Stephen, His Majesty doesn't care a whisker about a few ragged children. Don't be so literal about it all. Terrible waste of time, you know. Besides, that soft kind of talk is all very fine in Oxford. One needs tougher measures in this sort of backwater.'

Stephen was unable to resist saying quietly, 'Tough measures have an unfortunate habit of driving people into the enemy camp.'

Darbier smiled. 'In Cornwall, maybe, but not here. Trust me, Stephen, I know this part of the world better than you ever will. Turnip-heads like these will jump for whoever cracks the whip loudest.'

Stephen was debating whether to pursue the argument

further since it was, after all, one on which he felt strongly, when he realised he no longer had the major's attention.

'Here we go,' said Darbier, brightening visibly, 'What did I tell you?'

Following the direction of his gaze, Stephen saw the tall figure of the woman who had watched them that morning from the edge of the wood. She was standing by the market cross and talking with a farmer's wife over some items the country woman had in her basket. A little girl with a mass of red-brown hair under her white cap was holding her hand and sneaking an occasional glance in the direction of the soldiers. For no reason that he could have possibly explained, Stephen was filled with a sudden foreboding.

Major Darbier stretched his legs with the contentment of a cat, and stood up. He strolled over and introduced himself to Sir Diggory Page. Sir Diggory asked him if he could by any chance be the same Major Darbier who was a nephew to Lord Bewell. On being told that this was indeed the case, the grey-haired gentleman reaffirmed his desire that the officers would consider themselves his guests at Furleys for as long as was necessary.

'Most kind,' drawled Darbier, not committing himself. 'Tell me, Sir Diggory, who is that dark-haired lady by the market cross?'

Sir Diggory looked and cleared his throat awkwardly. Being short-sighted, and too vain to admit the fact, he had some trouble answering. It was the landlord of The Lion, who happened to be passing with yet more ale for the soldiers (and wondering when or if he would ever get paid), who said, 'That is Mistress Taverner, sir.'

'Doll Taverner, of course,' said Sir Diggory hurriedly, 'I was not quite sure whom you meant. An excellent lady.'

'And her husband?'

'Josiah Taverner is one of Tilsbury's leading citizens. He came originally from a Catholic family, but put all that nonsense behind him as a young man. I believe he made his fortune in the German wars.'

'Can we see his home from here?'

'You would have passed it as you entered the town. The Priory House. First place you come to after that ruined tower. Used to be a convent there, you know,' said Sir Diggory, glad to be able to assist this nephew of Lord Bewell's, 'Perfectly reasonable house too, I dare say. Some of your men would be quite comfortable there.'

Darbier turned to the billeting officer. 'Captain Sutton and I will lodge at Master Taverner's home, to begin with, at any rate. It commands an excellent strategic position. Have our baggage taken there at once.'

'But—' the billeting officer peered down his beaky nose at his list, 'But—'

'Just do it, you imbecile,' snapped Darbier.

Sir Diggory had not given up altogether. 'You must dine with me at Furleys today, Major. My wife will be delighted to make your acquaintance. I believe that she and your aunt were once—'

'Maybe tomorrow,' Darbier cut in. 'Or next week. One is going to be busy training the men, and so forth. But if you have any decent wines, have them sent to our billet. Good day, sir.'

He walked back to Stephen, leaving the baronet as little satisfied as the billeting officer.

'That's settled then. More ale?'

Stephen smiled. 'I don't know if your reasons for choosing a billet follow any known military principle,' he said.

'It's the Darbier principle, Stephen. Enjoy yourself while you can. When the natural order is turned upside down by war, the opportunities for pleasure are wonderfully increased.'

Stephen, who had seen the dread on the faces of the townspeople as they marched in, said, 'Not many would agree with that.'

'Good God, man, one doesn't want agreement. Can't imagine anything more tedious.'

The two men lapsed into silence. They were both scanning the crowds around the market cross, but the tall lady with the dark hair and the little girl at her side was no longer to be seen.

By the time she sat down with her family for their midday meal, Mistress Taverner had developed a throbbing pain behind her eyes. The table had been laid as usual according to her precise instructions, one dish followed another in smooth succession, the children observed their customary silence. On the surface at least, all was as it had ever been. Yet all was utterly different. Tension crackled in the air. The children, usually so well behaved, had barely any appetite and were frantic for the meal to end. Harry had overheard one of the outside men saying the soldiers were bound to be on the look-out for decent horses, and

35

his pony was the best horse he knew. Just the thought of his precious Bonnet being stolen from him by some brutish cavalryman and most likely shot in battle – for he knew that soldiers were trained to shoot at the horses, not their riders – drove him to despair. Philip was furious because, despite all his best efforts he still had not managed to escape his grandmother and run down the street to see the soldiers. Since he had been sleeping soundly, he had missed seeing them when they marched past the house earlier and he was now convinced that he was the only person left on earth who had never set eyes on a real live soldier. Beth, as well as struggling with her own anxieties, was alert to the anguish of others.

Her mother's for instance. The severity of Doll Taverner's expression as she followed the ritual of their midday meal was almost frightening. She did not look beautiful now, her strange eyes were far too ferocious. But what disturbed Beth most was that her mother had an air of fragility, like something that could be shattered at a single touch. Beth was reminded suddenly of the edifices that Mabs concocted of fine-spun sugar, delicate as cobweb lace, but brittle as ice. Seeing her mother in that light gave Beth a tingling sense of impending disaster.

Even her father, who could usually be relied upon for an indulgent smile whenever their eyes met across the long table, was today thoroughly out of sorts. He snapped at the servants, kicked out at the dogs when they came too close, scowled at everyone. And, still more remarkably in a man who was gaining a reputation for gluttony, he barely touched his food.

Doll also noticed his abstinence. She wondered what had caused his disquiet. He had every reason to be complacent at having hidden part of his fortune so cleverly. It occurred to her that it might have been the reminder of the Jesuit priest, the last Catholic to use the secret route before it was discovered, which had spoiled his temper. She had seen before how he hated any mention of it. Josiah had been a child when the priest was dragged from the house by the pursuivants; the horror of it must have affected him deeply.

Only Nona appeared unperturbed by the tension. She was bent over her plate and attacking her food with the dedication of one who has known real hunger in her time. Because her teeth were few, she had evolved ways of chopping and mashing on the plate which occupied her full attention. Beth was grateful for her grandmother's reassuring sameness.

There was a sudden banging noise and the sounds of servants' feet hurrying down the screens passage. Doll turned pale and her knife clattered to the floor. Beth, who was always dropping things herself, had never seen her mother do so before, and sudden alarm gripped her. Even Nona looked up from her chopping and her chewing.

Mabs burst into the room. Her cheeks were red and her cap askew.

'There's soldiers at the door!' she gasped, 'They say they're stopping here.'

'No!' Doll's denial was instant, 'Not in my house. Never here!' She had caught hold of the edge of the table and her knuckles were white.

'Don't be a fool, woman,' snapped her husband.

'Send them away! Now!'

'Impossible.'

'You must.'

Josiah stood up. He walked the length of the room to stand beside her. 'Control yourself, Doll.' His hand gripped her shoulder, 'If this is to be our hour of trial, then the Lord will give us the strength to endure. Listen to me, all of you,' and he turned slightly to show that his instructions were for the entire household, 'These men are not our enemies. We are His Majesty's loyal subjects. We pray for eternal damnation to the perfidious rebels in Parliament. Is that understood?'

Doll removed his hand carefully. She did not look at him. She did not look at anyone. 'Very well,' she said at length, 'I understand.'

'Soldiers, at last. Hurray!' squealed Philip and, slipping down from his chair he began to race across the room to see them properly. His mother reached out a swift hand and caught him by the scruff of his neck.

Josiah turned his attention to Mabs. 'Don't just stand there, woman. Show them in at once.'

But there was no need. Major Darbier, who was not accustomed to being kept waiting, and certainly not by merchants, strode into the room. Stephen Sutton followed more slowly.

'Gentlemen!' exclaimed Josiah at once, it being obvious from his dress that Major Darbier at least was a high born officer. 'Welcome, welcome to my humble home.'

Moving painfully, as though it cost her great effort, his wife

37

rose slowly from her seat and, with a rustle of skirts, took up her position at her husband's side.

And then she too smiled, as if to welcome the soldiers.

Chapter 4

❧

Stephen's first impression on coming face to face with Mistress Taverner was that he had been wrong to think her tall. It was the straightness of her bearing that made her appear so; in fact she was of only medium height. This was swiftly followed by a stab of rage at the way Paul Darbier was bending over her hand. The major's flourishing courtesies rendered Stephen stiff and awkward by comparison, so that when he was introduced in his turn he confined himself to a brisk. 'Your servant, ma'am,' accompanied by the merest inclination of his head. Suddenly he was painfully aware that he had slept in his clothes for at least three nights and that his linen was showing the effects of their long march.

Master Taverner was meanwhile emphasising that they were his welcome guests, though he felt it only fair to point out that the comforts they were accustomed to would be more readily provided by Sir Diggory Page at Furleys. Stephen was repelled by his pompous manner.

Wishing to stem the tide of the fellow's insincerity, he said, 'Your home will provide all the luxury we require, Master Taverner,' but as he spoke he was startled to feel his sword being slowly eased from its scabbard. He grasped its basketwork hilt and his hand closed around something small and soft. A boy of perhaps three or four, with the same exquisite black eyes as his mother, was gazing up at him.

Stephen at once released the little hand. 'I trust I have not startled you,' he said gently, 'Would you like to see my sword?'

The child was nodding a vigorous 'yes' but his mother at once drew him back to her side.

'The children will not be permitted to inconvenience you, gentlemen,' she said, and Stephen noticed at once that there was something unusual about her voice, which was pitched low and throaty, 'Philip, go with your grandmother at once.'

'Don't send them away on our account,' protested Stephen.

'You will not find them a nuisance,' she said again. 'Go on now, children. All of you, go with Nona.'

A woman, short and stout and of great age, and dressed from head to toe in black, herded the three children from the room. Their excited voices faded as they climbed the stairs. As soon as they were gone, Mistress Taverner was once again smiling and serene.

Perhaps fearing his wife's coolness had offended the officers, Master Taverner said with an attempt at familiarity, 'Captain Sutton, I can tell from your voice you are a stranger to these parts.'

'My home is in Cornwall.'

'Ah yes, a West Country accent never fades entirely. Cornish, eh? You must have fought with my old comrade Ralph Hopton.'

'I served him at Lansdown and at Bristol.'

Master Taverner was nodding vigorously. 'And I myself fought with him in Bohemia when you, sir, must have been no older than my own little lad. So we are comrades in arms. after a fashion, eh?'

Aware that Mistress Taverner was observing him once again, Stephen found himself at a loss how to reply. It was Darbier who looked up from the piece of cold meat he had picked off a serving plate and enquired, 'You are a soldier, Master Taverner?'

'*Was* a soldier. My military days are over, alas. As a young man I served the Protestant cause in Europe for over ten years. His Majesty's sister Elizabeth had no more loyal champion than I.' He patted his ample stomach complacently. 'Sadly my present infirmity no longer permits me to bear arms. But all that I have is yours, gentlemen, since you are fighting in my place.'

Darbier's smile was tinged with malice. 'Sir, you are too kind.'

But later, when he and Stephen had retired to the room that had been assigned to them, Darbier, sprawling in a chair while his manservant struggled to remove his boots, asked casually, 'Do you suppose our fat host meant to include his delectable wife in his offer to share all he had with us?'

'The man may be a pompous ass,' said Stephen stiffly, 'but

hat's no reason to abuse his hospitality.'

Darbier burst out laughing. 'Nonsense, Stephen, his kind of conniving hypocrite deserves to be cuckolded. And did you see how wretched his wife looked? Imagine such a beautiful young creature being condemned to a lifetime with that monstrous fellow. Good heavens, man, it is practically our patriotic duty to bring some pleasure to her life.'

'You talk like a damned fool.'

'And you, Stephen, are only angry because I saw her first.'

Stephen's face broke into a grin. He was too honest not to admit that there was some truth in his major's words, and he had no intention of falling out with a superior officer over a married woman, however attractive that woman might be.

All the rest of that day the house was in turmoil. Beds and chests were moved, rooms were rearranged and cleaned, maids and serving men carried and shifted and scrubbed until all was ordered to Mistress Taverner's satisfaction. The two officers were given the bedchamber at the front of the house that Nona had previously shared with Philip and the baby, the large room where the two women had danced the previous evening. Nona and the little ones were moved into the room which since the birth of the baby had belonged to Harry. He was obliged to share a room with Beth once again. The serving girl Cary, who had been hired to help out with the baby, had slept in the attic with Mabs and the other women until now. She was told to move her few things down so she could share a chamber with the two older children. Doll did not intend any of her family to sleep unattended so long as there were soldiers in the house. Mabs and the others were instructed to return to their families in the town. The officers were accompanied by a couple of grooms, who were to lodge above the stable, a serving man and about three troopers who were assigned to the attics. This war had already produced stories of outrage in plenty, and Mistress Taverner was not going to risk leaving any of her female servants close to the kind of riff raff who called themselves soldiers.

Paul Darbier and Stephen were meanwhile busy with arrangements of their own. Having supervised the installation of their baggage – two large trunks together with several smaller items for the major, and a modest portmanteau for the captain – they passed the afternoon in meetings with the town worthies and the constable, checking the deposition of sentries and organising the scouts.

As they were riding back towards the town, they heard the unmistakable sounds of a drunken brawl coming from a small farmyard near the road. They wheeled their horses round and instantly identified the cause of the trouble: one of the Welshmen who had arrived with them that morning. A short, stocky fellow, he had evidently taken possession of a blackjack of the strong local cider and was already fighting drunk. A young lad with a bloody nose and an elderly farmer cowering behind a water butt were testimony to damage already done; having exhausted his human opposition the soldier was trying to smash a stable door with fists and feet while the women of the farm shrieked in horror.

'Damned rogue,' exclaimed Darbier, and then more loudly, 'Hey, fellow, stop that at once.'

For reply, the man spun about and took a swing at the major's horse, which reared up in fright, not used to being hit on the nose.

Darbier, who had difficulty keeping his seat, was outraged. 'I'll teach you—!' he began, pulling out his sword, but Stephen intercepted him.

'Wait!' he said, sliding from his horse. He advanced rapidly on the man, who was now roaring at everyone in Welsh. No great knowledge of languages was necessary to comprehend the gist of his words. He raised his fists to take a swipe at Stephen.

The soldier had only a hazy notion of what happened next. One moment the stern-looking officer was coming towards him and he was preparing to send him flying, and the next he found his arms pinned to his side, his feet knocked from under him and his head immersed in the icy water of the butt. The terrified cries of the women watching from the safety of the house had turned to howls of laughter.

When Stephen calculated the man was either sober enough, or sufficiently cowed to cause no more trouble, he released him. Spluttering wildly, the soldier shook his shaggy hair like a spaniel, and was promptly sick.

'Well done, Captain,' said Darbier. 'We'll have him flogged and thrown out for bad behaviour.'

'I doubt that will be necessary,' said Stephen mildly. 'Such fighting spirit only needs harnessing. A night in the stocks and he'll be quiet as a lamb when their training starts tomorrow, wait

42

and see.' He turned to the soldier, who had recovered and was dripping quietly in a corner. 'What's your name?'

'Owen,' was the reply.

'Good heavens,' said Darbier, 'They all have the same name, these Welshmen, however will we tell them apart?'

As if to demonstrate his lamb-like nature, Owen waited meekly while Stephen said a few words of apology to the elderly farmer. As Stephen remounted his horse, Darbier could not resist giving the soldier a prod with his sword before sheathing it once more.

'I never saw anyone overpowered that way before,' said Darbier as they left the farmyard. 'What's the trick?'

Stephen turned to him, and a sudden smile lit his usually grave face. 'The Cornish are famous for their wrestling, didn't you know? Among my countrymen I'm a novice, but here it has the advantage of surprise. The secret is to unbalance your opponent while hooking his legs from under him. If your adversary happens to be well on in drink, then he does much of the work for you.' He glanced back at Owen. 'We'll have no more trouble from our pot-valiant Welshman, I warrant you.'

They had reached the edge of the town, where the still-imposing ruins of the Old Priory were set back a little from the road. 'You go on, Major. I thought I'd have a look at the tower.'

'Sightseeing, Captain? Whatever for?'

'If it is safe, then that tower will make an excellent look-out, don't you agree? I want to see how much ground a sentry can cover.'

'Not a bad idea. I was thinking the same myself. Well, go ahead then. I'll leave you to sort out the details.'

The two men separated. Darbier was dimly aware that Stephen had already taken responsibility for several decisions. He had been scrupulous in emphasising to all the men the importance of paying for everything above the absolute necessities. 'Our task is to win these people over to the King's cause, not to alienate them,' he insisted. Major Darbier made it plain he thought the captain was wasting his time, especially as the men's wages were hopelessly in arrears and hardly any of them could afford even the price of a penny loaf. But already Darbier had known Stephen long enough to realise that the Cornishman, though superficially amiable, had a habit of tenacity which would make him a dangerous opponent, especially where principle was involved. Since Darbier had no principles himself, only his good manners and his honour as a gentleman, he found Stephen's stubbornness both curious and likeable. At least for the time being.

He was aware that Stephen had a reputation for professionalism, and thought such a captain would be useful in easing the burden of his own responsibility. Darbier was guided by only one precept: to do always what promised pleasure. He was healthy and energetic and, having been privileged since birth, he was a stranger to anxiety. Since he believed his good fortune was due to superior character and abilities, he took it for granted he would make an excellent soldier with no need for effort or adjustment. At present he found Stephen an agreeable foil to his own exuberant style.

It was typical of the two men that, as dusk fell on their first day in Tilsbury, Paul Darbier was contentedly wallowing in a tub of hot water which had been arranged at considerable difficulty in his bedroom, while Stephen was making his final checks on the billets for his men.

Darkness had fallen by the time he returned to the Priory House. He slid from his horse and led it round to the stable block at the back. He felt unutterably weary. From the loft he could hear erratic snoring, which he recognised as that of the groom's boy. He was just about to call out and wake him when he heard low voices coming from the smaller stable to the side. He recollected that the family had agreed to have their own three horses moved there, leaving the larger free for the soldiers'. Soft lantern light was shining on the chaff and straw in the entrance. Without knowing the exact reason for his silence, Stephen moved quietly towards the half-open door.

Mistress Taverner was standing there with her two older children while a small brown pony was contentedly guzzling from the manger. Although some kind of argument seemed to be taking place, her expression was more exasperated than angry. It appeared that the boy, whom Stephen had heard called Harry, was in trouble. He was hanging his head, but the stubborn angle of his bottom lip showed that he had not yet admitted defeat. His arm was draped over the pony's neck. The little girl, whose name Stephen could not recall, was evidently an anguished witness of the conflict. Both the children had their father's heavy features, but they still retained a singular charm.

'In the name of heaven, Harry,' Mistress Taverner was saying in that deep, rather husky voice of hers, 'what can you be thinking of? You've been with Bonnet the whole afternoon. Now you must come in to bed.'

The boy's head drooped a fraction lower, but a mumbled, 'I'm staying here,' could be heard quite clearly.

His mother snapped her fingers in irritation. 'Tst. You deserve to be whipped.'

'But Mother—'

'Don't interrupt, Beth. This does not concern you. Harry, come inside with me at once.'

Again the mumbled but defiant negative.

Then Mistress Taverner put her hand to her forehead where a stray wisp of hair had escaped to soften the severity of her face, and she said with sudden gentleness, 'Lordy, Harry. Today of all days—'

Stephen was entranced. He had been surrounded for so long by soldiers and the necessities of warfare. This scene reminded him of his own home and the person he had been before he set out on this endless journey. He remembered suddenly the time when he must have been about Harry's age, and had run away from home for a whole night and a day to prevent a litter of puppies from being drowned. He did not know the reason for the boy's disobedience, but he recognised the desperation that lay behind it.

And Mistress Taverner, alone in the lamp-lit stable with her two children, was revealed afresh. That morning, when Stephen had seen her as she stood on the edge of the wood she had appeared like some figure from an old story, beautiful and forbidding. Later he had seen the competent housewife, ordering her affairs with a minimum of fuss. Now he was observing her in an altogether more intimate light. Unaware that she was being watched, she appeared much younger, baffled by this wayward child as, Stephen guessed, she would never allow herself to be baffled by an adult.

'Harry,' she drew in her breath and tried a fresh tack, 'You've never defied me before so I'll overlook it this one time. But you must leave off this wickedness and come inside with me *now*.'

'But Mother—'

'Silence, Beth. Well, Harry, are you coming?'

'No.'

'I've never known you like this. What has got into you?'

The drooping head shook slowly from side to side. On his

sandy lashes something that might have been tears glistened briefly and the lad shifted a little closer to the comfort of the pony's shaggy neck. Bonnet, quite unmoved by the attention, shifted from one foot to the other and blew thoughtfully into her oats.

Mistress Taverner raised her hands slightly, then, defeated by Harry, normally the most pliable of her children, let them fall once more to her side. 'There's no more to be said. It's quite out of the question for you to remain here any longer. There are soldiers everywhere, the town is not safe. I shall have to give orders for Gerard to carry you in. You'll be confined to your room without food and not even see Bonnet until—'

At this the boy's courage failed and, he flung his arms around the pony's neck and sobbed broken-heartedly while Beth, unable to contain herself any longer burst out, 'Oh Mother, no! You can't do that! It's the soldiers, don't you understand? Harry thinks they'll steal Bonnet and she'll have to go into battle and be shot and killed and—'

An expression of amazement spread across Mistress Taverner's face as she looked, first at the desperate face of her daughter, then at the sobbing boy. 'Heavens above, Harry. Is this true?'

'Yes, yes, it is,' again Beth spoke for her brother. 'We heard the soldiers will take all the horses. And Harry has sworn they won't have Bonnet—'

Mistress Taverner's expression softened; she seemed to be on the verge of laughter. Stephen judged the time had come to make his presence known. He cleared his throat and moved forward from the shadows.

'Mistress Taverner,' he said, 'Please forgive me, but I could not help overhearing your daughter. I believe I may be able to help.'

The laughter died in her eyes and her expression changed with the speed of a vice closing.

'Captain Sutton—'

'I did not mean to startle you.'

'Are you in the habit of spying on people?' she asked sharply, 'You're as silent as a thief.' Instinctively she had gathered the children to her side. Stephen realised she was wondering how much he had overheard.

To give them all time to adjust to his presence, Stephen stepped over the straw and briefly fondled the pony's nose. He was reminded suddenly, and painfully, of the little dappled creature who had been the first mount he had shared with his brother Nicolas. They had driven their old groom to despair by mounting one behind the other and stealing off to gallop over the moorland when they were supposed to be under his tuition in the meadow. He turned to Harry, whom he judged to be a boy of few words but much pride.

'Is this your pony, Harry?'

The boy nodded, then wiped the last of his tears on his sleeve.

'And her name?'

'Bonnet.'

'Listen to me carefully. I am Captain Sutton. Major Darbier and I are in charge of all the soldiers who have come to Tilsbury today. Our task is to make sure that no horses are taken without the permission of their owners, and we will pay for those we need. Do you understand?'

The boy sniffed and glanced at his mother, who was watching with undisguised cynicism.

Stephen persevered. 'I shall leave instructions with my groom, but to make doubly sure your pony is safe, I'll draw up a document for you to keep. It will state that Bonnet must never become a soldier's horse.'

As Stephen was speaking he reflected that there were few soldiers on either side small enough to covet the little brown pony. Harry, who had been listening intently, now released his hold of Bonnet and came to stand before Stephen.

'Can you really do that?'

'I can. And I will.'

It was the captain's tone of voice, that and the grave expression of his eyes, that convinced Harry, more than the words. He nodded his hesitant agreement.

'Now, Harry, your side of the bargain is that you must obey your mother.'

'Very well.'

They shook hands.

Mistress Taverner moved forward. 'Inside now, children. At once.' Her voice was harsh. 'Harry, we'll talk of this again in the morning.'

Harry gave his pony a farewell pat on the rump and moved towards the doorway. Beth looked up at Stephen and seemed to be on the point of saying something, but a quick glance at her mother's face persuaded her to depart immediately.

When they had gone, Stephen said, 'I'm sorry your son was frightened.'

She did not look at him directly. 'Children are always frightened in wartime,' she said.

'I can assure you, they have no reason to fear us.'

'No?'

Stephen persevered. 'The presence of soldiers in your town is an inconvenience, I grant you that. It will not be a danger.'

'Words, Captain. Words are easy. But you know full well this war is not being fought with words. And when the killing begins, no one is spared.' She glanced at him briefly, and then made a little dipping motion with her head, as though to distance herself, before repeating in a low voice, 'No one at all.'

She reached out and laid her hand on Bonnet's dusty rump and her eyes were opaque.

Stephen asked softly, 'You speak from experience?'

She darted him a furious glance before replying, 'Only fools think otherwise.'

'I wish there was some way to persuade you we intend no harm to you or your family.'

'That could not be simpler,' she said with a bitter laugh. 'Take your men away with you and leave us in peace.'

'That is not possible. My orders are to establish a garrison in Tilsbury.'

'For how long?'

'That I cannot say.'

'And you will obey your orders, of course. And if you are told to raze this town to the ground and make all its citizens homeless, then like a good soldier, you would do it. So do not pretend to me there is no danger.'

'It is not likely.'

'Maybe not. But there is another danger, less obvious perhaps, but one I mean to guard against if I can.'

'And that is?'

'I wish no familiarity to develop between my children and your men. Not even with you, Captain Sutton. They would quickly become a nuisance and besides, the company of soldiers is not good for children. They are young and impressionable. Since you are guests in my husband's house, we shall do all that is necessary for your comfort. But I must ask you to respect the privacy of my family. Do I have your word?'

Stephen did not answer right away. He was aware that

48

Mistress Taverner was far from pleased with his interference in her domestic drama, but his attention was wholly absorbed by the way her dark eyes flickered back and forth as she spoke, lighting briefly on his face, then turning as if to look inward once again. Her pupils had grown very large in the dim light from the lantern and Stephen had the impression that all brightness was swallowed up in their depths. He was aware of the blue shadows ringing her eyes, the feathered arch of her eyebrows, the glimpse of white teeth. He was aware of her rapid, shallow breathing and the faint movement of her fur trim against the ivory pallor of her throat. He was aware that he was in the presence of a woman unlike any he had met before, and the knowledge was unsettling, but a pleasure, too.

She made a small gesture of annoyance. 'So, Captain Sutton. Do I have your word?'

He tried to collect his erratic thoughts. 'What, precisely, is your request, Mistress Taverner?'

Her frown deepened. 'I thought I had made myself plain. I do not wish my children to have any contact with the soldiers. I would like you not to talk with them at all.'

'Some contact is inevitable, if only for courtesy.'

'Then please keep it to a minimum.'

Afterwards Stephen thought of a hundred ways he might have prolonged the conversation and come away with more credit: he could have persuaded her that he represented no threat to her children; how, on the contrary, they reminded him of the little brood of nieces and nephews he had left behind him in Cornwall; and that he would do everything in his power . . . but somehow, at the time, he was conscious only of her frosty gaze and, wishing to convince her that she need not fear him, all he said was, 'As you wish, Mistress Taverner.'

She nodded. 'Excellent. I shall see you at supper. We dine within the half hour.'

And he was alone. Only the slight fragrance of the flower water scent she wore lingered after her. His weariness forgotten, Stephen took the lantern and went to tend Breda his mare. The groom's boy still snored in the loft above, but Stephen did not bother to wake him. The familiar actions of grooming and feeding were soothing; he was troubled by his encounter with Mistress Taverner, without understanding the reason, and he needed some moments alone.

* * *

Supper that evening was an impressive affair. Sir Diggory Page had sent over from Furley Court a quantity of claret and sack and a haunch of venison. Mabs had cooked it to perfection and, at her mistress's instructions, had raided their dwindling stores of crystallised fruit, marchpanes and sweetmeats. The table had been laid with the best Venetian glass and finest china. All their silver and brazen ware (or at least that which Josiah Taverner had admitted to possessing – plenty more was hidden beneath a loose slate in his back room) had long gone to be melted down at the royal mint at Oxford, but sufficient elegant holders had been found for the candles to give off a good light.

Paul Darbier, who had slept soundly after his bath, was discussing with Master Taverner the breakdown of the recent efforts to broker peace between King and Parliament. Stephen, who had not slept a wink in nearly three days, had trouble keeping his eyes open, and, when they were open, found it difficult to focus on anything except Mistress Taverner.

Clearly, she too was exhausted, and Stephen wondered again why she had been standing on the road above the town when the soldiers first arrived. Yet despite her obvious fatigue she sat, upright and apparently serene at the head of the table, and supervised the smooth progress of the meal. From time to time she offered more food, nodded to the servants to fill a glass, move a plate, put fresh logs on the fire. She was wearing a dress both modest and elegant; its deep indigo colour glowed darkly in the candlelight. She was gracious and smiling when required, attending to the words of the men when they spoke, acting her part to perfection. Yet Stephen, who watched her with the strange clarity of a man who is past all exhaustion, yet who nonetheless feels that he is awaking from a long sleep, knew that it was a performance only. Under the surface of the good housewife, calm and competent beyond her years, he sensed something feverish and brittle. He had learned that she was twenty-eight, only a year younger than he was. Sometimes, when she was acting her part well, she looked much older. But at other times, she seemed scarcely older than her children, and neither gracious nor serene. The hatred he had seen by the roadside that morning, the hostility behind her words to him in the stable, those had been real. And they remained, he knew, beneath the quiet gestures and the polished phrases of their hostess in her dress of glowing midnight.

Paul Darbier dominated the conversation. His speech was

with Josiah Taverner, but his intended audience was the merchant's wife. Undoubtedly he cut a fine figure. His long and fashionably curling hair framed a handsome face. His cheeks were flushed with wine and his full mouth glistened. He had changed into a doublet of raised red velvet which was open, revealing the extravagant lace of his shirt. Heavy gemstones shone from his fingers. Stephen, who had merely changed one buff coat for another, and whose linen, though clean, was unadorned by any trimming, could only reflect that to be dressed as a gentleman in Cornwall was to be less elegant than many a serving man in this more wealthy heart of the kingdom.

'We are here to harry those damned malignants in Gloucester,' Darbier was saying. He spoke in an expansive drawling voice that did not invite comment, still less disagreement. 'We must stop any supplies reaching them from around here, that sort of thing. And strangle their trade with London. It won't be long before Massey is routed. Garrisons like this one will be used in the final assault. I may lead it myself.'

Josiah Taverner put his elbows on the table and rested his fingertips together in an upside-down V before him, his favourite pose when about to treat his listeners to one of his weighty opinions. 'I was not aware His Majesty's position was so strong. Isn't it less than a month since Parliament took Shrewsbury?'

Darbier dismissed this with a jewelled wave of his hand. 'A place of minor importance. I dare say we could take it again tomorrow if we so desired. However, our priority is to strengthen the army for the final assault on London. I have it on excellent authority that the whole business will be resolved by summer's end.'

'Let us hope you're right, Major. But I fear that a young man like yourself does not comprehend the fundamental importance of trade. Parliament commands the sea, and holds London too. What do you – what do *we* have to set against it, eh?'

'The finest army in the land, that's all.'

'And yet they say that Parliament also is raising a new army.'

Darbier laughed comfortably. 'The desperate act of a losing side. Their commanders are hopelessly divided. Waller and Essex would rather see each other's downfall than the King's. The rebels are doomed and they know it.'

Stephen wondered if it was perhaps a wish to impress their hostess that made Darbier paint such a rosy picture of their fortunes. He himself had lost track of the number of times he had heard the confident assertion that the rebels would be crushed by midsummer, or Michaelmas, or Christmas, or the following summer . . . He saw no reason why the royalist victory should be swift. His Majesty's generals were quite as skilled at quarrelling among themselves as Parliament's; last year the King's great victory at Lostwithiel had been precisely balanced by his great defeat at Marston Moor. As one town was captured, somewhere else another was lost. Stephen thought it possible that this cruel chess game with the people and places of England would continue for many years yet to come.

He hoped however that Darbier's optimism was justified.

'The New Noddle Army,' the major laughed, throwing his napkin down on the polished surface of the table, 'that's what my friend Digby calls it. We have nothing to fear from Captain Cobbler and his cronies, have we Stephen?'

Stephen was beginning to see that Darbier was one of those people who feel they only need to want something enough for it to be a truth. He said wearily, 'Let's hope you're right, Major.'

'Of course I'm right, dammit. Let's drink a toast to the King.'

Stephen raised his glass, and the men removed their hats.

Mistress Taverner smiled and raised her glass also, but, like Stephen, she only sipped the wine. She was measuring the two men carefully. All soldiers were her sworn enemies, but since she must share her home with these two, she wished to assess their calibre.

Major Darbier she had quickly dismissed. She judged him to be the kind of spoilt and self-indulgent youth who is easily managed. So long as his vanity was pandered to and the servants gave him all the luxuries he had been accustomed to since infancy, he would be easy to manipulate. She had considered instructing the servants to be less than efficient. The occasional cold bath or badly cleaned clothes might induce the young major to seek more congenial lodging with Sir Diggory. But she had overheard him bawling at the maids that afternoon as his bath was fetched, and had decided it was wisest to accommodate him, for the time being at least. The man would be a nuisance and a bore, but nothing worse.

Captain Sutton, however, was another matter altogether. She watched him now, but covertly, from under her lashes. He had just been served a piece of Mabs' taffety pie. She guessed he was too exhausted even to know what he was eating. His face had probably been handsome, but now was lean almost to the point of gauntness, and his clear grey eyes were ringed with dark shadows of fatigue. There was a spareness about him, an economy of movement and gesture which, had he not been a soldier, might have been attractive. Unlike the ebullient major, he looked as if this war had already cost him dear. Mistress Taverner hoped he had suffered badly and would suffer more in the future. Her head pulsed with rage as she remembered how he had tried to insinuate his way into the children's affection just now in Bonnet's stable. As if the troubles of one small child concerned him in the slightest. As if he had not already done more than his share to make widows and orphans. A soldier was evil enough, and this one was a hypocrite into the bargain. She detested the Major Darbiers of this world, but what she had never thought to encounter and hated most of all was a soldier who prided himself on being an honest killing man.

'This pie is excellent, Mistress Taverner.' As Stephen looked up from his plate he caught her eyes on him; a glimpse of venom before the gracious smile slid down like a veil.

'Mabs will be delighted that it pleases you,' she said.

But she coloured slightly as she spoke, aware that he had already seen more of her than she wished to reveal. Inwardly she writhed. No doubt the contemptible rogue considered himself to be perceptive, as well as a man of honour.

As if his sort could ever know what honour was.

While their parents were dining below with the officers, Harry and Beth were discovering the dubious delights of sharing a room with Cary. She was a strongly built girl, with chestnut curls and a face that made her seem younger than her seventeen years. It was her air of industry combined with innocence that had persuaded Mistress Taverner to take Cary on after her last confinement. Her large brown eyes shone with freshness and honesty: she had the look of someone who did not even understand the meaning of wrongdoing, let alone practise it herself. Until now she had been employed as an extra pair of hands for Nona, and she was sufficiently in awe of the aged foreigner to curb her busy tongue. With the children, there was no such restraint.

Harry and Beth's two beds had been placed one on each side of the glowing fire. Cary's little truckle bed was in a corner by the window. The children, left to their own devices for once because of the demands made on all the servants that day, had

53

washed and changed and said their prayers before she came in. They had spoken little: Beth knew that Harry was ashamed of his show of weakness in the stable, and she was too tactful to add to his woes by talking of it.

Cary was delighted to have traded her bed in the cold attic for a chance to share the children's comforts.

'Oh my, a fire to undress by!' she exclaimed as she stood by the hearth and stripped down to her shift. Her firm shoulders were pink in the firelight. 'What a topsy-turvy day this has been, I never saw anything like it. *Poor* Mabs just said that if she has to cook a meal like that every evening she'll be dead by Easter, and I told her she must speak up and say she needs the extra help because we'll all be run off our feet, especially if the gentlemen keep wanting hot baths and heaven knows what else at all hours of the day and night. *Poor* Mabs barely has the strength to get herself off to her sister's, and it'll be the same again tomorrow.'

Beth had propped herself on one elbow and was attending closely. She had always loved listening to the servants. 'Will it?' she asked. 'Will it really be the same?'

'Sure to be.' Cary was holding her broad hands to the fire. 'Worse, probably. Master Bussell said he'd heard talk of more soldiers coming in a few days. And just where they think they'll all sleep is a mystery. Tilsbury is crammed to bursting already. They're six to a bed at The Lion. And *they're* the lucky ones.'

She thumped across the room and climbed into bed. It struck Beth as peculiar that Cary, who was so much larger and longer than either she or Harry, should have the smallest bed, but she was old enough to know that nothing would be gained by commenting on this, so she merely said, 'Then who are the *un*lucky ones?'

'Sentries,' said Cary firmly, 'The soldiers have to take turns keeping watch. To make sure the town isn't attacked and all of us slaughtered in our beds while we sleep.'

Harry, who had been only half listening as he was still thinking of Bonnet, was immediately all attention. 'Slaughtered?' he asked.

'In our beds. Or worse,' added Cary in an ominous voice. There was a brief silence while Beth and Harry tried to imagine what could possibly be worse than being slaughtered in your bed. Cary was plumping up her pillow. 'That's why they put the sentries about the place. But it's a terrible job. They dare not fall asleep, no matter how tired they are, because they get horribly punished, so they try all sorts of ways to keep awake.'

'Like pinching yourself?' queried Beth, thinking of the horrors of long sermons.

Cary was thoughtful. 'That sort of thing. I heard there was once a soldier who was so desperate to stay awake he sliced off his big toe. He thought the pain would help.'

'And did it?'

'For a short while. But then the effect wore off. So he had to cut off another toe, then a third. By morning he had only two toes left and the sentry post was a sea of blood and his feet swelled up and turned green. Then the poison spread right through his body and he died anyway.'

'Oh no, poor man.'

'Hmm.' Cary, unperturbed, was settling herself for sleep. 'Mind you,' she went on in a low voice, 'there's one sentry tonight will be lucky if he survives until morning without losing his mind entirely, never mind a few toes.'

'Why?'

'They've put a sentry in the Old Priory tower. Mabs' brothers are laying bets to see if he lasts until they change the watch. I think when the next one goes to take his place they'll find him dead of fright. Have you ever seen a man who died of fright? I did once, his eyes were staring and his tongue was—'

Beth interrupted swiftly, 'But what's so bad about the Old Priory?'

'Surely you know no one goes there even in the day time. My uncle tried to ride his horse there once, for a wager, but the animal wouldn't go near the place, though he beat him till he bled. They say even foxes and rabbits won't make their home there.'

'Is it haunted?' Beth had heard vague rumours, but her mother had always told her to ignore them.

'Haunted? Of course it's haunted. Don't you children know anything? The spirit of the Grey Lady will stay in that tower for ever and ever.'

'Why the tower?'

'Because that's where she threw herself from.'

'Why?'

'I thought everyone knew. You poor ignorant children, you have been kept in the dark. I suppose I ought to tell you, for your own safety, really.' Mistress of the dramatic pause, Cary was silent for a moment or two before beginning her story, 'Years ago, when King Harry ruled in England, the Old Priory was home to a company of nuns. Grey clothes they wore, all of them, and they couldn't so much as *speak* to a man, let alone marry one. Poor things, I suppose they must have grown used to it eventually. Then King Harry decided he wanted no more monks and nuns so all the convents and priories had to close. Most of them didn't mind too much, but the woman in charge of the Old Priory here said she would never give up her vows, and some of the other women stayed there with her. So King Harry sent a bunch of soldiers to turn them off the land, and they were a horrible bloodthirsty pack of men who couldn't wait to ravish all the nuns, and murder them too, probably. But the Grey Lady escaped and climbed to the top of the tower. It was much higher then than it is now, of course, even higher than the tower of Tilsbury church. When the soldiers started to climb the tower after her, she stood on the topmost ledge, and jumped.'

'Oh no.'

'Yes. But she didn't die straight away. Her skirts stopped her from falling so fast. But she was terribly injured, and she lay in awful agony at the foot of the tower, her back all broken and bleeding. But the soldiers were so wicked they wouldn't allow anyone to help or comfort her. In fact they just laughed. And then they took their pleasure of her anyway, all twisted up and screaming in agony as she was.' Cary paused for effect while Beth and Harry wondered what kind of pleasure could have been had of the poor nun, before she concluded briskly, 'And then she died.'

Beth was weeping silently. 'How terrible,' she whispered under her breath.

Since there was nothing Cary enjoyed half so much as a tale of disaster, she carried on blithely, quite unaware of the impact her story was making on her audience. 'Then, as she was dying, the nun forgave them all their sins for what they had done, because she was a proper Christian woman, even if she was a Papist. But God saw what had happened and, do you know, every single one of those men who had done that terrible thing to her died before the end of that very year? One died of a poison snake bite, one was bitten by a mad dog and died foaming and raving, one fell from his horse and broke his neck, one stuck a knife inside himself and all his insides tumbled on to his breeches . . . I can't remember all of them now,' she added, almost apologetically, 'But I do know they all died gruesome and unnatural deaths. Serve them right, too. That's why no one will go near the Old Priory, especially not at night. Lots of people have seen the Grey Lady, or heard her singing. It's a sound that drives folk to their deaths, even now. Well, good night children, we'll have to wait for the morning to see how that poor sentry has fared. I'm glad I'm snug in here, aren't you?'

And with that, Cary rolled over, pulled her blankets around her ears and slid instantly into a dreamless sleep. Harry and Beth, wide-eyed and too terrified to move or speak, lay awake for a long while, watching the shadows from the fire flickering strangely on the ceiling.

Beth was still awake when the fire had died down completely. And, after Cary's horrible stories, it seemed to her an altogether expected thing, when she heard her mother begin to scream.

Doll was in a small, cramped space. Her cheek was pressed against cold stone, her body was twisted and numb with cold and shock. There was a searing pain across her shoulders, and a smell of burning, a smell of fear.

She knew she must make no sound, and yet in her terror it seemed that her heartbeat and her agonised breathing must be heard far beyond her dark prison.

Noise was boiling up inside her head, a hammering of fists against a door, musket shot and cannon fire and a great roar of men's voices. And then the screaming, women and children screaming in terror and pain. All she could see, from her cramped and frozen place, was a hideous dance of feet, women's feet fleeing, men's pursuing, and then a man was pulling her free, a man with a pale face and hair and eyes the colour of broken glass. The only colour was in his lips, red fleshy lips that smiled at her as he lifted the dagger and came towards her. As the scream broke from her body, she grasped the dagger from him and plunged it into his face, again and again, and still the red lips smiled and she hacked at his terrible mouth. He smiled; he was shaking her. And she opened her eyes and saw Josiah, Josiah who was shaking her awake. Then Nona appeared beside her bed, carrying a tallow and muttering consolation.

Stephen, who had been in a light sleep, also heard the sound: a series of high-pitched wails of terror followed by the noise of doors opening and closing, and the rapid tread of feet. He sat up.

Beside him in the big bed, Paul Darbier, who had consumed copious amounts of Sir Diggory's sack as well as Master Taverner's brandy, was dead to the world. Stephen's first thought was that one of his men must have frightened a serving maid. He lit a tallow, flung on his breeches, and pushed open the door on to the landing.

He was just in time to see Mistress Taverner, a shawl draped over her pale cotton shift and her hair in a long braid, cross the landing with her grandmother who seemed to be guiding her while she muttered soothing words. When the door of Nona's bedchamber closed behind them, he heard more low-voiced speech, then a quiet, chanting song. In all his life he had never heard a song like it: the same phrase repeated time and again, yet never growing monotonous. It reminded him, as he stood there on the empty landing, watched only by a couple of ghostly portraits, and the candle wax dripped over his hand, of an incantation.

A moment later a third door creaked open and a small figure hesitated only for a moment before padding over the Turkey rug to stand at his side.

'Good evening, Captain Sutton,' said Beth politely, though there was a tremor of fear in her voice, 'I hope my mother has not disturbed your sleep. She has these bad dreams sometimes. Not very often, you understand, but still . . .' Her voice faded uncertainly; she was gazing at the closed door of her grandmother's room as though she longed to be on the other side of it, but dared not enter.

Stephen said gently, 'We all have bad dreams now and then.'

Unaware of what she was doing, Beth had slipped her hand into his. 'I expect she's better now,' she said, comforting herself, 'Nona is singing to her. This is one of Mother's favourites. I think it must remind her of when she was a little girl and lived in Spain. Have you ever been to Spain, Captain Sutton?'

'No. I didn't realise your mother was Spanish.'

'She's English now,' Beth was frowning. 'But it's a shame you've not been there. I think she'd love to talk of it.'

Stephen remembered that he had earlier promised Beth's mother to keep contact with her family to a minimum, and he tried to extricate his hand. The child only held on more tightly.

'You must go back to your own room now,' he told her, 'The bad dreams are over.'

'I suppose so,' but she sounded doubtful, and still anxious.

The singing behind the closed door of the bedroom was fainter now, hardly louder than the drone of a summer insect. 'But I keep worrying about your poor sentry.'

'My sentry? Why?'

'All alone in the Old Priory tower. I hope he doesn't have to cut off his toes or anything. It's not his fault the poor Grey Lady was all broken and bleeding on the ground.'

'Of course it wasn't,' said Stephen with emphasis. He decided that Mistress Taverner was not alone in being troubled by bad dreams. He added, 'The sentries will be changing over soon, anyway. No one enjoys guard duty, but you get used to it and then the time passes quickly enough.'

His voice was reassuring. Beth was normally a shy child but she was a shrewd judge of character and had decided from the first that she could trust Captain Sutton.

She nodded. 'I'll go back to bed now.'

'Good night then. Oh, and Beth, your mother doesn't want you and your brothers to talk with us soldiers unless it is absolutely necessary.'

'Oh. I see.' Her voice was heavy with disappointment. Then she asked, 'Has this been absolutely necessary, Captain Sutton?'

Stephen considered. 'I expect it has.'

She sighed. Her mother was always stopping her talking to people. She thought of Jinny Crew and her most interesting family.

'Does that mean you won't talk to me any more?'

'I'm a soldier,' said Stephen with a smile, 'I'm used to obeying orders.'

Beth let go of his hand and moved slowly towards the door of her room. 'Oh dear,' she said, 'And I thought it was only children who always had to do what they were told.' She hesitated, 'Well then, good night, Captain Sutton.'

He bid her good night and returned to his own room, all the time wondering how it was that the same features, so unappealing in the father, could be so engaging in this homely but warm-hearted child. He decided that on balance Mistress Taverner's prohibition on contact between them was wise after all. It would have been all too easy to become attached to this unusual family – and such intimacy formed no part of his soldierly duties.

Chapter 5

❧

Jack arrived early next morning.

Stephen knew at once who it was when his bedchamber door was flung open, a deep voice boomed, 'I came as soon as I could, Captain Sutton, sir,' and a tall figure took two steps into the room, tripped on the edge of the half-open portmanteau and crashed to the floor in a flying heap of arms and legs. Darbier rolled over and groaned in his sleep. Stephen sat up and reached once again for tallow and light.

'Damnation, Jack,' he said, still in darkness, 'What in God's name do you think you're doing?'

The young man was scrambling to his feet. 'I did not want to wake you, sir,' he explained, 'So I waited at The Lion for a couple of hours, and then, finding the back door of the house was open—'

'But you *have* woken me, you idiot. It's not even light yet.'

'Yes sir. I arrived about midnight, sir.'

The light caught and Stephen had a clear view of the intruder. 'I don't care what time you arrived. You've no business bursting in at such an ungodly hour. Or at any hour, come to that.'

'No sir. I see that, Captain Sutton. Tell me, is your wound healed now, sir?'

'Yes it is, dammit. Now get out of here.'

'Yes, Captain Sutton, sir.'

The young man stood immobile. He was very tall, with black eyebrows that grew together above his nose, giving him an undeserved air of ferocity. He was glaring down at Stephen with utter devotion.

'Go on, Jack,' said Stephen wearily, 'Go downstairs. When the servants wake up – but not a moment before – tell them you're to have a mattress in the attic with the other men. And be ready to muster at daybreak.'

'Yes, Captain Sutton, *sir*.'

Jack spun round and strode from the room with such a martial air that he crashed the door behind him, finally jolting Paul Darbier awake.

'What the devil was that?'

'That was Jack.'

'Who?'

'Ensign Skipton. A young soldier who saved my life during the assault on Bristol. Or maybe I saved his, I forget now which it was. Anyway, we survived together. Since when, he has held himself personally responsible for my well-being.' From the foot of the stairs came the sound of a halberd or two clattering to the ground. 'Yes, that's Jack. Prince Rupert had his dog Boy and I seem to be stuck with Jack.'

He smiled ruefully as he climbed from the bed and began to dress.

'It's far too early to get up,' said Darbier.

'Go back to sleep then. I'll check the sentries.'

'Are there no servants in this wretched house? Are we supposed to fend for ourselves?'

'I'll have one sent to you at daybreak.'

'Hot water, ale, something to eat. Someone to light the fire and my man to attend me.'

'Anything else?'

Darbier missed the irony in Stephen's voice. Unlike Stephen, he saw no reason why the war should require any reduction of standards, quite the contrary, in fact.

'Yes. Some water now.'

Darbier drank from the jug. Apart from his thirst, he was remarkably unaffected by the vast amounts he had consumed the previous evening.

'Tell me,' he asked, just before sinking back into a deep sleep, 'Is your friend Jack a complete fool?'

Stephen considered this for a few moments before replying. 'Far from it. In many ways he is brighter than most. His only handicap is a singular excess of enthusiasm.'

Stephen had need of Jack's enthusiasm as his first full day in Tilsbury progressed. Most of the men he had brought with him from Oxford were newly recruited from the Welsh hills. Many did not have weapons, and those that did were uncertain how to use them. Increasingly, as the war dragged on, the royalist ranks were being filled by men who had been pressed into service and were likely to desert at the first opportunity.

At the lower reach of the town beyond the Priory House and the old ruined tower, a wide meadow lay in a curve in the river. In peacetime this was where the local men had practised at the butts, where the maypole had been placed and the Whitsun Ales celebrated. Women sometimes brought their washing to be beaten on the flat stones of the shore. Today the hard and frosty ground echoed to the tramp of marching feet, the roars of the sergeants and the sharp rat-tat of the drums as the men were put through their paces. Stephen, watching them, assessed the task ahead: he must double their strength if he was to have a strong company ready for the start of the campaigning season. Besides training, the soldiers were in desperate need of equipment and clothes. Half these men had walked here bare-legged, even stockings were in short supply. And they were hungry. Stephen did not underestimate the difficulty of providing supplies without earning the hatred of the local population. For that reason alone he hoped they would soon be ordered to move on. Meanwhile he was supposed to harry the rebel garrison at Gloucester and prevent any contact between them and their parliamentary allies. For that he would need the assistance of cavalry.

But the cavalry, on that bright March morning by the bend in the river, was conspicuous only by its absence. Major Darbier, whose instructions had been the same as Stephen's, had left his troopers to their own devices while he rode over to Furleys to pay his respects to Sir Diggory and ensure the continued flow of wines and good food in the direction of the Priory House.

Stephen was frowning as he walked along beside the river and watched the men who were being instructed in the rudiments of musket drill. There was a problem of language with most of the Welsh recruits. Those who understood were translating for the benefit of their fellows; Stephen dreaded to think what essentials were being missed in the process. Jack was demonstrating, with his usual panache, the procedure for load, aim and fire to a handful of rustics who looked as if they had never handled any implement more warlike than sheep shears before. They kept edging away from their instructor, eyeing the burning match warily and leaping backwards at each explosion. As well they might, thought Stephen: Jack performed the sequence with such exuberance he was likely to blow his own head off one day.

But none of these problems caused the frown which now shadowed his face. He had turned less able men into a serious fighting force before this, and he knew that within six weeks this rag-tag collection of hill farmers and country boys would be ready to kill or be killed for King Charles. Stephen was well suited to the task ahead. He had first taken up arms to fight in the white and blue colours of the Grenviles in 1639, when King Charles had marched against the Scots. By the summer of 1642, when the quarrel between King and Parliament had escalated into open warfare, Stephen already had considerable experience of military life. That was almost three years ago, though it seemed to Stephen a lifetime. Throughout that time he had dedicated himself totally to the King's cause, believing that present harsh measures would be justified only when peace was restored and the nation's suffering came to an end. For nearly three years he had thought of little else.

Until now.

He had reached the furthest stretch of meadow, where the pikemen were stamping up and down with their pikes held level. Yet his mind was not on their efforts and he had to force himself to notice that several were practising with short willow poles and he must find proper weapons for them without delay. But then a picture of Mistress Taverner floated into his mind. She was lit by the soft glow of a lantern and confronting her wayward son. 'Lordy, Harry,' he heard her say, 'Today of all days,' and he saw her raise her hands slightly in a gesture of exasperation. He paused. Beside him, the river was in full spate after the winter rains. He found himself listening to the way it bubbled over the polished stones. He looked up. Untroubled by the martial activities in the meadow, a pair of moorhens was busy in the rushes by the far bank. Small details: the kind of observations he might have made years ago when he was free to roam the Cornish countryside with no thought of teaching men the art of killing their fellows.

That was it. He remembered now the expression on Mistress Taverner's face when her guard was down. All the hatred that civilians feel for fighting men had been visible in her dark eyes. He wondered if she loathed all soldiers in general or if, unlike her husband, she was especially hostile to royalists. He found that he was both sorry, and yet glad as well, that when Mistress Taverner was troubled by bad dreams, it was to her grandmother, not to her lumpish husband, that she turned for comfort.

Stephen frowned. From the edge of the meadow nearest the town there came a roar of laughter. He strode over to investigate. Then he too was obliged to smile.

A small child had wormed his way in amongst the soldiers and was endeavouring to lift a musket by the butt, while half a dozen men stood round him offering their encouragement and advice. It was Mistress Taverner's younger son, the dark-haired boy who resembled her so closely. Stephen groaned inwardly. After his attempts to reassure his mother the previous evening, it was a bitter irony now that her child had decided to seek adventure less than a dozen paces from a budge barrel full of powder.

'What's all this?' he demanded sternly.

'Here's a new recruit, sir. Says he'll do without the King's shilling, he's so keen to be a damn soldier.'

'Mind your language in front of the child or you'll be put on extra duties.'

Hearing the anger in their captain's voice, the soldiers fell back and began to look sheepish. Only Philip was unaffected. In fact he was so busy struggling to shoulder the musket, he had not even noticed Stephen's arrival.

Stephen removed it firmly from his grasp and handed it to the sergeant. 'Young man,' he asked, 'whatever do you suppose you're doing?'

'I'm a soldier.' Deprived of his precious musket, Philip looked up cheerfully. Stephen realised that at least one of Mistress Taverner's children was not at all frightened by soldiers, far from it.

'Who brought you here?'

'I brought myself. I was in the kitchen and Pedlar Sam came by to show Mabs and Nona what he had and while they were talking and looking, I got away. Now I'm a proper soldier.'

'No, you're going home where you belong. Don't argue with me,' Stephen's voice could be fierce when he chose and he calculated that this was an occasion requiring fierceness, 'I'm taking you back to your mother myself and I never want to see you here again.'

65

'But—'

'No buts. Come with me. Men, back to your drill. And if any
other children see fit to play at soldiers, they're to be sent
packing at once, is that understood? There'll be no accidents to
civilians while I'm in charge.'

Philip was contemplating disobedience, but he saw how all
the other soldiers obeyed their captain, so reluctantly he fell in
beside Stephen. Slightly breathless from keeping up with
Stephen's long stride, Philip panted, 'Why can't I be a soldier?'

Not slowing his pace for a moment, Stephen glanced down at
him. The child had his mother's ivory pallor and velvet dark
eyes and the energy of a firework. Stephen remembered only
too well the frustration of being denied treats because of age at
a time when childhood seemed likely to go on for ever, so he
said, 'Because you have much to learn before you can be a good
soldier. You must be able to read and write, and you must learn
to do as you are told. No one can give orders until he has learned
to obey. One day you'll no doubt be an officer and a boy must
prepare himself if he is to serve King Charles.'

Here Stephen broke off suddenly. Behind him on the muster
ground, a loud cheer had erupted from Jack's recruits as the
ensign's hat was blown clean into the river by an untimely
musket shot.

Stephen was so absorbed by his small companion that he did not
notice the newcomer until he had reached the gate of the Priory
House. A well-dressed woman was waiting for him to catch up
with her. She was perhaps in her early thirties, and attended by
a manservant who was wearing some rudimentary livery. Had
Stephen not been preoccupied, he might have noticed a certain
familiarity in her features.

He held open the gate. Before passing through ahead of him,
she looked up with studied amusement. 'Has Doll Taverner
already enlisted your services as a nursemaid?'

Stephen grinned. 'Children and soldiers are a poor mix,' he
said.

'Nonsense, Captain Sutton, you are too modest. The child is
clearly devoted to you already.'

She had the kind of deliberately soft voice that very
determined women sometimes adopt in order to mask their
steel. She had an abundance of mousy hair and her features
were far from beautiful – slightly protuberant eyes and a chin

that would soon be lost in a series of doubles – but she had the imposing manner of a woman who expects to be admired. And who, in consequence, almost always is.

'You have the advantage of me, ma'am,' said Stephen, 'since you already know my name.'

'Of course I do,' she said, sailing into the house ahead of him and letting her cloak fall into the arms of the little maid who had opened the door, while her manservant retired to the kitchens, 'You and Major Darbier are already famous throughout the entire length and breadth of Tilsbury. It's hardly to be wondered at. Your arrival has been the greatest excitement in our little world since the Flood.'

Her breathy voice had an air of mockery. She had paused in front of a round mirror to touch her hair and adjust the kerchief at her bodice. She caught Stephen's reflection, observing her, and held his glance for a fraction longer than was prudent, causing him to forget that he still held little Philip by the hand.

He remembered a moment later when Mistress Taverner swept down the stairs and caught the boy in her arms in a barely disguised tumult of relief and anger. 'You wicked boy!' she hugged him furiously, 'How dare you run off and make us all worry so?'

Philip wriggled. 'When I can read I'm going to be an officer in the army!'

'Never!' Doll darted a furious glance at Stephen. 'Don't even joke about such things.'

'Then I suggest you keep a better watch on the boy,' said Stephen, who was not prepared to take the blame for Philip's military ambitions. 'A muster ground is no place for a child.'

'Captain Sutton,' her flaring nostrils alone betrayed her rage, 'I do not believe you have anything to teach me about the dangers children run in time of war.'

The visitor, who had observed the reunion between mother and son with an expression that might perhaps have indicated envy, interrupted smoothly, 'Doll, my dear, you must not be so fierce. I am sure Captain Sutton did not mean to imply criticism. Everyone knows you to be the most devoted of mothers. Now I want you to put him out of his misery since I know he is consumed with curiosity to know who I am and I do not have the time to tell him myself. Is your grandmother in her room? I need to speak with her urgently.'

Remembering her duties as a hostess, Doll embraced her

visitor, though with more politeness than affection, before saying, 'No, all the rooms have been changed around. Ellen will take you. Everything is upside down today.'

'I don't believe you, Doll. You're always so wonderfully organised. You put me to shame.'

The two women eyed each other warily for a moment. Stephen was struck by the contrast between them: Mistress Taverner was all unconscious beauty, with a touch of wildness about her, while her visitor was a study in artifice and social poise. Just as Ellen began to lead her up the wide stairway, the stranger threw Stephen a final, teasing smile.

Mistress Taverner, still holding her son tightly, settled on the lowest stair. She seemed to have forgotten anyone else was there as she scolded Philip tenderly. With the swift transitions possible in the very young, he had shifted from a would-be soldier to a rather sleepy small boy, and was contentedly sucking his thumb.

'Your visitor's name?' Stephen asked.

She shifted her position slightly to accommodate Philip's weight before answering, 'Mistress Corinna Rogers. Like many people in this town, she believes my grandmother can see into the future. That is why she comes to consult her.'

'And do you also believe in your grandmother's powers?'

She did not answer him straightaway. She appeared uneasy, and Stephen wondered suddenly if she had seen him on the landing when she had been troubled by her dream. Blue shadows ringed her eyes. Then she gave an odd little smile. 'Of course I do,' she said, 'But then, my case is different.'

'How so?'

'Nona's powers have always been my only protection. I *must* believe in them.'

'Are you in such need of protection?'

She did not respond straight away, but rested her chin thoughtfully on her son's black crown of hair. Then she said, 'Unlike my grandmother, I cannot answer questions about the future.' Suddenly she was brisk and businesslike again. 'My family will take their midday meal in the winter parlour. Food has been laid out for you and Major Darbier in the hall, if you require it,' she indicated the room in which they had supped the previous evening, on the other side of the passage. 'Ellen will see that you have all you need.'

She stood up and was about to lead Philip up the stairs when

Stephen said, 'Mistress Taverner, wait.' All morning he had been rehearsing how he might convince his reluctant hostess that he regretted the difficulties caused her by the soldiers, but the look that she now turned on him was so frosty that the words he had prepared seemed clumsy and inadequate. He was nothing if not tenacious. 'Our presence here is a nuisance for you,' he said, 'I wish it could be otherwise.'

'How so, otherwise?'

'I wish the war may soon be over.'

'In Germany the fighting has already lasted for a generation.'

'Pray God that never happens here.'

'When both sides pray to God so fervently I am sure He knows not which way to turn.'

Though the words were lightly spoken, Stephen could sense the tension that lay behind them.

He said, 'Then I shall confine myself to hoping that the garrison is soon removed from Tilsbury.'

'Do you indeed, Captain Sutton?' she asked sceptically, 'How very kind of you.' Then she smiled. 'But really, you know, the inconvenience is nothing. My husband and I are delighted to make a contribution, however small, to His Majesty's noble cause.'

Stephen could have shaken her for the insincerity of it, yet he found himself instead on the verge of laughter. Then again, he thought what a fine thing it would be if he could take her hand and persuade her that she had no reason to fear.

And Doll inclined her head and went on up the stairs with her son, leaving him alone with his confusion.

Stephen was washing down the bread and cold meat with a glass of ale when the door swung open, and Corinna Rogers swept in. He stood up.

'Captain Sutton, don't let me interrupt your meal.'

'I was just finishing, Mistress Rogers.'

'That's good, you know my name, so we may consider ourselves introduced. How are you enjoying your stay in our little backwater?'

'Your town has much to recommend it, I am sure, but I have not been sent here to enjoy myself.'

'So stern, Captain. But perhaps your views will be tempered by and by. We shall endeavour to see you are entertained.'

Stephen smiled at the playful teasing implied by her tone,

such a contrast to Mistress Taverner's suppressed anger. He asked, 'How was your meeting with the old woman?'

'Good heavens, Captain, are you trying to probe my secrets already? How audacious. Luckily for you I am not someone who easily takes offence. Besides, I am an open book,' her eyes dilated slightly, 'Ever since my dearest husband went off to fight – for His Majesty, of course, like yourself – I have been in a *ferment* to know how he does.'

The look she gave Stephen as she uttered the word 'ferment' was anything but wifely.

'Whose regiment did he join?' asked Stephen, enjoying himself.

'He is with the dragoons. They say you fought with Sir Bevil Grenvile and his Cornishmen.'

'That's right.'

'I can tell from your voice. I have never been able to make up my mind whether a Devon or a Cornish accent is the most attractive in a man. Now that we have met, I rather think it may be the Cornish. When we are both at leisure, you really must tell me of your adventures. In the first year of the war it was news of the Cornish victories that kept us from despair.'

The smile died on Stephen's face. 'They were hard won,' he said tersely.

'Of course they were. All the more reason why you should allow yourself a little indulgence now that you have found safe harbour in Tilsbury. I trust you are being made comfortable?'

'We have been treated handsomely.'

She was drawing on her gloves. 'Excellent.' She tugged the soft leather down over her fingers one by one, with slow precision, then raised her eyes to Stephen's face with a look of great directness. 'But I feel it is only fair to tell you that Doll, who is a dear friend and quite above reproach, is nonetheless a foreigner, and her ways are not always ours. Moreover, I have heard that she sometimes finds company irksome. So, Captain Sutton, if the hospitality in this house ever begins to pall, please remember that my husband and I are also eager to do our part for His Majesty's forces. As it happens, dear Tom is absent from home, but I know he'd want me to make you welcome.'

It was not so much the words that took Stephen aback, more the expression that accompanied them. He had observed that look many times before in the eyes of whores in Bristol and Oxford, but never in his life had he seen it in the eyes of a respectable wife in a small market town.

He was smiling again. 'You are most generous, Mistress Rogers.'

She turned away and into the screens passage where the maid was holding her cloak and her manservant was waiting to attend her, and she said with a clear, bright laugh, 'There, Captain Sutton, I can keep nothing from you. I am generous to a fault. Until our next meeting, then.'

She sailed with majestic confidence out into the noon sunshine. And the house seemed a smaller, emptier place once the front door had shut behind her.

Nona was coming down the stairs and her face was creased with smiles.

'Was Mistress Rogers pleased with what you told her?' asked Stephen.

'Of course. She always likes what I tell her.'

Nona grinned even more broadly, showing her three remaining teeth in all their lonely glory. She patted Stephen on the arm and waddled past him into the dining hall. Stephen followed. She began helping herself to ale and bread, pulling out the soft middle and throwing the crusts to a couple of overweight spaniels who lay on the hearth.

'Miss Corinna is my best visitor. Always has been,' she explained between mouthfuls, 'No one else ever gives poor Nona a penny for her trouble. But Mistress Corinna is a good girl. So I am careful what to tell her.' Her laughter made her face collapse into a thousand wrinkles.

Stephen was about to question her more, when Mistress Taverner came into the room. 'Why are you bothering Captain Sutton, Nona? I've told you twice already this morning that we are to dine in the winter parlour from now on. You never listen to a word I tell you.'

'Stop fussing. I forget – too busy,' and she beamed at her granddaughter and patted the money pouch that hung from her waist. 'How can I remember all these changes now, eh?'

'You can remember well enough when it suits you. Just because you've a few coins in your pocket—'

'*Your* pocket. Here – ' Nona tossed the purse towards her granddaughter, 'You be glad Nona still makes money for you. Now, stop bothering me. I'll finish my food here. This soldier is glad of company, eh?'

71

'Delighted,' agreed Stephen easily.

'Tst. You're a wicked old nuisance,' exclaimed Doll, as she stalked from the room.

Nona chuckled unconcernedly and patted the chair next to hers. 'Pay no mind. When she worries, she's cross. Here, drink some ale.'

'No one likes to have soldiers billeted on them,' said Stephen, taking the seat she had indicated, 'I'm sure your granddaughter has good reason to be annoyed.'

The small black eyes observed him shrewdly. 'More than you know, soldier man,' she said softly, and suddenly her laughter was very far distant. 'Dola has a good memory, and good memories are bad, eh?'

'Why should she—?'

The old woman interrupted him. 'Our past is not your business. We talk of Miss Corinna. You like Sir Diggory's daughter?'

'Sir Diggory?' Stephen was silent for a few moments, absorbing this. Yes indeed, there was a definite resemblance between the patrician face of the elderly gentleman who had pressed them to share his hospitality at Furleys, and the forthright Mistress Rogers.

Nona poked him with an arthritic finger. '*That* surprises you, eh? Plain Mistress Rogers now, but she was grand enough before. Never marry for love, and that's the truth. Not that she did. She says she marry her Tom Rogers for love. Huh, to avoid a scandal, that's all. And now her handsome man goes off to war and leaves her all alone in her big empty bed, and she wonders will he return or not? Must she enjoy herself while she can, or does she have the widow's freedom ahead? Such problems these grand ladies suffer from, eh?'

Stephen grinned. 'And you told her what she wanted to hear?'

'Naturally, that's what she pays me for.' More chuckling, 'Her Tom will come home when he's good and ready, that's what I tell her. But many changes happen first, some good, some not so good!' At this she was almost overcome with merriment, and it was some moments before she could speak again.

Stephen was watching her with some concern. He was very much afraid Nona might choke. He noticed that Ellen had come in while they were talking and had lingered over her work, no doubt eager to pick up the details of their conversation. Discretion did not seem to be part of the service Nona offered.

'Tell people what they want to hear,' she told Stephen when she had caught her breath, 'But add in some trimming, make it sound good.'

'That's the code of honour of every charlatan,' commented Stephen, who was beginning to warm to the old woman.

At once Nona was serious again. 'Oh no, I'm no charlatan. You believe what you want, it make no difference. I never make up anything important, only select the right bits.'

'So you think you can see into the future?'

'Sometimes.'

'And what do you see there for me?'

'You want to know?'

'Yes.'

Nona sat very still for a little while, then turned slowly to face him. Her tiny eyes were almost closed and he could see the whites below her irises. Her head was tilted slightly backwards. Then she raised her hand and touched him, very gently, on the side of his face. Stephen, who had only asked in jest, felt a shiver run down his back.

She opened her eyes and beamed toothlessly. 'No need to look into the future to know about you,' she chuckled, 'It's written all over your face!'

'What do you mean?'

She slapped her knees with delight and chuckled, but no matter how Stephen cajoled, she refused to tell him any more.

Corinna Rogers walked slowly down the main street, her manservant following at a respectful distance. She was enjoying the bright March sunshine and was in no hurry to return home just yet. The Rogers' home in Distaff Lane was considered quite large by Tilsbury standards – though not as large as the Priory House – but Corinna found it practically a hovel compared to Furleys, where she had grown up.

Not that she had any regrets. Corinna Page had forsworn regrets when she was only sixteen and her brother's new tutor had shown her, in exquisite and memorable detail, exactly what the Prayer Book meant when it referred to 'the sins of the flesh'. Her only surprise then was that people ever bothered to spend their time doing anything else. John Bellman was an attentive lover, and she had been distraught when he suddenly left to take up a post in Leicestershire. Looking back now, she suspected he must have grown weary of the demands of a young girl who had nothing more to fill her time beyond scheming their next assignation. Also, no doubt, the whispers were beginning to crystallise into rumour and he needed to move on before scandal ruined them both. All in all, Corinna realised she had many reasons to be grateful to the memory of John Bellman, and her distress at his leaving lasted only until she made the discovery that there were plenty of other men in her father's household ready to be just as attentive. In the years that followed she had become adept at fending off respectable suitors while developing a sixth sense about which men could be relied on to be discreet. Tom Rogers, she remembered, had been employed to repair some damage done by a runaway cart to one of the gateposts at Furleys. She vaguely intended to continue with her amusements for as long as possible, until a wealthy marriage with one of her father's neighbours became inevitable. She had an idea that once married she would settle down and change altogether, she would produce a string of children and become fat and good. But long before she was able to test this out, her younger brother Frederick discovered her and Tom Rogers energetically occupied behind the dovecote. Although a profligate himself, Frederick had fixed ideas about the behaviour proper to young ladies: before the day was over she found herself betrothed to the young stonemason. She did not waste time being sorry. He was strong and handsome and totally besotted with his bride. Her father, who had not been told the full story, settled some money on the young couple and they moved into the house in Distaff Lane. Tom took on a couple of workmen to help him and for a few months all was contentment.

Children did not follow, nor did Corinna's hoped-for goodness or fatness. She was still fond of her handsome Tom, but during the long hours that he was busy at his trade, her old boredom returned. And Tom was often bad tempered. He was an excellent stonemason, but a hopeless employer and had no head for business. Several times Corinna had to appeal to her father for help in paying their debts. Moreover her husband had no intention of letting her amuse herself with anyone but him. On several occasions her gentle Tom had become quite violent when he suspected she had been flirting.

All in all it had been something of a relief when he took the King's shilling and enlisted with a local regiment. Of course she hoped he would return safely – but not just yet. She wanted to have a little more entertainment before finally settling down to be a dutiful goodwife in the town. The other townswomen regarded the arrival of the soldiers as an unmitigated disaster. Corinna hoped to turn it to her own advantage. She had observed the two officers the previous morning when they sat outside The Lion. Major Darbier was the most obviously handsome; she was the first to appreciate his dark good looks and his air of pleasure-loving energy. But he also looked self-indulgent and boastful. The last thing she wanted was a lover who would brag of his exploits. Nothing must spoil her reunion with Tom. So she scrutinised the other officer and found him entirely to her liking. He had lean straight features, a firm mouth and clear grey eyes. His pared-down gestures indicated a man who had experience of warfare but no social affectation. That combination of strength and gentleness was one she had always found deeply appealing.

She had gone to visit Nona that morning, not out of any urgent curiosity concerning Tom's return, but because she had learned that the major was visiting her father and she wanted to make the most of this chance to meet the handsome captain alone. As she walked home she considered that her first meeting with Stephen Sutton had been highly satisfactory. He had been impressed – as had been her intention – and had looked at her with that hungry expression men have sometimes when they have been too long denied the company of women. There was an air of raw energy about him: she guessed him to be a masterful soldier who was a novice where women were concerned – a thoroughly delicious combination, in her opinion. And someone whose discretion she could rely on.

Her friend Doll was clearly treating the soldiers with the coolness one would have expected. Corinna had always been puzzled by Doll. The foreigner's affection was all for her children, she was unlikely to provide a warm welcome for the poor lonely soldiers.

Corinna remembered the stories that had circulated about her neighbour when she first arrived. She remembered too the first time she had seen her in church with her husband. Corinna had been appalled at the sight of someone so young, barely more than a child, entering the church on the arm of such a grotesque and old-looking man. And Doll – what a terrible name to be burdened with. Though if Josiah Taverner had thought he was bringing a child's plaything home with him from the wars, then he must surely be a disappointed man now. She could imagine her treating the soldiers with the frosty politeness of a thrifty housewife who sees her precious stores being squandered by the minute. Such details were of no concern to Corinna. She would merely send to Furleys if her own supplies ran short. She knew her father had been complaining for some time about the heavy burden of taxation and the levies imposed to support King Charles's forces, but she had been brought up in abundance: impossible to imagine Furleys as anything but a bottomless pit of good things.

With no fear that any problem might arise in her campaign to enjoy the Cornish captain, Corinna began to plan her next move.

Stephen was not the only person to have been impressed by Corinna Rogers that morning. Josiah, dining with his wife and children in the winter parlour, had heard her voice in the passageway and had resisted the urge to go and speak with her. Corinna Rogers had been much in his mind recently. He had heard the rumours, had dismissed them as malicious gossip, but then, when he saw her walking in the street, or passed her as she rode out to visit her father at Furleys, something in the frankness of her gaze, the way she placed her foot on the groom's hands as she mounted her horse, set him to wondering.

Ever since he was a young man, Josiah had both feared and craved the sexual act. He had been brought up to believe it a sin and, during his years as a mercenary in Europe, he had seen plenty of evidence to support this idea. His marriage had been in part an attempt to atone for his frequent thoughts and occasional acts of lust. But if he had hoped that marriage would bring him relief from the fires that drove him, then he was only partially satisfied. Never once had his Doll rejected him, but he knew that his attentions sickened her. If abstinence had been one kind of torture, then this was just another. Not for one moment had she enjoyed him.

He had glanced out of the window of the winter parlour and caught sight of Mistress Rogers' distinctive walk, the walk of a woman who revels in her awareness of men's desire. His thoughts raced ahead of him. He had lain with prostitutes who received him because they were paid, and with his wife who did so because she must, but never in his whole life had he had intercourse with a woman who did it for the sheer pleasure of the act, as Corinna Rogers was said to do.

Chapter 6

❧

Mistress Taverner was stitching gold coins and precious stones into the seams of her husband's black coat.

It was late, the rest of the household was asleep and she was exhausted. She sat on a high-backed chair by the fire in their bedroom. Josiah watched her as she worked. The material of his coat was thick and she had a hard job sometimes to press the needle through. Besides, her hands were shaking.

She glanced up at him swiftly: her eyes were large. 'Why are you going?'

'It is very tiresome to have to repeat everything, Doll. If you would only listen when I explained the first time – but there, you are worse than the children at paying attention. As I told you before, it is necessary to spread the risk. If our hiding places here are discovered, we'll still have something put by in London. Never put all your eggs in one basket, that's my motto. Nor all your pearls in one coat lining, eh?' He wheezed dry humour at his own joke. 'That's enough in there, Doll. Put those others inside my beaver hat.'

She set the coat aside and picked up the hat which was trimmed with Russian fur. 'You told me we'd be safe. You said—'

'Plunder, Doll, plunder. That's the danger now, as I told you before. The English soldier is not in the habit of killing women and children – except in Ireland, of course, but that's different – but he'll help himself to another man's property if he gets the chance. I do not mean to part with more than I must.'

'Then why leave us unprotected now, of all times?'

'You must accept that I only act in my family's best interest, Doll, and cease plaguing me with your questions.'

She picked up the scissors and stabbed at the lining of the hat with such ferocity that Josiah said, 'Watch what you're doing there, Doll. That's my best hat, as well you know.'

Turning away to hide her irritation, she said, 'What chance does a foreigner like me have when men go to war?'

'Tst, Doll. You think only of yourself, whereas I must consider what is best for all of us. Besides, what are you fretting about? I've told you, and I really have no wish to repeat myself, they may tear the house apart from roof to cellar but they'll find little of value, I've made sure of that.'

The prospect of her precious home being ransacked was hardly comforting. 'If there's such a danger, why not take me and the children with you to London?'

'And leave my home empty? That would just be an invitation to plunder. Besides, so long as you are entertaining our officer friends, we show our loyalty to His Majesty. If the King succeeds, we will be rewarded. While I am in London I intend to let it be known that my real sympathies are with Parliament. You see, Doll, no one can tell which way the tide will flow. But Josiah Taverner will be on the winning side when this fight is decided. I'll not see my life's work undone by a damned war.'

Doll could see the logic of his plan, but logic had nothing whatsoever to do with the panic which burned inside her.

'You are determined to go, then?'

'Tomorrow morning.'

'The roads are not safe, you've said so yourself. Supposing—?'

'We must place our trust in God, my dear, having done all that is humanly possible, the rest, I am sure you agree, is up to divine providence.' Josiah often used God to clinch a debate when his mind was made up. Doll knew that argument was useless, had known it from the beginning, but her fear was so overpowering that she had been pleading in spite of herself. She had never done so before. In the past, her husband's absences had been a welcome respite, but now that the town was full of soldiers, everything was changed.

He leaned forward once again. 'I am gratified by your concern for my safety, Doll. You have not been so forthcoming on previous occasions and I must say that has saddened me.' She glanced at him swiftly to see if he was mocking her, but it was impossible to say. He went on ponderously, 'Marriage is of course a holy sacrament, but I believe it is also a kind of bargain. One does not usually choose to spell it out precisely, but in a time like the present a little plain speaking is in order. I am leaving you here alone, Doll, not out of regard for my own safety, far from it, but because I believe that it is necessary for our future prosperity. This means that I must place a heavy burden of trust on you. I hope and pray that you will show yourself worthy of that trust. I do not need to remind you, Doll, just how much you owe me—'

She shielded her eyes with her hand. 'No—' She was willing him not to go on.

'Every wife owes a duty to her husband, but you, Doll, are beholden to me even for your life. Everything that you have, your very existence, is the result of what I have done for you. Without me—'

She stood up. 'I know,' she breathed, 'I know. You need not—'

He rose to his feet also. 'I wish I did not feel the necessity, Doll, for us to talk in this way, but I must say that in recent times I have often had cause for disappointment. Our marriage, as I am sure you are aware, has not turned out as I expected. I will not go so far as to say that you have failed me, and God knows, I am a patient man. But still, this hour of danger is your chance to repay some little of the great good I have done for you.'

The constriction that Doll felt around her chest made it difficult to speak, but she managed, 'I have never given you cause to complain.'

He lowered his head slightly, as a bull does, thrusting his large face towards her and said, 'Doll, you have never given me anything.'

She flinched. 'I will endeavour to protect our home.'

'Good.'

A familiar rage began to bubble up inside her. 'Just let them try to touch it, I'll kill them every one, and gladly.'

'Yes, my dear, I believe you would. But that is not my intention at all, far from it. You will be gracious to the officers while I am gone, Doll. There will be no fits of temper, do you understand? Nor do I wish to hear that they have suffered any mysterious ailments, none of your grandmother's heathen potions, or you'll have me to answer to when I return. Use your womanly arts, my dear, the soldiers' goodwill is your best protection.'

'I will try.'

'Be sure you do. Because believe me, Doll, I shall be kept informed of all that goes on here, no matter how far away I am. I will receive regular reports. Do I make myself clear?'

Again the constriction in her breathing. She placed a pale hand against her upper chest, as though to slow the rapid beating of her heart.

'Bussell?' she queried. She had long suspected the steward of being her enemy.

'Why would I name my informer? Besides, I may have more than one. You should know by now that I leave nothing to chance.'

Suddenly her clothes hung from her limbs like lead weights, and the air in the room was grown thick and putrid. She stood up and crossed to the window, fumbling with the latch in her eagerness to open it. Just a breath of crisp night air, and Josiah had pulled the window closed again.

'Do you want me to catch my death of cold?' he asked angrily.

'I cannot breathe.'

'What nonsense. Of course you can. Return to your work.'

'Let me open the window.'

'No.' He placed his bulk four square in front of her. She raised her hands in protest. Her lungs were burning 'You think you can get rid of me by freezing me out. Not this time, Doll.'

They stood face to face.

'I must have air.'

'Enough, Doll. You have work to do. Sit, and sew. It is not so much to ask when I have given you everything.'

His words fell like dead weights upon her. 'No –' she breathed. She swayed, her eyes grew dark and she raised her hand, as though to push him aside. He parried her blow easily, and, at his touch, she crumpled to the ground in a faint.

It lasted only for a few moments. Josiah was standing over her when she opened her eyes.

'Fetch Nona,' she murmured, 'I am not well.'

Josiah smiled. 'None of your foreign tricks, Doll. They don't work on me like they used to. This last evening is for us together, and alone.'

It was a few moments before her strength returned. She rose slowly to her feet, and returned painfully to her chair. She was shielding her eyes with her hand. Josiah resumed his seat and waited patiently until she picked up her sewing once again.

And so they remained together by the fireside, a tranquil image of marital harmony, the husband smiling as his wife stitched on into the small hours of the night.

* * *

No one watching Josiah's departure the following morning would have suspected the painful scene that had occurred. Both husband and wife were concerned to present a united front for public viewing, Josiah because he liked to be seen as a devoted family man, his wife because her authority in the house derived from her position as his deputy. At first light Josiah had been closeted for over an hour with Bussell and she had no wish to find herself playing second fiddle to his long-nosed steward.

Despite her superficial calm, Doll was in a state of turmoil. Her faint the previous evening had been no trick, nor had it been unprecedented. From time to time over the years her rage and frustration had grown to such a pitch that she felt she must burst or destroy something or go insane. Her fierce self-control would not permit any show of weakness. The explosion was inward: she blacked out. Never for more than a moment or two, though she would feel unsteady for some time afterwards. Until now she had usually contrived to keep these little deaths, as she saw them, secret from everyone but Nona.

Now she tried to obliterate all memory of her humiliation the previous evening. If she thought of Josiah's words at all, they only baffled her. What more could she possibly have given him?

As always she had performed her morning tasks efficiently. There was reassurance in the practical and routine. If she could only concentrate on sweeping and polishing and the ordering of meals, then there was less room for thought. She might be able to block off the dark and nameless fears that lingered in the spaces between activity. When she had returned to her bedchamber just now, she had imagined she saw a movement of the panel that hid the priest's hole. And all at once she knew that behind that smooth surface of oak, a man could be concealed. A man, it might be, with a pale and bloodless face, and eyes like broken glass.

Small wonder, then, that she did not experience her usual fierce elation when she saw Josiah's portly back recede into the distance as he rode away. Usually on the days of his departure the servants would be startled to hear her singing as she went about her work, and the children were petted and given special treats.

But today was different. Today a group of soldiers were tramping down the street on their way to the muster ground. The townspeople watched them with blank faces. The air itself seemed heavy with dread. Only little Jinny Crew and her

81

brothers skipped along beside the men, hopping from one foot to the other in time to the drum's steady beat.

Josiah was no longer visible. She was alone. Alone for the second time in her life in a foreign land where soldiers held all the power. The years were slipping away as if they had never been. She closed her eyes, summoning all her strength. When she opened them again, it was to see Major Darbier sliding from his horse and coming forward to greet her.

'I hear your husband has been obliged to leave us,' he said. His cheeks were glowing from the early morning ride. He had glimpsed the fear in her eyes when she first noticed him. He was gratified that the cool and aloof Mistress Taverner regarded him as a threat, and he added, 'You are alone, then.'

It occurred to Doll then that her husband would be gone for some time, whatever reports his spies sent back to him. She had a sudden wild impulse to tell the odious major that he was no longer welcome in her home and he must leave at once. The storm would follow eventually, but would it not be worthwhile to have had the satisfaction of speaking her true mind, just once in her life? She heard Josiah's voice inside her head, 'You will be gracious to the officers, Doll. Their goodwill is your best protection.'

She turned to Paul Darbier but avoided looking at him directly, 'Yes, he asked me to convey his apologies to you and to Captain Sutton. I am to see that you are well looked after, in his place.'

Darbier grinned like a fox who has just been given the keys to the chicken coop. 'How very gracious of him. We must endeavour to entertain ourselves as best we can while he is gone.'

He offered her his arm. Doll hesitated only for a fleeting moment before taking it, and they walked in apparent amity up the wide path that led to her home; her skirt grazed the leaves of rosemary and thyme which gave off a pungent scent as she passed.

If his wife had been dismayed by the events of the previous evening, then so too was Josiah. Like her, he refused to show his feelings.

From boyhood he had known himself to be a creature of little charm. With his big head and his ponderous manner he had never learned the art of winning affection. Even his mother, his gentle, pious mother, had preferred his brothers and sisters. They were far livelier than he, they laughed together and had games from which he was excluded. Clumsy Josiah, the lumbering nuisance, the child whose absence was never missed.

He was born in the Priory House, and he had been reared in the Catholic faith. Almost before he was out of skirts he had overheard the rumours surrounding his home and his family. Because the Taverners had grown rich and then built their home by the ruins of the old convent, it was widely believed that the family was ill-fated. Certainly no Taverner father had yet lived long enough to see his heir reach manhood. Even in those times of high mortality, they were more unfortunate than most. Josiah's own father had been thrown into prison when the priest was discovered in their home; he had died of plague before his case ever came to trial. Josiah had been nine years old. From then on he had begun to conceive a passionate hatred for the religion that had cost his father so dear, and to which his mother still clung with pathetic devotion. He kept his thoughts to himself. His opinion was seldom requested, anyway.

But gradually he discovered his sole accomplishment: he could survive. One by one his pretty little sisters and his charming brothers succumbed to accident or sickness until only he and his eldest brother remained; their mother, too stricken by grief to carry on, retreated to the darkened bedchamber in which she was soon to die. That was when Josiah left his home and became a mercenary in the German wars. He half-hoped to lose his life in a glorious cause, since his survival seemed in some strange way to be an affront to the siblings who had perished. He knew that his mother was wondering what cruel trick of fate had left her with the child she cared for least.

He fought for the Protestant cause with the passion of a convert. To begin with, he was appalled by the sufferings of the ordinary people in the land through which the war had passed. In time, he ceased to notice it.

Until he found Doll. She had been so alone, so helpless. He was all that stood between her and annihilation. For almost the first and only time, when he gathered up her lifeless body in his arms, he saw himself transformed from an ugly misfit to a valiant knight. To the rest of the world he might be one of nature's cruel jokes, but this fragile child would be forever in his debt. She was another Ruth, friendless among the alien corn, and he, like Boaz, must raise her up. And she would be grateful. His little Doll: it was surely fortuitous that the English version of her name was that of a child's toy. At last in his beautiful Doll he had discovered the one person who must return his love.

It was a little while before he realised that this dream, like all his others, was unattainable. She was so shocked, in those first months and years, that it was easy to find reasons for her coolness – for nearly two years she never even spoke. But the time eventually came when he could no longer ignore the subtle alteration in her each time he entered a room, the way she broke off her singing or her talk, the way her expression became fixed and cold. Nor could he deny the look of disgust, quickly suppressed, whenever he approached her in their bed.

And she never allowed him to watch her dance.

If she had shown any fondness for him, he would have endeavoured to be a reasonable, even a kind husband, but, it seemed, she had not one grain of affection to offer him. She was never defiant, never opposed him directly, but neither had she taken a single step towards him. Never once had she sought out his company or come to tell him some piece of trivia concerning the children or the household. He knew too well how she brightened when he was planning a journey, how she sank into lethargy on his return.

Years ago he had rescued her, yes, but the rescue had not set her free. On the contrary, his action had made her his prisoner, and she, in her turn, did not allow him to forget her chains for a moment.

Josiah had lost track of the number of times he had toyed with the idea of getting rid of her. She had no family in this country to protect her interests, so it would not have proved difficult to do – messy, perhaps, or unpleasant, but perfectly reasonable. He told himself it was only the fear of her grandmother, that old witch who had stood guard over the girl since the first day he met them, which prevented him; but here, as in so much else, Josiah deceived himself. He could have got rid of the old woman somehow had he been determined enough. The truth was that he feared a scandal. Knowing himself to be little liked, he clung all the more tenaciously to the trappings of respectability. His many enemies would have been only too pleased to see his reputation in tatters. He would not give them that satisfaction. His marriage might be a hollow sham of the happiness he had hoped for, but it would not be made a mockery.

Besides, deep down, Josiah Taverner still hoped that his beautiful wife might one day come to feel, if not love, then some small glow of gratitude, or even affection.

Dear God, was that so very much to ask?

He knew he had small reason to complain. There had been compensations in plenty along the way: his elder brother had died a few months before he returned from Germany, leaving him to inherit the Priory House and his family's faltering business. Applying the ruthlessness he had learned in the wars, Josiah turned trade around and discovered the addictive delights of making money. It mattered less now that people disliked him: he had their fear and respect and that was a reasonable substitute. He became a person of modest importance in the county. Power, like money, was a potent drug: on a few occasions he had ruined smaller traders just for the satisfaction of demonstrating his strength.

So too with his wife. Doll did not – apparently she could not – care for him. Very well, his pleasure would come from the certainty of his power over her. He provided her with fine clothes and expensive jewels, knowing he could take them from her any time he wished. He delighted to see her with their children: those too she would forfeit if ever he had reason to cast her off. Once or twice he had considered the idea of sending her away unless she allowed him to watch her dance, but for some reason, at the last minute, he always held back; some lingering shred of humanity, perhaps, or a reluctance to play his final hand too soon.

Strangely enough, as he rode away from Tilsbury with a fair proportion of his worldly goods sewn into the seams and linings of his clothes, Josiah Taverner was not in the least troubled by doubts about his wife's fidelity. He had observed her often enough to know that the loathing she felt for him was extended, in some degree or other, to all of his sex. His warning to her the previous evening had been a reminder merely that though he himself might be absent, his power over her remained absolute.

Stephen spent most of that day reviewing the boundaries of the town to see what work would be necessary to make it defensible. Since Tilsbury was little more than a straggle of houses on two sides of a wide main street with the market cross in its centre, its defences would have been a futile task had it not been for the river which ran alongside the gardens and orchards to the south, forming a natural boundary. If a ditch and mound were dug along the hedges of the northern perimeter, the garrison could probably defend itself for some time. He also examined the priory ruins more closely to see if they could be used as an ammunition store: he had seen the results once when a munition wagon exploded near houses and it was not a sight he wished to see again.

Towards late afternoon, as Stephen was riding back towards town, he saw a column of soldiers making their way wearily down the hill. Though their colours were unfamiliar, he guessed at once that they were the extra troops he had been expecting.

The column was led by two men who looked like an illustration depicting Good and Evil. The younger of the two was a youth of almost girlish beauty, with light brown curls, creamy skin and almond-shaped hazel eyes. His companion looked as though he would have been more at home in bearskins than a buff coat. He was a hairy monster of a man with features as gnarled and rugged as the roots of an ancient tree.

'Captain Sutton?' queried the beautiful one.

Stephen nodded.

'I am Lieutenant Charles Donnelly, and this is Sergeant Michael O'Rourke. Our orders are to report to you, sir.'

Stephen surveyed them soberly for a few moments. 'Are you *all* Irish?' he asked.

'Yes sir.' Lieutenant Charles Donnelly stood a little straighter and his cheeks were touched with pink, 'We docked at Chester last November.'

Stephen's heart sank. Not that he himself had anything against the Irish, but he knew the likely reaction of the good folk of Tilsbury to having not just more soldiers inflicted on them, but Irish ones to boot. Already in this war the Irish had gained a reputation for savagery that was only partly deserved; unlike their English comrades they did not have the option of surrender. Irish prisoners ran the risk of being hung like common criminals when captured by Parliament.

But none of these thoughts were visible on his face as he said, 'Very well then, Lieutenant Donnelly, follow me. We'll find billets for your men by nightfall.'

As they approached the town, Stephen happened to glance towards the orchard beyond the Priory House garden. What he saw made him first grin, then frown and, leaving the Irish to find their own way to The Lion, he went to investigate.

86

A joust was taking place. Harry, mounted on Bonnet and carrying a hazel twig under his arm, was pitted, somewhat unequally, against his little brother, who rode high on Jack's shoulders.

'Faster, faster!' shrilled Philip, kicking his mount without mercy.

Jack obligingly whirled about, clutched the flailing legs with his hands and charged against the little pony. Harry urged Bonnet on with a bloodcurdling yell and all four collided in a tangle from which only Bonnet escaped, sensibly trotting away before pausing to observe from a safe distance.

As Stephen strode towards the laughing heap of bodies, he found it was all he could do to maintain a serious expression.

'Ensign Skipton, what do you think you're doing?'

Ensign Skipton, known for the time being as 'Horse', removed a small leg from across his face and sat up laughing. 'I'm establishing good relations with the civilian population, sir,' he said.

'I'm sure you mean well, but Mistress Taverner has made it perfectly clear that she does not wish any familiarity between her children and the military.'

Having scrambled to his feet, Philip now launched himself broadside against the ensign, who obligingly tumbled over.

'Jack, stand up at once.'

'Yes, Captain Sutton, sir.'

'That's better. I'm sure you have more important duties to attend to.'

'But there was no harm in it, Captain Sutton, it was only a game.'

'No more games, Jack, that's an order.' Stephen saw it would be useless to try to explain the problem to his ensign, who was all overgrown child himself. 'Off you go.'

As Stephen himself left the disappointed children behind, he reflected that war had a way of presenting problems that were never mentioned in the military manuals.

If Tilsbury had been crammed to bursting already, by the time the forty Irish were accommodated there was not an inch of space left anywhere. Only the Priory House was spared an extra influx, though a couple of soldiers were squeezed into the loft above the stable. Josiah had been right at least when he said the officers' goodwill was their best protection: Paul Darbier had no intention of sacrificing his comforts because of the arrival of more troops. Others must shift, not he. His attitude was that he was doing King Charles a mighty favour merely by his existence as a loyal officer; any actual exertion was thus superfluous. Doll was relieved their home had been spared, but still, the proximity of so many more soldiers was impossible to ignore.

Suddenly this little town, where everyone had always known everyone else and where nobody's business remained secret for more than an hour or two, was teeming with strangers. The Lion echoed with voices that roared out songs and jokes in unfamiliar accents. And how was anyone to manage with so many extra mouths to feed? The servants, who all came from local families, were preoccupied and anxious; already there was talk of fights breaking out; the locksmith was doing a brisk trade; one or two housewives had complained of thefts to the Justice, but he merely referred them to Major Darbier and it was common knowledge that soldiers always looked after their own.

Doll would have been surprised to discover that the two people in Tilsbury most deeply affected by the arrival of the Irish troops were her own Harry and Beth.

The previous evening Cary, when she joined them in their room, had told them some of the gorier details of the recent siege of Shrewsbury. As she sank into sleep herself, Cary was blissfully unaware that Beth had continued to weep in silence for some time. She had been tormented to think of all the poor cats and dogs who had been dropped over the walls of the town at night with smouldering match fastened round their bellies. The panic-stricken animals had hurtled through the besiegers' lines causing pandemonium, as had been intended and also, added Cary, a good deal of amusement to those behind the walls before they were all either killed or died from their burns. Beth could not believe people could be so cruel. The following evening she took great care to make sure that both her favourite cats accompanied her when she retired to bed.

She waited with some dread for Cary's arrival. Her heavy footsteps on the stairs, the door creaking open, Cary's face of blameless innocence. Beth crept a little deeper in the bed and wondered what horrors this evening would bring.

'Irish,' announced Cary ominously, as she shook out her thick brown hair, 'We thought we had troubles before, but my heavens we didn't know how lucky we were. Tilsbury has been overrun by Irish papist devils, and the Lord knows where it will end.'

'Devils?' prompted Harry, who found Cary's stories thrilling as well as frightening.

'Every last one of them.'

'But aren't the Irish fighting for King Charles too?'

'Only so long as it suits them. Once Parliament is defeated, they'll turn on the King without mercy. And all the English. Such heathens, all they understand is bloodshed, they couldn't stop murdering people if they wanted to.'

'Heathen?' asked Harry, who had a precise turn of mind, 'I thought you said they were papists.'

Cary fixed him with her remarkable stare, a look of such purity that no one could ever doubt her words, 'Disciples of the Anti-Christ,' she said firmly, 'Have you never heard what kind of people the Irish are?'

'No.' Harry was prepared to admit any amount of ignorance if it meant hearing another of Cary's amazing stories. Beth wanted to shut her eyes and stop up her ears, but somehow she was watching and listening more than ever.

'They are a nation who do not know what pity is. When they rebelled against the English three years ago it was the most terrible, barbarous, horrible rebellion there ever was. Do you know what they did?'

'Kill people?' suggested Beth, hoping to get it over with quickly.

'Tst. Everyone kills in wartime, but the Irish were much worse. They forced mothers and fathers to watch while their children were tied to spits and roasted like pieces of meat. They washed their hands in the blood of their victims. And heaven help any pregnant woman they found: they cut the babies out of their stomachs and skewered them on a pike while the mother watched, and *then* they cut off their heads. And some of the old people were cooked alive in a baker's oven and it was *ages* before . . . Beth, are you feeling all right?'

'I think she's being sick,' observed Harry.

'No I'm not,' Beth snuffled indignantly, 'But I'd rather not hear any more about the Irish, not tonight, anyway.'

Cary stumped over to her bedside and regarded the child thoughtfully for a few moments. 'Is it something you ate?' she asked kindly.

Beth was deeply ashamed. 'I'm fine, really I am. I think I'll go to sleep now, Cary.'

'That a good idea,' said Cary encouragingly as she returned to her own bed, 'Best get all the sleep you can before the murderous Irish go on the rampage, eh?' And she fell instantly into a deep and untroubled sleep, as was her custom.

Small wonder then that when the newly arrived Sergeant Michael O'Rourke arrived at the back door of the Priory House the next evening Beth could hardly suppress her scream. She had accompanied her mother to the kitchen to check the final preparations for the officers' supper, and, at the sight of the Irishman, she turned very pale and sat down suddenly on a little stool beside the open fire.

O'Rourke was indeed a fearsome sight and if Beth could imagine any human being capable of the atrocities Cary had described, then this was the man to do them. A scarred and craggy face, a wild mane of brindled hair and eyes that peered out from under huge and whiskery brows. And when he spoke, his accent was quite unlike any she had heard.

She was not the only person in the busy kitchen to be nonplussed by the stranger. Mabs shrieked and dropped her ladle, and Doll drew herself up very straight and said coldly, 'You must have come to the wrong house. We already have our full quota of soldiers.'

He touched the top of his massive head and said, 'I'm looking for Jack, ma'am.'

'Who?'

'Ensign Jack Skipton, ma'am. He's invited a few of us round for a jar of ale and some music.'

'*What?*'

Beth watched her mother anxiously: she knew only too well the kind of explosion that often followed this ominous self-control.

'I was looking for Jack, ma'am.'

Mabs, who had retrieved her composure at the same time as she had picked up her ladle, explained, 'He means the young fellow who arrived in the middle of the night. The one who's a friend to Captain Sutton.'

'Do you mean the idiot who's always knocking things over?'

Mabs smiled indulgently: Jack was already a favourite, 'That's the one.'

'He's not here,' Doll told the soldier firmly. 'Unlike you, he probably has work to do. Besides, he knows better than to go bursting into houses where he's not wanted and—'

As Doll's scolding continued, Beth grew seriously alarmed: to antagonise one of the murderous Irish papists was an act of foolhardy desperation. Had Beth been less blinded by panic, she might have observed that the terrible rogue O'Rourke was beginning to retreat towards the kitchen door.

'And as for dancing,' Doll was summing up in no uncertain terms, 'I will not allow any heathen capering on my premises. Ensign Skipton had no right to invite anyone here without asking me first, and I'll thank you to remember that in future and stay away.'

'What's all this talk of dancing?'

Doll spun round. Paul Darbier had come into the kitchen behind her and was picking at the edge of a pie crust. Beth, who had been smacked many times in the past for less offences, held her breath.

'You will kindly inform your soldiers, Major, that they may sleep in this house, but that my hospitality does not extend to revelry—'

'Revelry, eh? Sounds like the best idea I've heard all day,' said Paul amiably. 'Come now, Mistress Taverner, don't be so stern.'

'If they want music and dancing, they must go to The Lion.'

'Surely you don't want to spoil their pleasures. We'd be as bad as those miserable puritans in Parliament if we try to stop music and dancing. Why, it's almost a loyal duty to encourage them. What had you in mind, O'Rourke?'

'Just a bit of a tune, sir. One of the men is a champion on the pipes and I scrape at the fiddle a bit myself. We'd keep to the stable-yard, ma'am, and not be any trouble at all.'

Doll was on the point of telling him exactly how little trouble she intended him ever to be in her house, when Darbier cut in quickly, 'There you are, Mistress Taverner, you have the fellow's promise as clear as can be. Go ahead, O'Rourke, I'm sure no one could possibly object. Captain Sutton and I might join you ourselves when we've supped. And I dare say Mistress Taverner herself will be tempted, just for once. What do you think?'

Doll had turned very pale. Two spots of colour burned on her cheeks. Beth closed her eyes and waited for the heavens to fall and the world to come to an end, but then, to her complete amazement, she heard her mother say, with terrifying sweetness, 'Of course, Major Darbier, if entertainment is what you require, then I would not dream of standing in your way.'

Chapter 7

～

Torches had been set against the walls of the stable-yard and the figures of the soldiers moved strangely through the flickering yellow light. The frosty night air was filled with the smell of pitch and horse dung. Above the steeply-angled roof of the house, a fragment of moon was visible in a sky scattered with bright stars.

For a while the men had been content to sit around and talk while Jack plied them with ale and listened to their stories. With his usual swift enthusiasm he was already well on the way to becoming an Irish patriot. Charles Donnelly, the young lieutenant whose angelic appearance was in such contrast to O'Rourke's, had explained to Jack how the London parliament had promised to parcel out Irish land to any who helped in the nation's defeat. Jack was instantly outraged at the injustice. Michael O'Rourke nodded his shaggy head from time to time as the young man told their country's tale, but he added little, contenting himself with picking out the faint notes of a tune on his fiddle.

Soon it grew too cold for idleness. Besides, the evening meal was finished in the house and the maids were beginning to peer cautiously round the kitchen door and debate among themselves if they should pluck up courage and join in the fun. Harry and Beth would have been astonished to see that in the end it was Cary who, despite her opinion of the murdering heathens, was the first and boldest. Pulling a short coat around her shoulders and ignoring Mabs' doomish warnings, she stepped boldly out into the yard. Jack, who had a tendency to fall in love at a moment's notice, bounded up to her at once and invited her to begin the dancing with him.

'I might do,' she gazed at him coolly with her large untroubled brown eyes and Jack felt his heart turn over inside him, 'But don't expect me to loiter out here all evening. I've the two children to attend to in a moment.'

'Are they your own?' Jack had suffered in the past for failing to make sure potential partners were free to enjoy themselves.

'Good heavens no,' Cary giggled. 'I take care of Mistress Taverner's children.'

'That's all right then,' said Jack with such obvious relief that Cary, who had intended to be aloof and distant for at least five minutes, burst out laughing, and before she knew it, his arm was around her waist and she was whirling away into the dance. More than once during that first circuit of the yard, she debated whether to withdraw before her reputation was ruined. She had to keep glancing across at Mabs and Ellen, watching cautiously from just inside the kitchen doorway, to reassure herself that she was still on the Taverners' property despite the outlandish music, and could slip inside the house again at any time she chose.

Harry and Beth, listening to the fiddle and the pipes from their fire-warmed bedroom, waited with a mixture of trepidation and excitement for Cary to come and join them. Beth had been alarmed at first when she saw the great crowd of men who had congregated in their little stable-yard, but after a while she began to find the strange tunes comforting. Harry was still troubled.

'Do you suppose Father would mind?' he asked. Since Josiah had left, Harry was painfully conscious of being the oldest male of the family, and felt a weight of responsibility that was quite new to him.

Beth had a solution for this one. 'Mother said that Father wanted the soldiers to be happy here so it must be all right.'

Harry was still uneasy. There was a new tension in the house since Josiah had gone, a tension that he was far from understanding, but which troubled him all the more. Eventually, when Cary still did not come, both the children fell asleep, and the music and the laughter and the singing continued unabated.

Nona supped with the children; Doll took her evening meal alone. She had no wish to eat with the officers: what had been acceptable while Josiah remained was unthinkable now she was

94

alone. She had a tray sent up to her room, but when Ellen came to collect it a little later, the food had barely been touched. The maid was not to know that the few morsels that were missing had been eaten by the dogs.

Doll herself was far too agitated for hunger. Although her room was at the front of the house, the sound of voices and music floated up from the stable-yard. She felt like someone who has been seduced into thinking she inhabited a home of sturdy brick, but now found every brick turning to sand; all her hard-won security was crumbling into dust around her.

But she knew instinctively – no one better – that one must bow to what cannot be changed. To his credit, Bussell had understood this also.

'The soldiers plan to enjoy some music in the stable-yard this evening,' she had told him when the household was dispersing after evening prayers.

'Music? At the Priory House? Master Taverner would not like it.'

Yes, thought Doll, and you will waste no time in sending him a full report. As usual she avoided looking at her husband's assistant, who was rather grandly titled his steward. She did not like or trust Bussell in the least, and he was of singularly repellent aspect, with watery eyes the colour of sand, and red flaking skin all over his thin face.

She said coldly, 'My husband has left me to deal with these problems as best I can. He stated quite clearly that we must do all we can to meet the soldiers' needs.'

'I see.' Bussell stroked the side of his face with long fingers, a habit he had when busy with calculations. 'Then we have no choice but to fall in with their wishes. It is regrettable – but if we protest, we run the risk of being overruled. We must hope this does not become a regular occurrence.'

It was the nearest they had ever come to an amicable conversation. On reflection Doll thought she preferred her husband's steward when he was downright disagreeable. His smooth courtesy was more odious than his enmity.

She stood up and began pacing the room. From the stable-yard came a burst of loud laughter and what sounded like a raucous cheer. It was too much. She stepped briskly towards the door, determined to turn the whole noisy rabble into the street; then she checked herself. The gamble was too uncertain. She was mistress of this house, in name at least, but the soldiers ruled the town and she knew, better than any other inhabitant of Tilsbury, that a pack of soldiers, especially when well on in drink, were beyond any law but that of brute force.

For a few moments she remained motionless, then a smile spread slowly across her face. Josiah had taken his new pair of pistols with him, but his old ones remained in the chest in the corner of their room. She fingered the keys which hung from her waist: the stillroom, the buttery... and that chest. If force was the only language understood by such brutes, why not speak to them in their own language for once? Why stay forever powerless in the face of aggression?

The keys fell from her hand. Her smile died. There would be an impossible price to pay for her brief moment of satisfaction. She must try subtler measures to keep what control she could over her little household. She knew she should go down and confront the scene, but the very idea appalled her. Major Darbier had been looking at her with a new boldness since Josiah's departure. She loathed the spurious intimacy of his glances. Perhaps she had misjudged him that first evening. He had the manner of a youth who is in the habit of picking fruit from any tree of his choosing, no matter that it belongs to someone else. All her adult life she had been shielded by the fact of being Josiah Taverner's respectable wife; now, for the first time since her arrival in Tilsbury, she found herself exposed, and vulnerable.

However, her whole life here had been a lesson in self-discipline, and it did not desert her now. The moment she left her bedchamber and swept across the landing and down the broad stairway to the screens passage, she betrayed no trace of the fears and furies that had so absorbed her through the day.

She passed into the kitchen. All was scrubbed and neatly tidied away; the embers from the day's fire still glowed on the hearth but, unusually for this time of day, the place was deserted. Even the scullion who should be curled up in the kitchen corner by now was missing. She felt a sharp increase of anxiety; lifting her chin a little higher, she went to the half-open door and looked beyond into the wavering torchlight of the stable-yard.

The first thing she saw was Cary, her eyes glowing as the tall soldier who accompanied her whooped his delight and leaped into the air with such panache that a couple of less energetic dancers were almost knocked off their feet. Jack's apologies were typically profuse, but nothing could dampen his enthusiasm for long, and within the instant he was off again, Cary laughing and breathless as she struggled to keep up.

The scene was even worse than Doll had expected. Not only the soldiers, but her entire staff, from the steward to the lowliest lad who was employed to clean the drains, was enjoying the Irish soldiers' music and Jack's liberal supply of ale. Doll observed with horror that even Bussell himself, normally so dour and straight-laced, was tapping the toe of his boot in time to the music.

The two officers were lounging against the sill of the kitchen window. Both had tankards in their hands. Captain Sutton was watching the festivities with quiet amusement. The major was grinning at some witty comment he himself had made, but just then he turned and caught sight of Doll standing in the doorway. With a smile that indicated he had only been waiting for her arrival for the real fun to begin, he sauntered over to greet her; the slight roll in his walk betrayed his acquaintance with the contents of Josiah's cellar.

Doll half-turned to retreat into the house, but she was too late.

'Mistress Taverner, I was on the point of coming inside to track you down. These heathen Irish have a cunning way with a tune, even if it does sound somewhat barbaric to a cultured ear.'

'I know nothing of their music.'

'It surely makes you long to dance.'

'I never dance.'

'Nonsense, everyone dances – such a pleasure, don't you think? Here, let me show you, the steps are really very simple.'

Darbier placed his jewelled hand under her elbow and inclined his head with what was presumably intended as a persuasive smile. Doll managed to disguise the revulsion, so strong it was almost a sickness, that passed through her body at his touch; she merely lifted her arm free of his grasp and said with an icy courtesy, 'I told you, Major Darbier, I do not dance.'

But the young major was as single-minded as a dog with a bone. 'You delight in teasing, Mistress Taverner. You mean to enjoy yourself, but you wish to hear me beg first. Come now—'

'You could not be more mistaken, Major. I merely came outside to recall my servants to their duties.' Doll glanced with some agitation through the throng of bodies to where Mabs, solid reliable boring middle-aged Mabs, was shrieking with laughter at some obviously improper remark made by a trooper with a bald head and a coat that must have been made for a man half his size. 'If you will excuse me—'

But that was precisely what Darbier was not prepared to do. 'Why so hasty? Here, let me fetch you some drink.'

'No.'

Stephen had joined them. Since he observed the scene with eyes less blinded by self-interest than Darbier's were, he saw the emotion which simmered under Mistress Taverner's brittle calm.

With a slight bow, he said, 'Good evening, Mistress Taverner. I hope you do not object to the men's entertainment.'

Doll raised a single eyebrow in mocking enquiry. 'And if I did, Captain Sutton? I cannot imagine that my wishes would be of the slightest concern to you or those ruffians you choose to call soldiers.'

Stephen frowned. 'I was led to understand you had given your permission. Jack is not in the habit of abusing hospitality.'

Doll's anger only increased. At least with the odious Major Darbier she knew precisely where she stood. She loathed the way Captain Sutton pretended to be adhering to the social code which had existed in peacetime and which had nothing whatsoever to do with a pack of Irish scoundrels cavorting around her stable-yard and undermining her authority.

Controlling her irritation as best she could, she began, 'Captain Sutton—'

But Darbier cut in with a brisk, 'Don't fuss, Stephen. The men need to divert themselves occasionally. I'm sure our lovely hostess is holding out simply for the pleasure of being persuaded . . . she'll soon be enjoying herself as much as anyone. I was just saying—'

'Excuse me, gentlemen.'

For the music and the dance had ended. Doll lifted her skirts clear of the cobbles and swept over to where Cary was deep in conversation with Jack. At the sight of her mistress, the girl was suddenly all doe-eyed sobriety.

'Cary,' said Doll tersely, 'If you value your position in this house you will go inside to your duties this instant.'

One look at Mistress Taverner's expression told Cary that argument would be worse than useless. With a subdued, 'Yes, ma'am,' she bobbed a small curtsy and ran back to the house with never a backward glance to the loose-limbed young ensign. She was hoping vaguely to give her mistress the impression that she had somehow got tangled up in the dancing against her wishes and was glad of the chance to escape.

But when she was back in the upstairs room and found both children sleeping soundly, she regretted her sudden departure. She pulled a blanket around her shoulders and sat by the window, gazing at the dusting of stars across the night sky. For once in her life sleep evaded her. She looked down on the lamplit scene and heard the music and the voices floating up, and she thought wistfully of the dashing young ensign, so different from the local boys she had so far encountered. She was sorry her pleasure had been brief, and consoled herself plotting the next day's encounters.

Jack, meanwhile, was prepared to take all the blame, pay any price, just so long as the beautiful Cary did not get into any trouble. He soon found that Mistress Taverner had no interest in his explanations.

The music had begun again. Doll looked about her for Mabs and Ellen, but for the moment they were hidden in the throng of bodies. She began to feel something close to panic. Once again, Darbier appeared at her side.

'Oh come now, Mistress Taverner, you are being too harsh on your servants.'

'On the contrary, Major, this indiscipline will be their undoing.'

Stephen too had joined them. Was she never to be free of this ubiquitous pair? He said, 'Mistress Taverner, if you wish, I will dismiss the men immediately.'

'Nonsense, Stephen,' exclaimed Darbier, 'the fun is only just beginning and I'm certain Mistress Taverner did not mean—'

Stephen said firmly, 'I'm sure our hostess can speak for herself.'

But Doll did not answer straight away. She sensed a subtle trap. Certainly she longed for normality to return to her home, but she recoiled from the thought of being indebted to one of the hated soldiers. Captain Sutton, for all his pretended civility, was making the point that his power was now superior to hers. The revelry would end only when he gave the word. Better not to rule at all than concede that her authority depended on their help.

She said curtly, 'You must do as you think best. Your men are your concern, my business is with my servants. I will bid you both goodnight.'

This time even Darbier could not misinterpret her purpose. As she walked away he shook his hand ruefully, as though he had just been burnt, and grinned at Stephen.

'Your Cornish courtesies are wasted on that one,' he said, 'Her type understands nothing but a direct approach.'

Stephen did not catch the nuance underlying Darbier's mention of 'her type'. He was watching Mistress Taverner as she approached Bussell, then spoke briefly to Mabs and Ellen. Within a few moments all her servants were safely inside and the kitchen door had been closed against the corrupting festivities. The music continued, but it was grown more pensive. Darbier, annoyed that Stephen had not risen to the bait, said pointedly,

'That sort of woman is always the worst for putting on airs and graces. Believe me, Stephen, I saw through her from the first.'

'Whatever are you talking about?'

Darbier smiled. 'I thought perhaps you had not heard. Our proud Mistress Taverner was nothing but a whore when her clod of a husband found her. One of the scum following the Duke of Alva's army, so I'm reliably informed. Old Taverner got more than he bargained for when he laid her. He didn't dare give her the treatment she deserved because her old witch of a grandmother threatened to shrivel his manhood for ever unless he married the trollop. Now you see why she puts on such ladylike airs, it's only because—'

'Not another word!' Stephen was speaking through clenched teeth. He was startled, not so much by Darbier's slander, which he did not believe for a moment, as by his own blinding flash of rage at hearing it. It was all he could do not to floor the young idiot right there and then. He said slowly, 'Listen carefully, Major. If I ever hear you repeat those foul lies to me or anyone else, I swear I'll ram them down your throat, superior officer or no—'

Darbier was caught off his guard. For one thing he had not meant a word of what he said. It was merely an embroidered version of some gossip passed on by his manservant when riding back from Furleys. The man had heard that Mistress Taverner had gypsy blood. Darbier had never bothered to distinguish between gypsies and whores, and the attack on his hostess had merely been intended to relieve his wounded vanity. He did not take kindly to rebuffs. He was not, however, too drunk to recognise Stephen's threat as an act of gross insubordination. Briefly he considered insisting that Stephen retract. He hesitated. Although Stephen had not raised his voice, there was a ruthlessness in his eyes that Darbier had never seen before. He calculated their friendship was still likely to be useful to him in all manner of ways. Much better to treat the whole business as a joke.

His face broke into a wide smile and he clapped Stephen on the shoulders. 'Good heavens, man, don't take it so seriously. Of course it's a pack of lies. I just thought you'd be amused to hear the gossip—'

'Amused, Major? You don't know me, then.'

'Don't be so damned sensitive, man. There, I'm sorry if I've offended you, let's have another drink and forget about it.'

Stephen relaxed his hand, which was gripping the pommel of his sword. 'I accept your apology, Major. But I'll not have more drink. And the men should be dismissed. They've no more business carousing than the servants. I'm taking a patrol out tomorrow and they'll need their wits about them.'

Now that the immediate danger was past, Darbier began to resent that he was the one who had apologised. 'A patrol, eh?' he said, amiably enough, 'Excellent idea. I might come along too, if the mood takes me. Get the lie of the land and pull in a few more recruits, that's the way to do it, eh? One gets fidgety cooped up in a dreary spot like this.'

Stephen walked over and spoke to the musicians. The party was breaking up anyway; with the departure of the servants much of the animation had gone out of the gathering. Mist was spreading up from the river, obscuring the stars and making the night air clammy and cold.

Stephen had harsh words for Jack, who had invited the Irishmen to the Priory House without first considering its proprietor. Jack, who regarded any place where soldiers lodged as an inn or tavern of sorts, was aggrieved to begin with, but then, seeing that Stephen's displeasure was not to be countered by argument, he sank into a state of near despair. It was of no consolation to him to know that he had been a great success with all the maidservants or that, in his enthusiasm for the Irish dancing, he had left no greater damage than a broken stool.

By the time the sun rose over the ridge of hills behind the valley, the little troop of men were already some miles away. Corinna Rogers, learning of the previous evening's entertainment, was only sorry she had missed it. She had noted the arrival of Lieutenant Charles Donnelly the previous day. Observing his delicate, almost feminine beauty, she had reminded herself that although Stephen would suit her very well indeed it was always advisable to have more than a single string to one's bow.

Cary, as she went about her morning chores, searched in vain for Jack and planned how their most enjoyable flirtation should proceed. She sang so merrily but with no regard for melody, that those servants who were suffering with headaches shouted at her to stop. She ignored them, thinking only of Jack.

But Jack had other matters on his mind. For once the black line of his single eyebrow really did denote a frown as he schemed how he might perform some act of heroism which would restore him to Stephen's favour.

Chapter 8

❧

That morning, just before it grew light, Doll had taken the baby into her own room and was feeding him when she heard footsteps on the stairs. A little later came the crisp tap of horses' hooves ringing on the frost-hard ground at the front of the house. She pulled a shawl around her shoulders and, leaving the baby to enjoy the warm bed, she crossed the room and looked out of the window.

Three horsemen were visible in the grey dawn: Captain Sutton, Major Darbier and the one they called Jack. Although it was still too dark to see them clearly, there could be no doubt as to their identity: the major sat astride a fine horse, a high-bred prancing animal that skipped sideways and tossed its head, causing its rider – and Darbier was more asleep than awake – to curse it loudly. Jack as usual was all arms and legs. Captain Sutton sat very straight and still on his strong bay, watching while the men came running from their billet at The Lion or one of the many lodgings in Tilsbury. They were pulling their apostles over their heads, grabbing a quick bite of food, blowing on their fingers to warm them. Their voices were low and subdued. Then the drummer began to beat a steady rhythm and the group moved off, away from the town, over the bridge and out of sight.

Silence.

Doll stood by the window for a little while longer, looking down into the empty street. Silence. A huge weight was sliding from her shoulders. The hated soldiers were gone. Not all of them, it was true, probably less than half, but they included most of those who were lodged at the Priory House. Just for this morning, just for today, her home was her own again. Who could tell, they might all be killed, or the earth might open up and swallow them, or maybe they would simply decide to march and march and never come back.

Whatever might happen in the future, for today they had gone.

And Josiah had gone as well.

Doll let out a long breath, then stepped lightly across the room and beamed down at her baby. He was waving his arms and legs and grappling with a smile.

'My little heart,' she addressed him in Spanish, 'Today we are free to be happy.'

She tickled the shell-pink soles of his little feet and he flapped his arms with pleasure.

Doll lifted him up and slipped back into the bed; when she opened her shift, the baby nuzzled towards her and began feeding again. She stroked the silky crown of his head and whispered endearments in the language of her childhood.

She loved all her children: she loved Harry for his solemnity and Beth for her tenderness; she loved Philip with a fierce devotion because he alone of all her children reminded her of the faces of her youth, but she had loved each one in a different way before they could talk.

There was an understanding between her and Nona to speak Spanish only in the privacy of the stillroom, where there was no chance of being overheard. Her children were English-born, and she would never speak a word to them in Spanish once they had begun to talk. Very occasionally they might watch and listen while she and Nona danced and sang; but the music was a kind of addiction of which she could never quite be cured. At times it was the only way she knew to ease the unbearable ache inside her. But she always refused to translate the words.

With a baby she did not have to guard her speech. It was dangerous, she knew, to give your heart to babies. She had lost two before Harry's birth, and whenever she thought of those little graves beside Tilsbury church, the pain was as fresh as if they had died yesterday – but in this matter of loving babies, as in so much else, she had never learned to be prudent. So she cuddled the little lad who would one day be known as Robert, but who now, alone in the secrecy of her four-poster, she called 'Bobo', and sang to him a lullaby about an old woman whose donkey was idle and whose vines bore no fruit but who was happy nonetheless because the sun shone in the olive groves and she had once upon a time lain in the arms of her lover.

They both fell asleep in the big, curtained bed, and when, much later than usual, Doll awoke, the sun was shining outside the window and her home was still mercifully free of soldiers.

The servants, who had expected to be still in disgrace as a result of the spontaneous merry-making the previous evening, were astonished when their mistress appeared to be in an excellent good humour that morning. She praised Mabs warmly for all her hard work and the special dishes she had prepared, which made the cook blissfully happy. Mabs was devoted to her mistress. All her motherly instincts – and she was well-endowed with those, as with much else besides – had been alerted by the arrival of the dark-eyed child-wife, a stranger in a foreign land. It was Mabs who had guided her in English ways, Mabs who had laid the foundations for Mistress Taverner's reputation as an efficient manager. Mabs would have done much more, only the strange bond which existed between Doll and her grandmother had kept her at arm's length.

This morning Mabs was especially proud of her young mistress. Doll helped Ellen carry down the rugs to be beaten outside; she had Cary clear the old rushes and sweep the floors before laying fresh; she ordered the officers' bedchamber to be scoured from floor to ceiling. By the time she and Beth set off for their morning walk to the market cross, the house was scrubbed clean and smelled of fresh baking and sweet strewing herbs. Doll felt she had cleansed the house of the last traces of the soldiers – her only sorrow was that she could not throw their trunks and bags out into the street after them.

Nona too had been busy. A countrywoman came to the back door of the house with a gift of preserved damsons 'for the grandmother'. She was invited in to sit by the hearth. A long discussion then ensued, which only a practised eye would have recognised as a lengthy negotiation. A variety of topics were touched on, during the course of which the woman mentioned, though with no particular emphasis, that her husband was beginning to be troubled with pain in his bowels. They went on to talk of other matters. Only when the woman stood up and said it was time to be about her business, did Nona fetch a small gallipot from the stillroom and press it on the visitor 'for that problem of your man's'. More courtesies followed before the meeting ended. Everyone was satisfied, especially Nona, who had a particular fondness for preserved damsons.

During her morning walk into town, Doll collected butter and eggs and paused to talk with Corinna Rogers, who commented amiably, 'I hear the Priory House is grown famous for its merrymaking. Are you not worried how Master Taverner might react?'

'No.' Doll's answer was tense. 'The nuisance was kept to a minimum and I believe no great harm was done.'

Corinna disguised her envy with a compliment. 'Having the officers in your home clearly agrees with you,' she purred, 'Be careful, Doll, you look so radiant this morning you'll make me quite jealous.'

Doll, not believing any woman could actually desire to have soldiers billeted in her home, merely smiled. 'It's a mercy they've gone off on some business or other today. We have a chance to clean the place without them forever tramping in and out.'

'The officers are in your way?'

'Of course.'

Corinna was thoughtful. 'Never mind,' she said at last, 'They won't be here much longer. Once the campaigning season begins again, they'll be off to join Prince Rupert's army.'

'You're very well informed, Corinna.'

'It is interesting to hear the soldiers talk.'

Again, Doll was baffled. She was not aware of either liking or disliking Sir Diggory's daughter, but she often found their lack of common ground made conversation difficult. With mutual relief, they soon parted.

That afternoon Doll went down to the orchard with the children and Bonnet. Since the arrival of the soldiers Harry was forbidden to leave the property, and he was so grieved by this restriction that Gerard the groom had offered to teach him in the orchard. Gerard was infinitely patient; in fact he enjoyed instructing the three children. He mentioned to Doll that Harry was growing too old for fat little Bonnet.

She agreed, but added, 'There's no point buying new horses so long as the soldiers remain.'

Gerard grinned, 'At least Bonnet is safe.'

There had been some amusement in the stables when Harry had turned up with a grandly worded 'Warrant of Indemnity' signed by Captain Stephen Sutton to the effect that the pony known generally as Bonnet was henceforth to be exempted from all military service. Harry had wanted to hang it from a nail in the stable, but Gerard had persuaded him it would be best to keep it safe in his room.

Doll said tersely, 'That document is no more use than the certificates they hand out instead of money. No soldier was ever stopped by a scrap of paper.'

'At least it has put Master Harry's mind to rest,' said the groom.

But not, apparently, Beth's. There were dark circles shadowing her eyes. When it was her daughter's turn to stand and watch the others, Doll asked gently, 'Is anything troubling you, little Bee?'

Beth shook her head. Having been spared Cary's horror stories the previous evening because of the dancing, Beth had fallen asleep earlier than usual, only to be woken by a dream in which a band of Irish soldiers, who all looked identical to the terrifying O'Rourke, had cut the feet off Mabs and Ellen to stop them from dancing. In the bright sunshine of the orchard, with Bonnet and Gerard and her mother and brothers, she was ashamed of her cowardly dream.

It's the soldiers, thought Doll. She put her arm across Beth's shoulders and together they watched as Philip took his turn. Unlike his older brother and sister who were both conscientious and generally did as they were told, Philip soon found walking and trotting and riding over tiny jumps to be extremely boring. He wanted to liven the afternoon by sitting facing the pony's tail, or kneeling on the saddle. Gerard tried to be angry with him, but was unable to keep his expression serious for long enough. Doll was about to scold him, when she saw how Harry and Beth were clutching their stomachs with laughter. It was so good to see them both enjoying themselves that she decided to make an exception just this once.

And then Philip fell off and bumped his arm and had to be taken inside and the lesson was over.

Towards evening Doll was sitting with the children in the bedchamber at the back of the house that Nona now shared with Philip and the baby. Beth's spinet had been moved in there when the rooms were changed around, and she was practising. Beth enjoyed her music-making. She had square, capable hands. She liked the way the notes responded to her touch and the smooth feel of the ivory beneath her fingers.

Doll had fed the baby and now he was sleeping in her arms. Nona was dozing in a chair. Philip sat by the window, gazing out into the dusk, while his older brother knelt in front of the fire. Harry was lost in thought; Doll knew that he was missing his father. She had often found herself wishing the children enjoyed Josiah's absences as much as she did – then, all would be perfect.

They were the nearest she ever came to true contentment, these moments alone with Nona and the children while Beth practised. Though her daughter would never be a very accomplished musician, Doll found a special charm in the stilted jerky rhythms. She knew precisely where to expect the hesitations in each piece, so that when the teacher came and demonstrated, it was the correct tempo that sounded awkward.

She shifted slightly; her arm was beginning to tingle where the baby's weight lay. She did not want to wake him.

Beth's piece had ended. She turned to her mother.

'Did you like it?'

'It was beautiful, Beth. Can you play us something else?' The child glowed, and Doll smiled her further encouragement. 'You're much improved.'

'I could play you the new piece I'm learning. It's not very good yet but—'

A horrifying shriek ripped through the stillness of the house. Beth turned white and gripped the edge of her stool. Nona awoke with a start. Harry turned to his mother, his eyes round and questioning. Philip leaped down from his window seat and raced across the room, struggling to open the heavy door.

There was a sound of sobbing.

'That's Cary,' said Doll, rising to her feet and handing the baby to her grandmother, 'Whatever can have happened? Stay here with Nona, children. Philip, stay here.' She pulled her son firmly away from the door and he burst into disappointed tears. The baby, woken from his rest, also began to cry.

Doll stepped out on to the landing and it seemed as if the whole house was suddenly echoing with grief. A growing dread took hold of her as she hurried down the stairs.

She swept into the kitchen. 'What is – ?' she broke off, appalled by the scene that met her eyes. There was a small pool of blood spreading across the floor near Stephen's foot, and at the sight of the soldier's leather boots and the patch of bright and growing red, she became fixed and still. Another time and place were pressing against her skull. She put her hand to her mouth and raised horrified eyes to Stephen's face.

Mabs caught her by the hand. 'One of the soldiers has been hurt!' she exclaimed. 'Oh the poor lad, just look at the state he's in!'

The patrol had begun routinely enough. At each village they came to, Darbier summoned the constable and told him that, as the levy due from each parish for the maintenance of His Majesty's forces was in arrears, the soldiers were entitled to take whatever was necessary instead. This was generally the cue for the wretched constable to protest that his village's loyalty was matched only by their inability to provide one more crust of bread for the men or forkful of hay for their horses. Everything they possessed had already been taken by Massey's men from the parliamentary garrison at Gloucester. Darbier showed his contempt for this tale of woe. The soldiers then assembled at the church gate where the trumpeter summoned the population – mostly old men, women and children – and offered a shilling and a new pair of boots to any man enlisting in the royal army. By the time they marched out of each village they were lucky if they were the richer by a handful of meagre provisions and a couple of new recruits.

By early afternoon they had reached a ridge, overlooking one of the main routes between Gloucester and London. Will Dower, the local man whom they had taken with them as a guide, assured Stephen that in time of peace, traffic along that road was brisk, with herds of sheep and cattle from the Welsh hills being driven to the richer markets of the south, and a constant flow of wagons and pack-horse trains and wealthy merchants. Now it was all but deserted.

Darbier rode alongside. He was bored.

'Jesus, what a dreary place. What's that along there?' He was pointing to a dilapidated house a little further ahead with a few penned fields and a hanging sign that was all but obliterated by wind and weather. Will Dower informed him that this had formerly been a drovers' inn. Their animals could be penned in safety while the drovers were accommodated in the house.

'There's been no one there for over a year,' said the guide.

'Indeed?' Suddenly Darbier's face brightened. 'Then who the devil is that?'

A figure had appeared behind one of the sheds and took off,

racing across the first two enclosures. Darbier clapped his heels to his horse's sides and with an excited 'Hulloo!' he set off, as though he were in pursuit of a fox. The men laid down their packs and prepared to watch the sport. The boy was sprinting across the furthest field but he tripped as he tried to vault a low wall, and Darbier was upon him. It was not long before the runaway had been herded towards the group of soldiers.

Stephen saw that he was very young, hardly more than a child, with curly hair and a snub nose and freckled face. Despite his obvious terror of Darbier – of Darbier's two pistols, at any rate – he was pleading all the while to be released.

'My sister!' he choked, 'I can't leave my sister. Please sir, don't make me go, she's all alone. She's ill, she and the baby. They need me, please sir. She's all alone. I was going for help. Please sir, I have to get help for them.'

Darbier cut him short with a brisk, 'Silence, there. No one cares a damn about your sister.'

'But here, sir, it's the truth, sir, I'll pay you all I have. But I cannot go with you—'

Darbier prodded him with the tip of his sword. 'Stand up straight, man, you're a soldier now. You want your sister to be proud of you, don't you?' When the lad began babbling once more, Darbier said, 'That's enough. Get in line. You're in the King's army now. And any soldier who tries to desert is shot at once, do you understand?'

'But sir, my sister—'

'Shot. At once.'

Leaving the youth to the sergeant's mercies, Paul rode up to Stephen. The brief gallop and the chance to exercise some arbitrary power, seemed to have cheered him up enormously.

'That's the way to recruit, eh Stephen? I never could understand why we bother bribing them with shillings and shoes and God only knows what promise of luxury. Round 'em up like sheep, much simpler altogether.'

'Do you think so?'

'Of course.'

'In my opinion, you're wasting your effort.'

'Why so?'

'Your young lad will have deserted by the end of the week.'

'He'll never dare. I told him he'd be shot.'

'The men will tell him the truth, though, soon enough. Besides, that lad was desperate. I think his story was true.'

'And what if it was? If we release every idiot whose sister is having a baby, there'd be no soldiers left.'

Stephen did not answer.

Paul continued irritably, 'Maybe I should have him flogged. As a lesson to him and a warning to the others.'

Again, Stephen remained silent. In the present state of relations between them after their argument last night, Stephen realised that the lad would only suffer more if he tried to plead his case. Darbier would not hesitate to use him as a means of revenge. So Stephen's face remained carefully neutral as he replied, 'You must do as you think best, Major.'

But later, when Darbier was occupied in terrorising an elderly farmer into handing over a quantity of cheeses, Stephen dropped back among the men and came alongside the youth, whom the men had already nicknamed 'Rabbit' because of his unusual recruitment.

'What's your name, lad?' he asked.

He had to repeat the question again before the filthy, tear-stained face was turned towards him. The boy rubbed his eyes with his fists before saying, 'Tully.'

'Tully, *sir*,' corrected the sergeant who was walking beside him.

'Tully, sir,' he repeated in a dazed voice. He never so much as looked at Stephen or the sergeant, but stared straight ahead with clouded eyes. Stephen understood then that Tully – and he did not know if that was his family name, given name or a nickname – was oblivious to the people around him and saw only his forsaken sister and her child.

The incident depressed Stephen, though he knew that Darbier was right in some respects and that nearly every man in the army had a similar tale of woe, whether an abandoned sweetheart or an elderly mother or a hungry family. A prey to disconnected thoughts, he chose for a while to ride at about twenty paces to the side of the column. He realised with some dismay that he was beginning to dislike Paul Darbier intensely. Everything about the man, from his idiotic self-confidence to his strident, slightly whining voice, set his teeth on edge. It was no way to be feeling about a fellow officer.

Stephen remembered how he had had to fight down the urge to knock Darbier senseless the previous evening when he had slandered Mistress Taverner. Even at the memory, Stephen felt hot rage mount in his throat. He smothered it at once. But then he drifted into thinking of Mistress Taverner, the tilt of her neck when she was angered, the mocking way her eyebrows rose when she rebuffed his offers of help. He found himself wondering if she was one of the strongest women he had ever met, or one of the most vulnerable. There was intense pleasure in the speculation. In fact he relished the solitude simply because it allowed him to luxuriate in thoughts of the many-faceted Mistress Taverner.

They had reached the furthest extent of their day's journeying and were now wheeling in a wide arc towards home. Their way led through bleak upland country. No lush pastures here, no plump farmsteads. This was the home of high soaring hawks, a few stone cottages crouched against the weather, a handful of scrawny sheep cropping on thin grass. Not much here of use to His Majesty's army, neither supplies nor men.

Stephen was deep in thought when he became aware that Jack had come to ride alongside. The young ensign always appeared longer and less coordinated when mounted on a horse. His great feet hung down below the horse's belly and he seemed often on the verge of tumbling off – though in fact he was a reasonable rider and seldom did so.

They rode in silence for a while. Jack had intended to wait for Stephen to speak first, but after a few minutes, he could bear the suspense no longer and ventured, 'That young Tully's in a fair old state, Captain Sutton, sir.'

'He'll get over it,' replied Stephen tersely.

'Yes sir. Still, I'll keep an eye on him, just while he settles. I think maybe the major was a bit hard on him.'

These remarks were by way of a peace offering and Stephen knew it. Jack had been with him long enough to know how Darbier's bullying would displease him, and he had noticed him talking quietly to Tully earlier. Stephen glanced at Jack, now regarding him with the ferocious anxiety of a devoted worshipper who yearns to be returned to favour. But for once Stephen was not inclined to be forgiving. He was too irritated by the intrusion and by the whole business of disrupting the lives of ordinary people of which Tully's tragedy had been a small part – and Mistress Taverner's displeasure was another.

He said, 'Major Darbier is your superior officer and I'll tolerate no criticism of him. Get back with the other men.'

Jack drooped. 'Yes, Captain Sutton, sir.' His disappointment was absolute. Stephen wondered briefly how he had come to be saddled with a junior so totally dependent on his goodwill.

He remembered the first time he had noticed Jack; it was towards the end of the assault on Bristol, when Stephen had been so dazed by the massive slaughter of his fellow Cornishmen that he had, perhaps, grown careless, and had knelt down beside an old fellow who had been gravely injured and whom he had known since childhood. He had heard a boy's voice shouting, 'I'll get him for you, Captain Sutton, sir!' and had glanced up in time to see Jack lunge towards the parliamentary soldier who had been about to drive his pike into Stephen's back. Jack's valour had almost cost him his life, since he was no match for the pikeman. Stephen had dispatched the soldier himself: from that moment on Jack had been his devoted shadow.

He was unable to remain irritated with Jack for long. He glanced at him now, so cast down by Stephen's displeasure he was oblivious to all around him. One word of encouragement and he would be all buoyancy again. Stephen was about to ride over and offer him the friendly remark that would end his misery at once, when there was a shout from the head of the column.

They had reached a group of buildings that were spread out around an old farmhouse. Half a dozen women and children of all ages and in considerable distress were scurrying around the farmyard. A few chickens squawked and flew up into the air. Will Dower emerged from one of the sheds. He was grinning and waving something round his head like a flag.

'Here's stockings for your men!' he shouted, 'Dozens of them. All finished and ready for us to take.'

'You can't!' screamed one of the older women, 'They're ordered and paid for! We'll be ruined.'

Darbier laughed. 'Already paid for? Even better.'

Stephen cantered into the farmyard. A good supply of stockings for the men was a valuable prize indeed.

He spoke to the woman. 'Who ordered them? We'll pay for what we take.'

The woman eyed him suspiciously. 'Are you parliament men?'

'We are for His Majesty.'

The woman dropped her gaze. Stephen asked, 'These were for Massey at Gloucester?'

She did not answer.

113

Darbier was delighted. 'Massey's rebels must go barefoot then. And good riddance.'

Half a dozen soldiers staggered out of the building with their arms full of stockings. One or two of them, whose hosiery was worse than the rest, pulled them on then and there. The women fell back, defeated and despairing. Since they were nearing the end of their day's march a few men were busy trapping chickens to take back for the evening meal.

'We'll see you have tickets to be redeemed for cash, never worry,' said Stephen, but the woman merely looked at him in disbelief.

'Over there!' Will Dower had caught sight of a figure escaping from the rear of the farmhouse. The fugitive was hampered by the weight of what he was carrying.

Stephen wheeled his horse around to give chase but the oldest of the women leapt forward and caught hold of his horse's bridle. Having no inclination to fight with old women, Stephen was momentarily checked.

Jack, seeing his opportunity, roared out, 'Don't you worry, Captain Sutton sir, I'll get him for you!' and, legs flailing wildly, he kicked his horse into action and went careering after the flying figure. Just as he was galloping past the last of the buildings, a man stepped out from behind a low wall with a long-muzzled fowling piece in his hands. There was a sudden explosion and Jack let out a high-pitched scream and fell forwards on to his horse's neck.

Spurring his bay to a gallop, Stephen was alongside him in an instant. Jack's horse, terrified now by the weight across his neck, was at full tilt, and Stephen had a hard job to catch hold of the reins and slow down its flight before Jack fell. Slithering off his own mount he was just in time to catch Jack as he crashed towards the ground.

Stephen cradled him. 'Oh Captain Sutton sir,' gasped Jack, his face already ashen, 'It's my side, sir, he got me in the side.'

'I can see that, you fool,' said Stephen, with rough tenderness, for blood was pouring from a wound just above and slightly to the right of Jack's groin. Quickly Stephen unbuttoned his buff coat and pulled his shirt over his head to make a temporary bandage. Jack shouted out in agony as Stephen applied it, and his cry almost blotted out the sound of the pistol going off as Darbier executed his attacker.

'We'll get you back to Tilsbury,' said Stephen.

'Yes Captain Sutton sir.'

It was some time before they were ready to leave. The scout reckoned they were about six miles now from Tilsbury. Stephen thought of taking Jack back in an old two-wheeled cart he had noticed propped against the side of the house, but then decided that to be jolted over rough ground would be an intolerable agony. He opted to carry him on his own horse. For once he was glad that Breda, though no beauty, was strong enough to bear two, even at the end of a long day.

The old fellow whom Jack had been chasing was apprehended by a couple of soldiers. He had been trying to escape with several dozen more of the precious stockings. Darbier ordered him to be hanged from an old apple tree and then had the soldiers set fire to the hayrick and barn for good measure. Stephen, who had been too occupied with Jack's wounds to see what Darbier was up to, was sickened by the whole business. Jack was shivering violently and Stephen had a hard time to hold on to him as they rode away from the farm. The women, who had protested so vehemently against the removal of the precious stockings, were stunned into silence by the death of the two men. The last of the soldiers were tramping down the hill in the direction of Tilsbury when Stephen heard a loud wailing break out behind him, as the dead man was cut down from the tree.

Darbier rode up beside him.

'That should teach those peasants to favour Massey's rebels,' he said cheerfully, 'We'll have no more trouble from them.'

'I wonder,' said Stephen.

'Hullo, what's up now?'

The sergeant was running over to join them. It seemed that Tully, the young lad they had apprehended at the drovers' inn, had taken advantage of the commotion at the farm to make his escape. His taste of freedom had been short-lived, however, and he was now under guard, with a swollen lip and a cut above one eye.

'Well done,' said Darbier to the sergeant, 'I'll make an example of the rogue by and by.'

Stephen could not resist saying bitterly, 'Haven't there been examples enough today already?'

'What do you mean?'

'Let me deal with the boy.' As soon as he had spoken Stephen knew his request had been a mistake. All day Darbier had been looking for an opportunity to make up for his humiliation the previous evening.

'No, I'll do it myself,' and then, when Stephen did not answer, he added coolly, 'A shame about your friend, though. I expect he'll pull through.' When Stephen still did not answer, Darbier said, 'You should get someone else to carry him. There's blood on your coat and breeches already. They'll be ruined.'

Stephen felt a kind of black despair come over him. Taking Stephen's silence as a sign that he had once again accepted his superior authority, Darbier said brightly, almost by way of a peace offering, 'But all in all, this has been a pretty successful day, eh Stephen?'

There was no reply.

They returned to Tilsbury by the road on which they had first arrived only a few days before. The sun had sunk behind massed up clouds and the town lay in shadow. Stephen remembered how on that first magical morning, it had seemed to him to be an enchanted place; now it looked all too ordinary. Just another huddle of buildings, some grand, many poor, where people lived in dread of the soldiers. On the level ground by the river he could make out a small band of men still practising their pike drill. When they reached the bend in the road where he had first caught sight of Mistress Taverner, he half-expected to see her again. He remembered how it had seemed to him then that she could have been placed there by the townsfolk to put a curse on the invading soldiers; now he saw how wrong he had been. It was he and his men who were bringing misfortune to the people of Tilsbury. For the first time in his life he felt himself to be an agent of disaster.

Chapter 9

❧

Stephen, his face grey with strain, stood in the centre of the kitchen and held Jack's long body in his arms. There was such a quantity of blood everywhere that Doll thought at first both men had been injured.

'Jack has been shot,' said Stephen. Cary threw up her hands and howled all the louder. She was on the verge of hysterics. Making himself heard above the din, Stephen went on, 'I mean to put him in my own room, Mistress Taverner. The attic is far too cold.'

'Of course.' Doll's response was automatic, 'Here, let me help you. Cary, stop that noise this instant and help Mabs get hot water and clean linen.'

Stephen nodded his thanks and then, adjusting the weight in his arms, he turned to the young man he was carrying and said, 'Nearly there, Jack. Just a little longer.'

Doll took a taper and led the way up the stairs and into the officers' chamber which she had cleaned with such pride that morning. Within moments the fresh rushes were spotted with blood. She stood to one side while Stephen stooped and laid the youth with great gentleness on the large bed.

'There, Jack, rest quietly. We'll find you something for the pain. You're home now.'

Doll, seeing the delicacy of Stephen's touch as he set down his burden, felt an unwelcome tightness in her chest. To mask her confusion she said tersely, 'I'll fetch Nona to help you. She has experience of treating injuries.'

The gratitude on Stephen's face was painful, somehow. 'Thank you, Mistress Taverner,' he said gravely, 'I cannot bear to see him suffer.'

117

Unable to meet his eyes, Doll turned away and fussed with the bed hanging while anger began to well up inside her. 'What nonsense, Captain Sutton. Why spend your days training men to kill and maim each other if you do not care for suffering? Someone has injured your friend, but haven't you done the same to others, and been proud?'

Stephen gazed at her without speaking. Suddenly afraid of what she might say or do if she remained, she turned and hurried from the room without another word. As she crossed the landing she noted with irritation the blood that had already fallen on the rugs. She pushed open the door into the children's room.

'One of the soldiers has been shot.' Her voice was deliberately colourless. 'The one they call Jack. It's all right, Beth, he's only injured, not dead. Nona, can you come and look at the wound?'

Leaving Harry to watch over the younger ones, Doll waited on the landing while Nona went into Stephen's room. Cary hurried up the stairs with a pitcher of hot water. Though her broad face was still damp with tears, Doll was pleased to see her hysterics had been averted by the necessity for action: an altogether sensible girl. Jack's moans turned into howls of pain, presumably as Nona removed his temporary dressing.

Doll paced up and down, pausing occasionally to glare at one of the solemn portraits. She reminded herself of her earlier wish that all the soldiers might be killed, and wondered why she should be sorry now if one happened to be injured. But she was haunted by the expression she had seen on Stephen's face as he set his friend down on the bed.

Nona emerged from the bedroom, her hands covered in blood.

'Can you help him?'

'I can try,' said the old woman, 'It depends.' Then she wrinkled her nose in the familiar gesture which Doll had always found annoying, 'But this is just the beginning. These soldiers are bringing death into your house.'

A shiver travelled down her spine. For a moment she was unable to move or speak. Then she pulled herself together.

'None of that fortune-telling nonsense with me, Nona. Others may be taken in, but I'm not so gullible. Go and do something useful for once.'

Nona chuckled and said something in Spanish that Doll chose

to ignore. She was about to go down to the stillroom when they heard Darbier, who had paused to help himself to some food in the kitchen, coming through the screens passage to the stairs. Doll's first impulse was to retreat to the children's room, but she stopped herself. She had no intention of letting the soldiers force her into skulking and hiding in her own home.

Darbier greeted her cheerfully enough. He had a mutton bone in one hand and a wine skin in the other.

'Good evening, Mistress Taverner.'

'Major Darbier.'

'You'll be glad to know, Mistress Taverner, that we've had an excellent successful day. Several eager new recruits and enough stockings for a whole regiment of men.'

'You must be very pleased with yourself, Major.'

Nona began to giggle again, but Darbier had not noticed the acid tone in which Doll spoke. At that moment his bedroom door opened and Cary emerged with several items of bloody linen in her arms. Jack's moans could be heard quite clearly.

'Sweet heavens,' Darbier exclaimed, turning to Doll in disbelief. 'Whatever is Stephen thinking of, to put that fellow in my room? It's outrageous.'

Stephen had followed Cary on to the landing. 'Jack will have our bed until he is well enough to be moved again,' he said.

Darbier was on the point of protesting but he saw the steel in his fellow officer's eyes. As usual he opted for diversionary tactics. 'Mistress Taverner, I throw myself on your kindness. My chamber has been turned into an infirmary. I must request that you find me another.'

'I regret, Major, but as you yourself know, all the rooms in this house are occupied already.'

'You surely don't expect me to share my quarters with a sick man?'

'What you do is your concern. I cannot help you.' Then, fearing she had been too brusque she added, 'But I'm sure they can find room for you at The Lion. Or Sir Diggory would be delighted to accommodate you at Furleys.'

Darbier made a gesture that verged on petulance. 'I wish to stay here,' he said. He turned to Stephen. 'See what trouble your fussing over that boy has given me.'

Doll said, 'I'm sorry I cannot help you, gentlemen,' and was just continuing on her way when Darbier's next words brought her to an abrupt halt.

'Mistress Taverner, your own bedchamber is tolerably large, I believe.'

She turned round slowly, her eyes enormous. No doubt Darbier intended it as a smile, but the expression on his face looked to her like a blatant leer. For a few moments she felt a pinprick of memory blot out the present. Instinctively, she glanced at Stephen and, to her confusion, saw that his own fury equalled her own. The silence that followed was broken by a pitiful groan from Jack. Before she had a chance to consider she said, 'Very well, Major, I shall sleep with Nona and the little ones tonight. You may have my room until your young friend is better.'

'Ma'am, I shall remain eternally in your debt, your humble and most devoted servant.' The smile that accompanied Darbier's half bow managed to express something a good deal more insulting than gratitude.

Stephen sat all night by Jack's bedside. The local apothecary had been summoned, but seeing that the soldier's vital organs had been ruptured by the wound he did not want to risk his reputation with a failure. He therefore pronounced that Nona's care would be sufficient. Nona applied poultices and gave him soothing brews, but Jack's suffering continued. From time to time during that first night Stephen wiped the sweat from his face with a towel or administered sips of the wound drink Nona had mixed for him, or put more logs on the fire.

'Are you still there, Captain Sutton, sir?'

'Yes, Jack, I'm here.'

He took his hand; the shaking was grown less, but his pain was too acute for sleep. What Jack liked best was to hear the sound of Stephen's voice. So Stephen talked.

He talked of the men, how the soldiers were learning fast and would soon be ready to join the large army that was to be assembled after Easter; he spoke of the campaigns they had fought together, of Jack's own bravery and how Stephen had relied on him. In the very early morning, when Jack had drifted into a brief silence and Stephen's own eyelids were heavy, he heard the thin wail of the baby coming from another room. Footsteps, then the crying ceased abruptly. And Stephen was briefly comforted: he was not the only person awake in this dark night. He imagined Mistress Taverner taking the tiny child in her arms, putting him to her breast . . . and he almost smiled.

'Are you still there, Captain Sutton sir?'

'Yes, Jack, I'm here.'

And now Stephen found himself talking of the home in Cornwall where he had grown up; the beautiful spread of weathered stone buildings that should have gone to his older brother Nicolas. But Nicolas had died of his wounds after Lansdown and now the property would go to his eldest son. Stephen remembered his nephew as he had seen him last, curly-haired and bonny as Nicolas had been at the same age. No longer wondering if Jack was following his words, Stephen began to explain that he had never had any particular purpose in his life until this war began. As the second son, he had known Rossmere would never be his, and there had been little money to spare for his education. He had passed his time visiting the homes of friends and relatives all over Cornwall, in hurling matches and cock fights and card games, all pleasurable and aimless.

Until Bevil Grenvile set out in 1639 to fight with King Charles against the Scots, and Stephen was one of the first to answer his call and take up the soldier's life, and had done so readily again when Civil War broke out in 1642. The military life had suited him well. He was hardworking and brave, popular with the men, yet firm when firmness was needed. He believed passionately in the justice of the royalist cause; that if Parliament was allowed to overthrow the lawful King, then chaos would follow and in the chaos it was the poor and the weak who would suffer the most. Stephen believed that only in an ordered hierarchy could all members of society be protected

'Yes, Captain Sutton sir, that's right.'

But it was no longer only Jack to whom he was talking. It was as if he hoped to reach out to that other watcher in the night and answer her bitter question: why train men to fight and kill?

It was a question he had never needed to ask himself before, but which he asked himself now with a desperate urgency. It was not to slaughter civilians that he had put on the white and blue colours of the Grenviles, not to terrorise country folk for a few dozen knitted stockings that his brother Nicolas had given up his life. For the first time he felt himself to be a part of the disease that was afflicting the country, and not its cure. He thought of Tully, the Rabbit, whom Darbier had consigned to the town cage to teach him not to run away again. Was it possible that the boy's sister and her baby were more important than this army of the King's after all?

In the town cage that night Tully also found sleep impossible.

'Stop, please! Don't shut me up.' He had cried out to the sergeant who placed him there, 'I must get back to my sister!'

But, 'The Devil take your sister,' had been the reply, and Tully had broken into a sweat, as if at a premonition.

For what no one but Tully ever knew was that he was father as well as uncle to his sister's week-old baby. Since their grandfather's death a year since, the two children had been alone at the drovers' inn. There had been little trade, and they had often gone hungry. Tully had set snares and had gone begging in the nearby village. But their neighbours had little to give them, and gradually he and his sister had sunk into a silent and primitive existence, their only comfort the sharing of each other's bodies at night.

His sister's pregnancy had terrified them both but, dimly aware of their crime, they had not dared to seek help. Tully was still stunned by the horrors of the birth. He had done the best he could, but eventually even he realised that the girl and her infant were in desperate straights; he had been about to go down to the village to try to find the old midwife, when the soldiers had appeared and taken him by surprise.

'You'll come straight home, won't you, Tully?' she had raised her grey face from the pillow as he left.

'I'll be back before dark, never worry.'

And now she would be waiting, and wondering, and increasingly afraid. Tully had known hardship in plenty during his short life, but this disaster was enough to drive him clean out of his mind.

The following morning Darbier, though he had slept in the best bed in the house, complained of a headache. He felt far too delicate for any heavy work. As he left the house, Stephen chose to assume that Darbier did not feel up to his duties in Tilsbury either: he ordered Tully to be released from the town cage. Handing the lad over to Sergeant Morish, he ordered him close-watched but to be fairly treated. Morish knew his captain well enough to understand what he meant by 'fairly' and Tully was given a good breakfast before being taken down to the training ground and issued with a pike.

The weather had turned grey and wet. Darbier, alone at the

Priory House, grew increasingly bored. The parish clerk called on him towards midday with some complaint about a soldier who had been causing trouble at The Lion. Darbier told him airily he was far too busy to be bothering with such trivia. Then, as the clerk was ushered out, Darbier slumped back in his chair and wondered irritably how he was supposed to amuse himself now.

At that moment he heard the front door close. It was Mistress Taverner returning from her morning walk to the market cross. For once, Beth had not accompanied her. The previous evening Cary had given the children such a vivid description of Jack's wound, and followed this with so many other stories of horrific accidents, that Beth had hardly slept at all and was too listless to do more than sit by the kitchen fire and watch Mabs at her work.

Despite the dismal rain and her daughter's malaise, Doll was feeling pleased with the day. Dame Tucket had kept back a generous quantity of violets for her. As she set the basket down on the chest and the rain-damp flowers filled the screens passage with the scents of earth and spring, she thought happily that it was lucky the soldiers had no use for such luxuries. She was busy planning how she would use them – half she would crystallise and half would be used for scented water, and Beth could help her – when there, emerging from the winter parlour, was Major Darbier. Not content with disrupting the entire household, he apparently expected to be entertained as well.

'Good morning, Mistress Taverner. Let me tempt you to take a glass of wine with me by the fire. We can amuse each other on this dreary day. I'm not feeling at all well, and solitude is especially troublesome when one is unwell, don't you agree?'

Doll was about to say she was far too busy, but she hesitated. She had already seen enough of Darbier's evil mood that morning to know how he could vent his spleen when thwarted. Mabs was beginning to mutter darkly about being better off at home than here where she was treated no better than a slave, and they had problems enough already with the soldiers and now Jack to attend to without losing servants into the bargain. So she slipped off her cloak and shook the rain from her hair, and even managed a smile of sorts before saying, 'I'd be delighted, Major, but I cannot spare much time. Ellen, have Mabs prepare a jug of warmed wine and bring it to the winter parlour. And take these violets and place them in

123

the pantry. I'll deal with them myself by and by.'

Within a few minutes they were sitting one on each side of the bright fire and Ellen had placed the tray of wine on a small stool.

'Your health, Mistress Taverner.'

She raised her glass. 'I trust you were comfortable last night, Major.'

'It was tolerable,' he replied, and Doll noticed he made no mention of her own inconvenience at having to move from her room. 'But I was much disturbed. The cries of that boy are most irksome.'

'I'm sorry to hear it.' Doll was discovering that being polite with this spoiled youth was a kind of game. He so expected deference that he never noticed the irony that would have been evident to anyone else.

She said, 'Your poor ensign is in a good deal of pain.'

'Oh him.' Darbier frowned. 'Boys like that have no fortitude. My own head is hurting me terribly, but I do not complain.'

Doll smothered a smile. 'You are an example to us all, Major.'

He looked at her oddly for a moment and she wondered if she had gone too far, but then he said, 'Never mind about that tiresome boy. I'm interested to know more about you, Mistress Taverner.' He poured himself more wine. 'What brought you to Tilsbury?'

'I came here with my husband.'

'Yes, but what were the circumstances of your courtship? After all, you're not even English-born. Surely you're an unusual wife for a fellow like him.'

'You must ask him about that.'

'But he's not here.' He moved his chair a little nearer. 'One might wonder why a man would decide to leave his wife all alone when his home has been overrun with soldiers. It's an odd thing to do, don't you agree? I mean, if the man values his wife, and so on.'

Doll was genuinely puzzled. 'What are you suggesting, Major?'

'Oh, this and that, Mistress Taverner, just speculating, to pass the time, you know. I understand you met your husband in Germany. And yet you are of Spanish birth. It's all most intriguing.'

'Why? My story is of small interest.'

'You are too modest, Mistress Taverner. One is always curious to know about one's friends. Presumably, being Spanish, you were raised in the Catholic faith? Not that I've anything against Catholics, you understand—'

'I should hope not, Major. Your Queen herself is one.'

'Quite so, but tell me, I've always wondered, is it difficult to abjure the church in which one has been reared?' His dark-fringed eyes were smiling at her with a spurious intimacy.

Doll did not answer. It was unclear if she had heard his question. Her gaze was blank, but she fingered the fabric of her skirt, rolling a small section nervously between thumb and forefinger.

'Just as I guessed,' said Darbier, with an attempt at playfulness, 'you're hiding a dark secret.'

Her eyes slid round to focus on his, then looked quickly away. 'A secret, Major? Whatever are you talking about?'

'Your mystery, Mistress Taverner. I wish to know all about you.'

'There is nothing to know.'

'Oh, come now. Don't be angry. Talking about oneself is always agreeable. You may ask me whatever you wish to know about my life. I promise not to take offence.'

'But Major, your life is of no interest to me.'

'You *are* angry. I wonder why. You see, my problem is that with no certain *facts* to go on, I am likely to be misled by rumour. You know what gossips are like in a small place such as this.' Darbier was observing her shrewdly. He believed he had manoeuvred her cleverly into a trap.

Still avoiding his eye she said, 'No. I never pay any attention to gossip.'

He could tell she was agitated. He slung one of his long legs over the arm of his chair. 'You would be interested to know what they say of you, I'm sure.'

'No, Major Darbier, I can think of nothing more tedious.'

'Indeed?' he thought for a few moments, all the while stroking the jewel in his signet ring. 'It really is most unfortunate Master Taverner had to be called away on business so suddenly. I am surprised your husband did not consider how vulnerable a woman on her own must feel at a time like this. You know, war, and all the rest of it.'

Doll did not answer. Her hands were clenched in her lap. The scent of an old fear was in her lungs and it had grown difficult to breathe.

Darbier was jerking his booted foot to and fro; he turned to her with a smile. 'Soldiers are not always reasonable, are they, Mistress Taverner?'

She stood up swiftly and put her hand to her forehead. Speaking with obvious difficulty, she said in a low voice 'I must leave you, Major; there is much to be done.'

'But you've hardly touched your wine.'

She did not answer, simply turned and hurried from the room. For a little while, until his boredom and his headache reasserted themselves, Darbier was well satisfied with his efforts. Mistress Taverner was obviously hiding some shameful secret.

Uncovering the mystery might prove an agreeable means of passing the time while his talents were being wasted in this desolate backwater.

The household knew that Mistress Taverner had been distressed by her interview with the major when they heard the stillroom door close with a bang. The measure of her distress would be revealed by the length of time she remained secluded behind its locked door.

She stood quite still for a few moments in the centre of the room. She was unable to focus her eyes on the objects around her: the ordered rows of pots and bottles and jars, the alembic and the chafing dishes, all the familiar things which normally held a comforting power, were fading, and in their place was the smell and taste of an old terror. She gripped the sides of her head and closed her eyes. The torment intensified. She heard a roar of voices, shrill screams. There was a sudden image of boots covered in dark blood. She opened her eyes again and took hold of the edge of the slate shelf.

Take hold of Now.

War, and all the rest of it . . . how vulnerable a woman on her own must feel . . . soldiers are not always reasonable . . . What vicious instinct had guided Darbier to seek out her weakness? What local gossip could he have heard of her?

In all the years she had lived in Tilsbury she had hardly given any thought to how she was regarded by her neighbours. In fact, she came from so very far away that the local imagination had suffered a kind of paralysis. Had she derived from two villages distant, or even as far as Bristol, her foreignness would have been a matter for comment. But Spain via Germany was too exotic to be easily comprehended. Besides, she had been so young when she arrived: all her adult life had been spent in their town so that she was generally regarded as practically 'a proper Tilsbury woman'. There was even a certain local pride to be gained from her living there, as though her presence proved that there was no better place on earth. It had generally been enough that she was Josiah Taverner's wife, and the mother of his children.

Darbier's odious smirk, though, had hinted at some hidden knowledge. It was all nonsense, of course, yet she felt tainted by his pretended intimacy. Reason told her he knew nothing that could harm her, but still, she felt exposed and vulnerable. Lies can be more dangerous than any truth.

A key was turning in the lock.

'Who is it?' her question was shrill, though she knew only one other person had a key to this room.

Nona shuffled in. She had come down to mix fresh salves for Jack's wounds. She took one look at Doll's stricken face and said in Spanish, 'What's the matter with you?'

'When will the soldiers leave, Nona?'

'Why ask me? You say it's all nonsense and then expect me to tell you the future. Wait and find out for yourself.' The old woman's vanity had been ruffled by Doll's dismissal the previous evening and, worn out by tending Jack, she was not in an especially forgiving mood.

'I want them to leave.'

'So does everyone. Not much we can do about it. I can tell you one thing, though: that young fellow they call Jack won't be with us much longer.'

'He's dying?'

Nona nodded. 'Though it may take a week, or even more. Poor boy.'

Doll merely said, 'I wish their major was dying.'

Squeezing a cork back into a bottle of ointment, Nona agreed, 'The major is a nuisance.'

'He's worse than a nuisance.'

'Maybe so.'

Doll was eyeing the unmarked bottles that were ranged along the highest shelf. She reached up and selected one.

'Nona, what is this?'

'Never you mind.' Nona tried to take it from her, but Doll, who was considerably taller, kept it out of reach.

'You should have taught me your secrets by now.'

'Later.'

'Tell me now.'

Nona shook her head.

'Why not?'

'Because you're too angry.'

'No, I'm not. I was angry with the major just now, but that's over. Tell me how these medicines work.'

'One day, maybe. And you are still angry. I don't mean the major, that's nothing. You've been full of it ever since the day we came to this town.'

'What rubbish you talk, Nona.' But she put the little unmarked bottle back on its high shelf, knowing there was nothing to be gained by argument.

She watched Nona for a little while without speaking. The old hands were wrinkled and veined and covered in brown marks, and the knuckles were swollen and painful, but they worked with their habitual skill. Doll began to feel calmer.

Eventually she asked, 'Do you think people talk about us in Tilsbury?'

'They talk about everyone. And we are foreign, and so more interesting.'

'What do they say?'

Nona looked up from her work and grinned. 'Oh, nothing much. Just that you were once a gypsy and I'm an old witch.'

'What?'

'They also say that you are a good wife and mother and that I can be useful sometimes. No need to worry about the gossip. Now, stop holding me up, I've work to do even if you haven't. I'd better give Cary a few drops to soothe her. She's more of a hindrance than a help at present.'

'What about Beth? I'm worried about her. It's not like the child to be so distressed. Nothing has been right since the soldiers came.'

'Calm down,' said Nona irritably, 'Save your fussing for later. This is just the beginning. I don't need any magic powers to know everything will become much worse before the soldiers leave.' And then, seeing the expression of horror on Doll's face, she gathered up her medicines and departed, chuckling to herself with satisfaction.

Jack remained in the officers' bed for over a week, and throughout that time his suffering grew worse. It was especially bad at night, and there was little sleep for anyone in the house. Darbier fell into the habit of drinking himself into a stupor each evening, so he could have slept through Armageddon, but his resulting sore head the following day did nothing to improve his temper.

Stephen was utterly wretched. He was away from the house through most of each day, and if he did return for any reason, he went straight to Jack's bedside. At night he found sleep impossible; his visits to the sentries became so frequent that he was rumoured to have a mistress in the town. One morning the grooms climbed down the ladder from the stable loft to find him fast asleep against a bale of straw.

Stephen had no idea why Jack's ordeal should have affected him so deeply. He thought he had grown hardened to the horrors of war by now – heaven knew, he had seen enough of them – but Jack's long agony touched him more deeply than the hellish aftermath of Lansdown and Bristol had ever done. Perhaps it was the manner in which he had been attacked: the desperate futility of sacrificing his young life for a few dozen knitted stockings. Or he wondered if it was perhaps because of a childlike quality in Jack's nature, a kind of ongoing innocence that had made him different from other soldiers. Or perhaps it was simply that Jack had made him laugh – and now their laughter had been brutally extinguished.

Stephen, always a conscientious officer, now worked harder than ever. Much of the drilling of the men he left to Sergeant Morish and the two Irishmen, Donnelly and O'Rourke. Most days he left Tilsbury at daybreak with half a dozen horsemen to find provisions for the men and seek out new recruits. Once or twice they encountered parliamentarians from Gloucester and drove them scurrying back to their garrison. A couple of his men were injured, but not seriously. Stephen was heartily relieved that Darbier showed no further interest in these expeditions. The major preferred to while away the hours visiting Sir Diggory Page or holding court at the Priory House. Being so preoccupied with Jack and the work that needed doing, Stephen did not notice how Darbier was changing.

The young major had lived all his life in a world in which his position was clearly marked and in which he was treated with automatic deference. The first years of the war had not altered this. As Lord Bewell's nephew he had been given a commission despite his youth and inexperience: he was burdened with few responsibilities, he had believed himself popular. Even his two brief tastes of battle had done little to challenge his complacency since he had remained far from the actual fighting – but this stagnant garrison life was altogether different.

For a start, the soldiers and the townsfolk alike soon fell into the habit of bringing problems to Stephen, rather than to his major. It was Stephen who punished the two soldiers who had been causing trouble at The Lion, Stephen who tracked down and disciplined the man who had stolen a couple of horses and tried to sell them in the next town. What Darbier found impossible to understand was how Stephen could mete out pioneering duties or a spell in the stocks and earn the men's respect, while when he punished a fellow the resentment and hate rose from the onlookers like a black steam. Darbier had been happy enough when it was simply a matter of letting Stephen do all the work; he was less content now that he felt himself superfluous.

By some devious leap of logic, Darbier contrived to lay the blame for his own misfortunes on Jack. He believed his troubles had begun on the day of the ill-fated patrol; he was aware that Stephen had cooled towards him since that date (but had forgotten their argument the previous evening when he had said Mistress Taverner had been a whore before her marriage). Thus, in his view, it was all Jack's fault. If the young ensign had not been so reckless then he would never have been injured, Stephen would still be in good spirits and there would consequently be no ill-feeling between them.

In his confused way, Darbier was beginning to be frightened. The Priory House was not large enough for him to avoid the horror of Jack's suffering. For the first time in his life he was brought face to face with the reality of pain and imminent death. He began to have a morbid fear of the fighting that would come inevitably once the campaigning season began. His courage until now had been due to his sense of his own invulnerability; but listening to Jack's agony he began to fear for himself. Gruesome images of death and mutilation crowded his mind. The only remedy he knew was drink.

Several times he considered taking up Sir Diggory's offer and going to stay at Furleys. Once there he would feel himself to be Lord Bewell's nephew and invincible once again. But he was prevented by an obscure sense of pride. He feared that to leave the Priory House now would be seen as an admission of defeat.

He felt himself to be in competition with Stephen, both for the respect of their soldiers, and for Mistress Taverner's admiration. He had no intention of backing down and leaving Stephen in full possession of the field.

One night Stephen came in dog-tired from his customary rounds of the sentry posts. Darbier had been supping alone in the hall and called out to Stephen to join him, but Stephen was past hunger. He paused only long enough to pick up a jug of spiced wine, before mounting the stairs to Jack's room.

For the first time, Jack did not recognise him, but his delirium had in no way eased his pain. Stephen sat beside him for a little while, drinking the wine and wondering how anyone could endure for so long. He was filled with a bleak rage against a universe where such suffering was possible.

After a little while he was startled to feel someone stroking his head. He glanced up and saw the old woman, her white hair wispy and untidy. He found he was unable to speak.

'Stop torturing yourself,' said Nona, and on her face he saw the tranquillity that comes when suffering has been accepted. 'There's nothing you can do for him now.'

Stephen stared at her blankly. 'Is it hopeless?' he asked at last. 'Yes.'

He could not think what to say. For over a week he had clung to the hope that despite all Jack's wretchedness, he would pull through eventually. Now he knew he had been deluding himself. One glance at the death's head on the pillow, and anyone could see it was almost over.

After a while he asked, 'How long does he have?'

'Who can tell? Hours, maybe days. Weeks, even.'

Stephen sat for a few minutes more, vaguely aware that Nona was filling the chafing dish with fresh herbs and sprinkling scented waters on the pillow and bed hangings. After a bit he discovered, somewhat to his surprise, that he had drunk all the wine. He stood up and went down the stairs. He felt curiously light-headed.

Darbier was sitting by the fire in the dining hall, his elegantly booted legs stretched out against the fender. He looked up as Stephen came in. 'Hellfire, you look terrible. Sit down and eat, for God's sake.'

Stephen slumped on to a chair, but pushed away the food.

Darbier said dryly, 'I take it your young friend is no better.'

'Worse.'

'He won't last much longer then.'

'The old woman said it could be days – maybe more.'

Darbier swore. 'I wish to God he'd hurry up and get it over with, then at least we can all have some peace.' Then he added more amiably, 'Cheer up, Stephen, have some more wine. That'll do the trick. Damnation, it's all gone. Where in God's name are all the servants?'

He shouted out angrily and Doll, who happened to be passing on her way to bid goodnight to Harry and Beth, pushed open the door.

'Is anything the matter, gentlemen?'

'Yes indeed it is. Your servants are too damned idle to look after us properly. I've never come across such a pack of lazy scoundrels in my life. More wine and be quick about it.'

Only the sudden flaring of Doll's nostrils betrayed her fury. She too had been kept awake by Jack's cries and the teething baby. All day she had felt as if a protective layer of skin was being peeled away, and her nerves were exposed and jangling. Try though she might to convince herself that a soldier's suffering was nothing to her, each time Jack cried out it was as though the pain was slicing into her own body. And now this spoiled brat of a major thought he could treat her like a tavern keeper's drab, and all because she was a woman alone.

She said hotly, 'Major Darbier, it may have escaped your notice – though heaven knows, you do not appear to be weighed down by responsibility – but my servants have been put to a good deal of work already to look after you and your men. If they are sometimes slow, then I can assure you they always do their best.'

'Well, it's not enough, that's all. Fetch more wine.'

'No, Major, I am not your servant. I shall ask someone to attend you when they can spare the time.'

She closed the door.

'Damned arrogant woman,' muttered Darbier, his face turning an angry purple, 'How dare she lecture me! What an upstart, I could soon put her in her place if I wanted to.'

'Don't make trouble for Mistress Taverner, Major. Her servants are doing what they can. And her grandmother has given Jack every care.'

'Jack, Jack . . . I'm sick of hearing about the wretched boy. I know, Stephen, let's go to The Lion and see if we can enjoy ourselves for a change. This damn place is about as much fun as a plague house. Come on, you've been going about with a face like doom all week. Anyone would think it was you who'd been shot in the belly.'

'I almost wish it was.'

'That's senseless talk. And most likely treasonous. You're much more use to His Majesty's cause than some hare-brained ensign. Let's go.'

He stood up. Stephen stared at his hands for a few moments and then, as if coming to some kind of decision, he said bleakly, 'Very well. I can do nothing for him. He didn't even respond when I said his name.'

'That's more like it. By the time we're finished, *you* won't remember your own name either.'

The two men went out into the screens passage. Mistress Taverner was coming down the stairs, a lighted taper in her hand. She was wearing a simple dress of grey worsted, her throat was bare of jewellery, but she moved with an unselfconscious grace. It occurred to Stephen then, light-headed with fatigue as he was, that he had never seen a woman so beautiful before in all his life, nor ever would again. In that brief moment, and for no reason that he could think of, he was quite ridiculously happy.

Darbier said with a sneer, 'Your slovenly household is driving us to seek our comforts at The Lion. I've never known such incompetent servants. They deserve to be whipped.'

Doll had reached the lowest stair. She said, 'Then perhaps you'd like to move elsewhere.'

'Are you hoping to be rid of us, Mistress Taverner?'

Doll's cheeks were bright with anger, but she said smoothly, 'I am thinking only of your comfort, Major.'

Stephen was smiling for the first time in days. He was delighted that Mistress Taverner so clearly found Darbier odious, yet always managed to negotiate a path on the safe side of courtesy. He rejoiced that Darbier was too puffed up with vanity to read the situation correctly. He knew that Mistress Taverner loathed all soldiers, not just his commanding officer. He thought it quite possible that she hated all men indiscriminately. For the time being this fact did not trouble him in the least, just so long as he was able to see her several times each day, and to hear her speak.

He said, 'Mistress Taverner, we are grateful for your trouble.'

Doll was gripping the end of the bannister which had been carved to resemble a roaring lion. She began, 'I thank you, Captain Sutton–' and then she broke off.

Suddenly she was ash-pale. From the upstairs room came an unearthly howl of pain, and then another. Stephen turned aside and pounded his fist against the panelled wall.

'My God, you wouldn't leave a dog to suffer so!'

'Then the sooner we leave—'

But Stephen interrupted him. 'You go, Major. I'm not fit company.'

'Nonsense.'

'I'll stay here with Jack.'

'Don't be—'

Anxious to forestall Darbier's objections, Stephen had raced up the stairs two at a time. Darbier, thwarted and afraid, slammed out of the house alone.

Jack's room was lit by a single candle. Jack, his face twisted like a gargoyle's, was writhing and shrieking in agony. Stephen went straight to his side and, repeating helplessly, 'Jack, Jack, oh poor Jack,' he gathered the boy in strong arms and held him tightly. The hideous cries subsided into pitiful moans. Hardly aware of what she was doing, Doll had followed him into the room, and stood just inside the doorway. After a little while, as if sensing her presence, Stephen looked up and turned to her, and she saw his face was streaming with tears.

Still holding Jack with one arm, he wiped his free hand across his cheek, the gesture of a child.

Doll found that her heart was beating fiercely, as if she was the one in mortal danger, and she said in a hushed voice, 'I never saw a soldier weep before.'

Stephen said bitterly, 'You see one now.'

It is not right, she thought, a man who kills has no claim on grief. She found she was angry with Captain Sutton for his show of feeling. Bewildered, yet not understanding why, she left the bedchamber to search for her grandmother.

'Nona,' she said, when she had found her warming some small beer for the children, 'We must do something, it is intolerable. You must give Jack something stronger for the pain. So he can sleep.'

The old woman's little eyes were suddenly very penetrating and for once she spoke in Spanish, though they were in the kitchen and Mabs was close at hand.

'What do you mean, sleep? What are you asking me to do?'

'I don't know . . .' Doll considered for a little while, biting her lower lip, before saying firmly, 'Yes, I do. We must ease his suffering somehow, that's all. Don't worry, I'll take the blame if . . .'

Nona interrupted her. 'Do not even speak the words, that's bad luck, and mercy on us, there's enough of that around without adding to it. Very well then, I'll help the boy, if you're sure that's what you want.' She ordered Ellen to take the children their evening drink. Together they went to the still-room. Doll stood in silence and watched while her grandmother took down one of the jars from the very top shelf. There was no writing to indicate the contents, but it was marked with a squirl, something like an exotic leaf, and the bottle was almost full. Nona mixed a few drops with a colourless oil and put it into a small earthenware bottle.

'Follow my instructions exactly,' she said.

When Doll returned to the upstairs room Stephen had not moved but Jack was lying back on the pillow, and though his breath was still laboured, he was quieter. Stephen seemed to be telling him some rambling story about a young ensign in Grenvile's army who had risked his own life to save his captain. He broke off as Doll approached and watched her questioningly.

'My grandmother has mixed him a stronger medicine which may help with the pain,' she said in a low voice, 'Here, if you hold his head steady I will give it to him.'

Stephen did as she directed. It took some time to administer the required six drops, because of the risk of choking.

'There,' said Doll, as Stephen laid him back against the pillow. 'In a little while he'll be more comfortable.'

Jack opened his eyes; they were cloudy and did not focus properly.

'Jack?'

'Is that you, Captain Sutton, sir?'

'Yes Jack. I'm here. Mistress Taverner has just given you something to help you sleep.'

'That's good. I'd like that.'

Gradually Jack's speech became slurred, then drifted into a mumble. Stephen and Doll watched in silence, Stephen still sitting on the edge of the bed, Doll standing beside him. She found herself noticing the ridges formed by the tendons on the backs of his hands, the strong angle of his jaw and the way he could sit quite still, just watching.

'Jack?'

This time there was no reply.

Because it seemed to be the most natural thing in the world, Doll said gently, 'Let me sit with him for a little while. You go downstairs and Mabs will give you some food. It is better for your friend if you are strong. Go on.'

Stephen was about to protest, but then, 'Yes,' he said, 'You're right,' and he stood up.

He hesitated. 'Mistress Taverner—'

'Hush. Go. I will call you if he wakes.'

'Very well.'

He went out, leaving the door ajar, and she heard his footsteps going slowly down the stairs. Doll sat on the chair which Stephen had placed for her beside the bed. For a little while her mind was empty of all thought as she listened to the small evening noises of the house; logs wheezing in the grate, servants talking and banging pots in the kitchen below, the sound of the children preparing for bed, Jack's shallow breathing and his occasional anxious muttering.

She turned to look at him and, for the first time, she was struck by how horribly young he was. Not so very long ago he would have been the same age as her Harry. At that thought, the barriers she had erected against his suffering came tumbling down. She sat very still, examining him. His single black brow gave him his habitual frown. To Doll, it looked as though he was afraid.

She dipped the corner of a towel into the basin of water beside the bed and squeezed a few drops of moisture against his lips, then wiped his forehead. His muttering continued. 'Sssssh,' she soothed, and then, since he seemed calmed by the sound of her voice, she began to sing to him the lullaby she had shared with Bobo that morning, the one about the old woman who was happy because once, when she was young, she had lain in the arms of her lover. Jack's breathing grew easier. She sang very gently, as much because she found it calming herself, a quiet crooning, hardly louder than a breath of wind.

She was still absorbed in her song when, some little while later Stephen returned. He stood for several minutes in the doorway, hardly daring to breathe for fear he might break the spell. He had seen her tenderness when she was with her children, but this was different. She was taking on the lad's suffering, as only those who have suffered greatly themselves can do. She looked much older than he had seen her before, as she intoned her ancient, hypnotic song. And, like the song, her face was too unusual to be called beautiful, but mere beauty would have been insipid beside either.

If there was a precise moment when Stephen lost his heart, then that was it. But he remained motionless, not wishing to admit such a dangerous transition, not even to himself. Then the candle guttered suddenly in the draft from the open door, and she turned swiftly to face him, instantly breaking off her song.

'Don't stop,' said Stephen gently, 'Tell me what the words were saying, it was beautiful.'

'Oh, just nonsense,' she said, standing up. She was very pale and she avoided his eyes. 'You may watch him for a while now if you wish, he is sleeping peacefully. If the pain comes back, give him six more drops from the flask. No more. It might be dangerous.'

'I understand,' said Stephen, and he was still trying to find the words with which to thank her, when she hurried from the room, closing the door silently behind her.

Chapter 10

❧

Stephen laid down his pen and looked out of the window. It was Easter Sunday, an April afternoon of rare warmth and fleeting sunshine. Spring scents and birdsong were tempting him out of doors, but the muster ground by the river was deserted for once, as the men enjoyed a day of rest.

Stephen wished he could be idling with them outside The Lion, but the task in hand could be put off no longer. He was sitting beside the table in the room in which Jack had died and which he was once again sharing with Paul Darbier. He took up his quill and wrote, *'Your son had every care that kindness and skill could bestow. His death was as peaceful as any could wish.'*

Again he laid down his pen. Jack had lingered for another two days after Mistress Taverner had sung him her Spanish lullaby. The drops that Nona provided had ensured his tranquillity to the end. Stephen had never inquired what the medicine contained; Jack had been able to die with dignity and for that he was grateful. Nor did Mistress Taverner nurse Jack again; she had left that to Cary and Nona, and to Stephen himself. In fact he had hardly seen her. Stephen wondered if she was perhaps disturbed by the fact that he had seen her gentleness with Jack, or perhaps it was something that she had read in his eyes when he was watching her.

But nothing could deprive him of the picture he held of her stooping over his dying friend while she crooned the gentle song with the words she claimed were only nonsense.

Stephen sighed. Thoughts of Mistress Taverner were his constant companions, filling the gaps in time when he could not see her, nor hear her voice as she ordered her household. He had stood a little way behind her in church that Easter morning, and had watched through the whole service for the moments when she bent her head to say something to Philip and he was able to catch a glimpse of her pale cheek and dark lashes. He knew by the tilt of her head when she had slipped into abstraction – now he recognised those temporary lapses from concentration with which she was sometimes troubled.

He no longer tried to stop himself from thinking of Mistress Taverner, but he was careful never to analyse the direction his thoughts were leading. That way lay danger.

He took up his pen once more, dipped it in the ink. *'There was never a soldier braver than your son,'* he wrote, *'I wish he had not died.'*

The words were wretchedly inadequate. Stephen, unlike Paul Darbier, weighed each word carefully, whether speaking or writing. He was incapable of making a florid statement in which he only half-believed. Before, when he had been obliged to compose these painful last letters, he had always been able to add in a sentence or two about dying in a noble cause, because he had believed that to be true. This time it was impossible. The manner of Jack's death was an outrage against nature, and Stephen could no longer dress it up with pious words about duty or His Majesty's loyal service. *'I wish he had not died...'* He looked at the sentence. It seemed too obvious to be necessary and briefly he contemplated starting the letter again, but then he left it.

Stephen felt that something of his own self had been extinguished with Jack's death, some last spark of faith that this war was a straightforward crusade of good against evil. There were too many Darbiers on the royalist side, too many men who took their right to rule over others as God-given, and who would happily crush any who dared to oppose them. Stephen would never turn traitor to the cause in which his brother and friends had died; he would fight on loyally and doggedly, would die for it if necessary, but from now on he did so from necessity only.

'You would have been proud of him,' he wrote at length, *'God grant him peace and comfort to you and your family.'*

That was it. All else was trimming. There was no certainty even that his letter would reach its destination. Perhaps when this war was over he would go and seek out Jack's mother and talk to her himself of her son. When this war was over. Perhaps.

Nothing that had once been certain was so any more.

Doll had returned to her own bedchamber, the room which she had shared with Josiah through all her married life and in which her children had been born. Darbier had quitted it the morning following Jack's death, and Cary and Ellen had helped her clean it from floor to ceiling, yet still she could not settle. Though she had placed a bowl of last year's rose petals on the table and put sprigs of lavender in the chest and under her pillow, though she had chosen sweet cypress logs for the fire and used the last of her woodruff with the strewing herbs, it seemed to her that the acrid smell of the major still permeated her room. There was a wine stain on the filet-work bed-hanging which she could not quite erase and a new burn mark near the hearth. She fancied that his hand prints were on the panelled walls and on the posts of her bed; she was restless and slept badly. The first couple of nights she had brought the baby in with her so she would not have to cross the landing, but her unease remained.

It was not just the major, though his bearing towards her was increasingly ill-mannered. If that had been her only problem, she thought she could have managed somehow. It was only what she had expected, and she had been prepared to defend her home against ruffians, whether common soldiers or gentry; she believed she had the resources to withstand their barbarism. But she had been taken all unawares by the sight of a soldier who wept at the bedside of his dying friend. It had been easier when her heart had been full of hate only. The hate had not gone, it was as fierce as ever, but with it were mingled other emotions, just as powerful, which were new, and which she did not understand. The confusion disoriented her.

So she kept her distance from all the soldiers, especially Captain Sutton, and prayed for the day when the campaigning season would begin and her home would be her own once more.

A few days after Easter, Stephen was busy overseeing the unloading of some ammunition from the powder mill at Chester. Supply had been interrupted since the fall of Shrewsbury in the winter and his own stores had sunk dangerously low. But to his relief a couple of wagons had arrived the previous day. He would not contemplate storing such a quantity in the town, where an accident would be disastrous, so had decided to store it at the Old Priory. The ruined tower would make an ideal munitions store, and besides, this gave him an excuse to keep six men on guard duty there at all times. Local rumours concerning the Grey Lady had been causing serious problems among the sentries: men who had withstood cannon fire and cavalry charges were liable to scatter like mice if they thought they had caught a glimpse of a ghostly figure moving through the ruined walls on a starlit night. Stephen hoped that six men would have the courage that one or two had occasionally lacked.

He had mounted his mare and begun to ride towards the muster ground when he heard a voice calling his name. He reined Breda to a halt and, turning slightly in the saddle, saw a woman riding along the river bank towards him.

'Captain Sutton,' exclaimed Corinna, 'What a pleasure to see you again.'

He lifted his hat with a slight flourish and said, 'The pleasure is all mine, Mistress Rogers.'

'We'll see about that.' She smiled at him comfortably. 'I was on my way to see my father. He has been much troubled with gout recently and cannot leave Furleys. Why don't you come with me? I'm sure he'd be glad of some fresh company.'

Just at that moment Stephen could think of no particular reason to turn down Corinna Rogers' offer. 'I'd be delighted,' he said, 'If you're sure I'd not be an encumbrance.'

At this, Corinna merely laughed and kicked her horse onwards to keep pace with his. She was mounted on a pretty grey and, in her wide-brimmed hat and her short cloak, she knew she was being seen at her best. She was no beauty, but she sat easily on her horse and her laughter was frequent and engaging.

By the time they had ridden the short distance to Furleys, Stephen was beginning to realise that he had spent so much time anticipating Mistress Taverner's tense silences and barely veiled hostility, that he had forgotten what a straightforward pleasure the company of an amiable woman could be. She listened carefully to anything he said, agreed or disagreed with equal warmth and sincerity, and looked at him with great directness.

Corinna meanwhile was thinking what a shame it was that Captain Sutton had been monopolised for so long by Mistress Taverner who was well known to have time only for her children. It was quite clear the poor man was starved of even commonplace civilities. She was more than willing to fill the breach, but was still undecided whether a direct or more subtle

142

approach would be most effective. But she had reckoned without Stephen's manner, which was both courteous and unaffected, not to mention the warmth of his slight Cornish accent, and by the time she slid from her horse and gave it to the care of her father's groom, she was so aroused that she settled definitely in favour of directness, wondering only why she had dallied so long.

Furleys was a large house, not quite a mansion, set in a wooded park at a little distance from Tilsbury. It had been built to a modern design by Sir Diggory's father and had been hardly altered since then. Square and plain, it had the beauty of simplicity. But even here, Stephen could detect those subtle signs of neglect that he had seen in every house in the area whenever he set out on a patrol. He noticed too, with some amusement, the way Mistress Rogers changed as soon as she was once more in her father's home: no longer the high-born but impecunious wife of the local mason, but the baronet's daughter, and feared by the servants.

They found Sir Diggory, warmly wrapped in an old-fashioned velvet gown and nightcap, seated by a fire with his foot resting on a padded stool. His initial friendliness towards the soldiers had been eroded by the joint efforts of Major Darbier and the quartermaster who between them had made serious inroads on his previously well-stocked stores. He greeted Stephen coolly.

After an initial commonplace exchange, he asked querulously, 'The King plans to have a mighty army ready for the summer campaign. Will that see the end of the fighting, do you think?'

'Let us hope so,' said Stephen, 'The rebels are much divided and their new army is reported to be a shambles.'

'So Major Darbier tells me. But all the same, this war . . . it's a bad business, y'know. Bad for trade. Bad for the land. All my plate has gone to the mint at Oxford. Every week I get new demands for levies and taxes and heaven knows what besides. If the war is not won quickly, there will soon be nothing left worth fighting for.'

'The King himself has staked everything he possesses on this fight,' said Stephen with some sympathy, for he saw in Sir Diggory much of his own father's distress. War was hardest for the elderly, he thought: just when they might expect to reap the harvest of their labours, all they had achieved was taken from them.

While the two men discussed the war, Corinna fidgeted by the window. Eventually she came across to her father, dropped a light kiss on his nightcap and said, 'You must not hold poor Captain Sutton personally responsible for all your woes, I'm sure he has plenty of his own. Now, Father dear, don't be selfish and keep him all to yourself. I promised to show him the picture gallery before he's obliged to return to town. He claims to be a connoisseur.'

Stephen suppressed a smile: there had been no mention of any gallery, and Stephen had certainly made no claims to expertise. Sir Diggory entirely approved of the plan and was only sorry that his painful foot prevented him from accompanying them.

'Next time, Father dear,' breathed Corinna sweetly as she led the way from the room.

The family's collection of paintings was indeed impressive and Corinna knew erratic and entertaining details about each one. Most were portraits which had been done in the past hundred years, with a few modern still lifes and depictions of allegorical scenes. Sir Diggory's father had been the main collector, and, in order to make room for as many paintings as possible, the gallery had been designed with a series of alcoves in which they could be displayed on three sides. Corinna kept up a flow of chatter and Stephen, whose days had been filled with problems of discipline and supply for as long as he could remember, began to feel as if he had travelled much further than the short distance from Tilsbury.

He was examining a portrait of a ferret-faced gentleman in a high Elizabethan ruff, when he realised that Corinna had fallen silent for the first time. Wondering if her silence signalled boredom, he turned to look at her.

She was leaning back slightly, her elbows resting on the stone sill of the latticed window, and gazing up at him with an expression of quiet amusement. He thought perhaps he had said something betraying his ignorance of painting.

'Captain Sutton,' she spoke his name with the breathy inflection that always signalled her determination to have her own way, 'You have clearly been denied female company far too long.'

'Why do you say that?'

'Here I've been endeavouring to make love to you for the past half hour and you insist on giving all your attention to the paintings.'

The offer was playfully made, almost teasing, yet there was no doubt of its sincerity. Stephen removed his hat and ran his fingers through his hair. 'I owe you an apology then, for being so tardy.'

'No doubt you'll make up for your slow start.'

'I will do my best.' Stephen smiled suddenly, and Corinna knew with a rush of pleasure that her direct approach had been the right one after all. 'I'm flattered, Mistress Rogers. But why me?'

'I am an excellent good judge of character,' she purred, 'I know I can trust you to be discreet. A lady must consider her reputation when she goes looking for her pleasures. Now, do you intend to waste more time in talk, or will you kiss me?'

'Here?'

'Why not?'

'Now?'

'When better?'

Stephen fancied that the expression of her ferret-faced ancestor grew a fraction more disapproving as he leaned forward and, putting his hands gently about her waist, pressed his lips against hers. With a little sigh of satisfaction, Corinna wriggled slightly before answering his kiss with a subtle artifice that took him completely by surprise. Suddenly he found himself remembering his words to Beth on the night of his arrival at the Priory House when he had said, 'I am a soldier, and used to obeying orders.' As orders went, this one was pleasanter to obey than most. The next moment Corinna did something unexpected with her tongue, and he forgot about everything else.

They separated. Corinna was smiling, contented as a cat. She reached up a small hand and patted her hair. In Stephen's eyes she could now see the beginnings of desire where before there had been only friendship. Endeavouring to collect his thoughts, Stephen said, 'Is it only my discretion that recommends me?'

'We shall see, won't we? Besides I've flattered you quite enough for one day. Here—' And she surprised him anew by taking his hand and placing it over her breast, half-closing her eyes with pleasure. Stephen put his arms around her and kissed her hungrily, but she soon pushed him away.

'A taste,' she said coolly, 'That's all I'm offering here. I've had more than enough of dodging my father's servants and living in dread of their tales.'

'So?'

'Don't worry, Captain Sutton, I do not play the tease. Come to my house in Distaff Lane tomorrow after it is fully dark. Bring no servant with you. If anyone suspects, you may tell them it is my maid Ann who is your paramour.'

'Is she so willing to forfeit her good name?'

'That is between her and me. But, since you ask, Ann lost her good name a long time ago and I was the only person to offer lodging and work for her when the baby came. So you could say we have reached an agreement.'

'I see. Can't I visit you tonight?'

'No. I shall see you tomorrow. And now, Captain Sutton, I am sure you've been kept from your work in Tilsbury quite long enough. Unfortunately I am unable to accompany you since I am obliged to spend a little longer with my father.'

Stephen could not help smiling. 'You are very thorough in your planning, Mistress Rogers.'

'Of course. While you men are so occupied with this endless war, we women must take control of the more intimate aspects of life. It is only right.'

Then she laughed softly and, reaching up to take his head between her hands, she brushed her lips against his in a deliberately teasing gesture. She stepped back, adjusted the kerchief that lay across her bodice and said, 'Have I convinced you of my sincerity now?'

Stephen nodded. He took her hand and kissed it briefly, then picked up his hat and strode away down the long gallery, not once turning to look back.

Corinna crossed to the window and watched as Stephen's bay was led forward by a groom. She saw him mount and, still without a backward glance, canter away down the drive towards Tilsbury.

She was smiling. There was nothing so pleasurable as the anticipation of a new conquest – apart, of course, from the union itself. Captain Sutton had been just as she had expected and hoped – surprised, and then ardent, but not shocked. Major Darbier, having no doubt heard the rumours about her, had made one or two crude overtures in the past week, but she had repulsed him firmly. She preferred a man who in no way anticipated what she was prepared to give. In her dealings with grooms and tradesmen she had grown accustomed to take the initiative and decide the terms. And Captain Sutton, though definitely neither a groom nor a tradesman, had a kind of raw innocence about him that she had recognised at once, and which she found most attractive. She suspected, rightly as it happened, that his experience so far had all been with harlots and girls like her own poor Ann. She was certain therefore that she had much to teach him, and there were few occupations Corinna enjoyed more than lessons with a willing pupil.

Sergeant Morish had to repeat himself four times before Stephen took in what he was saying.

As Corinna had calculated, Stephen spent the rest of that day in a state of pleasurable anticipation. He had been caught off-guard by her bluntness, but saw no reason to turn her down. He was flattered, of course. Somewhat to his surprise he found he admired her determination to see her desires met according to her own plan. He had never come across a woman like her before, though he had heard others boast of such acquaintances. If one of the women he had known while he was growing up in Cornwall had made a similar approach he would doubtless have been deeply shocked. But Tilsbury was not Cornwall. There was a sense of 'abroad' so far from home which made it easy to assume that such matters were arranged differently here.

Besides, a light-hearted dalliance with an agreeable woman would be a welcome interlude before the rigours of the summer campaign. There was no danger of his ever falling in love with Corinna Rogers – and he guessed that was the last thing she would want. In fact, now that his immediate prospects had altered so radically, Stephen was able to admit to himself that he was head over heels in love with Mistress Taverner and would never feel a fraction of that for any other woman. After his conversation with Mistress Rogers, Stephen was full of a protective tenderness towards Doll Taverner. Impossible to imagine her making such a straightforward bid to get what she wanted. Now that he considered the matter, he saw that the two women could not have been more different. It would have been easy to say that Mistress Rogers was worldly-wise, where Mistress Taverner was still an innocent, but he suspected that was only half the truth. Mistress Rogers had the supreme confidence of a woman who has always held a central place in her own narrow world, and who knows no other. Mistress Taverner, by contrast, had the wariness of someone who has seen and experienced far too much. Perhaps it was the baronet's daughter who was the innocent after all. But as it was patently clear that the woman he loved would never regard him with anything but dislike, his intended affair with Corinna Rogers was a quite unrelated fact.

The only problem he saw at present was how to wait patiently during the twenty-four hours before their assignation. And now here was Sergeant Morish, looking at him as if he was deaf and blind and telling him news he had absolutely no wish to hear.

'Tully has run off, sir. I thought I should tell you first, Captain Sutton, as the major is sure to be in a rare old rage when he hears.'

Stephen groaned. 'Damnation. When did the boy go missing?'

'Some time last night. The men who lodge with him had had a proper skinful and they only noticed at sun-up.'

'I suppose he's headed back to his sister and that baby he was so worried about.'

'I reckon so.'

Stephen remembered the lad's freckled, tear-stained face. 'I'd as soon leave him go,' he mused, half to himself, but of course, that was impossible. For some reason Darbier had come to regard Tully as his own personal contribution to the royal army. Others might desert with impunity, whatever military regulations said, but Tully would never be allowed to. Stephen said, 'Pick someone to go with you and take a couple of horses. Bring him back quickly. No need to trouble the major unnecessarily.'

Morish nodded his agreement and went in search of the scout who had guided them on their first patrol. A kindly man, Morish had rather taken to young Tully, who was far from stupid and had the makings of a useful soldier. He trusted his captain to deal with the matter humanely. Like most of the other men he no longer trusted Major Darbier at all.

Inactivity had bred in the young major a kind of malicious gloom. He was more and more idle and drank heavily. He told himself that like his hero General Goring he would be able to throw off his self-indulgence as soon as his circumstances changed: he was sure he would perform brilliantly on the field of battle. Meanwhile it was not his fault if his talents were being frittered away in this backwater where his only purpose was to get through each day with as little effort as possible.

He was becoming increasingly irritated by his romantic failures. The fact that he had made no headway with Mistress Taverner was bad enough, but when Corinna Rogers had turned him down flat and made it quite clear he need expect no alteration in future, his pride was badly ruffled. From time to time he had made use of one of the camp followers who appeared as soon as soldiers were in one spot for more than a day or two, but he felt that more sophisticated diversions were appropriate for the nephew of Lord Bewell. During the autumn in Oxford he had enjoyed an affair with a wealthy widow who adored him and lived in terror of his bad temper. In Tilsbury he found he was neither adored nor feared – and this rankled dangerously.

Seeing her every day, he found it hardest to forgive Mistress Taverner for her coolness. He knew that Stephen had taken a fancy to her and, in the state of rivalry that existed between them, this itself was enough to make her an object of desire. He was determined either to win her himself, or prove that she was not worth having. Always reluctant to admit he'd been in the wrong, Darbier had come to believe the truth of his idle remark to Stephen that she had been a whore before her marriage. Gradually this image of her worked its way into his mind, until he was convinced he was being snubbed by a woman who had once been a common drab, an insult which was well-nigh intolerable.

Late on the evening of Tully's disappearance, of which he knew nothing, Darbier had strolled calmly into Mistress Taverner's bedchamber. It was a genuine mistake, since he was well on in drink and it had been his own room during Jack's slow dying. Mistress Taverner, dressed only in a pale shift and with a loose gown draped across her shoulders, was seated in a chair by the fire. She had just finished feeding her youngest child who lay contentedly in her lap, gazing vaguely in her direction and making experimental shapes with his lips. Her hair hung loose over her pale throat, and over the exposed breast which was still swollen with milk.

At Darbier's entry, she gave an odd cry and instinctively lifted the baby and held him across her naked breast.

'Oh God, I forgot,' said the major, swaying slightly where he stood, 'I thought this was still my room.'

'Get out!' But there was fear behind her anger, and the major sensed it.

As surprise gave way to eagerness, a grin spread over his face.

'Now that I'm here – ' he began.

She rose to her feet and stood very straight and tall, flinging her gown across her chest, and grasping the baby so tightly that he began to whimper. 'How dare you! Get out of my room at once!'

The major thought that he had never seen a woman half so good looking and desirable as Mistress Taverner was at that moment. Her dark eyes were hot with fury. Her breathing was shallow and very rapid. With no very clear idea of what he intended to do, he took an unsteady step in her direction. He half-expected her to attack him, and he relished the prospect of a confrontation, was on his guard to snatch her wrists and enjoy the intimacy of physical contact.

Her response was completely unexpected. Suddenly all the fight went out of her, she opened her mouth as if to speak, but no sound emerged except an inarticulate groan, and she sank down in the chair.

Even in his befuddled state Paul Darbier could see that some fundamental transformation had occurred. A moment ago she had been as brim full of fury as a tigress, now she had crumpled entirely, and, he was certain, would offer no more opposition than a defenceless child. No sooner had he adjusted to this unexpected turn of events, and was about to take advantage of the shift in power between them, when the old woman pushed past him; she was shaking her head with disapproval and tutting like a broody hen.

'It's bad,' she said, taking the baby and adjusting Doll's dress at the same time. '*No puede ser.* You go away, bad trouble here.'

'How dare you try and tell me what to do, you old hag,' snarled Darbier. Disappointment always made him vicious.

Nona narrowed her eyes. 'Young man,' she told him, 'Don't take risks you don't understand.'

All at once her harmless old face grew sinister, and Darbier felt a shiver of fear, then, recovering his dignity as best he could, 'What a deal of fuss over nothing,' he said airily as he retreated from the room.

A little later, when Stephen came in from his evening rounds, he heard the sound of Nona's crooning coming from the chamber on the other side of the stairs. Paul Darbier was already asleep and snoring loudly. Hearing the strange song once more, Stephen assumed that Mistress Taverner must have been distressed by another of her bad dreams.

Chapter 11

❧

'Who's there?'

Doll sat bolt upright in her bed and peered into the darkness. She had been woken by an ominous creak from somewhere near the door. Her mouth was dry and her heart was racing. With trembling hands she fumbled with the tinder box beside her bed and lit a candle. The door of her room was closed. She was alone. Another false alarm.

She leaned back against the pillows and closed her eyes, but sleep was impossible. She had lost count of the number of times she had woken already that night – a mouse scrabbling beneath the floorboards, a fall of soot in the chimney, the slightest sound was enough to fling her into terror. And now, though she repeated to herself that she was safe in her own home, she no longer believed it. Her heart had become a sail and terror was the wind that blew it.

A tingling across her shoulders told her there was someone in the room, she knew there was. She had heard a movement by the panel which hid the priest's hole. She made herself climb out of bed and search every corner. It was empty, of course, she had known all along it would be empty. As if the action of preparing for the day could bring forward the dawn, she pulled on her clothes, bathed her face with lavender soap and brushed out her hair. All the time she had the sensation of being watched.

Moving restlessly about the room, she came to a stop by the little chest beside the window: its lid was covered with an embroidery she had done when she was expecting Beth, a stump work pattern of buds and leaves. She ran her finger-tips over its surface. Inside that box Josiah kept his pistols. He had taken his best pair with him on his journey, but the older ones that had belonged to his brother were there still. A little smile crept into her eyes. She could take one of the pistols, defend herself with it.

Dear God, if only it were that easy. Crossing the room she went to the window and looked out into the shadowy night. It had not been Darbier's blundering into her room that had set every nerve in her body aflame with foreboding, nor the fact that he had seen her nakedness. It had been the expression in his eyes when he took a step towards her. Not desire, or even lust, so much as a terrifying confidence in his own superior strength. He despised her, she was sure of it, he believed she was his for the taking and no one would raise a hand to protect her. She had seen that look in a man's eyes once before in her life – but had never thought to see it again after all these years within the four walls of her own home.

She tensed suddenly. There was an acrid smell filling her nostrils, a smell of burning. Pushing open the casement window she breathed deeply, but the night air was pungent with the dewy scents of spring. The river murmured gently beyond the orchard. All was well. . . .

Someone had come into the room while she was looking out of the window. She spun round so quickly that she jammed her wrist on the corner of the sill. There, there in the shadows beside the bed, wasn't that the face of a man staring at her, a man with colourless hair and cold pale eyes and fleshy lips glistening with saliva? The scream died in her throat, a deadly paralysis spread through her body. She stood motionless. When all the frippery of civilisation was stripped away, this was the only truth that remained: she was alone in the world, and weak.

Beads of sweat ran down between her shoulder blades, returning her to an awareness of the present.

Gradually she began to hear a new sound: someone or something was scratching at her door. She tried to think clearly but no thought came.

The face of the man with the pale and the pitiless eyes was no longer visible. Had she imagined it, or had he hidden himself, perhaps behind the bed hangings? Pushing herself against the wind of fear, she went to the door and opened it. One of the old spaniels nuzzled briefly against her palm before crossing the room to flop down by the hearth.

'Good dog,' she heard herself say, but her voice was unfamiliar and awkward. She tried to swallow, but the muscles of her neck had tightened, making even that simple action difficult. She had the sensation that a burning coal was lodged in her throat. The dog had a name, she knew it well, but just for the moment she could not remember what it was.

She looked around, but the man's face had not reappeared. On the road at the front of the house she heard the rumble of a cart and a farmer encouraging his horse. Framed by the window, the sky had grown paler. Dawn was not far off.

Her glance fell once more on the little embroidered chest, and she tried to mock herself for her night time fears. To think that just a little while ago she had considered taking Josiah's pistols for her own defence – the foolishness of it! She knelt down and took the little key that hung from her girdle, and turned it in the lock, raising the lid with a kind of reverence. The pistols were wrapped in a cloth of red silk, silk the colour of blood. She lifted them out and felt their weight against her palm, then the silk slithered over her hand and the weapons were revealed in all their lethal beauty. This was how soldiers created terror and pain – what was to stop her doing the same? She gripped one firmly and pointed it into the shadows where the man's face had been. She conjured up his image again, saw him cringe in fear while a giddy strength flowed down her arm and into the hand which held the pistol.

What was she thinking of, she wondered. Was she planning to shoot someone? She almost laughed. In the bedchamber across the landing, Darbier was sleeping. Supposing he were to wake and find her standing beside him with the pistol in her hand, would he ever dare to look at her so insolently again?

A child's cry broke the stillness, the baby was fretful and hungry. Did she hope to soothe her child while carrying a pistol in her hand? With a lingering regret she wrapped the guns once more in their silks and was about to put them back in the chest when she saw the glint of a dagger. She reached in and picked it up swiftly. It was one Josiah had purchased as a young man, the kind of short-bladed instrument they called a stiletto. It was a small thing, almost dainty. A womanly thing entirely, no harm in it at all. Without giving herself time to consider what she was doing she had tucked it into the pouch that she carried on her girdle, closed the little embroidered chest with her key and hurried to the baby.

Knowing that she carried the dagger at her side, as she walked silently over the carpets on the landing, was both a comfort and a terror of a new and unexpected kind.

Beth did not enjoy her expedition to the market cross that morning. For one thing, the country wives from whom they normally purchased milk and eggs did nothing but complain about how the soldiers had taken all they had, and were they now supposed to feed themselves with the tickets that were being issued instead of money? And then, when they were returning to the Priory House, there was an argument across the road between Jinny Crew's mother and one of the Welsh women who had arrived a couple of days earlier to join their menfolk.

'Why are they fighting?' she asked.

She had to repeat the question several times before her mother even heard her. Doll glanced at the two women contemptuously before answering, 'Have you never seen two dogs fighting for their master's affections? – And more fool them,' which Beth found a wholly unsatisfactory explanation but she dared not ask again, because, worst of all from her point of view, her mother was tense and distracted. She was gripping Beth's hand so tightly that it hurt yet she hardly seemed to know that she was there at all. She was glad when they returned and Doll told her to go and help Nona, for she had work to do in the stillroom.

Only when the stillroom door was locked behind her did Doll allow herself to breathe more deeply. It was true, there were many tasks that needed her attention at this busy time of year, but she was too distracted to do even one. There was a dull throbbing in her head and every time she closed her eyes she saw Darbier's flushed and greedy face. All morning she had felt as though she was on the point of vomiting. She wondered if she was with child again. Normally, pregnancy was a pleasure. Just at the moment, the thought of bringing new life into a corrupt world disgusted her.

Strange images and fragments of memory floated in her mind. Darbier's blundering had sprung the catch on a whole Pandora's box of half-remembered feelings and events: smell of burning, smell of fear, and chaos all around. There was a sharp pain across her shoulders, and, when she raised her hand to push back a strand of hair, her forehead was beaded with sweat.

I am ill, she thought – but she knew the illness was not in her body, but her mind.

Very carefully, as if fearing that her trembling hands would let them fall, she reached down one of Nona's nameless bottles from the top shelf. She frowned, trying to understand. Slowly the fog inside her brain began to clear. The bottle with the strange symbol on it which had been half-full at the time of Jack's death, now contained less than a quarter of the unknown liquid. She removed the cork and sniffed. The smell was strange – bitter, yet cloyingly sweet at the same time. She replaced the cork and put the bottle back. There was another one, next to it, identical in every way, except the second was full.

She puzzled over the meaning of the empty bottle. What had Nona been doing with the precious medicine since Jack's death? She shuddered. Perhaps she was imagining it all. Perhaps she had imagined the moment when Darbier had blundered into her room. Already the incident was gaining the stylised character of a dream. Perhaps the fragments of memory that increasingly teased at her mind were not memories at all, but fictions. Her hand fumbled at the pouch that rested against her hip and she felt the hard line of the stiletto. Why had she armed herself with a dagger within her own home? Was it a wise precaution or was it perhaps a symptom of approaching madness?

Towards the middle of the afternoon Mabs glanced up from the mound of wizened apples she was sorting, to see her mistress hurrying from the pantry, her face pale as death.

'Seen a ghost, have you?'

'It was . . . I saw . . .' Mistress Taverner stared back at her. The expression on her face suddenly gave Mabs the feeling she was not so very much older than Beth, after all. She was fingering the cloth of her skirt as she tried to frame the words. 'Only a mouse . . .' she managed in the end.

'A mouse?' Mabs had never known her to be frightened by mice before, or rats either, come to that. 'Here, ma'am, you don't look well at all. Come and sit by the fire in the parlour and I'll fetch you a drop of something.'

Mabs liked nothing better than a chance to mother her young mistress, and she chivvied her into the winter parlour, where a fire had already been lit. Major Darbier for once was absent, having gone to look at a couple of new horses that had been got for his troopers.

Doll consented to be fussed over and placed in a chair beside the fire; she was shaking, but not with cold. She had only lifted the cloth that covered the pitcher of milk. It was only a mouse that she had seen floating on the surface, its brown coat soaked with cream. Who cared about a mouse? No need to cry out in horror. Just throw the milk away, she told herself, give it to the cats . . . yet she could not shake off the thought of that tiny creature, falling over the lip of the jug, swimming so desperately, trying to scramble up the smooth sides, swimming on, round and round, exhaustion overcoming it. Drowning alone . . . Suffering and death had spread into every corner of her home. Even into a harmless jug of milk.

Mabs brought her buttered ale and was kind. But Doll found it hard to make out what she was saying because of the noise within her head that ebbed and flowed like a tide.

'You ought to lie down,' said Mabs. 'You're not yourself at all.'

But lying down was the last thing Doll wanted to do. She began to pace the room.

Then she stopped.

The portrait still stood propped against the wall near the window. Josiah had intended it to be hung over the fireplace in the dining hall but somehow, in all the turmoil before his departure, the job had never been done. Now the sight of that settled family group filled her with an irrational rage: how pathetically confident that woman looked now. If she had only guessed the dangers that lay ahead, she would never have stood so blindly calm.

'Quick, Mabs,' she said, 'Help me turn it around.'

'Don't you lift it. I'll fetch one of the men—'

'No, no. We must do it at once.'

Mabs saw her mistress must be humoured. But even when the figures had been turned to face the wall, Doll could not settle. Her pacing continued, anxious as before. She hardly noticed when Mabs retreated, baffled, to her kitchen. From time to time Doll touched the bag that hung from her waist, felt the weight of the metal dagger against her hip bone. 'Vengeance is mine, saith the Lord.' A mouse had drowned, slowly and horribly, and now she too carried death about her person. 'This is just the beginning,' Nona had said on the night that Jack was brought in wounded, 'These men are bringing death into your home.' There was a pounding beneath her ribs, a drumbeat telling her to run away while she still could.

But where?

She had paused for a moment by the window, watching but not seeing the activity beyond the gate, when Paul Darbier strolled into the room. She was so enveloped in her thoughts and fears and memories that she never even noticed him. He hesitated for a moment in the doorway, expecting her to turn and make some gesture of greeting, but when she apparently ignored him he smiled and walked slowly over to the hearth. All morning the picture of her as he had seen her the previous evening, her dark hair streaming across her naked breast, had stuck like a splinter in his mind. He assumed she was ignoring him on purpose, that she intended to provoke him. He was angry and stimulated at the same time. He thought she must be arousing him, deliberately.

He spread his ringed fingers in front of him and admired the rich clusters of jewels before saying, 'I wanted to congratulate you, Mistress Taverner. You're a damned fine actress, you know. Played your part well.'

She jumped slightly at the sound of his voice and then, turning to face him but remaining at the window, she frowned, not having properly heard what he was saying.

Darbier took her silence to indicate agreement. He went on, 'Others have been hoodwinked, eh? – but I'm not so easily fooled. Mistress Taverner, respectable wife and mother, that's a fine trick you've played on the good folk of Tilsbury.' He moved over to the portrait. 'You've turned it around, Mistress Taverner, I wonder why?' Then he smiled as if they did indeed share a secret. 'The past can never be buried completely, can it, Mistress Taverner?'

Her eyes were opaque. 'What in heaven's name are you talking about, Major?'

Darbier noticed with delight the way her sudden trembling caused the fabric of her dress to quiver. He was congratulating himself as he began to cross the room towards her, believing that he had at last found the secret to dealing with her veneer of hostility.

'No need to play the virtuous wife with me, you know... since you and I both know full well—'

A strange smile spread across her face. He did not notice her hand as it reached down to the embroidered pouch that hung from her waist.

'Yes, Major, what is it we both know?'

He stopped. Something in the manner of her question jarred on his confidence. He said, rather too loudly, 'What you once were – no need to spell it out. Just so long as we understand each other,' and he stood four square in front of her.

'Keep away.'

'And if I refuse?'

'Dear God, don't tempt me.'

He grinned, took another step towards her. 'Tempting you is precisely what I have in mind, don't you—'

'Mother, come quickly!' Beth catapulted into the room with such impatience that she barely noticed the major, certainly did not see his annoyance.

'Get on back to your nursery where you belong!' he burst out in a fury, 'Can't you see I'm talking to your mother?'

'It's Nona,' Beth was almost weeping, 'There's something wrong, she's—'

Above all things, Darbier hated to be ignored. 'Damn you,' he exclaimed, 'I thought I told you to leave us be,' and to reinforce his words, he reached out and caught the child by her arm. The impact was instant. Until then, Doll had stood quite motionless, but the moment he laid his hand on her daughter's sleeve, she was transformed. She sprang forward and snatched the child away.

'Don't touch her!' she burst out, in a strange, harsh voice, 'Don't touch her or I'll kill you!'

'Mother, stop.' Beth's eyes had filled with tears. 'Please stop.'

Darbier had backed off at once. 'Great heavens, woman, what a deal of fuss over nothing. No need to go making a song and dance,' he drawled, a hint of reproach in his voice.

Doll blinked. She relaxed her grip on her daughter. 'What's the matter, Beth?'

'It's Nona. There's something wrong. She won't speak to me or do anything.'

'There you are,' said Darbier, 'What did I tell you? It's just the old woman.'

Doll ignored him. She was still breathing heavily, but she said in a quiet voice, 'Don't worry, little Bee. I'll come with you now. It's all right.'

Darbier, watching Mistress Taverner with her daughter, could not decide which was the more enticing, her fury or her tenderness. He said, 'We'll have to continue our discussion, eh?

When there're no brats to come between us.'

In the doorway, Doll paused, and turned to him with a light in her strange eyes that put him in mind of the stories of her grandmother's arcane powers. She said smoothly, 'Major, you should be on your knees to thank little Beth. She may have saved your life,' but before he could say another word, she had left the room.

The major stood quite still for a moment or two, then crossed to the hearth and poured himself a mug of buttered ale. After a little while he had rearranged their somewhat odd exchange to his own satisfaction and managed to convince himself that he had in fact handled the whole situation rather cleverly. He was certain that veiled references to her scandalous past were the bait with which Mistress Taverner was to be hooked.

In the upstairs bedchamber, Nona was sitting in her usual chair by the fire. Although she was perhaps paler, and Doll thought she could detect a certain blueness around her lips, the old woman appeared otherwise unchanged. Except that she was angry.

'Now you've gone and bothered your mother,' she complained, 'There was no need for that at all, Beth. Nothing to make a fuss about.'

'But you wouldn't speak to me!' Beth was on the verge of tears.

'I don't have to speak if I don't feel like it.'

Philip was by the open window. As always he was more interested in observing the activities of the soldiers than anything that took place indoors. Harry sat somewhat apart, a small island of anxiety, listlessly arranging chequers on a board.

'What happened, Nona?' asked Doll.

'Nothing. Just a lot of fuss about nothing. At my age, you learn to expect an occasional upset.'

What kind of upset, Doll wondered. But she did not ask. Nona must never change.

'There you are, Beth, there was no reason for alarm.' She spoke as much to calm herself as her child, 'Nona's fine. Just a little bit tired.' She stroked Beth's frizz of hair. In the light from the afternoon sun it shone redder than usual. Hair the colour of blood, thought Doll. She glanced swiftly away. Sunlight lay in pools of blood across the floor. I am going mad, she thought, why do I carry this dagger at my side? She said softly 'Beth, will you play us one of your pretty songs?'

But Beth was not to be soothed. She could feel the tension sparking from her mother's touch.

Hunting for reassurance, she pleaded, 'I'd rather hear one of yours.'

'One of mine?'

'Yes, one of the Spanish ones you and Nona sing together. Then we can all be peaceful again.'

'Nonsense, Beth, yours are much nicer.'

'Please—'

'Well, maybe so. Why not?' Perhaps dancing would help. Heaven knew, she had never needed the balm of music more than she did now. 'What do you think, Nona?'

At that moment Philip let out an excited cry and peered so far out of the window that Doll raced across the room to catch hold of his skirts before he tumbled down into the flower bed below.

'Tully's back!' he squealed, struggling to keep his position. 'They've caught Tully. Major Darbier's come out and he looks mighty angry and, oh look, he's hitting him with a stick. And now here's Captain Sutton. And he's joining in, he's hitting him as well!'

Doll kept a firm hold on the boy, but she was mesmerised by the grim scene being enacted in the stable-yard. The major was thrashing the young runaway without mercy and looked for all the world as if he meant to kill him. And while Doll stood at the window and held her squirming son, she saw another Doll, a mirror image of herself, step out across the cobbled yard below the window, take a short-bladed knife in her hand and stab the major, stab him again and again, until he let go his vicious hold of his victim and collapsed in a bloody heap on the ground. And then she could see nothing, only blackness and emptiness, and Beth had pushed past her with a horrified cry, 'Oh, it's not fair! Poor Tully, how can they be so unkind?'

'Beth, don't look. Come here at once.' Just before she drew both her children away from the window Doll looked out once again: the shadow Doll was no longer there, but some kind of fight was developing between Captain Sutton and the major.

Beth was panting slightly as she returned to the centre of the room. 'It's all right,' she announced triumphantly to Nona and Harry, 'Captain Sutton wasn't hitting poor Tully. I knew he wouldn't. He was just stopping the horrid major from being cruel.'

That evening was particularly mild, a first breath of spring. Wood pigeons called to each other in the dusk and the village children ventured down to play on the field by the river where the soldiers had drilled all day with musket and pike. In the ruined priory the sentries relished the soft April evening and chatted to keep their spirits up while they kept a lookout both for Massey's men and the ghost of the Grey Lady. In the shed behind the stables Tully, bound and hungry, gave himself up to bitter despair, not because of the major's beating, which had been brief, but because when he returned to the drovers' inn high on the hills he found his sister and her baby had been dead and buried for over a week. The sexton and the constable had already disposed of the bodies, and the only home he had ever known was desolate, and strange. He had no idea what to do next and had been almost relieved when Sergeant Morish and the other man came and took him back with them to Tilsbury. But now, as dusk fell, the knowledge that he would never again see his sister sank in, and he was drowning in a sea of loneliness.

Cary, as she settled Harry and Beth for the night, gave them a detailed account of the fight they had not been permitted to watch but which she and Mabs had observed from a convenient window. How Major Darbier had roared that he would kill young Tully for running away again, and how Captain Sutton had come raging out of the house and ordered him to stop. And how, when the major had carried on anyway, Captain Sutton had caught hold of his arms and pinned them to his sides until the major had been forced to give in and let Tully be taken away to be dealt with by Morish. And then how Major Darbier had stormed and threatened Captain Sutton with all sorts of horrors, but the captain had just ignored him and gone back to his work, and then the major had gone inside and the servants heard no more.

And Beth had listened and worried more than anything. Everyone was fighting, she thought, it was as if the war took place not just on battlefields but in every room of every house in the land. Her mother had looked and spoken so strangely today that Beth was half-afraid of what she might do next. She longed to ask Harry what he thought, but her brother was withdrawn and hardly spoke to her these days. In fact Harry was as agitated as she was by these strange doings in the soldiers' world. He wished from the bottom of his heart that his father would come home and explain these adult mysteries.

Beth would hardly have been comforted could she have seen into her mother's thoughts. Doll had not eaten all day, but she had no hunger. She was exhausted and restless at the same time. In her mind Tully and the drowned mouse were becoming interchangeable. When she took a pitcher of water to the stillroom she half-expected to see Tully's face staring up at her from its dark surface. Terrified of her own thoughts, she went in search of Nona. The old woman had already retired to bed.

'Are you ill?' Doll felt a clutch of a new kind of panic.

'Only tired. Don't bother me with the baby tonight. I need a good sleep.'

'Very well.'

Philip, tucked up in his little bed beside his grandmother's, was humming to himself, his usual way of settling himself for the night. Alone of all the family, the boy remained unaffected by the tensions of the day. His elfin beauty and his fearlessness made Doll suddenly afraid for him: so content in his little kingdom, he was the one with everything to lose.

'Good night, Nona. Sleep well.' She gave Philip a kiss which made him wrinkle up his nose with pretended disdain, and then went to her own room. She was suddenly very cold. She pulled a warm shawl around her shoulders but the chill seemed to be coming from within. The baby was sleeping soundly in his crib, which had been moved into her own room. She half-wished he would wake.

Laughter from the stable-yard behind the house, then shouting, the beginnings of a quarrel. Panic rose like a sickness in her throat. Violence and fighting and death all around her. War was an evil flood and now the dregs were lapping through the doors of her very home.

Light was slipping away. With the approach of darkness, Doll felt a primitive fear of night, danger in every shadow.

Gradually she became aware that she still carried the dagger in the pouch which hung from her waist. A sudden cold wash of perspiration beaded her body: she had come so perilously close to using it on the major when he had talked to her in riddles in the winter parlour. How easy it would have been. 'Come closer, Major, closer still . . .' and then, just as he was about to touch her, the fresh blade sliced into his stomach, his heart, his loathsome, gloating face. Just like the scene she had observed when she looked out of the upstairs window and her shadow-self moved with such deadly grace across the stable-yard. . . .

She knew she ought to put the stiletto back into its little chest, but she had grown to like the feel of its weight against her hip. She would never use it, of course not, but just to know it was there, that in itself was a kind of comfort.

This is madness, she thought . . . and then she wondered why that must be so. Men carried swords and pistols and daggers all the time: why not a woman too? She began to pace the floor; each time she came to the little embroidered chest she paused, then turned away and walked again. Next time, she told herself, next time I shall put it back where it belongs. It seemed to her that the room, lit only by a single candle, was filling with faces and the sound of murmured voices. But she no longer feared them quite so much, having the dagger so close to hand.

Too exhausted for sleep she took the candle and went down the stairs to her stillroom: she would make herself a soothing concoction of camomile flowers, then she could rest.

Stephen had stripped to his breeches and was washing in a basin of water when Darbier came into their room. He cursed silently. He knew there had to be a reckoning with the major, but had been hoping to postpone it until after his evening with Mistress Rogers.

'You defied me,' said Darbier, only the slight slurring of his words betraying that he had been soothing his ruffled pride with drink. 'In front of all the men, openly defied me.'

Stephen splashed water on his face and neck before raising his head and looking towards the major. 'It was only Sergeant Morish and a couple of others who were there. They won't say anything.'

'Liar. The news will be all over this damned rat-hole by morning. You deliberately humiliated me.'

'I'm sorry Paul, but I'd do the same again. Better to stop you doing something you'd only regret. Tully deserved to be punished, not killed.'

'Damn you, Captain, I'm the major here. I decide those things. And what's the good of apologising when no one can hear you?'

Stephen was towelling himself dry. He gazed at Darbier with a cool appraisal that the other man found more vexing than outright defiance. 'Are you asking me for a public apology?'

'God damn your eyes, Captain, I don't *ask* for anything. I give

165

orders and I expect them to be obeyed. You will do whatever your commanding officer tells you.'

'Naturally.'

The single word was pronounced without any particular expression but Darbier eyed his opponent with suspicion. Was that 'naturally' sincere or mocking? He had no way of knowing. Recently he had found it safest to assume that everyone was against him.

'I shall make a report of this to our colonel.'

'You must do as you see fit. But it might be wise to consider—'

'What?'

'If a detailed investigation were made into your own recent conduct, you are unlikely to emerge with great credit. Far better if we sort this out between us.'

'A duel?'

Stephen smothered a sigh which seemed to imply that his major was little more than a child, and a thorough nuisance, but he continued evenly, 'If that is what you want. Or I'll make a public apology if you prefer. But I absolutely refuse to stand by and watch while you beat a lad senseless just on a vicious whim. You may tell that to our colonel any time you wish.'

Stephen flung down his towel and pulled a clean cambric shirt over his head. Darbier was beginning to realise that Stephen's anger was of an altogether different calibre from his own. Whereas for Paul Darbier anger was an excuse to let rip and do exactly as he pleased, Stephen was utterly controlled, and immovable. Darbier chose a different tack.

He said, 'You're getting damned smart, aren't you?'

Stephen glanced out of the window, but did not answer. He noticed only that it was almost dark.

'Are you meeting a woman?'

Once again, Stephen was silent. Even the most routine of lies had always been a problem.

'Answer me, man, are you?'

'I'll probably check on the sentries later.'

'So you *are* meeting a woman. Who is it?'

No answer.

'Some idle trollop, I expect. But no, you'd not get spruced up for a common drab.'

'It hardly matters.'

'I'll be the judge of that, Captain. So who is the lucky woman, eh? You're not telling. Well, it certainly isn't Doll Taverner, is it, though any fool can tell you're besotted with the woman. She'd never have you – and why not? Because you're so blinded by all your fine notions that you've missed the truth about the woman entirely. I've had more experience in these matters than you, Captain, and I know how to handle this kind of situation. I wouldn't be at all surprised if there were some interesting developments in that direction over the next couple of days. I'll let you know. I must say, though, I'm surprised at you, making do with second best when you've been so fired up about our Spanish beauty. But I tell you what, Captain, I'll make a full report of all her charms for you when I know them more intimately. You'd like that, wouldn't you?'

Stephen was suddenly very still. He knew that it would suit Darbier perfectly if he were to lose his temper now: to attack his major in order to save the life of a young recruit might just be defensible, to attack him over a woman was definitely not. Besides, he understood Darbier well enough to know that if he felt able to fling a few well-aimed insults, the incident over Tully would be forgotten all the sooner.

He said quietly, 'You know full well, Paul, you'll get nowhere with Mistress Taverner.'

Darbier eyed him closely. The way Stephen said the words convinced him, if he had needed convincing, that the best way to settle his score was to have first possession of the woman Stephen so clearly wanted. Once again the image of her pale nakedness came into his mind. But if Stephen meanwhile was enjoying himself elsewhere, some of his triumph was sure to be diluted.

He said slyly, 'Of course, I could order you to take first watch in the ruin tonight.'

Stephen wanted very much to keep his rendezvous with Corinna Rogers. He had thought of nothing else all day. Even while he had been washing, he had imagined how she too must be preparing herself . . . The possibility of disappointment was bitter.

He said, very quietly, 'Whatever you decide, Major.'

But in the silence that followed there echoed the light tread of someone going down the stairs, and both recognised Mistress Taverner's footsteps.

Darbier's face lit up. 'You may go to the devil tonight, for all I care. I've got better things to do. I'll decide how to deal with your foul insubordination in the morning.'

And with that he stalked from the room. Stephen breathed a sigh of relief, then spent a few minutes more making sure that he was fit for a lady's company. He realised he was as nervous as a schoolboy. It was a frivolous, pleasurable sort of nervousness, and a welcome change from the kind of dread that had become all too familiar over the past two and a half years.

He closed the door of his room and went quickly down the stairs. The house was already steeped in its night-time silence, all the servants either sleeping or occupied elsewhere. So much the better: he was mindful of the need for secrecy.

Just as he reached the bottom of the stairs he heard the sound of a man's voice, low and insistent, coming from the rear of the house. Darbier. He hesitated. Then there was silence. Some instinct of protection spurred him to check that Mistress Taverner was safe before he left. But then he considered how Corinna Rogers must already be waiting for him, and wondering about the delay . . . Besides, Mistress Taverner had made it plain on numerous occasions that she resented his interference and was well able to look after herself. But he had only taken a couple of steps towards the front door when there was another sound, an agonised groan that Stephen recognised only too well, and then the noise of pottery smashing.

He raced down the screens passage, reaching the stillroom in an instant. And then he stopped, appalled by the sight that met his eyes.

The man who would soon be still and silent for ever was rolling in wordless agony on the floor, blood pouring from a wound in his breast. And beside him, quieter than death, stood Mistress Taverner. As Stephen came into the room she let the stiletto fall from her hand, and in that instant, Darbier died.

Chapter 12

❧

During a long pause there was no movement in the stillroom, only the candle's shadows flickering in the draught from the open door.

At length Stephen said, softly, 'What in God's name have you done?'

Doll did not answer, did not even look at him. Her eyes were enormous, and her lips were parted in an odd smile. The hand which had held the dagger was raised slightly before her in a grotesque parody of a handshake.

He stepped forward to kneel beside the major. There was a spasm of movement but no trace of breath, and Stephen had seen that look in men's eyes too often to allow any false hopes now. He touched Darbier's lids with his fingertips and the eyes no longer stared up towards the ceiling. Stephen stood up and turned to Mistress Taverner.

'Why?'

At his question she made an odd sound, then slowly, very slowly, she began to crumple into unconsciousness. Instinctively Stephen slid his arm around her waist and caught her, a dead weight, before she struck the ground.

For the first time in his career as a soldier, perhaps for the first time in his life, Stephen had not the first idea what to do next. He was standing in the middle of the stillroom, a man lay dead on the floor in front of him and the woman who had apparently committed the murder was slumped unconscious in his arms. He had a sudden presentiment that the way he acted in the next few minutes, or hours perhaps, was going to affect the whole of the rest of his life, and the lives of those near to him, in a way that nothing had ever done before. He was aware that he needed to think clearly, but thinking clearly was just then the hardest of tasks. He listened intently, but the silence of the house remained absolute: no one but he had overheard the deadly scuffle that had just taken place.

In the silence Mistress Taverner murmured, 'Juana—'

'What?'

She was endeavouring to raise her head, but her eyes were still not fully open. 'My sister needs me,' she said.

'Your sister?' Stephen had never felt more helpless in his life. He wondered how often he had longed to hold Mistress Taverner in his arms; perhaps since that first evening when he had seen her talking with her children in the stable – and now he did so. She was pressed so close against his chest that he could feel her heartbeat and her black hair had spilled over his hand – and it was a disaster. His first task was to relieve the shock which had apparently overwhelmed her. With one arm still supporting her shoulders, he gently lowered her feet to rest against the floor.

'See if you can walk,' he said, 'I'll help you to your room and Nona will take care of you.'

But she did not seem to have heard him. '*Mamaita*,' she whispered, 'Where is *Mamaita*? They are killing my mother.'

'Who is?'

'All of them.'

Stephen guided her from the stillroom, taking care to pull the door shut behind him. But she could barely walk and as soon as they reached the screens passage he again lifted her in his arms and carried her up the stairs to her room, where he set her down in the chair beside the dying fire. He saw she was regaining her strength, though her eyes still had an oddly sightless look. A chill fear occurred to him as he gazed down on her: he had heard stories of people being driven into madness by some unbearable shock.

He said, 'I'll fetch Nona for you, Mistress Taverner. She'll be able to help.'

But she gripped the sleeve of his doublet. 'No, no, they've beaten Nona. Don't leave me here alone—'

At this last appeal Stephen felt something breaking inside him. He crouched down beside the chair and stroked her pale hand. 'There,' he murmured, 'You're safe now. Don't worry. You're safe.' And he thought how useless and untrue the words were. With Major Darbier slain in her own house, she had every reason to worry, and so did he.

He was still in this position when he heard a door opening across the landing and Beth, holding up her nightgown with one hand, came quietly into the room.

'Has Mother been dreaming?' she asked.

Stephen noted that Mistress Taverner showed no sign of having recognised her daughter's voice, but she had relaxed her hold on his doublet enough for him to extricate himself gently. He turned to Beth.

'Yes, I think so. We need to wake your grandmother.'

Beth nodded, and with her usual composure she crossed the landing and pushed open the door into her grandmother's room, Stephen following with the candle. From the high bed came a regular, wheezing snore. Beth put her lips close to Nona's ear and said, 'Wake up, Nona. Mother's had one of her dreams. Wake up!' But the sleeper's rhythmic snoring did not even falter.

'Here, I'll try.' Stephen shook the old woman with increasing roughness, but she merely grumbled and worked her way a little deeper into the bed. It was then that he noticed the glass phial next to his candle on the little table. He picked it up and sniffed it cautiously. An oddly familiar smell, though he could not, just at that moment, place it.

Beth explained, 'Nona says she is old now, that's why she needs a little something for good sleeps. Mother does not know.'

Stephen groaned. A drugged sleep, and just when the old woman was most desperately needed.

'She won't help you, will she?' said Beth, 'If you want, I could sing to Mother; that's what Nona does when she has these dreams.'

Stephen considered. He was still undecided how best to deal with this catastrophe, but already he had an impulse towards secrecy. Tempting though Beth's offer was, he judged it best that she did not hear what her mother might say in her present state.

There was movement in the smaller bed. 'What are you doing Beth?' came a sleepy voice, 'Why is Captain Sutton here?'

'Go back to sleep, Pip,' Beth spoke with all the stern authority of an eight-year-old for her younger brother, 'This is none of your concern.'

Telling Philip to mind his own business was a certain way to arouse his interest: all at once he was very wide awake indeed.

Stephen had no wish to alert the whole household.

'Here's what you must do, Beth, if you want to help your mother,' said Stephen in a low voice, 'Stay with Philip until he settles again. Then you must go back to your own room and try to sleep yourself.'

'But—'

'Soldiers' orders,' he said firmly, and, with a sigh, Beth knew she had to accept. But just as he was going to the door, she brightened.

'Captain Sutton—'

He turned. Beth was standing in the pool of light from the candle and her homely face was suddenly impish.

'What is it, Beth?'

'Now *you* will have to sing for Mother, won't you?'

If only it was so simple, thought Stephen as he returned to Mistress Taverner's chamber, apprehension a growing weight within him. He found her still seated, just as he had left her, her head resting on one hand, her dark hair beginning to fall across her face, eyes open but unseeing. He closed the door behind him and approached slowly.

'Mistress Taverner—'

She did not look up, but examined the backs of her hands intently. 'I couldn't help you, Juana,' her voice was oddly high and childish, 'I didn't know—'

Stephen found water in a jug behind a screen and poured some in a basin. It was icy cold. He dipped his hands in and smoothed some on her forehead and cheeks. She looked up at him and her expression was anguished.

'Stop them!' she wailed. 'For God's sake, make them stop!'

Stephen stepped back helplessly.

She was looking all about, but seeing nothing he could see. 'Hide, hide,' she sobbed, 'There's nowhere safe, nowhere to hide . . .'

Of all torments, this was the most agonising. As he watched her disintegrate in front of his eyes, he was finally compelled to understand the depth of his feeling for her.

He took her hands between his. 'Mistress Taverner,' he said, in the quiet voice he used to steady troops before a fight, 'Look at me. I am Stephen Sutton. You are in Tilsbury. I don't know who in God's name Juana is or was but there's no Juana here. Do you understand? Now, you must listen to me. A man lies dead in your house and you have killed him. We must consider how to act.'

She did not – could not – hear him. In growing desperation, Stephen took hold of her chin and forced her to look into his eyes. She did not resist. 'There is no Juana,' he told her again, 'You are in your own room, your own home. You have a husband Josiah. You have children. Look—' he pulled her to her feet and, catching her round the waist, he half-dragged her across the room to the wooden crib where the baby was sleeping. Once again he was holding her in his arms and she made no movement of protest. But though she leaned her body against his, he had never felt another human being to be so impossibly far away. 'Look, now,' he made his voice harsh, 'there lies your son. Look at him, he needs you. Here and now your children need you—' She shrank from the sight of the sleeping baby, but Stephen was relentless. 'Don't you understand that? You have done foul murder, and if we don't think of some way out of this then you will have to stand trial for your life and most certainly you will die. Mistress Taverner, I want to help you, but you must do your part too, I cannot act alone—'

Stephen broke off. What was he saying? But of course, the answer was very simple. He was telling her that he intended to do all in his power to save her from the consequences of her crime. There was no alternative. Darbier was dead, and all the judicial murders in the world would not bring him back to life.

The decision made was a burden lifted suddenly from his shoulders. He took Mistress Taverner's face between his hands and said gently and very clearly, 'You do understand, don't you? You have killed Major Darbier. Now, do you wish your children to be orphans?'

He held his breath. In the long silence that followed he saw her eyes begin to focus on his. He searched them for signs of recognition. Her lips moved, a slight groan escaped her.

'What has happened?' she asked, her eyes brimming with tears, 'What have I done?'

Stephen let his hands fall to his side, forcing himself to remain outwardly impassive.

'You stabbed Major Darbier,' he said, as she sank down on a low stool and covered her face with her hands, 'He is dead. It happened in your stillroom.'

She smothered a cry. Stephen wished he could comfort her, but he knew he must not, not yet. The baby stirred in his cradle, whimpered once or twice, then slipped back into sleep.

Stephen said, 'Tell me what happened.'

'I don't remember. I took the dagger this morning. Last night I could not sleep because the major had been in my room.'

'Darbier came in here?'

'He said it was a mistake. But it was the way he looked at me that was so . . . disgusting. I carried the dagger all day. I was going to put it back in the chest, but after that . . . there is nothing.'

'I don't mean just now,' said Stephen, who thought he could guess what had taken place in the stillroom. 'Tell me what happened before, that other time. Who was Juana?'

'Juana?'

'You talked about someone called Juana. You said she had been killed. And that Nona had been beaten. Was that a dream?'

She shook her head. 'No,' she said, 'That was my life.' Then she raised her eyes, looked at him very directly and it seemed to Stephen that their eyes met for the first time. 'Juana was my sister.'

She was still shivering, so he fetched a heavy shawl and placed it around her shoulders. He sat down on a chair at a little distance and waited.

'Tell me,' he said, 'I want to know everything.'

'Why?'

'Because I want to help you.'

'But we do not have time, the major will be found. What can I do?'

'I will think of something. Trust me, Mistress Taverner.'

'Why?'

'Must there always be a reason?'

Doll stared at him. All her life she had lived in fear of soldiers. This man was undoubtedly a soldier, yet she found she did not fear him, not in the least. Just for the moment, she was cleansed of all her fear. She understood that she had committed a terrible murder, but strangely enough, that knowledge was a kind of freedom, a loosening of bonds. As if she had been fettered all her life and now was free . . . it was madness, of course. Or perhaps it was simply the desperate freedom of someone who has forfeited everything they will ever have on this earth and so has nothing more to fear.

Her shivering had not lessened, despite the warm shawl, but

she said calmly, 'What is it you wish to know?'

Stephen was frowning. 'Just now, you seemed to be reliving something that happened,' he prompted her as gently as he could. 'Your sister was killed.'

She looked away. 'Many people were killed.'

He waited, but when she remained silent he asked, 'Where was this?'

'In . . . in Würzburg.' She appeared to have some difficulty saying the word for the first time, then she said again more clearly, 'In Würzburg.'

Stephen had heard of the town before, it was a name that carried dark associations, but he could not remember why.

He said, 'Will you tell me, Mistress Taverner?'

Her strange eyes were searching his face. 'Why? Why do you want to know about me?'

'I told you, I want to help you.'

She thought for a little while before saying slowly, 'And if I tell you, tell you everything, from the beginning, do you promise you will try to help me?'

'I promise.'

She nodded. 'Are you sure we should not act first?'

'It is only just midnight. We have plenty of time.'

'Very well then. I will leave it to you. What do you wish to know?'

'About you, your life. Where were you born?'

'In Spain.'

'And your family?'

'My family?' She thought for a moment, before beginning carefully, as though anxious to help him out. 'My father was an apothecary. When I was born he was already an old man. My mother was his third wife. His other children were all grown up, with families of their own. Two of his sons were older than my mother. She had two children, my sister Juana, and then me. My mother was still so young and beautiful that my father called us his three flowers. He was a wise man, and kind – too kind, my mother often said. He could not say "no" to anyone, and people took advantage of his kindness. My mother used to cry sometimes because he gave our money to a poor family, or gave away medicines and got nothing in return. Once I heard her complaining that he cared more for others than for her, but he just smiled. Then he said that he had the three most beautiful flowers in the world, why should he need more? But she was still cross and said his daughters needed shoes, how was she to pay for them? So he promised to find the money for our shoes, and *Mamaita* was comforted.'

She had begun her story to satisfy Stephen, but already she seemed almost to have forgotten that he was there. Now she was telling her story to herself, as if to make sense of the journey that had led her to this place and moment.

'Our home was by the shop, in the middle of the town. It had cool dark rooms, we kept the shutters closed against the sun. One of my earliest memories is of waking up from the siesta and looking at Juana who still slept beside me.' She was smiling now as she spoke. 'Her body was striped black and white from the sunlight coming through the shuttered window, and I thought she was changing into a strange animal and I screamed. Then everyone woke up and laughed at me for being afraid. I can remember the smell of orange blossom that seemed to be everywhere, and the smell of the dust in the streets, and the mystery of my father's shop with all its bottles and secrets. And the sunshine that dazzled us when we came out of the dark church on Saints' days and Sundays. On summer evenings everyone gathered in the courtyard and I would sit with my father while the women danced and sang, and sometimes I would try to join them.

'I think I must have been about five or six when we left our home. The Spanish army in the Low Countries needed men like my father, and maybe he had trouble with his debts. People used to come to the house and complain and my mother would cry and say what was she supposed to do, he was hopeless, he'd never change and we would all be ruined. And then there was more arguing because my father wanted to take Nona with us – Nona was his aunt, not really my grandmother at all, but she had always been like a big sister to him – and my mother was upset and said did he think she couldn't manage her own family? But she gave way in the end, and later she was glad, I think. The day before we left, my father produced new shoes for us all. Mine pinched my feet and I wanted to take them off, but they made me keep them on. So I cried when we left our home, not because we were leaving – I don't think I understood what that meant – but because my feet hurt me. Though if I could have known what lay ahead of us, I would never have gone. Never. And Father told me not to cry because when we came home again we would be rich and everyone could have as many shoes as they wanted.'

She frowned, and was silent for a few moments. So far the story had been easy enough to tell. When she began again, it was with a new caution, as though frightened of what lay ahead. 'I can't remember the journey at all. I remember talk of English pirates, but my mother and Juana were both so sick, I think they were too ill to be afraid. When we reached Flanders, there was snow and ice. I thought I would die of cold and I wanted to go home. We all wanted to go home. My mother became ill – she coughed all the time and could hardly leave her bed. Nona looked after her, and Juana and I were left to look after ourselves. I was so homesick, I wanted to die. The only times I was happy was when Juana let me dance with her and I began to learn the different kinds of dance. I can see her now, in that filthy Flanders hovel where we lived and the snow all piling up outside the windows, and Juana in the middle of the room with her head thrown back and her beautiful face all covered with tears while she danced.

'Then my father was ordered to one of the Spanish garrisons in Germany. As far as I could see, it was no better than the town in Flanders where we had been, but we had a proper house. My mother was impatient with me for still being homesick: she said this was our home now and we must forget about Spain.

'After a while I grew used to the place, Würzburg it was called.' She gave an involuntary shiver as she said the name, then carried on, 'But still at night I used to lie in bed and go over and over my memories of Spain. I think I was afraid that if I stopped remembering, I would never find a way to go home. I plagued the adults with questions: *Mamaita*, was the door to the kitchen the first one on the right, or the second? Nona, how many windows overlooked the courtyard? Juana, what was the name of the old woman who came to help with the washing? I kept asking, no matter how annoyed they were with me: I was trying to keep our home alive so it would still be there for us to return to.

'But I was not so unhappy in Würzburg. Some things were the same as always. My father still gave away medicines and cures to people who could not afford to pay, and my mother still got angry and cried. Then a new trouble came into my life; Juana was growing up. To me that felt like a kind of betrayal. She wouldn't play our old games any more. She was beautiful, and very shy with strangers. There was a young soldier who began visiting our house and trying to talk to her after Mass. Juana acted differently when he was near: I thought he made her sad, but she said I wasn't to make him go away. Then she began visiting the sisters at the Convent of Our Lady. My mother told me one day that Juana might become a nun. That would have been even worse than losing her to a soldier. For weeks I was in despair – whatever Juana chose, I knew I was going to lose her.

'I was so preoccupied with Juana's future, that I paid hardly any attention to the talk around me. Ever since we had arrived in Flanders the adults had talked about the war, and sometimes old soldiers came to my father and they had terrible wounds that had healed badly, but however dreadful the stories we heard, our lives were unaffected. The summer that Juana was trying to decide between her soldier and the convent, I heard the name Magdeburg often. Some people said it was a great victory against the heretics, but my father was angry with them and said the Holy Church did not prosper because whole cities were destroyed in her name.

'Then we began to hear talk of the Swedish king, Gustavus Adolphus. The Lion of the North, some people were calling him, and they began to be anxious because all the Protestant nobles in Germany were rallying to his banner. In our town everyone was working to build up the defences around the city wall, but my mother and I were only concerned to know: would Juana choose the veil or marriage? Then one day there was fear everywhere: the enemy was at the gate. Everyone was crying. Juana finally made her decision: she would offer up her life to the Church. I think she believed that her soldier might be spared if she made the sacrifice. If she had known what was to come, I swear she might just as well have made a pact with the Devil.'

She fell into silence.

Stephen said, 'You do not have to go on. If the memories are so bad—'

She rounded on him. 'You asked, Captain Sutton, you said you wanted to know. Well then, listen to me, listen to the end. And then you must help me as you promised.'

'Very well.'

She drew in her breath, steeling herself, then continued, 'When the first of the barbarians began to fight their way into the town, my father gathered us together in his shop and told my mother to take us all to the convent; he said we would be safe there. But my mother would not go. She was crying again, but she said if she was to die she wanted to be with him, so Nona and Juana and I went alone. And I was kicking and screaming so much to stay with my parents that I never even said goodbye to them, and Nona and Juana had to carry and drag me all the way to the convent.

'The sisters had always made a fuss of me, but recently I had been rude to them often because I thought they were stealing Juana from me. We went to the convent church. I had been there many times before, but never had I seen it like that. All the sisters were there, and the priest who used to serve mass, but also many women and children from the town. Some of the sisters were singing, but many were crying and afraid. And one was laughing, a terrible hysterical kind of laugh – and that was the worst sound of all. That was when I began to be truly frightened.'

She wrapped her arms around her chest and began rocking back and forth. 'Yes, now I am frightened. There is gunfire all through the convent, we can hear people screaming. The sisters hurry to close the big doors of the church and push down the big bolts, but it is too late, we can hear the men hammering against the doors. Now one of the oldest of the nuns finds me. I never liked her because she has big teeth like a rabbit and she always wants me to tell her about my sins, but now she is crying, she tells me to hide under a stone sarcophagus in the side chapel. "Hide, child, hide." She speaks to me in German, "You are too young and beautiful for this. Don't make a sound, pray to the Holy Mother." But there is not enough room, my face is pressed against the stone floor. I cannot see Juana any more, or Nona, just the feet of the nuns who are praying nearest to my hiding place. I cannot pray, I cannot move, I cannot cry. All the noises are inside my head, the singing and the crying and the shouting and the musket fire and the hammering on the door. They are getting louder and louder. My brains are going to burst. And then I hear a great roar of triumph, the men have broken down the door. I close my eyes and try to press myself down into the floor. I want to be stone, cold stone, but it is impossible. I open my eyes and see boots, big leather boots all covered with mud, only the mud is a red colour, I've never seen mud that colour before. Then I see that it was blood. And the screaming is different, it has changed, not just terror, but pain, inhuman pain. I think it will never stop, it goes on and on, I'm afraid it will go on for ever. I can't see the feet of the sisters any more, only the boots of men, and a hand, a child's hand, it must be, lying on the ground, not moving at all. And now there is blood, a pool of blood spreading across the floor to where I am hiding. I watch it coming towards me. I know that the instant it touches me, I will die, or go mad. It has come right up and I must move away. And the moment I move all the fear—' she gave a sob that was almost a cry of terror, 'all the fear inside me explodes, I cannot stay hidden any more. I struggle out from behind the tomb. I look around me, and I can see . . . I can see . . .'

Here she broke off. Her face was bathed in tears.

Appalled, Stephen began to speak, but she did not hear him.

'Terrible . . .' she struggled, 'So terrible . . . Nona is lying quite close to where I have been hiding. She is covered in one of the sister's cloaks and it is red with blood. I know she is dead. There is a priest lying near the altar: they have cut him – there – and he is bleeding to death.

'And now I see Juana. I think maybe she is already dead, I hope so, dear God I hope so. One of the heretics is just finishing with her: I do not understand then what he was doing, not yet, but I know it is a bad thing. He has no colour to him at all, pale hair and eyes, but his lips were red like blood, and then when he was done he took a knife from his belt and . . .'

'It is over,' said Stephen, 'It happened a long time ago.'

She ignored him. 'I want to scream but there is no sound. The man with the knife turns, he sees me. He smiles. He is walking towards me. His hands are covered with her blood, he treads on the dead child and he is smiling. And I want to reach out and take the dagger from him and push it into his heart. And this evening, when he came into my room, I did—'

'That was Major Darbier.'

'Yes, I know. I know that now.'

There was a long silence.

'It was the look in his eyes,' she said, 'the smile. I could not bear to see that smile.'

'That is . . . that is . . .' Stephen could not find the words, but she turned to him and held his gaze for an instant.

'Yes,' she said simply, and he saw that she had returned to the present.

After a while he asked, 'How did you escape?'

'By the time I crawled out from behind the tomb, other

soldiers had come into the church. I suppose they, must have been officers and were trying to restore order – but too late, much too late. One of them, a man with sandy hair and a big head, pushed the other one out of the way. He came over and picked me up. I thought he was going to destroy me. I suppose I fainted.'

'And that was Josiah?'

She nodded.

The next question was one Stephen could not ask.

She said, as if reading his thoughts, 'He did not . . . touch me. Not in that way. I only know what happened after that from what Nona told me. All I can remember is smells – the smell of burning and blood – and the feeling that the world had ended. And in a way it was true. My world did not exist any more. My mother and father had been murdered in our home, his apothecary's shop was ransacked. There was no Juana. I was very ill. I could not speak. I did not speak again for more than two years. Nona had to speak for me.'

'How did she survive the massacre?'

'She had pretended to be dead. She reasoned that an old woman like her would be left to last, so she pulled a cloak from one of the murdered sisters and lay down near where I was hiding. When she realised that the new soldiers were trying to end the nightmare, and that they were taking me away with them, she came forward. She looked after me while I was ill, and when I was getting better again she told me we could not get back with our own kind. She said our best chance was for me to marry Josiah and we could all live in England, which was a country without war. He had been giving us money. I think maybe he had planned to trick us, but then he thought Nona could make him ill – he gets pains in his stomach sometimes, and they started about that time. So he dared not go back on his word. All I knew of the English was that they were pirates and I imagined we would live always on a ship, but I did whatever Nona told me. I could not think for myself, not then. I can't remember anything about the wedding, or the journey. Everything was muddled for a long time. I was living in a mist. Not living, just existing, like an animal.'

'How old were you?'

'When the heretics came to Würzburg? – I was thirteen. And fourteen when I married Josiah. He was a kind man, then, and prepared to wait. But perhaps he did not wait long enough.

181

Perhaps I am still crazy. Why not? I have carried those deaths inside me to this day – can you understand that? – my sister's blood has covered my heart. Her death was my death. When my first child was born and I saw the blood spread over his head and body, I thought: that is Juana's blood, and I knew at once that he could not survive. That nothing good would ever come from inside me.'

'But Harry?'

'Yes, Harry was the beginning. After the second baby died, I think perhaps I was mad for a little while. Josiah went away and Nona cared for me day and night. She gave me medicines to clean up the rottenness inside; morning and evening she bathed me with scented soaps and covered my body with flower waters. She burned special herbs in my room so I would only breathe in pure air. And she persuaded me to dance with her again. One day when we were dancing, I began to sing. That was when I found that I could speak again. But now I had a new language as well as a new life. No longer a Spanish child, but an English wife. When Harry was born, and then Beth, I knew the miracle had taken place. Inside maybe I would always be unclean, but my children were no longer poisoned by my suffering – they were the new life.'

In the long silence that followed, the baby stirred and snuffled in his cradle. Stephen felt such a power of rage and despair that he found it hard to speak.

She said, 'There, Captain Sutton. You have heard my story. How do you like it?'

'I think it is the most terrible story I have ever heard in my life.'

She turned to him in scorn. 'You are a kind man, and you are shocked by what I have told you – but why should you be surprised? This is what happens when men decide to go to war.'

'Pray God it never happens in this country,' he said with a passion. 'And you were so young, just a child!'

'An *innocent* child? Do you think children are spared in wartime? How you delude yourself! And now my own children will suffer because of what I have done, and this war of yours is to blame. Because of your precious major—'

'What exactly did Darbier do?'

She looked away. 'I cannot remember.' She stood up suddenly and began pacing the room. 'Sweet heavens, I should have killed myself when I had murdered him. I do not regret his death. He deserved to die. And now I must suffer again. You cannot help me. It is hopeless. I will not be handed over to your army's justice. I will kill myself first—'

She had reached the small chest which held Josiah's pistols, but Stephen said in anguish, 'No, don't give up hope, not yet. If there was any way I could change what happened to you and your family in Würzburg, then I would do it. I cannot alter your past, Mistress Taverner, but I believe I can help you now.'

'How?' Her question was angry. 'That brute's body lies in my house, and I killed him. Don't raise my hopes with talk of miracles, that is not fair—'

'I know. But listen. Now Darbier has died, I am the senior officer in Tilsbury, for the time being, at least. And if I act quickly, you should be able to go free.'

She looked at him with sudden hope, and then a terrible despair swept over her. 'No, you are wasting your time. It is too late for me, Captain. I think perhaps I do not wish to live any more. There has been too much suffering already, and now this . . . I am weary of it all.'

'And your children?'

She shrugged hopelessly. 'Josiah will make provision for them. They would not miss me long.'

'That is a lie, you know it is.'

She sank down on the chair and buried her face in her hands. After a while Stephen asked, 'Do you want me to help you?'

She leaned back in her chair and looked up at him with a kind of anger. 'What choice do I have? For the sake of my children, I must say yes.'

'Then give me the key to your stillroom and wait here. Will you be all right on your own for a little while?'

She shrugged. 'Of course. I must.'

'I will return as soon as I can.'

Detaching the key from the chain at her waist, she reached out her hand and said to him with a mocking, bitter smile, 'Do not be anxious for me, Captain Sutton. I will do whatever you tell me. After all, what choice do I have?'

Chapter 13

❧

Stephen sat down at the table in his room and wrote a brief letter to his father. Now that he had fixed on a plan, his head was clear once more, and he acted swiftly. Having signed and sealed the letter, he drafted a vaguely worded travel pass, then took some coins from his leather pouch. He was just about to leave the room when, on an impulse, he took the least flamboyant of Darbier's doublets and breeches from the chest, and slung them over his arm.

Hardly making a sound, he went down the stairs. The stillroom was just as they had left it. Major Paul Darbier, stiff and awkward in death, lay stretched across the slate floor, a small pool of blood staining the dark velvet of his coat. Stephen observed that Mistress Taverner must have aimed her dagger with lethal accuracy at the major's heart – a professional assassin could not have accomplished a more efficient murder. Leaving everything just as it was, he turned the key in the lock and slipped it into his pocket before quitting the house by a side door and going to the stable-yard. He found Tully lying on a pile of sacks in a shed where buckets and other implements were stored. The boy had been bound hand and foot and, at Stephen's approach, he whimpered with fear.

'Hush, Tully, don't be frightened. Hold still while I untie these cords. I've come to help you get away.'

As soon as he was free, Tully scrambled across the shed and crouched in the furthest corner. Moving slowly and deliberately, so as not to frighten him, Stephen set his candle into a lantern holder to shield it against the night breeze.

'Listen Tully,' he addressed the boy in a low and urgent voice,

'Do you want to escape from here – properly escape? You know you can't go back home, but I can arrange for you to go to a place where you'll be fed and taken care of until this fighting is over. Would you like that?'

There was no answer.

'You'll have to speak, Tully. We haven't got much time. Trust me.'

'I want to go home.'

'I know you do, but that's impossible. Besides, your sister's dead, and her baby too.' Stephen drove home the truth as gently as he could, but briefly, as he spoke the words, he was filled with a weary despair. Mistress Taverner had been right, after all. Tully and his sister were two children whose lives had been destroyed by war, just as hers and her own sister's had been. He forced himself to persevere. 'If you attempt to go home now, the soldiers will only hunt you down again and bring you back here, like they did today. Is that what you want?'

A mumbled 'No, leave me alone.'

'I'm trying to help you, Tully.'

'But where can I go?'

'To Cornwall.'

'Where?'

'Listen carefully. Major Darbier has been murdered.' Stephen hesitated only for a moment before continuing, 'I don't know who did it, but when his body is found, people might think it was you. Because of the way he beat you this afternoon.'

'But I didn't, sir, I promise. How could I? I've been shut up here all the time—'

'I know that, Tully. Don't worry. I'm only saying how it might look. And I'm offering you the chance to escape from this. Listen, I need someone I can trust to take an important message to my father in Cornwall. Can you do that?'

'What message?'

'I have the letter here. It is sealed, and you must be very careful to hand it to my father, Sir John Sutton of Rossmere, and to no one else. Do you understand?'

'Reckon so.'

'I've made out a pass for you in case you meet with any soldiers. Your way will be by Bristol, then Exeter. They're royalist towns so you should have no problem with parliament men. I've written down a list of all the places you will go through. I don't suppose you can read—'

'I can, sir, just a bit.'

'Excellent. See here, Tully, this is your route.' Stephen held up the lantern and pointed to the names of the towns. Tully repeated them laboriously. 'It will be a long hard journey, but I've money for you which will pay for food and lodging on the way.'

'Money, sir?' Tully's tone was noticeably brighter.

'Yes, quite enough for a long journey if you're careful with it.'

'I'm hungry now.'

'You'll have to wait, I'm afraid. I could not get you any food from the kitchen because the scullion sleeps there. But as soon as you're safely away, you may stop and buy yourself a meal. You can ride, I hope?'

'Yes, sir.'

'Good. Here's a fresh doublet and breeches for you. We must hurry. You want to be well away before daybreak when they'll raise the hue and cry. I'll prepare your horse while you change your clothes.'

'Yes, sir.'

Stephen noted with satisfaction that Tully was sounding quite purposeful now. Shielding the lantern with his palm, he picked up a handful of sacks and crossed the yard to the stables.

He chose his own bay, Breda, since she was the most sturdy and dependable of all the soldiers' horses, and the one most likely to endure the long journey to Rossmere. Besides, he had his own reasons for wanting to make sure Tully's journey was trouble-free. He knew that he was using the lad as an unwitting accomplice to Darbier's murder, but he consoled himself with the thought that, if all went as he planned, the boy might avoid risking his young life in a cause he barely understood. If, by any mischance, Tully was ever apprehended and charged with the murder, Stephen realised he would have to take the blame himself. So far, however, he was pleased with the speed at which Tully had adapted to this sudden change in his fortunes, and he began to think his strategy might have some chance of success.

He had just finished wrapping sacks around Breda's hooves to deaden their sound, when Tully came in, warmly clad in his new coat and breeches. The two men led the horse to the front of the house and a little way down the road away from the town before either spoke. Tully had decided that Captain Sutton himself must have murdered Darbier as a consequence of their quarrel that afternoon – and a good thing too, in Tully's opinion: he was happy to help the captain cover up his crime, especially if it meant a soft billet for the rest of this war. Stephen was relieved to see that dawn was still a little way off.

He broke the silence. 'With luck Major Darbier's body will not be found until you're a good few miles from Tilsbury. Take the sacks off and hide them before it gets light. Whatever you do, don't attempt to go back to your own home, that's the first place they'll look for you. Try to keep a steady speed, at least until you're south of Bristol. Here's the money, and the letter and your pass. Keep them all safe. Remember, if anyone questions you, you're taking an urgent message to my father. You know nothing of the major's death. Never speak of this to anyone. Should anything go wrong, enlist in another regiment. Whatever you do, don't come back here. Never come back.'

'Yes, Captain Sutton. I understand.' With his money and his new clothes and the open road ahead of him, Tully seemed to have grown in stature and confidence. During his childhood in the drovers' inn he had often heard men talk of the towns they had journeyed through, and now it was his turn to see something of the world. 'Will you and I meet again, sir?'

'I hope so. I intend returning to Rossmere as soon as this fighting is done. Good luck, Tully, and God's speed.'

Tully slipped his money and documents into the front of his doublet, before swinging up into the saddle. Then he rode away, Breda's muffled hooves making no sound on the soft earth of the road.

Stephen waited for a few moments. The night air was cool and clean against his face. He walked thoughtfully back to the house. He felt like someone who has entrusted his safety to a fragile agent, a messenger pigeon, perhaps. The 'important' message to his father, which Tully now carried within his doublet, was brief and to the point:

My dear Father,
I am fully recovered from the injury of which you heard, and I trust that you continue in good health. The boy Tully who brings you this letter has done me a signal good service and I wish him to be found employment at Rossmere until I am able to come home. He has no particular trade, but I believe he will prove quick to learn.
Remember me to my sister-in-law and her children. God keep you all safe,
Your loving son,
Stephen.

* * *

Dawn was approaching. Darbier's body could not be left in the stillroom, but Stephen dared not risk being observed dragging the corpse outside the house. In the end he laid it in the screens passage, near the foot of the stairs. Then he returned to the stable-yard and flung the dagger into a clump of nettles where it was sure to be found before long. Finally, leaving the side door ajar as if someone had quitted the house in a hurry, he returned to Mistress Taverner's bedchamber.

She was seated in a tall, tapestry-covered chair, her head leaning against its back, with her eyes half-closed and her hands resting loosely on her lap. For a moment Stephen was anxious that during his absence she had lapsed into her former state of delusion, but he need not have worried. She glanced up at his approach, and her expression was direct, and very calm.

So many violent sensations had flowed through her in the past twenty-four hours that she was drained of energy, and she noted Stephen's return without any particular emotion. The agitation which had been driving her for days – perhaps ever since the night when Josiah had told her that soldiers were coming to Tilsbury – had been swept away. Despite her serene appearance, she did not feel calm just now, nothing so soothing, but she was experiencing a kind of detachment, as though the human body can only absorb so much emotion and her quota had been all used up; she was left with nothing but a strange hollowness.

So she turned to the man who at this moment held her life and her family's happiness in his power and asked quietly, 'Well?'

Stephen came to stand in front of her; she listened in silence while he told her what he had done. Still she felt no emotion, except perhaps a quiet satisfaction at a scheme well executed.

'You want me to pretend I know nothing of the major's death?'

Stephen nodded. 'When his body is found, we must both feign surprise.'

'Don't worry, Captain. I'm an expert at dissembling.'

'Then you have the advantage of me,' said Stephen with a rueful smile, 'I was obliged to lie to young Tully just now. It was not easy.'

She dismissed this as of no consequence. Still leaning back in her chair, she was examining Stephen's face carefully. She realised that by his actions during the past couple of hours he had implicated himself in the murder of his fellow officer. If the truth were ever to come out in the future, Captain Sutton would henceforth be held accountable for at least some of the events of this night. Like everyone else, she knew that there had been increasing friction between the two men, and she wondered if it now suited his purposes to have the major removed from the scene. But this still did not explain his willingness to help her.

'Why, Captain? Why lie to save my skin?'

Stephen looked away. 'Must there be reasons?'

'In my experience there always are.'

Stephen walked a little distance away, out of the ring of candle-shine, and frowned. When he spoke again, his words were hesitant. 'I did not see that there was anything to be gained if you were found out. The major is dead. I am sorry it happened, but your punishment would not bring him back to life. We must consider the living. There are your children . . . I know you did not wish it, but I have grown fond of them . . .'

His words faded into silence. Still Doll looked at him, trying to understand.

She said, 'Are you telling me you have risked your career, perhaps your life even, for the sake of my children?'

'I did not want to see them suffer . . .'

'You expect me to believe that?'

Stephen took a step forward into the light and the expression in his eyes gave her the answer she had been seeking, and which she found she had no wish to see. 'I expect nothing of you, Mistress Taverner,' he said.

She smiled. 'There, Captain Sutton, you do not know your own skills. You are a practised liar after all.'

She stood up and crossed the room to the fireplace where she rested her forearm on the mantel. She was still smiling at him, but it was an odd, bitter smile. Only half-aware of what he was doing Stephen went over to her, then he caught hold of her hand and raised it to his lips.

'I only know,' he said, releasing her hand at once, 'that I would do anything to make you happy.'

'Oh Captain Sutton,' again that bitter smile, 'how easy you make it sound.'

'Maybe it is.'

She did not answer. Slowly the smile faded from her face and she turned away from his gaze. Her former sense of detachment was ebbing swiftly away and the feelings she was left with were raw and ugly. She was aware that he was standing very close to her, and waiting.

At last she said, 'So, Captain, you wish to be the agent of my happiness?'

Stephen heard the mockery in her words, but did not understand it. He asked simply, 'Why are you surprised?'

'Oh no, I'm not surprised. It is only what I expected. But I warn you, I don't believe I have ever known what happiness was. You are more ambitious on my behalf than I have ever been. All I ask is that my children are safe and that I may remain at liberty to care for them.'

'Unless Tully betrays us, you will have both wishes.'

'Thanks to your kindness and quick-thinking, Captain.' She slid him a sideways glance: the words themselves expressed gratitude, but the meaning behind them was far more devious. Stephen frowned. He began to speak, but thought better of it and stopped abruptly.

She stepped away from him, then turned and said with a little laugh, 'How can I best repay you? How can I show my gratitude to the man who intends to save me from a felon's death? The law is cruel to women, we both know that. I have seen women dragged through the street to the gallows, I have seen them stripped to the waist and whipped. I am not very brave. I could not stand such a thing. Better to die by my own hand than face such shame. And the children, let us never forget the children, my babies, the scandal would destroy them . . . of course, no price is too high to pay for their safety. There is nothing—'

Her voice was beginning to rise and Stephen realised that she was verging on hysteria.

'Stop,' he told her in a low voice, 'Do not distress yourself more. You will wake the servants and you must be calm to play your part in the morning.'

'Play my part? Oh, have no worries there, Captain, I shall play my part to perfection. I have had practice in plenty. It's easy, see, let me show you—'

'Hush, please hush. Don't spoil it all now. Here—' In an effort to calm her Stephen took hold of her hands which were trembling violently and pressed them against his chest. 'It will be all right, I promise. Only stay calm. Hush now—'

'Yes, you're right, of course you're right. How could it be otherwise?' She leaned back slightly, but made no attempt to free her hands, only looked up into his eyes, and when she

191

laughed, her laughter was brittle like something precious that is easily broken. Then she said in a low voice, 'Don't worry, Captain, I put myself under your protection. See, now I am quite calm again.'

Just before she closed her eyes, she saw the way his expression changed from concern, to bewilderment, and then to a slow warmth. She breathed a sigh of relief as she reached up and touched his lips with her own: the bargain was really very simple after all, and this was a small price to pay for her own life and the protection of her children. All she had to do now was ignore the bitterness that swamped her heart and the revulsion that rose like a sickness in the throat. Just play her part. God knows, she had done so often enough in the past, and it would be worth it surely to be free of the debt she owed this man.

But his touch was light, and quickly over. She opened her eyes. His expression was almost fierce. She said softly, 'Here, Captain Sutton, here is your reward,' and moved towards him once more.

'Mistress Taverner—' His words were a kind of groan.

She smiled, a small, sphinx-like smile, and set herself to remember the pattern of the vine shadows in the courtyard where she had played as a child and the sound of women's voices that had drifted from her mother's kitchen. 'Don't stop, Captain, morning is coming and we do not have much time. Here—' As he bent his head to kiss her once again, she reached up her hand to unfasten the lacing of her bodice. Her fingers brushed against his, and she felt his hands grasping hers as he pressed his face into her dark hair and said, 'I've wanted you—'

She tried to find words to answer his, but found she could not speak. She forced her lips against his, but in those few brief seconds she felt the old familiar numbness spreading outwards from her heart and she could no longer either speak or move.

Still cradling her in his arms, Stephen said gently, 'Do you want me?'

Immobile, she could only stare at him.

'What's the matter?'

'Nothing,' she managed a whisper, 'I want you to. It's what you want . . . We must . . .'

Stephen was gazing at her blankly. 'What is it? I don't understand you,' he said.

'Don't try. Hurry.'

'Why?'

'You want me, don't you?'

'Of course, but—'

'Well, then.'

He stroked her hair. This time there was no mistaking her tremor of distaste. Stephen felt a great weight of sadness and self-loathing. He drew back and said in a low voice, 'Now I see. You think you have to do this, don't you? That it's the only reason I helped you. Because I wanted—'

Doll was waiting for the familiar numbness to pass.

'Stephen,' she said.

'Why are you doing this?'

'Does there have to be a reason?'

'You were the one who told me there always is.'

'Yes, so I did. Well, maybe I was wrong.'

He took a step away. 'More wrong than you can imagine,' he said.

'Are you angry?'

'I don't know. I think perhaps I feel sorry for you.'

She closed her eyes to hide the panic that rose inside her at his words. 'You mean to betray me after all?'

He laughed, an ugly-sounding laugh. Then he said, 'Look at me, and tell me what you see.'

She lowered her eyes. She felt a slow anger begin to burn; he had no right to trick her in this way. 'No,' she said, 'I don't understand what you want.'

'Just tell me, what do you see when you look at me?'

Still she did not look up. He took both her hands in his. He said, 'You see a soldier, don't you? But Doll, I was a man before I was a soldier. Can't you understand that?'

She flinched when he spoke her name for the first time. No, she did not understand him, not at all; he was playing this game by rules she had never come across before, but one thing was suddenly very clear to her indeed. She pulled her hands away and looked at him directly as she said in a cold voice, 'No. I do not. I do not understand you at all. But I tell you this: I was Dolores before I ever became an English Doll. Never call me Doll. It was Dolores who killed your vile major and she doesn't regret it, not for a second. I'm glad she did it. And if you dare to call me Doll again, I think maybe I will kill you too.'

To her astonishment, Stephen smiled. 'Amen to that,' he said gently. 'I'd rather have you murderous than selling love. I never

193

wanted that.' He took her hand and raised it to his lips. 'You think I need payment? Well then, I have taken it. There, you owe me nothing.' He released her hand and stepped away with sudden briskness. 'It's late. Soon it will be light and we must not be found together when the servants discover the major's body. I'll leave you. You should have given me some lessons in lying when we still had the chance.' Then he smiled. 'But maybe you did.'

She was staring at him very intently. 'Will you carry this deception through, in spite of—?'

He said, 'Your question is insulting. Trust me,' he hesitated then, 'Trust me, Dolores.' And with that he turned and left the room, closing the door gently behind him.

She remained motionless for a few moments more, savouring the silence in the empty room and looking towards the window for the first pale signs of the dawn, before hurriedly stripping to her shift and laying herself beneath the bed covers. She had barely closed her eyes when the house was roused by a piercing shriek and the sound of running feet: Darbier's body had been discovered.

Mistress Taverner remained closeted in her room for three days. For most of that time she lay on her bed, too exhausted to move but unable to find rest in sleep. It was generally assumed that the shock of the major's death had caused a temporary relapse, similar, now people came to think of it, to the melancholy that had afflicted her following the deaths of her first two children. Her milk supply dried up suddenly and a wet-nurse had to be found for the baby: luckily Cary's older sister Joan had recently given birth to a strong infant and her milk supply was ample for two. Only Nona was allowed to attend the invalid. She told her grandmother there had been a mishap in the stillroom, some medicine spilled on the floor with the broken china that needed to be cleared up. Nona made no comment, but then, they had never been in the habit of confiding in each other.

She heard, with mixed feelings, that Captain Sutton left Tilsbury almost immediately to make a report to his colonel of what little was known of Major Darbier's murder. Arrangements had been set in hand for the funeral. She was relieved to learn that the general opinion was, as the captain had intended, that Tully was the culprit: the dagger had been duly found in the stable-yard and no one but she knew its provenance. If Nona guessed, she kept her own counsel, as always. All the evidence pointed to the runaway. One of the grooms mentioned that he thought he had heard Captain Sutton in the stable late that night and a few of the soldiers came to share Tully's belief that Captain Sutton himself had been the murderer, but they kept this opinion to themselves. They trusted their captain: once the campaigning season began again they would have to trust him with their lives and they were prepared to accept that he had acted with good reason.

Only Mistress Taverner did not dare to trust him. He had sent her no word of reassurance before riding off next morning and she thought it more than likely he had come to regret his impulsive chivalry. Why should he bother to help her if he was taking nothing in return? Surely, when he came to make his report to the colonel he would choose to tell the truth. Hadn't he hinted as much when he told her how difficult he found it to lie, even to a boy of no consequence like Tully?

At the thought of the events that would inevitably follow his disclosure, she became consumed with terror. Female felons were abused and humiliated by their captors in peacetime, how much worse would it be under military rule? On the second morning a loud beating at the front door hurled her into a state of such panic that she sped across the room, took the little ivory-handled pistol from the casket and was endeavouring to load it with trembling fingers when Nona came to tell her that Sir Diggory, having heard of her indisposition, had sent his manservant over with a gift of carp from his fishpond to speed her recovery. After that she kept the pistol loaded and ready under a shawl on the little table beside her bed: better to end her life by her own hand than allow herself to be tortured and killed by strangers.

But while there was still a chance that Captain Sutton might stay true to his word, she could not take that final step. Her will to survive was strong: it had been forged by events that would have destroyed a weaker child. She had reasons enough for wanting to live. During the long hours that she lay on her bed, she listened to the everyday sounds of her home: Philip pleading with Nona to be taken to the muster ground to watch the soldiers; Beth stumbling over a new tune on her spinet; Harry calling the dogs to accompany him to the orchard and his daily lesson on Bonnet; Mabs and Cary and Ellen gossiping and laughing as they went about their tasks. But she found that above all she wanted to live, not just for her children and her household, but for herself. For Dolores.

During her occasional fragments of sleep she was tormented by dreams of bloodshed and accusation, but while awake she had no regrets about having killed Major Darbier, no matter how high the price she eventually had to pay. This puzzled her. She had been less than honest with Captain Sutton when she told him she did not remember the events in the stillroom which had culminated in the murder; the fact was that she remembered every detail precisely, right up to the moment when she took the dagger from its embroidered pouch and felt its tip pierce the soft fabric of his doublet: a moment's resistance, then a sudden yielding, as though his flesh had no more substance than a peach. She even remembered his first response, an expression of almost comical bewilderment and disbelief. It was only after his death that her memories became confused.

She had lied to Stephen because she knew she had to win his support. He was most likely to help her if he believed she had acted in self-defence. In a way, perhaps, she had. But how to explain that the major had only been his usual odious self, a nuisance, yes, but not dangerous? Perhaps the difference this time was that he had followed her into her stillroom, slipping in after her before she had a chance to lock the door. The stillroom was her own private sanctuary, more so even than her bedchamber, which, after all, she had always shared with Josiah. No one, apart from her and Nona, had set foot in that room as long as she could remember. So that when she saw his insolent face, leering at her in the one place where she had always felt safe, her horror made her confused. She had seen on his young shoulders the image of the ghostly pale soldier who had walked towards her with her sister's blood covering the blade of his knife. And so she had accomplished what the young child had been unable to do, but had dreamed of in horrifying detail from time to time ever since. She could not unravel the sequence. But gradually, as she lay and listened to the relentless tolling of the funeral bell, she came to understand that the murder she had committed had been simply the most recent in a chain of events that had begun on that terrible day in Würzburg.

And she came to realise also that Darbier was not the only

casualty of that night: Josiah's helpless Doll had been destroyed also. The mute child he had brought to Tilsbury all those years ago had grown outwardly into a competent and assured woman, but inside she had still been haunted by the terrors that had paralysed her as she hid beneath the stone tomb. No longer. If Captain Sutton reneged on his promise, if Tully was captured and pointed the blame towards her, she would kill herself without hesitation before ever again submitting to men's tyranny.

Yet, despite her new-found resolution, she had been prepared to trade her body for her freedom. That oldest of transactions was one that she understood, having made it many times before with Josiah, and though it might be unpleasant, it was a small fee to pay for the precious gift of survival. As well as the inevitable revulsion, she had experienced a sharp sense of relief when she thought she had deciphered the riddle of the captain's unexpected help.

But Stephen Sutton had turned her down. Far from reassuring her, this fact was troubling. Not merely because she felt it made his betrayal more likely, but because she feared he might be planning to exact some still higher price. Despite his protestations, his actions had put her in his debt, and sooner or later, all debts must be paid. But how? Must she pretend to love the captain? Even Josiah had never insisted on so impossible a price, though he had yearned for some sign of affection. Better by far her benefactor should take her body, and leave her spirit free.

Through the three days that she remained in her room, Mistress Taverner was prey to intense bouts of confusion, terror and despair. But right from the beginning there was another emotion and, as the days passed and the shock receded and still no soldiers came to drag her from her home to stand trial for her crime, that new emotion began to dominate all the others. It was a form of elation, a glimpse of freedom, a belief that, when and if this present nightmare ever ended, she might at last begin to lead a different kind of life.

Doll had always been fearful and restrained. Doll had been a shadow, a cipher, Josiah's dutiful wife, responding to circumstance but never daring to take control. Doll had been a terrified child inhabiting the body of a grown woman. But Doll existed no more.

She had no clear picture of the person who was replacing her, but she knew no one would ever call her Doll again. From now on until the day she died she would carry the name of Dolores, the name given to the Mother of Sorrows, the name she had been given in infancy in that distant land she could barely remember, but would never allow herself entirely to forget.

Chapter 14

❧

Stephen wished he was confronting a battery of cannon fire rather than the small penetrating eyes of his colonel.

'Captain Sutton, let me see if I have understood you correctly. You say the major's body was found at the foot of the stairs in the house where you were both billeted?'

'Yes, sir.'

'A house belonging to one Josiah Taverner who is absent on business?'

'Yes, sir.'

'A house at present maintained by his wife?'

'Yes, sir.'

'And that this boy Tully who deserted the same night is assumed to have been the culprit?'

Stephen looked towards the window. 'Yes, sir.'

'And that no one else had any reason to quarrel with the major?'

Stephen glanced at the floor. 'No, sir.'

'And that you questioned all members of the household before reaching this conclusion?'

Stephen looked towards the empty fireplace. 'Yes, sir.'

'And none of them had any information that could help you shed light on this unfortunate event?'

Stephen stared hard at his mud-spattered boots. 'No, sir.'

'And that you have done everything possible to see the villain Tully apprehended?'

Perspiration gleamed on Stephen's face. 'Yes, sir.'

The colonel flung down his pen in exasperation and leaned back in his chair. 'Captain Sutton, I don't believe a word of it.'

Stephen continued to stare at his boots.

'The murder of one of His Majesty's officers is a damned serious matter, Captain.'

'Yes, sir.'

'So you have absolutely no idea how the boy Tully escaped from his place of captivity, entered the house, stabbed Major Darbier and then made his escape on your own horse, and all without anyone noticing anything?'

Stephen looked at the floor, the window, his boots and the empty fireplace before answering, 'No, sir.'

'I trust you are a better soldier than liar, Captain Sutton.'

Stephen made no comment. The colonel sighed with annoyance, but he did not waste too long in speculation. He knew Captain Sutton to be a man of stubborn honesty and courage, just the kind of experienced and dedicated soldier he most needed at this present time. Despite the self-congratulatory reports young Darbier had sent from Tilsbury, the colonel had no doubt who was really responsible for the damage being done to the Gloucester rebels. Like Tully, the colonel thought it most probable there had been some quarrel between the two men and the major had come off the worst. In fact Major Darbier's death was no great loss. The royalist ranks were thickly populated with high-born and ineffective officers, many more officers, in fact, than they had troops to lead.

The colonel said slowly, 'Now, sir, answer me one question, and this time I want only the truth. Can you look me straight in the eyes and tell me that you have at all times acted honourably in this matter of Major Darbier's murder?'

Stephen considered for some time before raising his eyes and looking very directly at the colonel. 'With regard to Major Darbier's death and the events which followed, I would do the same again.'

The colonel held his gaze for a few moments. Though Stephen's face was still covered in the dust and grime of his recent long ride, his grey eyes were transparently clear.

'Spoken like a Jesuit. Very well then, that's all I wish to know.' Already the colonel was turning his attention to the next item of business. 'Leave a copy of your report with my secretary. It will sit admirably with the other fictions this war produces daily. Come back for your orders in the morning.'

'Yes, sir.'

Stephen stepped out into the spring sunshine and commotion

of an Oxford street and drew in a deep breath. He had not slept in two nights and he could not remember when he had last eaten, his clothes were filthy and now his cambric shirt was wringing with sweat. He noticed none of this. He gave sixpence to a passing beggar and, glad only that the ordeal was over, turned in at the nearest alehouse to celebrate Mistress Taverner's escape.

A couple of days later, as he rode back towards Tilsbury, his mood was grown sombre once again. He had talked with several friends concerning the likely progress of the war. Most of those whose opinion he valued – including, apparently, Prince Rupert – believed an outright victory over Parliament was now impossible. They were convinced the King should treat with the rebels for reasonable terms while he still could. His Majesty, however, would listen only to the wishful thinking of the ever optimistic Digby: a new army was about to be sent from Ireland; his wife the Queen was even now persuading the French to send a decisive force; above all, there was the incontrovertible fact that God would never permit His anointed King to suffer ultimate defeat. Meanwhile, Sir Thomas Fairfax and Lieutenant General Cromwell were putting their new army through its paces and preparing for an all-out assault.

When he had returned for his second, and far less arduous, meeting with his colonel, Stephen had been surprised by his orders. He was to send the bulk of his men to join the main field army that was now assembling for the summer campaign, but was himself to remain in Tilsbury with a garrison strong enough to keep up the pressure on Massey in Gloucester.

Stephen received these instructions with mixed emotions. Like everyone else he had assumed that the garrison would be quitting Tilsbury entirely within the next couple of weeks. To Stephen this change of plan meant above all that he would continue to be near Mistress Taverner. It had been difficult enough to feign indifference even before the major's death, surely it would be impossible now, with the events of that long night lying forever between them. All the problems that inevitably awaited him on his return would have been so much easier to deal with if he could have busied himself for an imminent departure.

He should have been disappointed by the order to remain. But of course, he was not.

When the colonel asked him if he had acted honourably in the matter of Darbier's murder, he had been unable to give an unqualified yes. Not because he had championed Mistress Taverner, but because he had allowed himself to make love to her at a time when she was too shocked and vulnerable to know what she was doing. Her assumption that his help was motivated solely by desire was deeply wounding to him, the more so because it contained a grain of truth. Would he have been so ready to lie for her if she had not been the most bewitching woman he had ever met? If she had been ugly, or merely plain? If he had not been head over heels in love?

The events following Darbier's death had led him to feel an extraordinary sense of intimacy with her, and for a few blind moments he had persuaded himself that she shared his feeling.

He had deluded himself then, but he did not do so now. He was more deeply in love with Mistress Taverner than before, and he understood now, with a certainty that at times verged on a kind of bitter resignation, that however long he lived he would never be free of loving her. But he also knew better than to expect any return of feelings. He had seen her distracted and murderous, he had seen her a grieving child. Most bitter of all, he had seen her counterfeiting the womanly emotions which he now believed were beyond her ability to feel. He told himself that, since he was to stay a while longer in Tilsbury, he must endeavour simply to convince her that her low opinion of him had been misplaced. Never again could he hope to make her care for him.

But because he rode through lanes that shimmered with the fresh green leaves of spring, and because he was in love, he did not give up hope entirely.

He found Mistress Taverner in the garden. It was the second day that she had left her room, and the first that she had ventured outside. Bussell had carried out a chair for her and had set it in a paved corner which was sheltered from the wind by a solid wall of box and holly. She was supervising the gardener as he cleared the beds and divided the stronger growing plants.

The garden which lay behind the Priory House was not designed to be a thing of beauty; its purpose was entirely practical. Rose bushes there were in plenty – at present gaunt shapes with the first green leaves emerging – but their flowers would be stripped before they were fully opened in order to make rose-water. Lavender, rosemary, thyme, sage, sweet marjoram and a host of lesser known herbs were grown simply for their medicinal or culinary properties, with no thought of how they might look. Even the clove-scented gilliflowers, which were just now coming into bloom and which filled the air with their heady scent, were valued by her only because they could be candied for winter dishes and cordials, or used at once in salads or sauces. Other housewives in Tilsbury arranged their gardens for pleasure as well as utility, and one or two of the more ambitious had laid out knot gardens of low box hedging around their herbs in imitation of the one which was so admired at Furleys – but such refinements had never even occurred to the mistress of the Priory House. She never saw the whole picture, only the individual items that were useful.

Nona had offered to bring the baby out to enjoy the sunshine with her, but Dolores had refused, saying it was too cold, which was palpably untrue. She had hardly seen little Robert since the morning after the murder, when he had fretted at the breast and squalled with hunger until the cause of his unhappiness was found. Perhaps she was avoiding him because he had been an innocent witness during those first few terrible hours; it was as if some of the horror of that time had adhered to him. Or maybe she simply needed solitude. She was relieved that Harry and Philip were busy with Bonnet in the orchard, and only Beth insisted on staying by her side. For one thing, Beth loved the garden, especially at this eager, growing time of year – but more than that, she had been shocked by Darbier's death and increasingly anxious and afraid during the days of her mother's seclusion. Her natural anxiety had been magnified by Cary's nightly descriptions of the details of the major's death, the condition of his corpse, the likely fate of his assailant when caught and graphic accounts of several other murders thrown in for good measure. So Beth stayed close to her mother now, straying only occasionally to watch the gardener or follow the progress of a fat bumblebee from flower to flower, before running back to ask the familiar questions:

'Are you feeling better now?'

'Much better, thank you.'

'You won't get ill again, will you?'

'I don't think so, little Bee.'

Dolores felt a knot in her throat as she looked into the face of her only daughter. With her sandy frizz of hair and her blunt, almost frog-like features, little Beth had neither beauty nor grace, but she had a charm that was all her own. How could she have put her innocent happiness at risk by committing senseless murder? And if Captain Sutton should change his mind, or fail in his mission, who would care for her then? The questions were too painful to contemplate, too pressing to ignore.

'Go and play, Beth. No need to worry over me.'

The child squatted at her feet. Dolores sighed. She did not have the heart to dismiss Beth but her nerves were still jagged. She had been expecting Captain Sutton's return for over twenty-four hours. If he was detained in Oxford then surely it was because his story had not been believed, perhaps even now a troop of soldiers were marching towards Tilsbury with orders for her arrest. Her imagination raced ahead: armed men trampling over her precious beds of herbs, little Beth thrust roughly aside, the fetters and the abuse. And she would be left no time to get her ivory handled pistol which she had left in her bedchamber . . .

'Mother, what's the matter? You look so strange.'

'It's nothing, Beth. I just remembered I left something in my room.'

'Shall I fetch it for you?'

'No, no. I'll be back before you know it.'

'I'll come with you.'

Dolores was about to protest when suddenly Beth let out a cry of pleasure.

'Oh, look, Captain Sutton is back, hurray!' And, forgetting that she was not supposed to be friendly with the soldiers, she raced down the paved walk of the garden and caught hold of his hand. 'Oh, Captain Sutton, I'm *so* glad you're back!'

Beth's enthusiasm nearly undermined Stephen's resolve. He had made up his mind to be courteous and restrained in all his dealings with the family and to do nothing that could be interpreted as an attempt to win their affections. The urge at least to grin and tell Beth that he had missed her too was almost overwhelming, but he crushed it and said merely, 'Good day, Beth, I hope you are well,' without even so much as a smile. But Beth charitably assumed that he was weary from his long ride and did not take offence in the least.

Dolores had half risen from her seat. She was suddenly very pale. She said, 'Captain Sutton, I trust you have been successful?'

Stephen cleared his throat. The gardener was out of earshot, but Beth was all eyes and ears, and to send her away so quickly would be sure to arouse comment. He said carefully, 'I told the colonel all that I knew concerning the murder of Major Darbier—'

Dolores found her mouth was parched and breathing had become impossible.

Stephen went on, 'He agreed that every effort must be made to apprehend young Tully, but in the country's present state of confusion he is unlikely to be found. Most probably he has enlisted in one of the rebel armies by now.'

Dolores sank back in her chair and covered her eyes with her hand. 'Thank you, Captain Sutton.'

It was only by supreme effort that Stephen was able to remain outwardly impassive. He said, 'I hope you will suffer no further inconvenience as a result of Major Darbier's untimely death.'

'Dear God, make it so.'

Beth was watching both the captain and her mother closely, and she was amazed to see that her mother's cheeks, beneath the shielding hand, were damp with tears.

Stephen also had noticed. He guessed they were tears of relief that he had, after all, kept his word, and his first impulse of compassion gave way to annoyance. He said sternly, 'I gave you my word, Mistress Taverner, that I would try to conclude matters with as little trouble to you as possible. You have no cause for surprise.'

Dolores looked up at him gravely. 'Are you telling me I have misjudged you, Captain?'

Stephen was unable to respond. At the sight of her dark eyes, fixed on his own, all the events of that night were suddenly as vivid as if they had occurred minutes ago: the memory of the touch of her skin against his cheek, the delicate fragrance of her hair and the press of her lips on his. Like Odysseus he wished he could be tied to the mast so as not to be disarmed by the sirens' song. The urge to throw himself down before Mistress Taverner and tell her he would have died for her and happily, if it had been any help, was almost impossible to resist – but he stood his ground.

Beth considered he had been unfair. She said, 'Captain Sutton, you must not be cross with my mother. She has been ill since you went away. Her milk has all dried up with the shock of what happened to Major Darbier and—'

'Hush, Beth, I'm sure Captain Sutton has no interest in our trivial worries.'

'On the contrary, I'm sorry. I did not realise you had been unwell.'

'I'm recovered, now. Beth, the captain must be tired and hungry after his journey. Run into the kitchen and have Mabs send out some refreshment.'

Reassured by what appeared to be a return to normality, Beth did as she was told.

For a little while neither Stephen nor Dolores could think what to say. The silence was filled with birdsong and the hum of insects, the far murmur of the river and the muted, spring afternoon sounds of the town.

At length Dolores said, 'You must be weary, Captain. I'll call Bussell and he can bring you a chair.'

'Thank you, but I prefer to stand.'

This time the silence was even longer. Both were painfully aware that Beth would return at any moment, and the chance to talk freely would be gone. But how much could be said, and how much must never be spoken of again? At some stage during that second silence, the moment when they might have discussed the events surrounding Darbier's death passed by. Neither could think how to broach the subject: it slipped into the region of matters that must not be talked of.

Stephen began, 'I have been ordered to dispatch most of the men here to join the King's main army. Many believe this summer's campaign will be decisive, one way or another.'

To Dolores' astonishment his news filled her with sudden alarm. 'You are leaving us, Captain Sutton?'

'No. My orders are to stay in Tilsbury with a few men. The garrison is still needed to keep a check on the rebels in Gloucester. Soldiers will remain a burden on this town for some time yet, though their numbers will be much reduced.'

'I see.' She was thoughtful. Why should the news that he was to stay be a cause for relief? She was beginning to understand that by making himself the custodian of her crime Stephen had bound her to him with ties stronger than kinship or affection. He contained within his memory a portion of her very self, and wherever he went, the secret of her guilt went with him. Better by far that he remain in Tilsbury; once he had gone, and she no longer knew where he was, an essential part of her life would be forever beyond her control. It had been bad enough when she had thought herself simply in his debt; but this went deeper. This was a bond without limit of time.

Stephen, seeing her concern but misinterpreting the cause, said briskly, 'I intend transferring my billet to another house. After what has happened, I'm sure you do not wish me to remain under your roof. We need not have any further dealings.'

Dolores was suddenly all confusion. She stood up swiftly. 'Captain Sutton, please do not think . . . I did not intend . . . you must do as you see fit but . . . no need to act in a hurry . . . welcome to stay here if you wish . . .'

Now it was Stephen's turn to be surprised. 'Mistress Taverner, are you telling me you *want* me to remain at the Priory House so long as the garrison remains in Tilsbury?'

'I suppose I must be.'

'Once the main force has left, I can arrange for your home to be free of soldiers entirely.'

Dolores pondered. To have the house to herself again was what she had longed for twenty times each day for over a month. But if Stephen Sutton left this place, where would he find lodging? At The Lion? And once the memory of his impetuous promise had faded, wasn't it entirely possible that one evening, after a mug of sack too many, he would find himself relating to an eager group of fellow soldiers the true story of Major Darbier's demise?

'Captain Sutton, let me say merely that I feel safer knowing you are in our house.'

'I'm delighted to hear it.' And now it was Stephen's turn to smile. 'I am very surprised. Mistress Taverner, you never cease to amaze me.' Then he frowned, fearing she might interpret this as a reference to the night that could neither be forgotten, nor spoken of again. He saw Beth emerging from the kitchen door; her progress was slow because she was carrying a large pitcher. Behind her came Mabs, with a tray, and behind her the kitchen boy with a rush-seated chair and a joint stool. He went on quickly, and in a low voice, 'Mistress Taverner, I do not pretend that I shall ever forget . . . certain events.' She looked away in sudden anxiety. 'But for my part I intend there to be no alteration . . . from what existed before. I am a soldier who happens, for the time being, to be billeted in your house. Over the next few days I will be very busy. We are not likely to be much together. I am sure that is what you want, and so it is my wish also.'

'Thank you, Captain Sutton.'

The refreshments arrived. A jug of Mabs' special juniper ale, some slices of game pie and a piece of cheese. Dolores was careful not to enquire as to the precise ingredients of the pie: since the soldiers had devoured almost all the available food in the area great ingenuity was required, and Mabs was more than equal to the challenge. She could accomplish much with a plucked jackdaw, a turnip and a handful of raisins. Mabs only perceived the war as it affected the supply of goods coming into her kitchen.

'Here you are, Captain Sutton,' she announced cheerfully, 'Some proper food for you again. I dare say you've been eating in taverns and heaven knows what low-down places. Good Tilsbury food for you again now.'

'Thank you Mabs. I have certainly missed your cooking.' Stephen grinned at the serving woman, who responded with a surprisingly coquettish smile.

At the sight of the easy familiarity between them, Dolores felt a sudden disquiet: a sense of matters slipping beyond her control. She had intended to remain with the captain a little longer to show that she could play her part as well as ever before, but suddenly the effort required was too great. She rose to her feet. 'Stay and enjoy your food. Beth will keep you company. I have work to attend indoors.'

She hurried away. The truth was, that Captain Sutton's presence troubled her in ways she only half-understood. She wished him to remain in her home, but it was difficult to be near him. She had assumed that once he came back and told her his mission had been successful, her worries would be at an end, but she found now they had merely been replaced by problems of a new and more complex kind.

Chapter 15

❧

Dolores did not know if she was glad or sorry when, over the next five days, Stephen was so much occupied that she barely saw him. Perhaps she was both glad and sorry. In those days her life was composed almost entirely of contradictions: she felt stronger, but at the same time more vulnerable than before. And while she scarcely spoke to Stephen, she was intensely aware of him at all times. It was as though the secret they shared was a net in which both were entangled: any vibration on the part of one was instantly sensed by the other. Sometimes, in moments of desperation, she thought all her present troubles would be ended if only Captain Sutton might stop an enemy bullet. Yet this solution, which was both practical and, in the present time, quite likely, did not cheer her in the least.

As was her custom she distracted herself by hard work. At this time of year there was much to be done in the stillroom with the first of the spring herbs and flowers. Since she was continually plagued with bad dreams, she was up most mornings before dawn and she kept herself so busy that she scarcely noticed that Nona, who usually shared the work with her, was seldom to be seen.

Ten days after the major's death, a letter arrived from Josiah. There was no return address, but she guessed it must have come from London.

My dear wife,
I was much troubled to learn that you had permitted dancing and riotous music to take place in our house. I must remind you of the

heavy trust I have placed on you for the welfare both spiritual and
moral of our children and servants—

She had crumpled it up, still only half-read. If Josiah knew what real crimes had occurred in his house, what would his reaction be then? The sin of music was a relative trifle and his reproaches merely irritated her.

And then, one morning at the very end of April, the soldiers left. Every last person in Tilsbury seemed to have come to their doorways to watch their departure. Sergeant Morish rode at their head with the scout, Will Dower: behind them marched one hundred musketeers and fifty pikemen. Stephen had done his job well and the raggle-tailed assortment of farm boys and drifters had been transformed into a troop that would do His Majesty proud. The rear of the column was less impressive. After the wagons of ammunition and baggage and tools came a sizeable number of women and children. Most of the Welsh recruits seemed to have got word somehow to their families who had been arriving in dribs and drabs over the past month. Stephen had not realised how their numbers had grown until he saw them all leaving.

After some consideration he had decided to keep the Irish soldiers with him in Tilsbury. They numbered about forty, the minimum amount necessary to continue the pressure on Gloucester; Lieutenant Donnelly and Sergeant O'Rourke, though so unalike in looks, were similar in their dedication and fighting skills. They were men Stephen knew he could work with well. And he had come to enjoy their company and their music.

A strange silence descended on the town as the last of the wagons rumbled out of sight on the Oxford road. Most of the local youths had enlisted, the troublemakers were all gone, The Lion was suddenly deserted. Even the animals made less noise: all the chickens and geese for miles around had long ago been eaten, there was hardly any livestock left, and nothing for the dogs to bark at. Stephen dispatched a dozen men on a patrol and, since the billeting officer was one of those who had gone with the main body of men, he devoted a couple of hours to rearranging the accommodation of those that were left.

Towards late afternoon, when his work was nearly completed, Stephen emerged from The Lion and almost collided with Corinna Rogers. She came to a halt at once and observed him coolly, all the while tapping her hand against her skirts as though suppressing her impatience.

Stephen coloured. 'Mistress Rogers,' he said, 'I owe you an apology.'

She replied briskly, 'Nonsense, Captain, you owe me nothing. Ten days ago, maybe, but the time for apologies is long gone.'

'I'm sorry.' Stephen apologised anyway, 'I should have sent you word at once. I was . . . unavoidably detained.'

'I do not doubt it, Captain. It never occurred to me you might have changed your mind.'

'No, no, of course not, but . . .'

'No need to explain.' Like several others, Corinna Rogers assumed Captain Sutton had spent that night in quarrelling with the major, 'If there's one thing I cannot abide it is tiresome and wholly superfluous explanations. Don't worry, Captain, I bear you no ill will—'

'I am delighted to hear it.'

She tilted her face upwards, and though her mouth smiled sweetly, her round eyes were hard as marbles. 'But remember, Captain, there are certain opportunities that come to a man only once in his life. I hope I make myself clear. Whatever the reasons, there are no second chances.'

'That is my loss, but I understand.'

'Good. Now, if you will excuse me Captain . . .' She swung past him and continued on her way down the street. Stephen watched her go with a grin of admiration, but, despite his words, hardly any regret. He found it difficult to recall with what eagerness he had been anticipating his rendezvous with her. The events of that night had wiped the memory clean from his mind, so much so that he had forgotten his broken promise until after his return from Oxford. In fact, now that he considered it, he discovered he was happy to be barred from trying to pursue the affair. Feeling for Mistress Taverner as he now did, it would have been impossible to pretend to make love to anyone else.

Corinna was also relieved, but for a quite different reason. She was heartily glad that she had not bumped into Stephen Sutton earlier. Had she encountered him during those first few days, she would surely have struck him and forfeited the last scrap of her reputation on the spot. Being jilted was an entirely new experience, and one she had not relished in the least; she had raged for days. This afternoon she had been able to dismiss Captain Sutton in a dignified manner: her serenity was a recent thing, and entirely due to the fact that just two days ago she had found a new and, in his own way, equally satisfactory lover.

Surprisingly, Dolores was less affected than almost anyone else in Tilsbury by the departure of the soldiers. From her point of view there was now only one soldier of any significance – Captain Sutton. As long as he remained, her circumstances were not altered. She could no more put him out of her mind than she could forget that she had committed murder. She was, however, relieved that the pressure on the Priory House was reduced: a couple of soldiers remained in the loft above the stable but the attics were cleared, and Mabs and Ellen were able to return to the house. Cary was resigned to taking her little bed back to join them, but Dolores stopped her.

'Stay with Beth a little longer,' she told her, 'Two deaths in the house in such a short space have clearly upset her. I'm sure she likes to have you near.'

'Yes, ma'am,' Cary agreed blithely. She too had noticed Beth's tired and wan appearance and was certain the girl would benefit from her company. Only the previous evening she had been telling her the fate of the Irish chieftain Connor M'Guire who had been imprisoned in the Tower of London throughout the war. He had been sentenced to a traitor's death by Parliament and, deprived even of the offices of a priest, he had been taken to Tyburn. There he had been hanged, but before he was dead, he had been cut down by the bloodthirsty sheriff so he might be fully conscious when the disembowelling was performed. However, the executioner, who was obviously a man of civilised instincts, had cut M'Guire's throat. 'Thus,' as Cary said with satisfaction, 'bringing his terrible suffering to a merciful end.' For Beth, who could picture the scene in every gory detail, it seemed little consolation enough.

The day the soldiers left, Beth clung to her mother like a frightened shadow. Dolores was concerned.

'Come along, little Bee. We'll go and pick dandelions together. The fresh air will bring some colour to your cheeks.'

Dolores took her largest willow basket and found a smaller one for Beth. As they pushed open the gate at the front of the house she was more than ever pleased they were leaving the town behind them. Over the road, an ugly scene was developing outside Mother Crew's ramshackle home. Mother Crew, looking for all the world like a goblin queen, was roaring abuse at a crowd who were surrounding her home.

Beth noticed it too. 'Why are all those people shouting?' she asked, gripping her mother's hand more tightly.

Dolores, who knew how Mother Crew was rumoured to have supplemented her income while Tilsbury was full of soldiers, said firmly, 'Because most people are ignorant and cruel, that's why,' and she strode on angrily. Beth did not really understand this explanation, but her mother's tone of voice was wonderfully reassuring.

So much so that when they reached the meadow beyond the second bend in the river she was almost able to forget the horrifying images that Cary's tales had printed in her mind. Even the war could not impede the coming of spring: in some ways this year was lovelier than ever, partly because it was such a contrast to the daily news of man-created ugliness, and partly because, with so many men away and fighting, the farms were suffering a neglect which allowed nature to flourish. Hedges which had not been trimmed in nearly four years were growing profusely; fields which should have been ploughed were lying fallow and covered in a bright lace of spring flowers. While Dolores and Beth gathered the dandelions, larks rose up and sang in the high clear air above them. Gradually Beth relinquished her night-time fears; she breathed more deeply and her lungs were filled with the sweet scents of the meadow. When her own basket was half-full she noticed that her mother, bent double and working quickly, was singing quietly to herself. Beth listened for a while, entranced, and worked her way closer, the better to hear the words. For once Dolores had forgotten her self-imposed ban, and was singing a song from her childhood.

At last Beth could restrain herself no longer. 'What are the words saying?'

Dolores stopped, put a hand in the small of her back and straightened herself. She was frowning. 'Nothing very interesting.'

'But tell me anyway. Please.'

Her mother smiled at her swiftly. 'Why so curious? It's only a piece of foolishness. All about a young girl who has been separated from the man she loves. It's night, and she asks the moon to look down and see what her lover is doing.'

'That's nice.' Beth was delighted. 'It has a sort of sad and happy feeling. I wish you would teach me the words.'

'Well, and maybe I will one day. Why not?'

Dolores patted her daughter's head. She was about to return to her work when she happened to glance towards the town. At first she thought that someone must have lit a bonfire, but that was hardly likely since firewood was now in such short supply. A large cloud of smoke was rising from somewhere in the region of the Priory House.

'Quick, Beth. Something is wrong.'

With their baskets still only half-full, they left the meadow and hurried back towards the town. As they rounded the last bend, they saw the smoke was coming from Mother Crew's house. All around was pandemonium. Mother Crew had never been liked, even before the soldiers arrived, and a good number of people were content to stand around and jeer as her home smouldered. Stephen had only just arrived on the scene with half a dozen soldiers. Buckets had been fetched from the vestry and he was organising a chain of men from the house to the river. But the river was too far and the buckets too few and the fire had already taken hold of the hovel.

Seeing the problem at once, Dolores raced into the Priory House. She ordered her servants – who had all gathered in the front garden to watch the drama unfold – to collect every pot and bucket that could be found and help Captain Sutton get the fire under control. She was pleased to see that Harry had already joined the chain of soldiers and was working hard. The servants sprang into action, and Dolores, carrying a large brew pan and an earthenware pitcher, led them down to the river. Beth, left behind on the edge of the crowd, watched the scene with growing horror.

It seemed to her that Captain Sutton was everywhere at once. He was shouting orders to the men, encouraging the water carriers to work faster while he organised another group to beat at the flames with shovels. At one moment Beth's heart almost stopped with terror when she saw him dash through the narrow front door right into the murky inferno of the house. When he came out a few moments later, his face was blackened by smoke, but he held a coughing child in his arms. And all the while Mother Crew, a terrifying figure of a woman at the best of times, was cursing the bystanders and screaming at the soldiers to save her home. Then Beth saw Donnelly and O'Rourke come galloping up to the house and leap from their horses and Captain Sutton was just giving them their orders when she saw the most terrifying sight of all. From a little opening below the thatch she

214

saw a child's terrified face peep out. Jinny.

'Oh jump, jump!' Beth screamed at the face, but it vanished into the smoke and dark. She dashed through the crowd to tell Captain Sutton of this fresh nightmare, but he had already seen it for himself.

'Get back, Beth,' he roared at her, 'the thatch will be alight any moment!'

There were no ladders to hand, no time to fetch any. The mood of the crowd had changed in an instant: suddenly all was concern, but no one had any idea how best to help. Beth, retreating from the house but unable to tear her eyes from the terrifying scene, saw Lieutenant Charles Donnelly, the man with the face of a young angel, say a few words to the fearsome O'Rourke who nodded and crouched down briefly. The next moment Donnelly was standing on the other man's shoulders and had hoisted himself up to the level of the window and reached inside and pulled first one child and then another from the house as if he were extracting kittens from a nest. He was just in time. He passed the children down, leaped from O'Rourke's shoulders, and the two men sprang back just as the thatch exploded into flame and the crowd was beaten back by the heat.

Recognising that their task was hopeless, the chain of men and women fetching water from the river paused in their work. They stood quite still, watching the flames leap up into the sky and listening to the crack of timber and collapsing walls. Stephen was about to urge them to redouble their efforts when he saw it was pointless. No one could get within ten yards of the blazing building; a hundred buckets of water would make no difference now. His main anxiety from the first had been that a spark might reach the ruined priory next to the Taverners' home. Although most of the ammunition and powder had been dispatched with the soldiers to the King's army, there was still a formidable amount stored in the ruins. He sent Donnelly and O'Rourke with half a dozen men to warn the sentries to be extra vigilant until the danger was past.

Beth understood none of this. She observed the townspeople as they watched the blaze from a safe distance; on a few faces she saw the cruelty and delight in the misfortunes of others that Cary had been telling her about almost every night for the past six weeks. On others she saw compassion – and shame, for no one had realised there were children still sheltering in the house. Now her mother was walking back from the river towards them. Philip, who had somehow escaped notice in the tumult, ran across the road to tell her what he had seen. Dolores took hold of his hand and went to join Captain Sutton, who was now standing quite still. Beth was about to go to her, when she noticed Jinny Crew, all alone, at a little distance from the crowd. Her face was devoid of expression. Beth took a few steps towards her, then stopped. Though they had lived opposite each other all their lives, she could not now recollect if they had ever exchanged two words before.

She said, 'Jinny—'

The girl turned suddenly. Her blue eyes were very pale and she looked as though she might burst out laughing. That thought was so alarming to Beth that she couldn't think what to say next.

Dolores was looking around for her daughter. She caught sight of her just as she was about to approach Jinny Crew. Still holding Philip firmly by the hand – she could not imagine how he had managed to break free of Nona and the others at such a dangerous moment – she went across to join them. Captain Sutton followed. Dolores also had observed the blankness on Jinny's face, and recognised the signs of imminent hysteria.

She said, 'Jinny, you poor child—'

The girl's chin wobbled.

Dolores turned to Stephen. 'Where is her mother?'

But no one seemed to know. Suddenly weary of wishing her neighbours to hell, Mother Crew had abruptly disappeared with her three younger children.

'Where can the child go?' asked Stephen. No one was likely to offer Jinny even a temporary home. Her mother had for a long time been the town's unofficial whore. Her activities had on the whole been overlooked but her zeal for the soldiers had made her an object of hatred. And Jinny, undernourished child that she still was, would soon be of an age to follow her mother's trade.

The same thoughts had been passing through Dolores' mind. She said, 'You had better come home with us, Jinny. Just for tonight at any rate. In the morning you can help us to decide what is best to do. Come along.'

Jinny, rendered stupid by shock, merely stared at her. Dolores placed Philip's hand in Beth's, and put her arm around the waif. 'Don't be frightened, Jinny, we'll find your mother later.'

216

The child let out an odd, gulping sob and pressed her face into Mistress Taverner's shoulder. Dolores was just about to set off towards the house when she caught Stephen's eyes on her. His face had an expression she had never noticed before and she could not tell what he was thinking. She had a strange sensation just beneath her ribs, as if some part of her were folding in upon itself. The way his clear eyes were fixed on hers made her feel both warm and yet uneasy too.

Turning away, she said quickly, 'Come, Beth. Time to go home.'

Beth nodded. It was only when she caught sight of their two willow baskets upturned on the edge of the road, and their precious dandelion heads strewn in the dust, all trampled and irretrievably smashed, that she began to lose control. Everything was being destroyed. The cry began somewhere deep in her chest and burst out as a thin high wail of despair.

Dolores, turning at the sound, glanced instinctively at Captain Sutton. Catching her eye for a moment, he stooped at once and picked Beth up. Still sobbing uncontrollably she crumpled like a rag doll against his buff coat. Philip, seeing his opportunity, was about to scamper off but Stephen reached out his free hand and caught hold of his arm. 'Not this time,' he said firmly, 'Home.' And Philip, for once in his life a little awed by the situation, did not protest.

Dolores nodded her approval and crossed the road to the Priory House. Jinny was clinging to her like a frail and foul-smelling vine, and Dolores wondered absently whether a session with soap and water would be one shock too many for the child on this most shocking of days. She was aware that Mabs and the others would have plenty to say if they had to share their quarters with her in her present state.

She was also aware, as she pushed open the gate and walked up the path to the house, that Stephen Sutton was following with her two middle children and that she, most protective and cautious of mothers, had trusted him with them entirely.

Early evening and Harry was in the kitchen with Mabs and Bussell when there was a timid knock at the back door. Mabs, grumbling, began to rise to her feet but Harry said, 'I'll go.'

It was Tom the Cooper, an old man who had never set foot in the Priory House in his life. He thrust something into Harry's hands. 'For the little maid,' he mumbled, and was gone again before Harry had a chance to thank him.

'Another present for Jinny,' said Harry, carrying the tray which was covered with a linen napkin.

Mabs was annoyed. 'Do they think we can't feed the girl without their help?' she asked.

Bussell merely looked down his long nose and said, 'Another bad conscience.'

'I don't understand,' said Harry, lifting the napkin and peering at the marchpanes beneath, 'Why set fire to her home if they're going to be sorry after?'

Neither Bussell nor Mabs had any answer to that. Harry sighed. If his father were only home, he could ask him, but he had wished Josiah back in Tilsbury a thousand times and still he did not return. He felt he had outgrown the comfort that Nona or his mother might offer, but so far he had found nothing to take their place. His sense of isolation was so intense it was almost a kind of sickness.

Mabs, who wanted a chance to discuss the day's events with Bussell properly, with no young ears listening, told him, 'Take the marchpanes to the girl. They'll cheer her up.'

Harry sighed again and set off towards the stairs. Captain Sutton was just coming in through the front door.

'Good evening, Harry,' said Stephen.

Harry mumbled a reply. Though not given to rudeness, the boy found it impossible to know how to act in Captain Sutton's company. He resented his presence in their home almost as much as he missed his father. At the same time he could not help admiring him; he had seen the way Captain Sutton took command of the situation that afternoon and had known exactly what to do, and Harry had been proud to be able to work with the men. But now even that memory left a sour taste in his mouth because of the outrage he had felt when the captain carried Beth into their house. So now, at the sight of him, Harry merely mumbled and went on up the stairs feeling more miserable and confused than ever.

The scene in the upstairs room was surprisingly tranquil. Jinny had been happy to submit to soap and water when told she might put on one of Beth's old gowns afterwards. It was estimated that Jinny was probably about three years older than Beth, but she was so skinny that the gown, though much too short in the hem and sleeves, fitted well enough around the middle.

Jinny herself was almost more stunned at being taken into the Priory House than by the burning of her home and the disappearance of her mother and brothers. For as long as she could remember she had looked across the road at the imposing facade of the Taverners' house, so close to her own and yet it might have been a hundred miles away. Each day she had seen the front door open and Mistress Taverner and her daughter issue forth wearing their beautiful clothes and walk down the street with their confident stride. Recently there had been officers going in and out of that door as well . . . but what lay on the far side it was quite beyond her ability to imagine. And now here she was, in another world entirely, a world of smooth oaken surfaces polished to a dull shine, of wide carpeted spaces and high ceilings with patterns of leaves and fruit worked in the plaster. She had walked up the stairs and been brought into this room where everything smelled as delicious as a hay meadow in June, and now she was even wearing some of their exquisite clothes. Everyone seemed to assume that she must be miserable, or anxious about her mother, but the truth was she had never been so blissfully happy. If this miracle were only to last for a single night, if tomorrow she had to put on her scratchy fustian dress and go home to her angry mother again, then at least she would have made the most of this brief interval of dream.

Beth was seated on a footstool by her mother's chair, her arm draped across Dolores's knee. Her fit of hysterical crying had left her with a peaceful kind of exhaustion, and the hot posset that Mabs had made for them all spread a warm feeling from the base of her stomach. Every now and then she felt her mother's hand lightly stroking her hair, and that was a different kind of warming. She wondered if the terrifying looking Mother Crew ever stroked Jinny's hair in such a comforting way, and she thought probably not. This was such a sad notion that Beth was sorry Jinny had been given an old gown to wear. She would have liked her to have the new green tabby.

After the dramas of the afternoon, Dolores was content just to have her family around her – and on their best behaviour too: the act of welcoming Jinny into their midst had created a temporary sense of harmony. The baby was propped against some cushions – in a week or two he would be sitting without assistance. Philip was playing with some wooden skittles and treating his baby brother to a garbled account of the burning house. Nona was seated on a low chair, her hands resting on her knees, her eyes half-closed.

'Tom the Cooper brought some marchpanes for Jinny,' said Harry, setting them down on a side table.

'Would you like to try one now, Jinny?' asked Dolores.

Jinny shook her head. She had already eaten more in her few hours in the Priory House than she normally ate in a whole week at home. She was afraid her refusal to eat them straight away might mean someone else would get them, so she added swiftly, 'But I'll have them later.'

'Don't worry.' Dolores smiled, 'No one will take them from you.'

Harry had gone to stand by the window. He said, 'Why is everyone giving Jinny things? Don't they think we'll take proper care of her?'

'It's not that, Harry,' said Dolores, 'It's their way of saying sorry. No one thought there were children in the house when they put the torch to it.'

'But why did the children go indoors?'

'Perhaps they were more frightened of the crowd than of the smoke,' she glanced warningly in Jinny's direction, 'Best not to talk of it too much just for now.'

Harry frowned. He still did not feel it made much sense. Dolores lapsed into thought. She had heard the front door open and close just before Harry came in, and she knew that Captain Sutton had returned. Now he would be eating his evening meal alone in the hall room. As always, her body monitored his whereabouts, but now she was beginning to realise that this was not simply because he carried the memory of her crime with him wherever he went. It was not because of their shared secret that she had known instinctively how to work with him during the crisis of the fire, nor was that the reason she had trusted him with Philip and Beth. She found herself remembering the way he looked at her when she took Jinny under her wing – and each time she thought of it, she experienced that strange, oddly pleasurable unease.

Beth twisted her head around and appealed to her mother. 'Will you and Nona dance for us tonight? It has been that sort of a day, hasn't it?'

Dolores smiled and looked across to her grandmother. 'How about you, Nona? I think Beth is right.'

'I'm too old and stiff.'

'All the more reason. Come—' Dolores stood up impulsively and shook out her skirts. She pulled Nona to her feet. She sensed that her grandmother was out of sorts, and she thought the dancing might boost her flagging spirits.

Nona was grumbling and smiling at the same time. The two women moved to the open space in front of the window. As usual they began slowly, almost tentatively. Their song was little more than a low repetitive chanting, their feet shuffled against the floor. Then gradually the music caught hold of them both, their voices rose more strongly and their bodies began to move with a slow swaying rhythm, feet stamping and heads thrown back. Beth glanced across to see if Jinny was surprised by this most private of family ceremonies, and wondered if she realised the honour of being permitted to watch. But Jinny had gone beyond surprise. After this day's upsets, if Mistress Taverner and the old lady had turned into a pair of ravens and begun flying in and out of the windows, she would just have helped herself to another marchpane and thought how pleasant life was in the Priory House.

Stephen Sutton, seated alone at the head of the dining table, put down his glass of wine and leaned back in his chair. There was a smile on his face. He had heard talk in the town of the foreigners' music and their dancing, but the sounds he heard now were stranger even than had been described. He tried to imagine the scene, but instead he kept remembering how Dolores had reached out to Jinny Crew when even the child's own family had abandoned her. Even now, he felt a huge sense of pride at her action. There was nothing possessive in his feeling of pride. He could not help loving Mistress Taverner, he would continue to love her no matter what she did, and yet it made him enormously happy that she had acted with spontaneous kindness. He did not begin to understand this, but then, there was no need for understanding. It was enough to enjoy.

And yet it was a kind of agony to be so close to the woman he loved, but to be unable to show that love in any way. It had become a physical pain, like a great weight constantly pressing on his chest. Sometimes he almost wished he had left with Sergeant Morish and the others. But at that moment he knew he would not have traded places with any man alive.

He heard the music stop abruptly. He waited for some time, but it did not recommence.

In the upstairs room, Nona, who had seemed to be enjoying the dance as much as Dolores had hoped she would, stopped suddenly and put her hands on the back of her chair, as though afraid of falling.

'Are you all right?'

It was a few moments before Nona could speak, but then she nodded, adding curtly, 'No more dancing for me, though. You carry on. You don't need me.'

Dolores hesitated. A sudden anxiety flooded through her, but she dismissed it swiftly. 'We're all tired,' she said, 'We've danced enough. Here's poor Jinny can barely keep her eyes open.'

She began chivvying the children to prepare for bed. Never in her life had she danced alone, and the thought of doing so now filled her with great sadness.

Chapter 16

❧

The old woman was sleeping herself towards death.

Dolores could no longer ignore the truth. Nona had taken to her bed the day after Mother Crew's house burned down, and now, a week later, she hardly left it.

'It's a cancer,' she told Dolores calmly, 'It's eating me up inside. And I'm tired. A couple of those special drops are what I need.'

Dolores sniffed the little bottle whose contents had made such a difference to Jack's last days. 'What is it?' she asked.

'I don't know the English name. Your father always kept some in his shop. I managed to save a few bottles when the soldiers came. He said it was for peaceful ends when all hope was gone. And it helped young Jack, didn't it? If I'm not too greedy, there'll be enough left for someone else. I'd better not wait around too long, eh?' And she grinned, not having the energy for her usual toothless chuckle.

She was so accepting of her condition that Dolores was inclined to disbelieve her. 'You'll be better again in a day or so,' she said one morning, but Nona was impatient.

'No foolish talk. I'm ready to go.' And it was only the truth. For Nona, the fifteen years since her family had been destroyed in Würzburg had been a kind of postscript to her life. The main thread had been broken, she had been forced to carry on as best she could, living from day to day. She enjoyed a good meal or a warm fire and asked for little more. She loved Dolores' children, yet the arrival of each baby had caused her unexpected heartache. It was not just that they reminded her of the lives that had been lost, more that they offered the illusion of new beginnings in a cruel world. For years now she had been more comfortable at deathbed scenes than births. She found great solace in the satisfactory completion of a life, the certainty that a peaceful end might conclude the daily struggle. She knew that she had taken risks with her poisons and her prophecies, but she had enjoyed the power it gave her too much to care about the danger. And now Dolores needed the knowledge herself.

'Listen,' she said, 'you must learn. The bottle on the top shelf, the one with the strange flower on the label, I had that from your father too, but I've never used it. Six drops of that in a man's drink will make him sleep like the dead for six hours and then wake with no ill effects. Remember now, six drops and six hours.'

And so she went on, whenever she was strong enough to talk, passing on to Dolores the accumulated knowledge of a lifetime. 'Remember what I'm telling you,' she repeated, 'That stillroom contains your weapons and your armour. Learn how to use them well, and you are a match for any man.'

'Tell me, Nona,' said Dolores one evening when the children were all in bed and the house was quiet, 'How did you give Josiah those stomach pains every time he was angry with me?'

'Ah, that.' This time Nona did manage a chuckle. 'Your husband fears his own evil thoughts, so he does the work for me. When we were still in Germany and I was afraid he'd go back on his promises, I think maybe I did drop a little something in his ale. I can't remember now exactly what it was, just a medicine that produces cramps, I think. But Josiah believed I could see into his soul. After that first time, I only had to look at him in a certain way – like this, see–' and Nona half-closed her eyes and looked up into her lids so that only the whites of her eyes were visible, before carrying on, 'and he'd get the pains all over again. As if by magic.'

'The fool. I never knew it was so easy.'

'Nothing simpler, so long as you don't give away your power.'

'*My* power?'

'You can rule him easily.'

'How?'

'You'll see. Once you stop hating. It's the hate has always made you weak.'

'Explain, please.'

But Nona's eyes were closing, and she waved her hand,

bringing their talk to an end. Dolores sighed. All their conversations were like this, now, brief windows opening into Nona's consciousness. Exhausted, but not yet ready for sleep, Dolores sat by her grandmother's bedside for a little while, mulling over what she had said. She had thought she was the only person awake in the house, but then she heard light footsteps on the stairs, the front door open and close. She stood up and went slowly to the window. There was no moon, and the sky was heavy with cloud.

And then, in the darkness, as she had surely known she would, she saw a figure with a lantern coming round the corner of the house, and she knew, from the energy that flowed through her, that it was Captain Sutton. And then, also as she had known she would, she saw the bobbing lantern come to a halt just below her window, and she saw his face upturned towards the place where she stood, a dim outline against the light from a single candle. Dolores felt the touch of his gaze on her but she did not step back into the shadows as she would have done ten days before. She stood quite still, and a tremor of a new kind of fear shivered through her. And she remained standing immobile at the window, long after the figure with the lantern had moved on, and out of sight.

The next morning she encountered Stephen in the screens passage. She found herself avoiding his eyes.

He said, 'I hear your grandmother is unwell.'

'She says she is dying.'

'I am sorry.'

'She is reconciled . . . I believe she is almost eager.'

Stephen thought for a moment before saying, 'Mistress Taverner, if she is well enough, I would like to see her. I never thanked her properly for the care she gave Jack.'

'Of course, Captain. She sleeps most of the time, but when awake, she's perfectly lucid. Do you want to see her now?'

'Thank you.'

Dolores led the way up the stairs. Knowing that Stephen Sutton was following, she felt suddenly awkward and conscious of her smallest movement. Having ascertained that Nona was awake she said, 'There, I shall leave you with her, Captain Sutton. Do not be alarmed if she falls asleep suddenly.'

She closed the door behind him – and made sure she was occupied elsewhere when he was finished.

Harry and Beth were less than philosophical about her present condition and Nona made it clear she found their gloom tiresome. Philip was altogether too boisterous for a sick-room companion and Dolores had moved him into her own bedchamber. Curiously enough, the one person who spent nearly as much time with Nona as Dolores did, was Jinny.

The girl had been so dismayed at the prospect of being sent back to her mother – who was reported to have taken up residence with her brother's wife in the next village – that no more was said on the subject. After the initial flush of goodwill had worn off, Mabs and the other servants lost interest in her, and Jinny was too much in awe of Harry and Beth to be comfortable with them. She was happiest when settled by Nona's bed. Dolores was teaching her to spin so she might make herself useful, and though the girl had no particular aptitude, she was pleased to have something to do and stuck to the task with determination. The sound of the spinning wheel was soothing to Nona, providing company without any of the weariness of talk. Every now and then she would hear Jinny curse horribly.

'Tst. Such bad language.'

'But I broke the thread.'

'Everyone does that when they're learning. Try again.'

Jinny would sigh, and mutter crossly, but in a few minutes the wheel began humming again and Nona would sink back into her slumber.

Dolores fell into the habit of sleeping on the truckle bed in Nona's room. Early one morning, when it was still dark, she awoke to hear Captain Sutton going down the stairs and out through the side door. She was still awake when she heard horses gathering at the front of the house. Though he had said nothing to her of his plans, she assumed he must be leading a patrol against the Gloucester rebels. Suddenly she was reminded of the morning when she had watched him setting off with Major Darbier on the patrol which had cost Jack his life. A sudden foreboding fell over her, and even though the horsemen had quickly trotted down the road and the house was once more enveloped in silence, she was unable to sleep again.

All day the anxiety nagged. Leaving Jinny and her spinning wheel to keep Nona company, she set out to gather cowslips. The town seemed unnaturally quiet. The soldiers that had not accompanied Captain Sutton were mostly occupied in sentry duty and there was only a handful of men still drilling on the muster ground by the bend in the river. The day was overcast and there was a chilling wind. Dolores forced herself to work steadily, but all the time there was a knot of anxiety in the pit of her stomach and she was listening for the hoofbeats that would signal the return of the soldiers.

Towards noon she heard the sound of two horses approaching along the Oxford road. Suddenly the knot of tension inside her tightened and her heart began to race. She picked up the basket of cowslips and walked briskly back to town.

And as she walked, she struggled to understand her agitation. Stay calm, she told herself, there is no cause for anxiety. If Captain Sutton has an accident, what is that to me? But since she so clearly *was* concerned, she told herself this feeling was entirely natural: after all, by his swift action he had saved her from imprisonment, trial and death – she had every cause for gratitude, so she was bound to hope he would avoid danger and come safely through this war.

Mabs was making pastry. She looked up. 'Will Dower came by,' she said, 'He had a message for Captain Sutton but I told him he'd not return till evening. Will's gone home for now, said he'd be back later. And he brought a letter for you.'

'Captain Sutton is not yet returned?'

Mabs shook her head. 'They're usually all day at their patrolling. I only hope he remembers to bring us some food. I can't keep on making meals from air.'

Mabs approved of patrols. Not that she had anything against the rebels in Gloucester, but Captain Sutton almost always returned with some useful item for her kitchen. She had only a vague idea of what the fighting was about and no particular sympathy with one side or the other. But she was passionate about the need for a full larder and would have given her instant allegiance to any soldier who could bring home a haunch of venison or a sack of coarse sugar or – another source of anxiety just now – a good quantity of bay salt.

Dolores took the letter, registering as she did so that it was from Josiah. And she marvelled only that she had not thought of him in days. It was not just the distance, nor the length of time he had been away: she realised that, recently, her husband had become quite simply an irrelevance.

She retreated with the letter into her stillroom, locking the door behind her before leaning back against the slate shelf and breaking the seal with her thumb.

> *My dear wife,*
> *Affairs of business require me to remain absent from Tilsbury for some little while longer. I regret the pressing obligations that keep me from home in these difficult times, but I trust you are continuing to be a worthy steward of our fortunes, for our children's sake as well as for my own. Please convey to Captain Sutton my condolences for Major Darbier's untimely death, and assure him that I remain at all times his willing host and devoted colleague in this endeavour.*
> *Josiah Taverner.*

A black mist was forming behind Dolores' eyes. Once again there was no address, but she was convinced it came to her from London. No doubt Josiah had decided Parliament was now the likely victor and preferred to sit out the remainder of the war in the relative safety of the capital. Suddenly his neutrality no longer seemed to Dolores so admirable. In fact, just at this moment she thought it was despicable. When men such as Stephen Sutton were risking their lives daily, what gave Josiah the right to take his fat ease among the self-righteous merchants of the City?

Nor did Josiah's purpose in mentioning Major Darbier's death escape her attention. He cared not a fig for any man's wellbeing but his own: his sole intention had been to remind her that he was kept reliably informed. Bussell . . . she thought absently. She had always assumed it was Bussell. And how would Josiah react if he were to receive an accurate account of the major's last hours? She gave a bitter laugh. If he had held the power in his hand, instead of Captain Sutton, would he have tried to save her? Or would he have seen it as an excellent opportunity to dispose of a woman who had long ago become more a burden than a blessing? Or, if he had chosen to save her skin, would it have been simply to avoid a scandal which would damage his reputation and the future prospects of his children? Not because he cared for her. Never because of her. Whereas Stephen Sutton had acted as he did because . . .

She checked herself just in time. She crumpled the letter into a ball and busied herself with tinder and flint before placing it in a shallow chafing dish and setting it alight. She was sure she had absolutely no idea why Captain Sutton had decided to help her. His motives did not concern her at all. He was nothing whatsoever to do with her. Nor could she imagine what had caused her anxiety that morning – whatever it was, it certainly was not concern for Captain Sutton. She was overwrought because of Nona, that was it. Her grandmother was dying so of course she was distressed. It had nothing to do with Captain Sutton and the danger of his patrol. She was so far from caring about him that he could be blown to pieces by one of Massey's henchmen and . . . the sudden image was so appalling that she clenched her fist and bit her knuckles to stop herself from crying out. She told herself that all suffering was regrettable, she was more tender-hearted than she realised. She had grieved even when Ensign Skipton had been wounded . . . and so her thoughts veered back and forth, like the shuttle through a loom, until her head was throbbing and the knot of tension deep inside her was drawn a little tighter than before. And Josiah's letter had burned to a fragile grey ash.

Dolores smoothed down her skirts, pushed back a few wandering strands of hair and composed herself for the necessity of facing her household and somehow filling the remainder of the day until the patrol returned safely.

Towards evening, Dolores was told a soldier was asking to see her. She went to the back door and was surprised to find O'Rourke, as unkempt as ever, but with a shifty expression in his eyes that immediately aroused her suspicion.

'Well? What is it?'

His agitation increased. 'May I speak with you privately, ma'am?'

Dolores would have dismissed him, but it occurred to her that he might have something to say which touched on Captain Sutton, or even the major's death.

'We can talk in the winter parlour,' she said.

Mabs asked, 'Shall I bring in some refreshment?'

'Certainly not. I'm sure our conversation will be brief.'

When they were alone in the winter parlour, O'Rourke stood awkwardly in the middle of the room. Dolores did not invite him to be seated. Fingering the edge of his doublet, he began hesitantly, 'I understand the old lady is . . . unwell.'

Dolores raised her fine eyebrows as though to ask what business that was of his, but she said nothing.

'They say she does not have long.'

'So?'

'It's just that I was thinking, ma'am, her being Spanish originally, and so of my religion . . . and I did not like to think of her dying without the offices of a priest, I know it is what we always fear, and there is a gentleman could come to her if she wished . . .'

It was a few moments before Dolores spoke. Then she said very quietly, 'Am I right in believing you are offering to bring a Catholic priest to this house so my grandmother may receive the last rites?'

'Yes, ma'am.'

'I never knew there was a priest near here.'

'There is almost always a priest somewhere nearabouts. Though naturally they do not trumpet their true identity.'

Again Dolores was silent. The soldier standing in front of her no longer looked shifty: merely anxious, and concerned for the dying hours of an old woman he scarcely knew, but who had once shared his religion.

At length she said quietly, 'Wait here. I shall go and ask my grandmother. This must be her decision.'

The priest arrived with such promptness that he must have been waiting somewhere on the outskirts of town. Nona had consented to see him with her customary style. 'Why not? Just think how angry Josiah would be if he knew he had been entertaining Catholic priests in his home. Besides, the fellow can do no harm.'

There was something about the man, who went by the name of Father Perry, to which Dolores took an instant dislike. Fair-haired and willowy, he was not much older than she was, perhaps in his early thirties, but his face had that ageless energy of the true fanatic. He looked consumptive; his eyes were dark and penetrating. As he came into the house, he raised his hand as though to bless her, but Dolores stepped back.

'Not me,' she said coldly, 'It is my grandmother who has agreed to see you.'

He nodded in silent agreement and followed her up the stairs. Dolores dismissed Jinny, telling her that Master Perry was a well-known surgeon who might be able to help Nona. She stood by the door of Nona's room and watched with resolute indifference while the priest heard Nona's confession. I am only doing this because it might bring some small comfort to Nona's last hours, she thought stonily – it is all nonsense, but Nona is old and there is no harm in it. She realised then that the last time she had seen a priest he had been lying at the foot of his own altar and dying from his terrible wound. She imagined him suddenly with the face of Father Perry. Never before had she considered the religion she had abjured; it was as though the Roman Catholic church itself had been wiped out by the massacre at Würzburg. She had taken on Josiah's religion as she had adopted his name and language and customs, without thinking, because she had no choice. Now, hearing the Latin phrases for the first time in what seemed like much more than fifteen years, she told herself that it was all a meaningless jumble of words that had nothing to do with Dolores Taverner, of the Priory House, Tilsbury.

But when the priest had turned from the bed and approached the silent woman standing by the door, he saw that her face was bathed in tears.

'Do you want to make your confession, my daughter?' he asked.

'Certainly not.'

'Then let me bless your children.'

'No. This is nothing to do with them.' Father Perry was about to argue with her, but she carried on, 'Come downstairs, Master Perry, and I will have food and drink brought for you.'

When they were alone together, Father Perry reiterated, as she had known he would, his request that she receive confession. To distract him, she said, 'You are the first priest to enter this house in a good many years.'

He nodded. 'There used to be a priest's hole, I believe, and a secret route going to some ruins.'

'It was blocked off years ago,' she said swiftly.

'That must have been after Father Tellam was taken. Did you know the pursuivants caught up with him when he was celebrating mass in this very house?'

'I had heard the story, but I never knew his name.'

That dangerous light was shining more brightly in the priest's eyes. 'Father Tellam made a glorious end. He is one of the blessed martyrs. We all pray that we may honour God by dying in his cause.'

'A glorious end? To be hung by the neck and then cut down before you are dead? To be cut open . . . I do not call that a glorious end, but a terrible waste of a life.'

231

'No life is wasted that has been dedicated to God.' He nibbled on a piece of cheese, but he was too highly-strung for hunger. 'Father Tellam was one of the finest of our order. He had dedicated his life to the care of children, and the sick. So much more tragic, therefore, that he was betrayed by a child.'

'A child?'

'I believe it was one of the children living in this house at the time. The pursuivant had used devious means to win the boy's trust, and persuaded him to reveal the hour that the priest would be serving mass in this house. That was how Father Tellam came to be caught. The boy's father was taken to prison at the same time. He would have been released, I am sure, but he caught the plague and died within the week.'

'Yes, I knew that part of the story. Do you remember the name of the child?'

The priest shook his head. It could have been Josiah, Dolores thought, it must have been either him or his older brother. Josiah had been eight or nine at the time of his father's death in prison. She remembered having once been told that converts are always more zealous than those who have been born to a faith. Josiah's youthful betrayal of his family's Roman Catholic religion might explain his long fanaticism for the Protestant cause in Europe. A way to shake off the burden of guilt. Hadn't Nona said that Josiah was afraid of his own wickedness? If he had been responsible for his father's death, then he had every reason for that fear.

'I know Father Tellam forgave all his persecutors at the end.' Father Perry spoke with reverence.

'No doubt, since he was so eager for martyrdom he should have been grateful to them.'

This idea seemed to annoy the priest, but he said smoothly, 'You seem much troubled, my child. Let me hear your confession and—'

'No, Father.' Dolores smiled at him strangely. 'There is no need for that. I lead such a blameless life, alone here with my children and my duties, that there is nothing for me to confess. If only there were some heinous crime I had committed then I'm sure I would be only too glad of your offices. Murder, for instance. What manner of penance would you impose if I had done a murder?'

'We are not here to talk of imaginary crimes.'

'But perhaps it is not imaginary, Father. Maybe I have done

murder. You are forbidden to repeat what is said to you in the privacy of confession, so I need not fear betrayal. I could talk to you quite freely, isn't that right, Father? And when you had heard all the details of my terrible crime, you would know what to do, wouldn't you? Just a few words of absolution, a penance or two, and I would be free of the burden of it for ever. Oh, Father Perry, how simple it all sounds, does it not? Just a little murder, after all.'

Father Perry was coming to the conclusion that Mistress Taverner was probably a trifle unhinged, and nothing would be gained by continuing their conversation. He stood up and prepared to leave; the food and drink that had been brought for him was barely touched. The woman was looking at him with contempt.

Just as he was about to leave, he reached into his purse and pulled out a small crucifix elaborately worked in silver.

'God bless you, my child,' he said softly, 'and bring you to an understanding of His grace. Take this . . . and keep it as a reminder of the faith in which you were born, and in which, God willing, you will one day die. May it guide your prayers.'

I am not your child, thought Dolores fiercely, and she was on the point of handing it back to him. But as she felt the cool metal against her palm, she thought of her prayer. Dear God, she breathed, bring Captain Sutton safe home from his patrol.

Nona was fretting. Jinny had been packed off to bed. A greenish light remained in the sky, but it was well past the expected hour of the patrol's return, and still there was no sign of them. Dolores stood by the half-open window, drumming her finger tips on the sill.

'What's the matter with you?' asked Nona irritably, 'You're as restless as a cat.'

'It's nothing.'

'Where's Philip? I want to see Philip. Did I ever tell you he's the image of your father?'

'He's in bed, fast asleep. It's late.'

'Then wake him up and bring him here.'

Glad of any distraction, Dolores crossed the landing and pushed open the door into the room where Philip was sleeping. It was still light enough to see without a candle. The child was lying on his back, sprawled like a puppy with his arms flung wide across the pillow. His long dark lashes were very clear

233

against the pallor of his cheek. For a few moments before she woke him, the love Dolores felt for this, the most beautiful of her children, flooded through her and swept all her earlier anxiety away.

He was wide awake in an instant. 'Is the patrol back yet? Has something happened to Captain Sutton? Is there fighting?'

'No, no, Philip. But Nona wants to see you.'

'Why? Is she dying already?'

'Tst. Such a question.' She took his hand and led him to his grandmother's bedside. Nona's face broke into a smile.

'Just look at him!' she exclaimed in Spanish, 'The little Spaniard. You'd never know he was Josiah's, would you? He's Miguel all over again.'

Dolores smiled, and answered in the same language. 'He's more trouble than all the other three put together.'

'Yes, of course. Your father was the same. This one will break a few hearts and cause plenty of mischief.'

'Was my father a heart-breaker?'

'What does it matter now? He's been dead for fifteen years.' She turned to Philip and addressed him in English. 'Never forget,' she told him solemnly, 'that you have Spanish blood in your veins.'

Philip looked at her with round black eyes. 'I saw blood today,' he said, 'Lots of it. Mabs' brother John had cut his foot with an axe and the blood was pouring out of his shoe.'

Nona giggled. 'Well, next time you bleed remember that the blood coming out is half Spanish, that's all.'

'Don't confuse him, Nona. He might have a foreign mother, but he's English-born.'

'More's the pity,' Nona grumbled. 'I'm going home soon enough anyway. But I shall miss the little imp.'

Philip said earnestly, 'Mabs saw elfin lights in the Old Priory. She said there were footprints by the river in the morning and they were much too small for human feet. She says they must have belonged to all the fairy folk who look after the Grey Lady and—'

'Get away with your nonsense.'

'Come along, Philip. Nona's tired now.'

Philip did not give up so easily. 'Gerard promised he'll find me a grass snake's nest this summer.'

'Say good night to Nona, Pip. I'll take you back to your room.'

But Philip had been excited by the unexpected summons, and

by the time Dolores had settled him again it was pitch dark. She returned to Nona's bedside to find the old woman in a deep sleep. She told herself to rest while she could, but her anxiety had returned, more violent than before. She went back to her bedchamber and looked out into the spring darkness. What had kept them so late? Previous patrols had always been back by dusk. Her ears were straining for the sound of returning horsemen and the faint sounds of the night were magnified. Half a dozen times she was sure she heard hoofbeats and hurried to the window overlooking the road and gazed out into the black night. The hoofbeats did not materialise. She thought of Philip and his elfin lights by the priory, and she began to wonder if perhaps there were phantom horsemen also whose faint tapping sounds were intended to torment those who watched and waited in vain . . .

And then she heard them. Slow steps afar off that broke into an eager trot as the horses sensed they were nearing home. By now her eyes were sufficiently attuned to the darkness to make out the shapes of the riders as they approached the Priory House. Then one figure detached itself from the rest and she heard Stephen's voice bidding goodnight to his men and heard their weary answers, and she turned and sped down the stairs and through the kitchen, where she paused only to prod the sleeping scullion and order him to find wine and food for the captain, and then out into the stable-yard where she heard him calling to his groom to tend his horse. He was just coming from the stable when he saw her.

'Mistress Taverner, is something wrong?'

She came to an abrupt halt. 'You were so late. I thought perhaps some accident . . .' Her voice was unusually harsh.

He approached her slowly. 'We've had a long day and done considerable damage to our friend Massey. Luckily none of ours is hurt.'

Dolores turned away without a word and walked briskly ahead of him into the kitchen where the scullion, more asleep than awake, was assembling wine and food. Her voice was still angry as she said to Stephen, 'Then you must be hungry. Go through to the hall, I shall bring you some refreshment.' And then, turning with exasperation to the kitchen boy she exclaimed, 'No, not that wine, you fool. Here, I'll do it myself.'

'Don't trouble on my account,' said Stephen, 'I'm so hungry I could eat black bread.'

'Not in my house, you won't. Go on, sit down, rest yourself. I'll be through in a moment.'

Wondering, in an exhausted way, just what he had done to offend Mistress Taverner – since she appeared angry – Stephen took a candle and went to the hall. No sooner had he sat down in the high-backed chair at the head of the table than weariness almost overwhelmed him. Every muscle in his body ached. He flung his hat down on the table and ran his fingers through his hair. He felt as if he had eaten and breathed nothing but dust for several days. He contemplated pulling off his boots, but since Mistress Taverner herself was bringing his food, he decided against it. Anyway, he had not the energy. Briefly, he leaned his head against the back of the chair and closed his eyes.

When Dolores, carrying a tray, pushed the door open with her foot a few minutes later, she thought he must be sleeping. She hesitated, setting the tray down carefully so as not to disturb him. His face and hair were covered in dust and his clothes were filthy. For a few moments she felt a hesitant tenderness, then she saw the bright stain of blood on the collar of his shirt and she burst out, 'Just look at you! And you told me none were hurt!'

Without raising his head from the chair back, Stephen opened his eyes. There could be no doubt that Mistress Taverner was in a fine passion for some reason. He sighed. There'd been conflict enough already today; he was not eager for more.

He said, 'You should be congratulating me, Mistress Taverner. I had the devil's own luck. A bullet came so close it must have caught the edge of my ear. Had I not turned my head at just that moment, I've no doubt it would have gone clean through my brain.'

'Oh!' Dolores sank down into a chair. 'Such foolish risks, and all for what? Here, have some wine. Eat.'

'Thank you.'

'I'll fetch some water and clean the cut for you. There is always a danger the poison will spread.'

'Don't trouble.' He touched his ear carefully, 'I believe it is healing by itself.'

'How can you tell?' Her voice rose. 'You cannot even see the injury. My Harry would have more sense. How did it happen?'

Stephen took a long draught of wine before answering, 'We'd been told that some of Cromwell's men were planning to link up with the Gloucester garrison. Our task was to prevent that. We caught up with them about fifteen miles north of here. There were more rebels than we had anticipated, about fifty, I should say.'

'But you were only ten!'

'Fourteen. We had the advantage of surprise and the ground was well set for an ambush. We must have killed half a dozen of them and wounded others. I think they took us for a formidable number because we chased them half way back to Cromwell's army.'

'Was that when you were shot at?'

Stephen nodded. 'But not by them. Massey's men had hoped to reach a rendezvous, and we only just escaped being ambushed in our turn. But escape we did, thank God.'

While he was talking, Stephen's weariness fell away; he was speaking now with an infectious enthusiasm, and for the first time Dolores glimpsed the possibility that fighting might sometimes be a kind of adventure.

She turned away in disgust. 'Will Dower returned this morning and was looking for you. He came three times this evening. We could not imagine what had detained you.'

'I'll see him in the morning. I'm sure his news can wait.' He spoke as soothingly as he could before asking gently, 'Is your grandmother any better today?'

She rose to her feet. 'No, she will not get better. But she's no worse either. She wanted to see Philip this evening.' She could not imagine why she had bothered to mention this detail.

'Philip?'

'Yes. She said he reminds her of my father. I believe my father was her favourite.' As she spoke, Dolores found that her eyes were suddenly and inexplicably filled with tears.

'I'm sorry.'

She rounded on him. 'Why should you pretend to be sorry? You've no more sense than to go and get yourself shot at and all the time I'm . . .'

She broke off. Stephen was staring at her. She had no idea at all just what she had been intending to say, she only knew that she was still angry and she was shaking. And then, all at once, Stephen understood the reason for her anger, the reason that was displayed so plainly in her dark eyes as they gazed down on him. His look of incomprehension gave way to a sudden, almost boyish smile and he said softly, 'Mistress Taverner, please don't worry about my safety.'

237

She stared at him in disbelief. 'Me? Why should I concern myself with—?' then she broke off. She was still staring at him as a glow of colour spread slowly across her cheeks.

Stephen tried to be serious, but was unable to smother his smile. For once her anger was a cause of pure delight.

Dolores drew in a breath as if to speak, then turned and swept out of the room without another word.

Chapter 17

❧

The following morning was mild and grey – a Cornish sort of
morning, thought Stephen cheerfully as he set about his work.
Will Dower had returned with the good news that King Charles
and the soldiers who had over-wintered in Oxford had met up
with Prince Rupert's forces at Stow-on-the-Wold. The men
whom Stephen had trained so well were now part of a mighty
army of eleven thousand men, and Will Dower spoke lyrically of
the fine display they had made. However, a large parliamentary
force was known to be threatening the royalist headquarters at
Oxford. Stephen did not underestimate the task that lay ahead
of them in the coming summer, but on that particular morning
he was filled with optimism: in war, as in life, anything was
possible. The expression in Mistress Taverner's dark eyes the
night before, when she scolded him for the crime of taking
risks, had been proof indeed that miracles were possible.

His men attributed his buoyant mood to his success on the
previous day's patrol. Stephen knew they must soon expect
some kind of retaliation by Massey's men, and he impressed on
the sentries the need for increased vigilance.

Dolores was keeping a vigil of an altogether different kind.
Nona's sleeps were deepening, her moments of consciousness
were very brief and her breathing was increasingly laboured.
During the morning a constant stream of visitors called at the
house to pay their last respects; Mabs and the other servants
filed in one after the other to bid her farewell, and an expectant
hush fell over the house. That afternoon the children were
brought into her bedchamber. Beth and Philip wept freely, Beth
because she was heartbroken at the prospect of losing her

grandmother, Philip, who did not really understand, because he was infected by his sister's grief. But Dolores' heart went out to Harry, who hid his sorrow behind a show of indifference. Afterwards, she drew him to one side and said, 'There's no crime in sadness, Harry. Captain Sutton was not ashamed to weep when his friend Jack was dying.'

Harry merely scuffed the toe of his boot against the edge of a chest and said flatly, 'Father would not cry. I'm going to ride Bonnet, now. You'd better look after Beth and Pip,' and he strode out, whistling.

Jinny hardly left the old woman's bedside. Although the girl obviously delighted in the role of nurse, Dolores was concerned that she was making too heavy an investment of affection when the result was sure to be heartache. Later that afternoon she said to her, as gently as she could, 'You know Nona is dying, don't you?'

'Yes, ma'am.' Jinny's pale eyes looked up at her imploringly, 'My grandmother was like this at the end. She was the only one who was ever kind to me. I like helping the old lady now. Please don't send me away.'

'Very well, we'll take turns watching her.'

That evening Dolores was the first to fall asleep on the little truckle bed. She had heard the door of Captain Sutton's room close and as always she felt both reassured and somehow unsettled by knowing he was in the house. Outside, a fine rain had begun to fall and its gentle patter muffled the rasping sound of Nona's breath. But, despite her weariness, Dolores' sleep was shallow and, as usual, shot through with poisonous dreams. She awoke suddenly to find Jinny's face, anxious in the candleshine and very close to her own.

'Are you all right, ma'am? You've been talking and saying all sorts.'

'Talking?' Dolores found her mouth was suddenly dry with fear.

'Yes, ma'am.'

She tried to recollect the substance of her dreams, but even as she clutched at them, they evaporated into air. 'Did you hear anything – in particular?' She tried to make the question sound unimportant, but her voice emerged taut with strain.

'Just something about hiding a knife and telling people to go away. It didn't make much sense, but then, dreams are a funny old jumble of stuff, aren't they?'

Dolores said casually, 'I've never paid them much heed.'

'I'm frightened of mine. Major Darbier shouted at me and my brothers once and the next night I dreamed I killed him. And then two days later, there he was, murdered, just like in my dream. It almost felt as if it was my dream that made it happen.'

Suddenly Dolores found she was icy cold. Was it possible this child had guessed the real circumstances of the major's death? Was her apparently innocent chatter intended to elicit some kind of confession? Her face was devoid of artifice. Perhaps Jinny was after all genuinely troubled by the thought that her dreams could have played some part in the major's death.

Dolores said coolly, 'You might have had a premonition.'

'What's that?'

'It's when you know something before it takes place.'

Jinny nodded. 'My grandmother used to have those.'

'But a premonition is just a way of seeing; it can't make the future happen. So you need not trouble yourself about Major Darbier's death.'

'That's good. I'd not want murder on my conscience.'

Dolores shuddered. 'No,' she said.

'I still can't understand how Tully got free to do the killing, though. The soldier swore he'd tied him firmly.'

'Jinny, you're a hopeless chatterbox. It's your turn to rest now. I'll watch Nona for a while.'

'Yes ma'am.'

Jinny stretched out on the small bed and in a few minutes she seemed to be asleep. Dolores could not shake off the notion that Jinny had had some hidden motive for talking as she did. What gossip might the child have heard about the major's death? Had Dolores betrayed her own guilt while she was sleeping? How would she ever again be able to rest peacefully when there was the chance that she herself might reveal her secret to the world? What could she have said to arouse the child's suspicions? She examined Jinny's face carefully in the candlelight, and for the first time thought she detected a hint of cunning in the twist of her mouth.

Then Nona breathed in a long rasping breath and Dolores forgot her own worries and went to sit by her bedside. She had told Jinny earlier in the day that Nona was dying, but she had not really believed it herself until this moment. It was such an exquisitely wizened and precious face that lay now against the pillow, a face that displayed the particular beauty of great age.

241

She felt grief, not for Nona herself, who was so ready to go, but for herself and the children, because soon they would be more alone than ever. She smoothed Nona's white hair from her forehead and lifted the frail hand to rest it against her cheek.

'I shall miss you, Nona,' she spoke in a low voice, 'I could never have survived it all alone.'

Nona's eyelids fluttered and she gazed up into her face. 'Dolores?'

'I'm here.'

So faintly that it was barely perceptible, Nona smiled. There was silence, a vast and solemn silence, with only the quietness of the rain falling in the still night air. Dolores' eyes were brimming with tears as she turned Nona's fragile hand and kissed the palm.

'Thank you, Nona . . .'

From far off came a sound that could have been a musket firing. Dolores heard it, then another and another, but the staccato bursts were no part of the huge tranquillity in which she felt herself enfolded. Nona drew in a long, harsh breath. And then, as if their din was coming from another world, the church bells began to ring out their warning and the musket shots were suddenly come very close indeed.

Jinny sat bolt upright. 'What is it? What is happening?'

'Hush, Jinny, Nona is awake. Don't alarm her.'

'But the bells—!'

The firing had reached the end of the street. In the attics Mabs and Ellen had awoken and were shrieking in terror; feet clattered on the stairs; there were hoofbeats pounding on the road. All over the town, soldiers were tumbling from their billets and hurrying to repulse the attack. Dolores heard every smallest sound, but it was as if the commotion was happening to someone else in another time and place entirely. As if all the events were taking place on a distant stage, she heard the front door slam shut and Captain Sutton's voice roaring out orders to his men as the enemy riders burst upon them. And Nona's hand, light as a withered leaf, rested still against her cheek and the calm of the old woman's dying flowed all around her.

Without turning, she said to Jinny, 'It's time now, Jinny. Wake the children and bring them here. Then tell Mabs and the others to stay safe in the kitchen until the danger has passed. Go quickly now.'

Jinny hurried from the room. Dolores heard her passing on

the instructions to the terrified servants.

The ancient face smiled up at her. 'We've come a long way, haven't we?' she murmured.

Dolores nodded, and a single tear rolled down her cheek. She sniffed.

'I'm going back,' said Nona.

Musket fire was right outside the house now, the fighting must be taking place just beyond their gate. A horse screamed horribly as it was hit, and men were shouting, and crying out in pain. Then a stray musket shot shattered a downstairs window. There was an explosion of splintering glass, Ellen began screaming and Harry and Beth burst into the bedchamber.

'What's happening?'

'I'm frightened!'

Even Harry allowed Dolores to put her arm around his shoulders as she drew them to their grandmother's bedside. 'Sit here, crouch down, we'll stay with Nona. We're safe enough, never worry. See how peaceful Nona is.'

The two children, huddled by the bed, regarded Nona with awe. She was pausing for so long between breaths that Beth kept thinking, 'Now, surely she has died,' and then the lungs filled one more time. Harry could not tear his eyes away: he was watching to see if there was a precise moment when a living person became a corpse. Would he see her soul leave her body? How could one be sure?

Nona seemed to be aware of their presence. 'Good children,' she whispered. Gradually the peace of Nona's dying moments transmitted itself to them also, and they sat very still and unafraid while outside the house the firing and shouting continued more furiously than before and the sky began to lighten with the coming dawn. Only when an especially loud shot burst out just beneath their window did Beth give a little start of fear. Then she smiled uncertainly at her mother.

'Nona doesn't hear it any more, does she?'

Dolores shook her head.

Nona was still smiling, a last echo of her old mischievous chuckle. Then she murmured, 'I'm taking the child with me.'

Now it was Harry's turn to appeal to his mother. 'Why did she say that?'

'Her mind must be wandering.'

Nona's next breath was a long time in coming. Inside the room there was utter stillness while from the street came the sound of horses' hooves galloping away, musket shot growing fainter. The church bells ceased their ringing and an eerie silence descended on the town.

Then Beth turned to her mother and asked, 'Where's Pip?'

Her gentle question was more shattering than any musket shot. Dolores looked around her in bewilderment.

'I sent Jinny to fetch him.'

'Maybe he's sleeping,' Harry attempted reassurance, 'He'll be furious at missing the excitement!'

But Dolores was already on her feet. 'Quick, tell the servants. Find him!'

Panic was hammering in her ears as Dolores sped across the landing to Philip's bedchamber. When she saw the empty bed she let out a wail of despair and raced to the window. The aftermath of the attack was plainly visible in the dawn light: a couple of horses lay dead just beyond their gate, while, by the blackened remains of Mother Crew's house, O'Rourke and another man were helping a wounded soldier to his feet. But no Philip, no Philip anywhere.

'No!' she groaned, 'Dear God, no. Not Philip!'

As she emerged from the bedchamber she encountered Mabs, still in her shift and with her eyes streaming with tears. 'Oh Mistress Taverner, he must have slipped out while no one was looking. I never saw him go, no one saw him, we would have stopped him. The men are gone now to hunt, but oh, if he's hurt—!'

'Be quiet, you fool!' Dolores was incandescent with rage, 'Find him! Don't stand there wailing, look!'

Mabs burst into loud sobbing and shuffled down the stairs. The whole house was in uproar. An injured man had been carried into the kitchen, but no one paid him any heed as panic for the missing child spread like summer fire. Harry had struggled into his breeches and was hunting through the stables, Beth, utterly bewildered, sank down on a chest on the landing and stayed there, too appalled to move. Even the baby had awoken and was howling for his wet nurse, who had fled from the house in terror.

Borne on a red tide of rage, Dolores swept back into the bedchamber where Nona was lying.

'What have you done with him?' She caught hold of the old woman by the shoulders and began shaking her, 'Where is he?

You can't take him with you, you can't! I won't let you!'

Beth had followed her into the room and stood sobbing by the door.

'Don't hurt Nona,' she begged, 'she's dying.'

At that moment her mother seemed to Beth utterly transformed. Her face contorted with grief, she arched over the old woman like a black angel of death and poured out a torrent of rage.

From below came a high pitched scream, rapid footsteps on the stairs and then Beth was thrust aside and a man's voice exclaimed, 'Mistress Taverner, have you taken leave of your senses?'

It was Stephen, angrier than anyone had ever seen him in his life before. He was dressed only in his shirt and breeches and boots, had not even had time to buckle on his sword or take his hat. Blood was flowing from a wound to his shoulder and there was blood on his hands, but Dolores saw none of this, only that he had Philip – Philip still barefoot and in his nightclothes, but very much alive and well – borne aloft in his strong arms.

She let out a sob of relief and let Nona's body fall back on the bed.

Stephen exclaimed angrily, 'He could have been killed. Can't you keep watch over one small child?'

Unable to speak, Dolores snatched Philip and hugged him so tightly that the boy began to feel frightened for the first time. He struggled and whimpered slightly, but Dolores wanted never to let him go.

'He could have been trampled by the horses,' said Stephen, still breathing heavily, 'If I hadn't noticed him when I did . . . why weren't you tending him yourself instead of attacking the old woman?'

Dolores looked up at him over the top of Philip's crow-dark hair; her eyes were ringed with dark shadows of shock. She said in a voice choking with dry sobs, 'Nona said she was taking the child . . . I thought she meant to have Philip . . . I was so angry and frightened, it was a kind of madness . . . if I lost Philip I would die . . .'

Stephen went over to the bed and stood for a few moments, looking down at the old woman, before pushing back a strand of grey hair and adjusting the coverlet. 'Your grandmother's dead,' he said at length, 'Didn't you know?'

Still holding Philip in a tight embrace, Dolores sank down in a low chair. Tears were covering her cheeks, but she made no sound.

Stephen's anger was ebbing fast. The sight of the elf-like child, ghostly in his cambric shift, dodging through the hooves of the enemy horses, had shaken him with a sense of horror he had thought himself past feeling. War tortured you with so many tragedies and disasters and then, just when you believed you had experienced them all, it found another that struck you to the marrow: it produced a child slippery as quicksilver who escaped his mother's vigilance because her grandmother was dying and flung himself into the thick of an enemy attack.

Stephen went to the window. The clouds that had brought rain in the night were rolling away, the sun was risen and the wide street was striped with shadow. Already men were attaching muddy ropes to the two dead horses to drag them to the shambles. Half a dozen hungry dogs edged round the scene and waited to lap up the spilled blood before it soaked into the earth.

He turned. Mistress Taverner was still holding the child as a drowning mariner clings to a fragment of wreckage. The last of Stephen's anger evaporated when he saw the anguish in her eyes. He crossed the room, stooped down and began prizing her fingers from their desperate grip.

'The danger is past,' he said, 'Massey's men will be half way back to Gloucester by now. Their honour is satisfied and they've paid in kind for the damage we did them. Let him go now.'

Philip was squirming, but Dolores did not release her grip.

'Your boy is safe,' Stephen spoke firmly.

All at once Dolores allowed her hands to drop to her sides. Philip scrambled down off her knees and was heading for the door, when Stephen caught him by the shoulders.

'Not so fast,' he said, 'Listen to me first. You will *never* run off alone like that again, do you understand? If I ever hear you've disobeyed, you'll have to answer to me. Is that clear?'

Perhaps because Stephen addressed him in the tone of voice he reserved for particularly troublesome young recruits, Philip was, for the moment at least, overawed, and he nodded a vague promise to be good in future. Dolores followed the child with her eyes as he thankfully left the room, then she rose to her feet and went across to the bed. For a while she gazed down in silence on her grandmother's face.

'Nona is dead,' she said simply, 'I thought she meant to take

246

Philip. I could not have borne to lose him.'

Stephen, watching, did not know what to say.

She sat down on the edge of the bed and smiled an odd little smile. 'It's strange, isn't it,' she said, 'Nona has always comforted us at times like this. And now, of course, we need her more than ever before, and there is no one – ' Her voice broke before she could finish, and she looked away to hide her tears.

Stephen took a step towards her, and then stopped. They had both forgotten Beth who had stood in shocked silence by the door ever since Stephen came in with Pip. Now, still dressed in her nightshift, with her hair all tousled and her face grubby with tears, she moved towards the empty space in front of the window. She was gazing fixedly at her mother as she began to murmur a few stray fragments of song and shuffled inexpertly with her feet. Then she seemed to gain her confidence: she threw back her head and shoulders, and arched her spine as she had seen the two women do so often in the past. Her song increased in strength, and though the words themselves made no sense, being simply approximations of what she had heard, the tune and rhythm were unmistakable.

Dolores had been watching, too surprised to move, but suddenly she sprang forward in fury. 'How dare you! You don't know, that's not your song!'

Beth flinched as her mother raised her hand to strike her, but carried on the dance, and Stephen caught Dolores by the arm in time to deflect the blow. 'Leave her be,' he commanded, 'Can't you see this is her way of helping?'

Beth's eyes were swimming with tears, but she was determined as never in her life before, and so she continued with her dance and her song, an odd little figure with her frizz of cinnamon hair catching the low rays of the morning sun as she repeated the steps she had watched so many times, but never until this moment dared to try herself.

When Stephen's fingers circled her arm, Dolores felt her anger fall away like an old, tired skin and it was all she could do to stop herself slumping against his side. She was no longer aware of the child and her garbled version of the ancient song, nor of her grandmother's corpse lying so still in the middle of the big bed. She was conscious only of the pressure of his hand against her flesh and of her own infinite sense of longing. Stephen, though neither had moved a muscle, sensed the change in her and could not tear his hand away, and so they stood side by side and watched Beth as she danced, and it seemed to them both that the touch was burning deep into their skin.

A little later that morning, when the town was beginning to return to normal and Stephen was occupied in making arrangements for the wounded, Ellen happened to go to the front garden for some sprigs of rosemary. A few seconds later, the whole house was pierced by her shriek of horror. She had all but stumbled over a thin, outstretched leg which was protruding from a clump of wormwood and bay. It was Jinny. A musket ball must have ricocheted against the front of the house and had caught her full in the chest, killing her instantly. Sergeant O'Rourke, who had been in the kitchen with the injured soldier, was recruited to carry her woeful corpse into the house.

Cary held the door open for him as he entered, and commented, 'The poor mite must have been killed while the old lady was dying, and no one thought to look for her.'

Beth, who was coming down the stairs with her mother just as the little procession filed into the house, gave a gasp of horror at Cary's words. She glanced up at Dolores in silent appeal, but saw from her mother's expression that she too had just connected Jinny's death with Nona's last words. Pip, all unawares and eager to absorb the scene, squeezed past them. Dolores took Beth's hand but had no words of comfort or explanation to offer. Both mother and daughter knew this mystery would be with them all their lives, and that they would never understand it fully.

Chapter 18

❧

Nona and Jinny were buried side by side in a quiet corner of the churchyard. Beth had insisted that Jinny be laid out in her own best green tabby. Mabs was scandalised but Dolores did not have the heart to contradict her. The church was crowded for Nona's funeral. Although no one in the town – apart from Stephen – knew her history, many people had cause to remember her with gratitude.

Jinny's funeral, the following day, was less well attended. Mother Crew sat through the service with a face like granite, and the three small boys who sat with her looked more confused than distressed. Dolores, together with her children and all the servants from the Priory House (except for the wet nurse and the baby) made up almost all the rest of the congregation. A few parishioners who remembered the burning of Mother Crew's house with shame stood towards the back of the church, as did Stephen, and one or two of his fellow soldiers. Afterwards Beth held her mother's hand very tightly as the coffin was lowered into the ground.

'Poor little mite,' said Mabs, blowing her nose, 'She was so content with her spinning, no trouble at all.'

'She must have left the house to hunt for Master Philip,' said Cary blithely, 'It's almost as though her dying was his fault.'

Beth gasped and Harry glanced first at Cary, then at his mother, with an expression of horror. 'Pip?' he said, 'How could he be to blame?'

Only Philip was unmoved by Cary's statement. He was observing with relish the number of worms there were in the earth being shovelled into the grave: coffin worms, Harry had once called them.

'Don't talk nonsense, Cary,' said Dolores sharply, 'Jinny's death was caused by the man who fired the shot, no one else.'

'Yes'm.' Cary looked subdued, but not convinced.

Mabs said, 'Could be the girl was running away. She might have thought she'd take the blame for losing Master Pip, even though it wasn't her fault. You never know.'

'Oh, quiet, all of you!' Harry burst out, 'Poor Jinny's dead, isn't she? What does it matter what she was doing, she's *dead!*' And he turned quickly and stumped across the graveyard before anyone could see how deeply the two deaths had hurt him.

Stephen was standing with the other soldiers a little distance away. He longed to go over and talk with Dolores and her children, but forced himself to remain apart. Sergeant O'Rourke went across to say a few words to Mother Crew: he had been shocked to the marrow by finding the child's body and his condolences were so obviously sincere that even Jinny's fearsome mother softened slightly in his company.

In contrast Cary was her usual serene and sunny self: when O'Rourke had finished talking with Mistress Crew, Cary left the Priory House group and went to join him. A strange friendship had sprung up between the two of them since the morning of Jinny's death: O'Rourke had been visibly distressed when he carried the little corpse into the kitchen and Cary, who never seemed to be distressed by anything much, had done what she could to comfort him. In her customary manner, her efforts consisted mainly of telling him of other children who had met with violent deaths, omitting no detail that would bring the tales to life. O'Rourke had become mesmerised by this blameless-looking girl who recounted histories so gruesome they made his stomach turn. Cary for her part was beginning to think the Irishman was probably quite handsome under all those whiskers.

By that time all who had come into contact with O'Rourke had learned that his appearance gave no indication of character. He might look like a heathen savage, but there was not a gentler man in the whole of Tilsbury. It was rumoured he had adopted a grey kitten that he had rescued from a drowning-sack, and that he carried the creature buttoned inside his doublet for warmth.

Dolores watched him now as he talked with Cary and looked miserably towards the open grave, and she thought how topsy-turvy everything was. She saw the Irish soldier's genuine unhappiness, her own young maid's apparent lack of concern. Nothing turned out as she would have expected. She had been very conscious of Nona's absence all through the day of Jinny's funeral. She was aware that in some way she did not understand she had postponed her sadness. Just now, with the war come so close and her little household depending on her, she could not afford the luxury of grief. But she knew also that however much she might miss Nona – and she would surely miss her for a very long while to come – she was able to face the future without her. Had Nona died six, or even two months earlier, she did not think she could have endured it. In some obscure way her new-found strength was connected with Major Darbier's death – but also with the Cornish captain who stood a little distance away across the graveyard, and observed her and her family with steady grey eyes.

She knew instinctively that he wanted to join her, sensed it because of the invisible net in which both were meshed. And though she held Pip by one hand, and Beth with the other, she felt a kind of incompleteness, because she, to whom her children had always been everything, wanted the soldier at her side as well. A twinge of guilt disturbed her: on the day of Jinny's funeral, and the day after her grandmother's, she ought not to be thinking of Captain Sutton.

'Take the children home,' she said to Mabs, 'be careful Cary says nothing to upset them. Heaven knows, they've had upsets in plenty in the past few weeks. I'll follow shortly.'

Delighted at the chance to spoil the children, especially as instructions to take the wind out of the bumptious Cary's sails were included, Mabs enveloped the children in warmth and promises of sweetmeats, and shuffled out of the churchyard with them.

Dolores moved across to Nona's grave: she had kept back a few sprigs of rosemary and she placed some first on the two little plots where her babies lay, and then on the freshly laid turves that covered her grandmother. Rosemary for remembrance – but she and Nona had witnessed much that was better forgotten. The events that she had recounted to Stephen had faded to pale shadow once again, and it was better that way. Random pictures of her grandmother floated to the surface of her mind: in most of them Nona was smiling. The old woman had had so many reasons for bitterness, but she had been more often cheerful than sad.

'How did you manage it?' she addressed the spirit of the old woman in Spanish, 'I wish I'd asked you before you died. What was your secret?'

It was then she realised there was no one left she could speak to in her mother tongue, and a wave of desolation passed over her. A moment or so later, there was a presence at her side, a hand lightly touching her elbow. Dolores felt the colour rush into her face as she turned to look up at Captain Sutton.

'If you'd prefer to be alone, I'll go,' he said, and stopped himself from adding, 'But you looked so sad . . .'

'No, don't go. There will be time enough for solitude.'

The last of the mourners were leaving the churchyard, and the grave-diggers were busy with their task. Dolores turned away from her grandmother's plot.

'Are you going back to the house?' asked Stephen, 'I shall walk with you.'

'I must see if I can comfort the children. There has been much to distress them recently.'

'Since the soldiers came?'

'Partly, yes. But you are not to blame for Nona's passing. She has always been a second mother to them; I think Beth will miss her most. I am worried about Beth, Captain Sutton. She always used to be such a placid child, and now the slightest thing upsets her.'

Stephen was silent for a few moments before asking, 'Do she and Harry still share a room with your maid Cary?'

'Yes, they seem to find her company reassuring.'

'Maybe so.' Stephen hesitated, not liking to interfere, then said, 'Cary is an honest girl, and good-hearted, and I know she is devoted to them all, but she does have an extremely lurid turn of mind. She may well be saying things that upset them – especially poor Beth. I know that her account of the Irish atrocities made a lasting impression on O'Rourke – and he is a hardened soldier.'

Dolores considered, frowning, then, 'How extraordinary. Do you know, Captain Sutton, I think you may be right. Just now Cary made some foolish remark about Jinny's death being all Pip's fault – that was why Harry ran off. Oh dear, and I thought they'd find her a comfort. Perhaps the medicine has done more harm than the illness it was supposed to cure.'

'It is often the case.'

She glanced at him swiftly. His expression was inscrutable as he walked along by her side, keeping at all times a careful distance between them. Impossible to read anything in that gaunt, impassive face. Dolores discovered that she wanted very much to know that his apparent coolness was superficial only: so much of her new-found strength was due to the certainty that he cared for her.

'Captain Sutton,' she began. And then she stopped. They had reached the lych-gate leading from the churchyard to the main street. A group of townsfolk had gathered near the market cross – a small group, but nonetheless one that gave off a distinct air of menace. Attention was directed towards the corner of Distaff Lane. The next moment there was a shout, and a carriage rounded the corner. As it approached the market cross the driver whipped his horses to a canter, but even so one or two of the stones that were thrown found their target. Curtains had been drawn across the windows of the carriage, and Dolores could imagine how frightened the passenger – for passenger there surely was – must be. A cloud of dust rose up behind the wheels of the carriage, and an old man spat contemptuously after it.

'What is happening?' Dolores asked, 'Surely that is Sir Diggory's carriage.'

'Have you not heard?'

'Heard what?'

Stephen realised that Dolores, quarantined from gossip by her dual bereavement, must be one of the few people in Tilsbury still ignorant of the scandal.

He said, 'I believe Mistress Rogers has decided to return to Furleys.'

'Why? Is there news of her husband?'

'No. Nothing is known. But her position in Tilsbury has become difficult, recently.'

'Why?'

'When Massey's men attacked on the night your grandmother died, one of the Irish soldiers, who had been billeted at The Lion, was seen coming from Mistress Rogers' house instead. He maintained that his rendezvous had been with her maid, Ann, but the good people of this town must have drawn a contrary conclusion.'

'I'm sure they have. Which soldier was it?'

'Lieutenant Donnelly.'

'Ah, of course. The good-looking one.'

Stephen, briefly, looked annoyed – and Dolores, for some reason, felt much better.

She said cheerfully, 'As Sir Diggory's daughter, I'm sure she'll ride out the storm. It's the Mother Crews of this world who come off worst.'

'Apparently she is more anxious about her husband's anger than her neighbours' disapproval. She told her maid that if the rebels don't kill her Tom, then her Tom will surely kill her.'

'They say he is a violent man. You seem extremely well informed on this subject, Captain.'

'As Donnelly is one of my officers, anything that concerns him is my business.'

'O'Rourke and Cary – and now Lieutenant Donnelly: your Irishmen are winning hearts all over Tilsbury. Strange, when you remember how much they've been feared. They have such a cruel reputation, but they seem no worse than others, perhaps better in some ways.'

'Are you revising your opinion of soldiers in general, Mistress Taverner?'

She looked straight ahead, but said nothing.

Stephen went on, 'They have earned their reputation. Do not be deceived: they are ruthless fighters. But then, they have to be. We are fighting for a cause, a principle – the Irish are fighting for survival. If Parliament wins it will be bad enough in this country, God knows, but ten times worse in Ireland. They give no quarter because they know they can expect none. As often as not they are hanged as common criminals when captured by the rebels . . . I apologise, I did not mean to distress you. My choice of subject matter is as unfortunate as young Cary's, considering you are returning from a funeral. I'll leave you.' They had reached the front gate of the Priory House. 'There are a number of new recruits recently come from Wales and I must decide whether to send them at once to join His Majesty's army or whether they need more training before they are fit. Good day, Mistress Taverner.'

Stephen had made up the excuse about the new recruits at the last moment. The conversation with Dolores – their first since Nona's death – had left him with an intense desire to wear himself out with hard work. Having seen to the new recruits and judged that they needed a fortnight's training at the least, he had his horse saddled and, taking only a couple of men with him, rode off at a fast pace on the pretext of checking some pike-heads which were being produced in a nearby village. His companions noticed that he was preoccupied, and they wondered privately if he had had some adverse news concerning the war which had been kept from them. The truth was very different: never had martial thoughts been further from his mind.

It had been a form of torture to have to walk beside Mistress Taverner – always at a suitable distance – and talk to her of the Irishmen, of her servants and children, of Mistress Rogers' misfortunes, and never to be able to say a word of the one thing that was uppermost in his thoughts. Not even to be able to betray his feelings with a look. Stephen was a poor liar and a disastrous actor, and he was finding that these dubious skills did not grow any easier with practice. It had been difficult enough in the days following his return from Oxford, but then he had been outraged by her contempt for his motives, and spurred on by a determination to make her see that she had been wrong. But since the evening after his skirmish with the enemy patrols, when he had seen, from her anxiety over his safety, that she was beginning to return his feelings, the charade was grown impossible.

Loving her as he did, he was surprised to discover that knowing she cared for him only increased his anguish. The bald truth was that there could be no future for them: she was a married woman and he a soldier who might be ordered to leave at any moment. And Mistress Taverner had no Furleys to retreat to if her reputation was ever compromised. Corinna Rogers was a woman who calculated the risks when she took them and could look after herself as well as any woman could. Mistress Taverner, however, was an outsider, and totally dependent on the goodwill of others.

But there were more compelling reasons why Stephen was beginning to consider asking to be replaced as commander of the Tilsbury garrison. He was a man of stubborn pride, and having been once accused of helping her in order to further his own selfish ends, he had vowed never to expose himself to such an accusation again. The fact of Darbier's death and its aftermath now seemed an impossible barrier between them: any hint from him of how he felt could always be regarded as a request that the account between them be settled. That was a risk he would never take, no matter that he saw an answering love in her eyes.

Even this constraint might have been tolerable but for the uncertainties of war: the news that trickled in concerning the progress of the fighting told of two massive armies which were gathering strength for what must surely be the battle of all and for all. Sooner or later the time would come for him to leave Tilsbury, in victory or defeat, and the certainty of impending separation made his enforced silence a greater agony.

All these thoughts were going through Stephen's mind as he examined the new pikeheads, listened to complaints about shortages, and the village people's anxieties about the coming hay-making and harvest. Several times he made up his mind to leave Tilsbury at the first opportunity – only to reflect bitterly that this was likely to be another of those occasions when the medicine is more bitter than the disease it seeks to cure.

When Dolores went into the Priory House she was told that Harry and Philip were in the orchard with Bonnet, and that Gerard the groom was keeping an eye on them. Going to the children's bedchamber, she looked out of the window. Beyond the stable-yard and her garden, the orchard was a pale sea of blossom. In fact everywhere one looked in Tilsbury in this May month there was blossom – apple and pear and plum – and the hedgerows were brim full of hawthorn and guelder-rose and the first creamy heads of elder. She had observed this event many times before, and had welcomed it as a sign that the hated winter cold was over, but she had always compared it unfavourably with the perfumed orange groves of her earliest memories. Now, for the first time, as she looked out of her upstairs window, she saw that it was beautiful. Tilsbury, decked out in its May-time finery of blossom and bluebells and young green leaves, was a huddle of pale stone in a frothing sea of flowers. How was it that her eyes had observed this annual miracle so many times before, yet she had remained impervious to the beauty lying all around?

She found Beth eventually, pulling rhubarb with Mabs – or rather, Beth was standing, thumb in mouth, and watching while Mabs hauled out the fresh pink stems, lopped off their tops with a short knife and laid them in a basket. For a moment Dolores could neither move nor speak. She never saw the flash of a knife these days, but she was reminded of the feel of the little stiletto against her palm as she drove it into the major's body.

'Beth!' she called, wondering, as they turned to face her, that they did not recoil in horror from the murderess, 'Come inside, Beth, I need your help.'

Beth removed her thumb from her mouth, wiped it dry on her skirt, and came eagerly enough to join her mother. But her eyes were ringed with shadow: Dolores wondered if Captain Sutton's diagnosis was right, or whether it was simply that four deaths in the household in such a short space of time had been more than even placid Beth could cope with.

'Here,' she said, pushing open the door of her bedchamber, 'My embroidery wools have become all of a tangle and no one is as good as you at sorting them out. I thought to start a new piece of work, now the baby is with his nurse, but this muddle has quite defeated me.'

Beth delighted in her mother's basket of embroidery wools and she set to work busily, while Dolores, who had always found that talk flowed more freely when the hands were occupied, picked up a piece of plain sewing.

After a little while she said, 'It was good of you to give your green tabby for Jinny to be buried in, Beth.'

The child nodded. All her attention seemed to be absorbed in separating an indigo thread from a tangle of tawny reds and browns, but then she said in a dry voice, 'It wasn't really Pip that killed her, was it?'

'Heavens no. Can you imagine little Pip killing anyone? Don't trouble your head trying to work out the causes of these things, Beth, only our Lord knows that.'

'I suppose so.'

'Does Cary ever talk to you in the evenings ... about the fighting, or accidents?'

Beth nodded, but said nothing. She had a sudden fear that to talk might get Cary into trouble.

Dolores continued evenly, 'Cary is a good girl, and a hard worker. I intend to keep her with us for a long time. But I think perhaps sometimes her tongue runs away with her. Maybe it is time she went back to join Mabs in the attic. What do you think, little Bee?'

Suddenly Beth found the coloured tangle had become a blur. As the first tear spilled out and rolled down her cheek she said, 'It's not fair, the things that happen, they shouldn't be so cruel.'

'I know,' Dolores laid down her work and waited, 'The world can be a terrible place.'

'All those poor cats and dogs with the match cord tied round their bellies burning to death, and the Irishman having his insides dragged out and just because he loved his country, and the poor Grey Lady all broken and ravished and—'

Dolores swooped Beth in her arms as the child broke down and sobbed against her shoulder. 'And then poor Jinny with the musket ball in her chest and Jack, and now Nona's gone, and Father's away and the fighting never stops and I'm afraid we'll all be killed and there'll be no one left, and what if anything happened to *you*!'

'Hush now, hush.' Dolores hugged her and rocked her back and forth as she had done when Beth was a baby. 'I'm not planning to leave you, little Bee, we'll see this war out, don't you worry.' And she marvelled at the strength she felt as she held the weeping child, strength enough and to spare. In that moment she understood how the necessity to care for her granddaughter had helped Nona to survive the horror of the Würzburg massacre.

After a while, as Beth's sobs diminished to a weary snuffle, Dolores began to sing to her, as if she were still a baby, a lullaby about an old woman who is content in spite of her misfortunes, because once she was young and lay in the arms of her lover. With a little sigh of satisfaction, Beth curled up in her mother's lap and closed her eyes.

'Do you want to rest now, or shall we dance together?'

Beth was wide awake at once. 'Dance?'

'Why not? It will be our secret.'

Beth scrambled to her feet and shook out her skirts.

'Here, watch what I do and you will soon pick it up. You already understand the rhythms, I could tell that when you danced the day Nona died.'

'When Captain Sutton watched me?'

'Never mind about him. Look, your head needs to be very high, make yourself as tall as you can, that's right. Now we move our feet like this, follow the song as best you can, later I shall tell you what the words mean.'

So they began. Beth had watched the dance, and felt its rhythms, so many times before that she moved with an instinctive grace. Dolores, seeing the child's tear-streaked face so absorbed in the melody and actions, was reminded of her sister Juana, tears of homesickness on her cheeks as they danced together in their shabby Flanders lodgings: Juana, so darkly beautiful, would seem to have nothing at all in common with her pale and homespun niece, and yet Dolores saw now there was an unmistakable similarity, a combination of gentleness and determination. Like Juana, Beth was shy with strangers, utterly devoted to those she loved. Suddenly Dolores was aware of the unbroken thread that linked all those she had once loved with those she loved still: her little Philip who had reminded Nona so vividly of his Spanish grandfather, and now this little English girl with the blunt features and cloud of red-brown hair who seemed to be moving with the gentle ease inherited from the young aunt she would never know. And instead of sorrow, she felt a powerful joy.

The words of the funeral service came back to her: 'In the midst of life, we are in death'. But now Dolores felt the opposite was equally true. With the war coming ever closer, and death a frequent visitor in her home, she found she was not miserable and afraid, as she would have expected, but more intensely alive than at any point since she came to England. The past was sadness and loss, the future impossible to guess, and all that mattered was this present moment, the child dancing at her side, the music pulsing through her body, while outside the countryside was decked like a bride in the white May-time lace of blossom and wild flowers.

It was late when Stephen returned, and all the members of the household had long since retired to their beds. Cary was once again settled in the attic with Mabs and Ellen. Though on summer nights the attic rooms were often stuffy, she was glad of the change, since she calculated it would now be easier to spend these light evenings walking and talking with Sergeant O'Rourke. Only Dolores had found it impossible to sleep. She had lain down for a while with Beth, whom she had moved into her own wide bed, but once she knew the child was sleeping peacefully, a strange restlessness took hold of her. She had no need of a candle, since the moon was near the full, as she went to the room now shared by Harry and Philip. She had warned Harry that on no account was he to repeat a single one of Cary's horrendous stories, but Philip had been so jubilant at moving in with his older brother that he had been a long time settling. But now both the boys were fast asleep, Harry still with a frown creasing his forehead – even at rest he seemed to worry – while Philip lay sprawled across the bed. In Nona's old room the wet nurse, Cary's sister Joan, slept with her own baby and Robert.

Dolores, closing the door of their room quietly behind her, reflected that the household had shifted beds and rooms more frequently in the previous two months than in all the years she had lived there before.

Horse's hooves clipping the hard ground beside the house. An irregular, lop-sided rhythm. Dolores sped down the stairs to the kitchen, where she lit a candle from the embers of the day's fire. The scullion, snoring in his corner, did not stir.

When Stephen came in by the back door, he saw Dolores standing in the middle of the large kitchen; she was holding the candle at shoulder height, and this time, her expression was far from cross.

'You had an accident?'

'My mare went lame about five miles from here, so I sent the men back ahead of me.'

'Are you hurt?'

'No. She fell as we were coming down a rough slope. Her legs are badly grazed but your man Gerard says she will be recovered in a fortnight.'

'You should have taken a horse from one of your men.'

'So they said. But I preferred to walk.' The truth was that Stephen had been glad of the long walk home alone and in the moonlight: it had given him the opportunity to reach his decision.

'Have you eaten?'

'No. But I have a gift for Mabs.' He set a brace of hares down on the table.

Dolores smiled. 'A better target for your pistols than rebel soldiers.'

'I'd never hit one with a pistol.' Stephen was not smiling. 'A sling is what we use in our part of Cornwall. I learned the knack as a boy.'

While Dolores was hanging the animals out of reach of hungry cats and dogs she said, 'Mabs will be delighted. I'll bring you wine and food.' She shook the scullion into reluctant wakefulness with orders to draw the hares ready for cooking the next day.

'Thank you, Mistress Taverner,' said Stephen, but his spirits sank. So much easier to say what must now be said if she had maintained her former hostility.

But Dolores was far from hostile as she set food and drink down on the table in the dining hall, lit the candles and poured them each a glass of wine. Since Stephen seemed disinclined to talk she said, 'You were right about my girl Cary: she had been filling the children's heads with all sorts of horrors – even a version of the Grey Lady legend which spared no details. I have sent her back to the attics and taken Beth into my own room. I hope she will soon be her old self again.'

Stephen nodded, but said nothing. Nor did he look at her. He was frowning as he took a long drink of wine.

Dolores went on, 'If so, it will be thanks to you, Captain Sutton.'

He set down his glass, and his hand, closed into a fist, rested on the table.

'Mistress Taverner,' he began, 'I intend to ask to be relieved as garrison commander here so I may join His Majesty's main army. I am sure there is no shortage of officers who would be happy to replace me. I hope to leave Tilsbury within the week.'

'Why?'

Stephen was staring at his fist. 'It is likely that this summer's campaign will be decisive, one way or the other. I feel that I can best serve His Majesty if I—'

'Save that version for your commanding officer, Captain Sutton. I want to hear the truth.'

He stood up abruptly and went to stand by the window. Looking out into the darkness, he said, 'The situation here has become difficult. No, not difficult – impossible.'

'Impossible? Why? You are comfortable in this house, are you not? The town's defences are all well prepared. You have no problems with your men. Most of the local people have become reconciled to having soldiers here.' She gave a little laugh. 'Why, Captain Sutton, even I have ceased to complain. Did you not notice?'

'Yes.'

'So why this talk of leaving?'

'I must go sooner or later. Sometimes sooner is . . . easier.'

'But what of the people here, do you not care about them?' Dolores' voice betrayed her growing agitation. 'They have grown used to you. A new garrison commander might not be so scrupulous. Have you considered that?'

He nodded. 'Believe me, Mistress Taverner, I have considered everything.'

'Everything?'

'Yes.'

'Is it—' she hesitated, then, 'Is it perhaps because of Major Darbier that you wish to leave? Yes, yes, I know we have never spoken of it before, but perhaps it is important. You did me a great kindness, Captain, one I can never forget, but perhaps, because you helped me, it now preys on your conscience and—'

'No. My conscience is clear.'

'So you will not go back on your promise—?'

'Mistress Taverner, you are unfair. Nothing will ever make me betray your secret. Our secret. You must endeavour to trust me. If you are able.'

'But that's just it, Captain Sutton. I do trust you.' The words were softly spoken, but carried a weight of meaning.

'Then trust that I know what I am doing now.'

With a rustle of taffeta skirts, Dolores moved across the room to stand beside him. 'And if you are wrong?' she asked.

'I have given the matter much thought,' he said stubbornly, still looking through the window, 'I believe it is best to quit this place.'

'And me?'

A long silence, then, 'Yes. And you.'

'What if I told you I wanted you to stay?'

A muscle flickered in Stephen's cheek. 'It would make no difference. We both know I must leave . . . in the end.'

'Much may happen before the end.'

He glanced at her swiftly, then just as swiftly, looked away. He said, 'I understand that you are concerned for the safety of your family and your home. Some of our commanders have a bad reputation, but I will make sure my replacement is a man of honour.'

'Tst. I am not interested in your replacement.'

'Then I regret it, but still—'

She touched his hand. 'Captain Sutton, is it truly your wish to leave this house?'

'My wishes are of no importance.'

'No? So what of mine, Captain Sutton, does that count for nothing?' Her voice began to rise in anger. 'You come into my home, you win the affection of my children, you teach me to trust you, and then you tell me that you are leaving, and all on a selfish whim.'

In black misery Stephen turned away and moved towards the door. 'I am sorry if my decision causes you distress,' he said, 'But my mind is made up.'

'Stop!' She caught hold of his sleeve. 'You cannot go now. You cannot just leave me.'

He stopped. 'Why are you making this so difficult, Mistress Taverner? I know you are concerned for the safety of your family, but another soldier will protect this town at least as well as I can – perhaps better. My attacks on Massey have put Tilsbury at risk – poor Jinny's death is proof of that. I can give you no guarantees.'

'I do not want guarantees.'

'What then?'

She stared at him.

'What is it, Mistress Taverner?' he repeated, almost angrily. 'What is it you want from me?'

'I . . . I do not know. I never thought. But I don't want you to go. I know I don't want to lose you, not yet.'

'What, then?'

She closed her eyes briefly, and then the answer came to her, and almost took her breath away. 'I want you to hold me,' she said, and suddenly her eyes were brimming with tears. 'I don't want to be alone, not now, not tonight. Nona has gone and . . . I don't want you to leave me too, not yet.'

Stephen did not move a muscle. He said, 'Mistress Taverner, you have had a distressing day. I chose the wrong moment to tell you of my decision and I apologise. We can speak of this again in the morning and—'

But she interrupted him. Suddenly decisive, she wiped away her tears and, with an odd little smile, she reached her hands up to his face and kissed him very deliberately on the lips. She was breathing rapidly. 'Does that answer your question, Captain?'

Stephen's hands were clenched at his side, but his face betrayed no emotion. He said, 'You are distraught, Mistress Taverner, you would not be acting this way otherwise.' Once before, he had taken advantage of her temporary weakness and he would never permit himself to make the same mistake again. He continued, 'In a day or so you will come to realise that my departure is the only way.'

'No, I do not want you to go.'

Stephen hesitated. The memory of her counterfeit passion lodged like a stone in his chest. He said bleakly, 'You fear for your family's safety. Very well then, if it means so much to you, I will stay here as long as I am needed, or until I am ordered to leave. You do not need to offer . . . inducements.'

She frowned. 'What are you saying?'

'Only that I expect nothing in return. I do it because I care for you—'

'How much?'

He sighed. 'You must know, Mistress Taverner, that I love you.'

'And do you desire me also?'

'Yes.'

'Then why will you not kiss me?'

'I told you, I will help you and your family without that. I will stay in Tilsbury.' He turned away and flung himself down in the chair by the fire. Keeping his face turned from her, he said in a low voice, 'I have given you my word, Mistress Taverner, please trust me.'

Dolores was frowning, then all at once her expression shifted from bewilderment to quick disgust. 'Now I begin to understand. I should not blame you for being suspicious, it is only what I deserve. Captain Sutton, I admit that I have been blind and foolish in the past, but now it is surely your turn. The night that your major died, I thought that you and I could make a bargain. I did not understand then that what you were offering was freely given. Well, Captain, and so is this—'

She crossed the room to stand in front of him. He raised his eyes to gaze at her. Slowly, and very deliberately, she bent down and kissed first his forehead, then his lips. She was trembling.

Controlling himself with a supreme effort, Stephen said, 'I cannot allow you to do this. The risk for you is too great and—'

But she was smiling, an odd smile. Some ugly chain that had kept her bound to Josiah was being broken, and she felt a kind of exultation.

'No one will ever know,' she said. 'This is just another of our secrets. You do not have to protect me, not any more.'

'I cannot let you do this,' said Stephen again.

'Why not? Are you still angry, because of the last time?'

'Of course not.'

'Then put your arms around me. Hold me.'

This time, when she kissed him, Stephen could no longer resist. With a groan he put his arms around her and held her tightly. 'Oh, my love,' he breathed.

Dolores seemed to crumple in his arms. He saw that her face was bathed in tears.

'I won't leave you,' he said and kissed her very gently, 'Not while you still want me here.'

She drew away from him and fussed for a moment with her hair, then said, 'Not here, it is not safe, the scullion might come in or . . . and I had forgotten your long day. Finish your meal, Captain. I shall not disturb you any more. We should make a bargain together now, a pact: that we will never make bargains with each other again. Is that a good idea? In the morning, if you still wish to leave Tilsbury, I shall not attempt to dissuade you. But for tonight, I suggest that you leave the door to your bedchamber unlocked.'

Chapter 19

❧

Stephen had watched the moon travel some distance across the night sky, before he heard the gentle 'click' of his bedchamber door opening.

Alone in her room, Dolores had felt such a turmoil of conflicting emotions that she half-wondered if she might be losing her mind. When she considered the scene that had just taken place with Stephen, a wave of giddiness swept over her. How could she have been so reckless? A long time ago, so it seemed, she had told him there are always reasons . . . but just for the moment she had no idea what her own motives might be. Since Nona's death she had experienced an appalling ache of loneliness . . . but then, maybe the loneliness had always been there and she had simply been unaware of it until the moment when Stephen caught her by the wrist and they watched Beth dance, and she had barely been able to stop herself from falling into his arms. It seemed incredible, but it was true, that she who had always been so disgusted by the touch of a man, wanted to feel Stephen's body against her own.

There were other, more practical reasons. She wanted to make sure he would never again talk of leaving her and her children unprotected while Tilsbury was full of soldiers – but he had already told her he would remain anyway, and she knew he would never go back on his word. In part, too, her invitation had been an act of defiance: though Josiah must never know of her crime, she had tasted a new kind of freedom when she kissed Stephen.

As she paced her bedchamber and pondered her next move, Dolores was careful not to go so far as to consider the details of what she was offering. If she could have won Stephen's love by making him her brother, she would have done so, but that was impossible. She wanted to forge a link between them stronger than mere friendship, and knew no other way of doing it. The sexual act – what the soldiers had done to the women in the convent at Würzburg, what she and Josiah had done over the years – had always revolted her, and even now she avoided contemplating it. But since Stephen returned from Oxford, Dolores had gradually come to realise that the feeling she had for him was unlike anything she had experienced before.

She knew that Stephen loved her. She did not think that she loved him, but she trusted him, and cared for him. He was holding out a glimpse of a new kind of happiness, the gift of being truly loved. Not with Josiah's kind of love, jealous and constricting, but with something else, something unknown. So why hold back? There had been safety in the familiar and the dull. Great happiness brings the risk of great sorrow. She had learned to survive on her diet of crumbs: would she be able to again, when the time came?

For over an hour she debated with herself, yet in the end, there was no real choice. She was not a coward, far from it, but for years she had lived like one. Josiah's little Doll would never in a hundred years have done what she was about to do. She had felt herself to be reborn after Darbier's murder; this, then, was the time to prove it.

As she passed into his bedchamber, she saw Stephen outlined against the paler darkness of the window. He was on the window-seat, one leg bent, his left arm resting loosely upon his knee. He had been attempting, with notable lack of success, to convince himself that he was glad Mistress Taverner had changed her mind. He turned at once.

'Stephen—'

He hesitated only for an instant before crossing the room slowly to stand in front of her. Taking hold of her hands in his he raised them to his lips and the shawl fell from her shoulders. 'I thought you had changed your mind.'

'Nearly,' she said, 'I nearly did.'

They stared at each other for a few moments in the moonlight. Stephen felt suddenly awkward, and unsure.

She said, 'Hold me, Stephen, I want you to love me.'

He hesitated, forcing himself to say, 'Are you sure of this.

268

Dolores? You know, don't you, that I will remain in Tilsbury as long as you want me to, whatever happens between us.'

'I know that.'

He touched her hair, the side of her face, 'Then I'm glad.' She could see his smile in the moonlight.

When he put his arms around her and kissed her, Dolores felt a sudden kick of pleasure which was so unexpected that she drew in a shallow breath. Stephen held her more tightly, and slowly, she felt the old panic begin to flow through her: the urge to push him away and escape to her own room was very strong. Stephen sensed the change in her and, fearing that his own eagerness was making him rough, he drew back a fraction.

'Don't stop, Stephen, we must not delay. Beth may wake, or—'

She kissed him again, swiftly, then stepped across to the bed and pulled back the covers. Stephen just remembered to turn the key in the lock before he joined her. For a moment he hesitated. She had lain down and her hair fanned like a dark wing across the pillows. There was an urgency in her eyes which it was easy to mistake for desire.

'Now, Stephen,' she whispered, 'Now. Don't wait.'

Stephen covered her face with kisses. His hand caressed her breasts, the round curve of her hip.

'Hurry—'

Her whispered command seemed a mirror image of his own great longing. He heard her stifle a cry, though whether of pleasure or pain, he had no way of knowing.

'Dolores—'

'Yes. Make haste—'

It was only too easy to obey. For years now he had followed the discipline of a soldier. He had trained his body to ignore cold and hunger and fatigue. When occasion dictated he had passed his nights in rainy fields with his men. The only couplings he had known during those years had been brief and impersonal, a quick release of tension. Now he felt himself drowning in flesh as soft as velvet that smelled of summer gardens and new mown hay.

When it was over he became aware that Dolores was lying so still beside him that he thought she must be asleep. He propped himself on one elbow: her eyes were wide open and staring at some point in the canopy above their heads. He kissed her gently and she gave a small shiver. Then she smiled at him quickly.

'It is well,' she said.

'Yes. It is very well.'

Stephen rolled on to his back. He had spoken more to reassure her than from any real sense of well-being. It nagged at him that their encounter had been in some way incomplete. But though his mind was troubled, his body was sated and content and, after the tensions of the day, a huge weariness was washing through him. Within a short space, he had fallen into a profound sleep. As the rhythm of his breathing changed, Dolores sat up and pulled her shift down over her knees, hugging them tightly. She looked down at him. Now that there was no longer any reason to dissemble, an expression of sadness spread across her face. She felt more alone than she had thought possible, and on the verge of black despair. If ever she could love a man, then surely Stephen Sutton must be that man. She trusted him, she cared for him, she wanted him near her so that she could see him every day, so they could talk and be together. And yet at the very moment when he took her in his arms she had felt herself to be sliding beyond his reach. She yearned for closeness, but always there was this aching gulf.

Taking great care not to waken him, she slipped from the bed, gathered her shawl from the floor and returned to her own room. Beth was sleeping quietly. As Dolores sponged her body with flower waters, she reflected bitterly that she was cutting a fine swathe through the Ten Commandments. First murder, now adultery. But God had abandoned her that day in the church in Würzburg, and she had no scruples now about turning her back on Him.

The following day a fine gusting wind sprang up. Stephen, feeling well disposed to all illicit lovers, instructed Lieutenant Donnelly to take a message to Sir Diggory Page at Furleys, and added casually that there was no reason to hurry back. When Donnelly did return, towards mid-afternoon, his angelic features looked more cheerful than they had done since the night of the raid.

By that time Stephen had gone down to the orchard where Dolores was observing her children and the inexhaustible Bonnet. His ostensible reason for seeking her out was to tell her the news that Governor Massey had left Gloucester with a troop of mounted cavalry and, in a move of great daring, had stormed the royalist stronghold of Evesham. But Stephen's real motive was that he had not seen her all day, and the time had felt far too long.

He found her standing beneath an apple tree. The wind was making a snowstorm of the blossoms and Beth and Pip were whirling about in vain efforts to catch them. Harry, more serious, was trying to execute some complicated manoeuvre on his pony.

Dolores was smiling at the children's antics, and did not notice Stephen's approach.

'Good day, Mistress Taverner.'

She turned abruptly, and the colour flooded her face. 'Captain Sutton—'

'I hope I did not startle you.'

'Of course not. It's a pleasure to see you.' And for the first time since they had met, he saw a hesitant shyness in her smile. A couple of white petals had become lodged in her hair, and it was all Stephen could do to stop himself from reaching across and brushing them free.

As impassively as he was able, Stephen told her what he knew of Massey's raid on Evesham. While she was listening to him, Dolores experienced a strange mixture of tenderness and apprehension.

At length she said, 'Has this news influenced your decision to stay or go?'

Beth, who had just flung a handful of petals at her brother, was suddenly all attention.

'Do you even need to ask, Mistress Taverner?' said Stephen. 'You know full well recent events have persuaded me to remain here until I receive clear instructions to the contrary.'

'Captain Sutton is not going, is he?' Beth asked.

'No, Beth. Not yet, at any rate, though of course he cannot remain for ever.'

'I don't see why not. I hope he stays for ever and ever and ever.' Stephen and Dolores exchanged a rapid look, but the next moment Philip had rammed a handful of grass down his sister's neck and she rounded on him in a fury.

Stephen watched while Dolores separated the two yelling children and reprimanded them both firmly.

'It was his fault!' raged Beth, 'He began it!'

'Yes, and you were happy enough to carry on. No more fussing, now, Beth. Go and tell Gerard it is time for your turn on Bonnet.'

When Dolores was free to turn her attention back to Stephen, his eyes were shining. Suddenly afraid that even at this distance her groom must surely notice the change that had occurred between them, she moved away slightly, composed her features into an expression of severity and said coolly, 'Thank you so much for bringing me the news about the fall of Evesham, Captain Sutton. I fear this will mean increased danger for your men. No doubt you are more busy than ever.'

'The men are well trained and know how to respond if we are attacked,' said Stephen, but he had heard the dismissal behind her words and he added, 'I'll not disturb you and your family further with reports of the war.'

Harry was approaching. Dolores smiled towards her son and then, without turning to Stephen, she added nonchalantly, 'In these dangerous times, Captain Sutton, what is your opinion concerning the necessity for locking bedchamber doors?'

Stephen suppressed a grin. 'I believe each person must decide for themselves, Mistress Taverner, but for my part I have never thought it necessary to bar the door of my room. I see no reason to alter my practice now.'

'Just as I had thought. I'm delighted to hear it, Captain Sutton. Good day.'

No one observing the tall soldier, as he strode up the path that led from the orchard to the stable-yard, would have suspected that he considered himself to be the luckiest man alive.

Dolores visited Stephen's room again that night, and on most of the nights that followed. Sometimes he was obliged to check outlying sentry posts, and once or twice she herself fell asleep before Beth and did not wake again until it was too late, but more often than not, when all the house was sleeping, she pulled her shawl over her shoulders and stepped silently across the landing and pushed open the door to his chamber.

She liked it best when their love-making was done; until then she felt awkward and anxious and she spoke little. Once or twice Stephen had attempted to vary the rhythm of their encounters, but Dolores always urged him to make haste: Beth might wake, she insisted, they did not have the luxury of time. But once his energy was spent, she began to relax and they talked, usually of neutral topics. Dolores told him about the children, Stephen recounted the events of his day. Without ever having discussed the subject, they seemed to have reached an understanding not to touch on anything serious: Josiah was never mentioned, nor the future. Often it was enough to lie together in silence. Once or twice, when Dolores had lain for some while with her head on his shoulder, Stephen began to be aroused again. But she moved away at once and said she should return to her own room. Both were anxious lest they fall into a sleep so profound that Dolores would still be in his chamber when the servants and children woke in the morning. On a few nights Stephen said he wanted only to hold her in his arms, nothing more. Dolores was relieved, and yet found she was uneasy, at the same time. She fretted that his feeling for her was fading: though she gained no pleasure from his love-making, she was surprised to find that she did not altogether dislike it either. She enjoyed the certainty that he desired her as well as the knowledge that she was breaking a fundamental tie with Josiah. But sometimes her inability to share Stephen's pleasure left her haunted by the fear of being incomplete, the anxiety that some essential womanly part of her was missing. And that in time this lack would cause Stephen to tire of her.

Yet why should she mind? She had his promise that he would not quit Tilsbury until ordered to move on – either by her, or by his military command – and she knew he was a man who never went back on his word. If Stephen no longer wanted her as his mistress, he would still remain her trusted friend. But friendship was no longer enough. She craved his loving, even though she herself could not return it.

One night, when he had fallen asleep, she lit a candle and, for a long time, sat on the edge of the bed and observed his face by its gentle light. The creases around his eyes, the straight nose, high gaunt cheek-bones, the narrow angle of his jaw and his lips, parted slightly as he breathed – asleep and awake, his features had become an essential part of her life.

Very carefully, she drew back the bed covers a little way and examined his long limbs, the muscles on his arms, the sparse hair on his upper chest and the pale scars on his flesh, some gained in boyhood accidents, the more recent ones from this present war. Only when she had covered his body with the sheet once again did she realise she was weeping, without knowing the reason why.

Chapter 20

❧

Not so very far from Tilsbury, two huge armies were on the move. A parliamentary force of thirteen thousand men under Sir Thomas Fairfax set siege to the royalist headquarters at Oxford. King Charles led his army into Leicestershire to draw them off; Fairfax raised the siege and followed. Like vast leviathans the two armies crawled over the countryside. Not just the fighting men themselves – cavalry and gunners, pikemen and musketeers – but a straggling city of servants and wives, carters and grooms, surgeons and ministers, bakers and vintners and tailors and an increasingly disreputable assortment of hangers-on. Cumbersome and ill-provided with news, each monstrous serpent devoured all that lay in its path as it endeavoured to manoeuvre itself into a strong position for what many now believed would be the decisive battle of the war.

At the beginning of June news reached Tilsbury that the city of Leicester had been sacked by the King's army. Reports varied. Royalist sources hailed it as a brave victory; parliamentary broadsheets condemned the slaughter of women and children, the wholesale destruction, pillage and rape. The people of Tilsbury heard this with a shudder of sympathy for the ordinary citizens of Leicester whose lives had thus been ruined, and offered up fervent prayers for their own safety.

But for the most part their concerns were more prosaic. The weather had been wet, the young men were all gone to the war and the hay-making was likely to be a disaster. One rain-dreary evening Sergeant O'Rourke found Cary unusually cast down. Bracing himself for yet another tale of mayhem and gore, he was taken aback to discover she was concerned for her family at the farm. Destitution lay ahead if first the hay, and then the harvest, were to be lost.

The following day O'Rourke asked Stephen if he might use his free time to help Cary's family at their farm. Stephen had no objection, so long as his garrison duties were not neglected. Stephen then made a few enquiries of his own and found that all the nearby farms were in the same predicament. As long as the bad weather continued there was little anyone could do, but towards the middle of June there was a change: a bright wind blew up, the rain clouds rolled away and the meadows steamed in the sun. Stephen reorganised the men and, leaving only the sentries and scouts at their posts, he grouped them into work parties and set them to help in the fields. Some grumbled, a few enjoyed the work, but most had by now fallen into the habit of obedience and complied without a murmur.

They began just before dawn and worked alongside the old men and the women, scything and raking and turning the hay. The smell of fresh cut grass and meadow flowers drifted through the town and briefly there was a sense of optimism, and purpose. Even those who had been most hostile to the garrison were now prepared to moderate their opinion: soldiers in general were undoubtedly a burden, and the Irish were known to be the worst – but these particular Irish soldiers were obviously the exceptions that proved both rules. Farmers who had claimed to be destitute miraculously discovered supplies of cider and small beer for the men; women who had grudged them a hunk of dry bread now shared whatever they had, and gladly.

Stephen joined them when he could. On the third afternoon he found himself working alongside Lieutenant Donnelly in a wide meadow a little way up the valley. He had grown to like the young Irishman. Though more reserved than O'Rourke, he was loyal and hardworking. The two men worked in silence for a while. Less experienced than the old countrymen who were making their way steadily across the field in an unbroken line, Stephen and Donnelly took some time to find their own slower rhythm. When the others took their ease in the shade of a large elm, Stephen and Donnelly still had a good distance to cover, which led to some good-natured mockery. By the time they had finished their strip, the local men had begun again.

'I'd like to see them handle a musket, that's all,' said Donnelly with a grin when he had flopped down in the shade and taken a long drink from a flagon of cider.

'Our clumsiness cheers them more than if we were twice as fast. They'll talk of this for years.'

'Just a week of practice and we'll be faster than any of them.' Donnelly did not like to be beaten.

'A week of practice and the work will be done.'

'True enough. So long as they're grateful.'

'You can be sure of that.'

Stephen stretched his long legs on the grass and looked at the young lieutenant. With his tumble of light curls and his delicate, almost girlish profile, he looked like a study for a painter's angel. Or, thought Stephen, in this rustic setting, he could have been the model for some pastoral idyll, a young Endymion perhaps, waiting for his Diana.

'How old are you, Donnelly?'

'Twenty-four, or thereabouts, sir.'

Stephen knocked off a couple of years for exaggeration. Donnelly was still young enough to lie about such things, though heaven knows, this war was being fought by youths. Prince Rupert and Governor Massey at Gloucester were both younger than Stephen.

'And where is your home?'

'I have no home, sir. The Protestant settlers drove my family off their land. My mother and father both died in the winter that followed.'

Stephen made no comment. He knew that sympathy was the last thing his lieutenant was looking for. In the silence, they could hear a cuckoo's fractured note, and the steady whisper of the scythes. It took a huge effort of imagination to believe in the reality of dispossession and death from cold and hunger while all around them was the gauzy beauty of the midsummer day.

'Back to work,' said Stephen, 'Or we'll be here till midnight.' And then, as they stropped their blades he added, 'It might be that I need another message taken to Furleys this evening.'

At once, Donnelly's face was radiant. 'You know how to make a fellow happy, sir, and that's a fact. I wish you had messages for Sir Diggory four times a day.'

Stephen grinned. 'Wouldn't that be too much?'

'Indeed it would not. Make hay while the sun shines, isn't that what we're doing now? Besides, if I don't find a way to make a certain lady happy, then she'll find someone else who can.'

'Is she so fickle?'

'No sir, not fickle at all. I did not understand at first, but she just takes her pleasure as she likes, as a man does. When I am with her, she thinks of no one else; as soon as I am gone, I'm sure she forgets me entirely.'

'How do you know?'

'She said so. An honester woman I never did meet, for all that she spins a web of lies when she needs to. And I don't mind in the least. If I die in Tilsbury, I shall die a happy man. It's like—' he paused for a moment, searching for the right words to express his thoughts, '—It's been like learning a whole new language. I thought I knew how to speak it well enough before but now I can see I was merely grunting. Now I can sing and—'

Stephen burst out laughing. 'Come on then, Donnelly. We'd best get back to work if you're going to have time left over for singing lessons this evening.'

'Yes sir, Captain Sutton.'

Donnelly set to work with such a will that Stephen had a hard job to keep up with him. Later, when Donnelly had raced ahead and Stephen was walking back through the early evening sunshine, he observed with satisfaction that several hayricks had been completed already. He had the pleasing sense of fatigue that comes from toiling in the fresh air, very different from the weariness that followed days of training, or patrols. He found himself almost envying the country folk who would take up the threads of their lives as soon as the war was over. For his part, he had no very clear picture of what the future would hold for him – nor, until this moment, had he given it much thought.

He entered the Priory House by the front door, and at once he was filled with a sense of well-being. Having told Ellen to fetch him ale and food, he pushed open the door into the dining hall.

The windows had been flung wide open, and the air was heavy with the scent of flowers and new mown hay. As he waited he became aware of the small sounds of the summer's evening: the scamper of children's feet across upstairs floorboards; voices from the kitchen; swallows dipping and swooping from the eaves, and, somewhere beyond the garden, a hen was clucking her satisfaction at a new-laid egg. Sunlight slanted through the mullioned windows and made a chequered pattern on the slate floor. And then, from one of the upstairs chambers, came the sound of a tune, haltingly played, on Beth's little spinet.

Tonight, thought Stephen, Dolores will come to my room. It seemed strange to him then that this moment of complete content, such as occur only a few times in a man's life, should visit him now as he stood alone in a stranger's house, his limbs aching with weariness, while the world beyond was being torn apart by war. And yet he knew that the wholeness of this time and place would never fade.

It was Dolores who brought in the tray of food, the scullion following with a jug of ale. She was wearing her plain dress of dark grey, a wide white collar falling from the neck, her dark hair almost hidden beneath her coif. The simplicity of her clothes set off her strange beauty in a way that brought an ache to Stephen's throat. As soon as the scullion who accompanied her had set down the pitcher of ale, she dismissed him and pushed the door closed.

'You look like a common hayseed,' she scolded, 'Not at all like an officer in His Majesty's service.' But her eyes were warm with approval.

'I think a rustic's existence would suit me better,' he said, 'Especially if it meant I could stay here.'

She did not reply to this, but sat and watched him as he quenched his thirst and ate Mabs' good food. Then, suddenly, her expression changed, and she tilted her head on one side.

'Listen.'

'What?'

'That song—'

The simple tune on the spinet had ended and Beth seemed to be trying to pick out a half-remembered melody.

Dolores said, 'That's the dance I've been teaching her.' She began to croon the rhythm softly. 'That's it. No, no, like this . . .' Then she smiled at Stephen as an idea came into her mind, 'Would you like to see the dance?'

'More than anything.'

She rose to her feet. 'Then you shall. This can be my gift for you, alone. Josiah has never seen it, though he always wanted to, very much.'

Humming a gentle accompaniment, Dolores began to dance. She had performed the movements a thousand times before, but almost at once she realised that this was different. Stephen's grey eyes, watching her, changed it utterly. She was becoming aware for the first time of the way her spine arched slightly backwards, of the tilt of her head and neck, and the energy that was flowing through her limbs. The actions were sensuous, and the song an invitation.

She saw the admiration in his eyes, saw also his desire. And, as she moved in the patch of sunlight and her feet scuffed the woodruff and strewing herbs on the floor, she found that she was no longer shrinking from the fact of his desire, she was revelling in it. A warmth was spreading all through her body. Her throat was dry, but not with fear.

Confused by the unfamiliar sensations beginning to stir inside her, she broke off suddenly. Her breathing was shallow and rapid as she stared at Stephen, and her arms hung loosely at her sides.

'Don't stop . . .' he told her. 'It's beautiful.'

'I didn't realise . . .' Upstairs, Beth had abandoned her efforts to pin down the dance tune and had returned to one of her set pieces, a plodding galliard. 'I've never danced alone before. There was always Nona. It's different, with you watching.'

'Maybe you should teach me, and we could dance together,'

Dolores' eyebrows lifted at this suggestion, then she turned away with a little shrug of the shoulders. 'Why not? Nona said that in the village this was a dance for the beginning of May, young men and women together.'

'We're a little late in the season then,' said Stephen with a smile, 'and perhaps not quite as young as we should be, but we can try, can't we?'

'If you like.'

He went to stand in front of her.

'Feel the movements,' she told him. 'I am the song, and you the echo. Like this . . .'

She raised her hands in front of her and Stephen mirrored the gesture so that their palms grazed lightly. At the touch, Dolores felt a spark of energy pass through her hand and up her arm into her shoulder. It was far from unpleasant, but it startled her, and she began to draw back slightly. Stephen twined his fingers through hers.

'Teach me,' he insisted.

She held his gaze for a moment, then pushed him away gently as she began to croon the old song. And now it was utterly transformed: she was performing the dance as if for the first time, while Stephen, barely moving, stood before her. His attention was all absorbed in trying to attune himself to the unfamiliar rhythms, and her attention was all absorbed in him.

Neither noticed the sudden sound of a troop of horsemen riding past the window. Dolores was aware only that for the first time in her life she wanted to feel a man's hands on her body; Stephen's hands. She was beginning to mirror the love that she saw in his eyes.

'Like this.' She made a sudden movement towards him and brushed his lips with her own before sliding away and twirling about.

Stephen grinned and caught her round the waist. 'And this—' he began.

There was a commotion at the front door. A familiar voice could be heard demanding to speak with Captain Sutton. They sprang apart just as O'Rourke hurried in.

'There are troopers at The Lion,' he said, 'They say they're Prince Rupert's men. There's been a mighty battle fought. They barely escaped with their lives.'

'A battle? Where?'

'To the north. Near Leicester, I believe.'

'And the outcome?'

'They say our army is destroyed. His Majesty was barely able to escape the scene and it is thought he is fleeing towards Wales.'

'I'll talk with them at once.'

'They've ridden on already, sir. They are making for Furleys. Sir Diggory's son is with them. I heard him say this is the death blow for the King. The war is as good as over.'

Dolores gasped. Stephen said firmly, 'First reports are often unreliable, O'Rourke. There have been reverses before. So long as His Majesty remains at liberty to raise a new army, there is always a chance of victory.'

'Yes, sir.'

Dolores had turned away and was fussing with the items on the tray. Her eyes were bright with tears and a fierce rage was gathering inside her: even so were the lives of ordinary people turned upside down by events they had no way of controlling.

A young man whom no one had seen before sauntered into the room. Beneath the mud and dust of a hard ride, his clothes were those of a gentleman of fashion.

'Captain Sutton?' The youth's natural arrogance was

heightened by the fact that this particular officer had the appearance of a yeoman farmer.

'Yes?'

'Cornet Trimball, sir. Major Ripley presents his compliments and requests you will attend him at Furleys at once.'

'Major Ripley?'

'He is taking over command of the garrison here. I advise you not to keep him waiting.' And with that the youth turned on his heel and strolled out.

O'Rourke raised a single whiskery eyebrow and then departed to find Cary. He wanted to tell her the news himself before he was obliged to hear a blood-curdling version of the same tale from her own lips.

Stephen turned to Dolores. 'Nothing need change,' he told her.

But she brushed past him angrily as she left the room. 'You fool,' she said, 'Everything is changed already.'

In the upstairs bedroom, Beth continued with her music practice, her fingers plodding and stumbling over the notes as they did each day, regardless of the fact that on a stretch of farmland not so very far from Tilsbury a multitude of men had lost their lives, and King Charles had begun the long flight that would end only when he stepped on to the scaffold, and laid his head on the executioner's block.

Major Ripley had a sallow, sunken face. He was well past the age when a man can endure a catastrophic battle and two days of hard riding without ill effects. His narrow features were shrivelled with discomfort and irritation, and a punishing headache throbbed behind his eyes. He had taken a few sips of Sir Diggory's remaining brandy, but more than that would play havoc with his digestion: there were no easy comforts in Major Ripley's life.

He was seated now in an oaken chair, and Sir Diggory's son stood beside him. Frederick Page was a large, pale, blubbery youth with his sister's tendency to a double chin, but with none of her charm.

'You will transfer the men to this house at once,' the major was saying, 'I can't think what made you decide to garrison the town. It's impossible to defend.'

Stephen remembered, with unexpected affection, Paul Darbier's unorthodox criteria for the selection of billets. He said calmly, 'The river forms a natural boundary on one side, sir. With the walls of the Old Priory, and the earthworks we have built—'

'Fiddling about, sir, just fiddling about. A waste of time. Move the men at once.'

'Yes, sir.'

'Tonight, Captain.'

Thinking of Dolores, Stephen said, 'That will not be possible, sir. The ammunition is all stored in the ruins of the Old Priory and it must be transferred first. Besides, the men are fully occupied until dusk. I can organise the whole operation at first light tomorrow.'

'Occupied, Captain? How, occupied?'

'Working, sir. The men have been helping with the hay.'

Frederick Page let out a snort of contempt. 'Farm work, Captain Sutton?'

'Yes, the people here—'

Again the major interrupted him. 'I have no interest at all in the people here. Nor do I expect my soldiers to work as farm labourers. This nonsense must cease at once. Bad for discipline.'

'On the contrary, Major Ripley—'

'See it is done. Orders are to be obeyed, Captain. I desire no advice from you or anyone else. The men will muster here at first light tomorrow.'

Stephen saw Frederick Page smirk at this rebuff. He understood that his own experience of the area after nearly four months in charge of the garrison counted for nothing. He hated giving up his command to this jaundiced looking officer, but he had no choice. Over the past few months, especially since Darbier's death, Stephen had grown proud of his garrison. Now it was his no longer. But at least he had achieved one final night at the Priory House.

As he went out into the twilight to the gravel courtyard where his man was waiting with his horse, Lieutenant Donnelly came running to join him.

'We are to move the garrison here,' said Stephen.

'I know, sir.' However hard he tried to suppress it, Donnelly's face kept exploding into a grin. 'God bless Major Ripley, I say. A patron of lovers everywhere.'

Stephen reflected ruefully that in his own case nothing could be further from the truth, but he kept his thoughts to himself and Donnelly was still grinning when, a little later, the two officers rode into Tilsbury to prepare the men for departure.

It was later than usual when Dolores slipped into Stephen's bedchamber. For a while they neither spoke, nor touched each other.

At length Dolores asked quietly, 'The news is bad?'

'Very. We must wait for further details, but it is a serious defeat.'

'Worse than before?'

'Perhaps. One thing is certain, my position here has changed. I am no longer in charge of the garrison. Major Ripley has ordered a transfer to Furleys.'

'Yes.'

'I will have to leave in the morning.'

'I know.'

'It will be better for you and your family. If the garrison is attacked, then Furleys will suffer, not the town.'

'I am not afraid.'

As she said the four words, she marvelled to know that it was true. The terrible paralysing fear which had gripped her when Josiah first spoke of the coming of the soldiers, the panic which had consumed her in the days following Darbier's death, all that was in the past. As she stood and faced Stephen in the candlelight, she knew that she would fight to the death to protect her children, but she was not afraid.

He took her hands in both of his, raised them to his lips, and kissed them.

'I wish with all my heart I could remain here with you,' he said, 'It will be hard for us to meet from now on. Perhaps impossible.'

'Nothing is impossible,' she said. She was thinking, in particular, of the way her body had warmed to his as she danced for him that afternoon. But when, a little later, he took her in his arms in the canopied bed, she felt herself slipping from him, as had always happened before. Their love-making was an event disconnected from herself. Her sense of isolation increased, as though her skin was a coat of armour, keeping them apart. Was there never to be hope of change? The thought of never feeling Stephen beside her again was intolerable.

Afterwards they lay together some time without speaking, and she understood that he too was thinking how sad it would be if this was the last time between them. Such a waste of loving. But she had no way to speak to him directly.

'I never imagined this,' she said at length. 'And now, God help me, I do not know how to act.'

'How so?'

'I have betrayed Josiah by loving you. If we are to find a way to meet again in secret, it will be a double betrayal.'

Stephen was silent for a long while before saying, 'Perhaps it is best, then, that we end this now.'

'No! I will see you. I would gladly betray Josiah a thousand times over.' Suddenly decisive, she climbed from the bed and pulled her shawl around her shoulders.

'But how? It will be too dangerous for me to visit you here, and you cannot leave the house without arousing suspicion. I will not let you take that risk.'

She laid her finger on his lips and smiled. 'There is a secret way, Stephen. Everyone believes it was blocked off years ago, but Josiah had it opened up just before you came.'

'A secret way? Where is it?'

'Here, in this house. My husband's family used to be Catholics. They had a priest's hole built in Elizabeth's reign. When Father Tellam was apprehended by the pursuivants, the secret became known. The route no longer had any value so it was blocked off. Now it is open again. It leads from my own bedroom to the ruined priory.'

Stephen took her hands in his and kissed them. 'Dolores, you work miracles.'

'Have you noticed, I did not even trouble to ask you to keep my great secret? I know you could never betray me. It is not in your nature. Aren't you proud of how I trust you?'

'Very proud. And honoured.'

'Josiah hated having to share his secret with me. He only did so because he put some of his valuables in the tunnel, and the children are to have them if anything happens to him. I cannot show it to you now because Beth is sleeping in my room, and your men are keeping watch in the ruins. Will they be gone in three days' time?'

'I shall make sure they are.'

'Then wait for me there, just after midnight.'

Since there was no future for them, Stephen and Dolores had learned to treasure the present moment to the exclusion of all else. Having found a temporary solution to the problem of the garrison's transfer, they were as delighted as if they had outwitted fate altogether, and were never to be parted.

Afterwards, when Stephen reflected on their conversation, he blamed himself for having agreed to her scheme so readily. He was afraid that Dolores was becoming reckless, and felt that he should be cautious for them both. The danger was all hers: a Cornish officer caught in an affair with a married woman would earn nothing worse than the envy of his fellows. Josiah the vengeful husband was not likely to pose much of a problem. But the penalty for Dolores if their secret ever became known would be incalculable. He should have taken greater trouble to make sure she was protecting herself.

But by the time he had considered all this, their plan was already fixed. He had no way of getting a message to her, and no wish to cancel their meeting.

Chapter 21

❧

As Midsummer's Eve approached each day brought fresh news of the disaster at Naseby. Some of the cavalry had escaped, the King himself remained at liberty, but the infantry, the backbone of his army, had been annihilated. A week after their defeat, the royalist prisoners were paraded in London, thousands of fighting men and over fifty captured standards. The city of Leicester was retaken by Parliament together with huge quantities of artillery and horses. Charles's cause was effectively broken. Most chilling, because most personal, was the news that many of the Welsh women who had left Tilsbury with their menfolk just over a month before, had been butchered when the roundheads plundered the baggage train. The most likely explanation offered little comfort to Donnelly and O'Rourke and their men: crying out in a strange language, the wretched women had been mistaken for Irish.

Whatever their sympathies, most people were simply relieved that the crippling stalemate had ended. A few local men were already beginning to come home: they had either been injured, or had deserted, or they had been released on a promise to fight no more. Among the first to return was Corinna's husband Tom. Some fragments from a mortar had lodged in his knee during the first assault on Leicester, and though the wound had healed, his soldiering days were over. Knowing Corinna as he did, the news of her infidelity did not come as a complete surprise. Just as he was working himself into a fury, he received a message from Sir Diggory telling him to regard himself as Corinna's husband no longer; a legal separation was being arranged. Insult was added to injury by the promise of compensation. When Tom's rage had died down he convinced himself he was well rid of the arrogant trollop. He resumed his former friendships and way of life but nursed a simmering bitterness against all the inhabitants of Furleys. After a brief struggle with his pride, he decided to keep the money.

In those midsummer days and weeks following Naseby it was hard to believe in catastrophe. The weather continued fine, the hay was gathered and stacked in tidy ricks, the women coped as best they could with a shortage of sugar and an abundance of elderflowers and roses, the townspeople began to look forward to settling back into their former routines. At Furleys there was a sense of being suspended in a dream. The royalist troopers who had arrived with Major Ripley lounged in the sunshine and smoked contentedly, teased the servant girls and speculated in low voices about their host's daughter. Their officers amused themselves at bowls and indulged in fantasies, which no one any longer believed, of His Majesty's miraculous recovery: he was even now raising a new and better army in Wales; a huge force was about to set sail from Ireland; the Scots royalists were on the brink of a massive victory and their conquering army would sweep south before the autumn.

Stephen found that, for the first time since he rode from home to fight under Sir Bevil Grenvile's standard in 1639, there was nothing very much to fill his hours. He quickly realised that despite Major Ripley's fine words, no real defence of Furleys was being planned. Stephen devoted a hot afternoon to assessing the earthworks necessary to improve its security, only to be told to leave well alone. The major was making his own superior – but so far invisible – arrangements. Stephen concluded that Major Ripley and Lieutenant Page wanted to offer only enough resistance to ensure generous terms for themselves and for the house. From what was left unsaid in their discussion of events at Naseby, he gathered they had fled as soon as the cavalry broke and the tide was beginning to turn against them. Although Stephen knew better than to judge action taken in the heat of a fight, he was sickened by their inactivity now. He could not devote himself to bowls while the cause for which his brother and friends had died was evaporating in a sunny haze of idleness and make-believe.

Moreover, his position at Furleys was incongruous. Unlike the Irish, who had been unceremoniously billeted in the outbuildings, Stephen had been given his own room at the back of the house. But the troopers looked down on him because he was an infantryman, and Frederick Page, though only a lieutenant, made it clear he considered himself Stephen's superior. Since Sir Diggory's son had Major Ripley's confidence, there was little Stephen could do to counter this.

Yet despite all these frustrations, Stephen was content – and all because he was continuing to enjoy his stolen hours with Dolores.

Three days after Major Ripley's arrival, Stephen had made his way to the ruined priory just after midnight. The last of the ammunition had been moved out during the day, and all that remained was a faint smell of gunpowder and the more pungent smells from the alcove at the foot of the tower which the sentries had used as a latrine. Had he been looking at the problem from a purely military point of view, Stephen would certainly have left a sentry here even after the munitions had been moved to Furleys. The tower commanded an excellent view over the lower part of Tilsbury, the surrounding fields and the first half mile of the Oxford road, as well as a good deal of the parkland at Furleys. But Stephen's efforts to deal militarily with the situation had all been overruled by Major Ripley, and he had dismissed the sentries that afternoon with only a minor qualm of conscience. No curious soldiers must remain to hinder his rendezvous with Dolores.

But now there was no sign of her. Stephen sat down on a chunk of fallen masonry and listened to his horse cropping the grass and watched the bats flit through the rafters. Thanks to local superstition, a good deal of the structure of the Old Priory remained intact. No one wanted to risk the bad luck which was said to be the fate of any building used with materials taken from the site. The Grey Lady was a more effective custodian of her territory in death than she had been while still alive.

There was a flicker of light near the foot of the old tower.

'Dolores?' Stephen stood up.

No answer. The tiny light shifted slightly, and there was a shadow of movement.

'Dolores, is that you?'

During the huge silence that followed, Stephen, most unsuperstitious of men, felt a shiver of breath on the back of his neck and, for a fleeting moment, would not have been surprised if the ghost of the murdered prioress had risen up before him.

Then he grinned and told himself not to be a fool. Striding

over to the tiny light he found Dolores, a lantern in her hand, crouched against the foot of a pillar. He reached down and she grasped his hand.

'Dolores, what is it? What is the matter?'

She stared up at him with huge and horrified eyes, and sudden apprehension gripped him. The last time he had seen that expression on her face was in the aftermath of Darbier's murder: it occurred to him that she looked like a woman who has just encountered a ghost.

Crouching down beside her, he said again, 'What is it?' Her hand was icy, and when he touched her forehead, it was beaded with sweat.

'I do not . . .' Some constriction of the breath prevented her from continuing.

Stephen said gently, 'Something has frightened you. What—?'

'Nothing,' she said, 'Nothing is wrong now you're here. But I do not much care for tunnels.' She was still gripping his hand. 'Let us wait here for a moment before going back. I'll be better in a moment.'

'Shall I extinguish your lantern? Someone might see it.'

'So much the better. Elfin lights at midnight will feed the rumours of the Grey Lady. There's no one in Tilsbury would dare to come and find out the cause. Put your arm around me, Stephen, I'm feeling braver already.'

Dolores was ashamed of her fear, and did not want him to know how dearly it had cost her to enter the black tunnel alone. She had been dreading it since the night she had arranged the rendezvous with Stephen. When she awoke that morning the sense of dread was a great weight oppressing her, and several times she had thought of sending word to Stephen that their plans must be changed. All day she had grappled with her panic, but as evening approached, she told herself fiercely that she had done it once for Josiah; surely she could do as much – and more – for Stephen. She had forced herself to close her mind to the horror of the narrow, airless space. She would only allow herself to think of Stephen: Stephen's smile, Stephen's strong arms, Stephen's sure love waiting for her in the ruins of the Old Priory.

'There, I am strong again.' Her speech was almost normal. 'Now I can show you our secret way. Look, over here. The stones can be moved just a little and the entrance is invisible – like this. Push them aside – so – and there is the tunnel. Do not let go my hand, Stephen. I shall be fine now you are with me.'

And so it was. Though her heart was pounding and a cold sweat of fear covered her shoulder blades, Dolores still felt confident enough to halt when they reached the alcove.

'Look, Stephen. Here is the reason Josiah had the tunnel reopened.' She raised the casket and lifted the lid. A bloom of mould had made its surface slippery to the touch. A strange expression spread over her face as she looked at the precious gems and pieces of silver.

'Such riches for a sober merchant,' marvelled Stephen, 'Your husband has an eye for beauty.'

Dolores shook her head. 'It is their value he loves, nothing else.'

'How did he come by them?'

'Plunder. He stole them when he was a soldier in the German wars. Each piece must have been stripped from the neck of some terrified woman, or dragged at knife-point from a helpless Catholic. He tells people he fought for the Protestant cause, but he fought only for himself.'

'With great success.'

'There is more which he has taken with him to London. When he left, just after you came, he had a quantity of gold pieces and some jewels sewn into his clothing. He believes always in dividing his risks.' She slid her fingers into the tangle of treasure, then let it fall. 'I never realised until this moment how much I loathe them. The spoils of Josiah's Protestant crusade. And I was just another item of plunder.'

She closed the casket and hurried on. It had been a mistake to show Stephen the jewels. Somehow the sight of them had made the tunnel a shade more oppressive, the air more difficult to breathe. She did not speak again until she had ascended the narrow stair, pushed open the panel and had inhaled the scents of fresh strewing herbs in her chamber.

Stephen, emerging a moment later, looked about him.

'I have not entered this room since Darbier slept here.'

'Beth was with me until last night. Now she is with the baby. We have become a family of gypsies, always moving from room to room.'

She pushed the secret panel firmly closed. 'There,' she said, 'It's done. Pray God I never have to enter that cursed tunnel again.'

Stephen stroked back a strand of her hair. 'Do you hate it so much?'

'I will learn to love it if it brings us together. But I can't help thinking of that priest who was caught there by the pursuivants.' For some reason she did not mention her suspicion that Josiah might have been the child who betrayed him. Whether it was the memory of the priest's grim fate, or the tunnel itself, or the oppression aroused by seeing the casket of treasure, they both found it impossible to shift their sombre mood. Stephen found he wanted only to hold Dolores in his arms and talk. Tonight especially he was reluctant to make love to her since his actions brought her no pleasure. Each time he took her in his arms he was aware of an increasing dissatisfaction with himself. Dolores was at first dismayed, seeing this as proof that he was growing tired of her. Only when he had convinced her that nothing could be further from the truth did she settle back against the heaped-up pillows and say, 'Then talk to me.'

'What shall I talk about?'

'Not this terrible war. I never want to hear another word about supplies or musters or campaigns as long as I live.'

'What then?'

'Tell me of your life.'

'This war has been my life.'

'But before the fighting. Tell me about your home, your family. What did you do all day? Tell me about this Cornwall of yours. Is it like the country around here?'

'It is not so fruitful. The land is mostly poor and life is harsher. Yet I cannot imagine a more beautiful place anywhere in the world.'

'How can it be poor and harsh, and yet beautiful?'

'I don't know how. But it is.'

'Describe it to me.'

Stephen was silent for a little while, hunting for the words. It felt as if some long unused part of his brain was being forced to function again. 'The trees are much smaller than they are round here,' he said carefully, 'Most of them are stunted by the wind, some are curved like a wave from long battering, though a few grow taller in the valleys. The buildings are smaller too, most are low-built and the stone is grey, not gold as it is here.'

'I do not much care for the sound of your Cornwall, everything so small.'

'Not everything. The sky is huge and changes all the time.

The sea lies all around the land, and the waves are big and always beautiful. You can sit beside them for hours. And the great winds come blowing in off the ocean and it makes you glad to be alive.'

She turned to him tenderly. 'Your Cornwall makes a poet of you, Stephen.'

'Maybe because it is a poem. As are you.'

'That is flattery, not poetry.'

'I wish—'

He did not finish his sentence, and they lapsed into silence. He had been about to say how he longed to show her the country where he had been reared. And she was thinking that one day, maybe soon, he would return there and they would never see each other again. Their separate thoughts laid heavy on them, and, each wishing to spare the other that heaviness, they did not speak of it any more.

A few days later Dolores was busy in her garden. Robert was sitting nearby on his nurse's lap. Joan kept up a constant murmur of conversation, half to the baby, telling him how clever and strong he was, and half to Dolores, repeating what she had just told Robert and adding his precocious reaction. Dolores had noticed recently with some concern that Joan was showing signs of preferring Robert to her own infant. It would soon be time for the boy to be weaned so that Joan and her child could be sent back to the farm.

At present, however, Dolores' attention was all on her work. She was gathering roses and dropping them into a large wicker basket. This was the second cutting of the season. It was a task that had to be done each year and, as usual, she worked with quiet efficiency, picking the blooms just as the buds began to open. Later she would tip the pile on the kitchen table, and she and Mabs would scissor off and discard the white base of each petal. It was slow work, but necessary, since vast quantities of rose-water had to be put by before the winter months.

She moved on to the next bush, a lax growing damask, and noticed with a twinge of irritation that she had missed a couple of blossoms when she had gone over the bush a few days earlier. Now they were too far open to be of any use. She cut off one head and tossed it aside, and was about to do the same with the second when she paused. A small nameless insect was lumbering over the petals. She looked at it more closely, and examined the difficult terrain through which it stumbled. For the first time in her life she noticed how the flower was constructed, the way the petals overlapped, row upon row like the most elaborate of trimmings. Then she saw its colour, a dense, deep red, wine red, ruby red, red with a hint of purple and a touch of pink, red like no other red in the world. Sun warmed, the flower released such a powerful fragrance that her chest tightened as she inhaled. She reached out her hand and touched it tentatively: a couple of petals flaked off and floated to the ground – such infinite beauty, and so fleeting.

She stooped and picked up the flower she had thrown down just a minute before and held it carefully in the palm of her hand, then walked slowly to a nearby seat where she sank down. The tightness in her chest remained and briefly, she was giddy. As she looked about her she heard the thousand insects she could not see, heard the birds and the distant ripple of the river. She recalled the day of Jinny's funeral when she had seen the beauty of Tilsbury for the first time. But this was a different kind of seeing. Then she had looked with her eyes, now her whole body was responding.

Unexpected tears suddenly blurred her vision and she could see only colours: the almost painful blue of the sky, the hundred shades of green where sunlight filtered through overhanging trees, deep indigo in the shadows. The greyness in which she had been immersed for as long as she could remember since the day of the massacre was dissolving in a rainbow of light.

I am lucky to be alive, she thought, and the commonplace phrase, which she had heard Nona repeat countless times in the past, struck her with the force of a vision. She understood that there are two ways of being alive. Since Würzburg she had survived, she had been not dead. Only now was she discovering what it meant truly to live, to be awake to every sight and sound and sensation in her world.

Her joy was so intense it seemed close to being a kind of sorrow. Stephen, she thought, Stephen has unlocked this door. And though he might one day exit from her world . . . No, she told herself firmly. One day, probably soon, he was sure to be only a memory . . . but whatever happened in the future, she was never going to return to that grey bleak prison of the spirit she had lived in before.

She, Dolores, was lucky to be alive.

It was not only Stephen. For a few moments she resisted the

subsequent thought, because it was so painful, but only for a short while.

Others were less fortunate, and would never have this chance to see the world with new-born eyes. Another man had played a part in freeing her from the misery of the blind and passive Doll she had been. A man who would never see the summer world which overwhelmed her now because she herself had murdered him. For the first time the enormity of her action weighed like lead. Darbier had been an arrogant fool, he had been a nuisance and insulting. He had not deserved to die. He had paid the price for another man's crime, and she had been the agent of his young death.

Remorse was a physical ache in the pit of her stomach. Yet she found the recognition of her crime to be more bearable than she had perhaps expected. It was all part of the new clarity with which she saw her world, her world where beauty and pain and happiness were so fiercely tangled they would never be teased apart.

There was a voice at her side. 'Are you all right, ma'am? The sun is very strong. Shall I fetch your hat?'

She turned and saw Ellen's always pale face gazing at her anxiously. Unused to seeing her mistress take her ease before a task was completed, the girl had assumed she must be unwell.

Dolores smiled and rose to her feet. 'Thank you, Ellen. And then take the roses into the kitchen and begin preparing them for the still. Mabs will show you if you are not sure how to do it.'

She went over to Joan and told her to take the baby in for his nap and then, tucking the damask rose into her bodice, she went to pick some sprigs of rosemary. The arrangement of this garden is all wrong, she thought, all the plants are set out with no more thought to their appearance than jars on a shelf. It must be changed.

With her wide-brimmed hat shadowing her face, she strolled to the centre of Tilsbury and pushed open the gate into the churchyard. The sexton was measuring out a new plot for a veteran of Naseby who had returned home only to die a few days later of an infection. He nodded a greeting and carried on his work. Since the death of her first child, Mistress Taverner had been a familiar figure in the graveyard. She dropped a piece of the herb of remembrance on the graves of her two lost infants, then on those of her grandmother and of Jinny Crew. It was only to be expected. The sexton looked up with surprise, however, when she moved over to stand by the grave of the young major who had been lodging in her house at the time of his murder. He noticed that she stood there for some minutes without moving at all, her hands folded in front of her, the expression of her face obscured by the falling shadow of her hat. Then, as though reaching a decision she took a full-blown damask rose from her bodice and laid that on his grave with her last piece of rosemary.

She looked up. So absorbed was she in her thoughts that it was a few moments before she noticed the small figure standing in the corner of the churchyard. He turned abruptly, as if wanting to escape detection then, realising it was too late, he waited while she walked over to him.

'Harry, whatever are you doing here?'

He hung his head. 'I saw you leave the house,' he said, 'I didn't know where you were going.'

The explanation was straightforward enough, except that for some reason he seemed ashamed.

Dolores said lightly, 'Why, Harry, have you been spying on me?'

The question was entirely frivolous, but no sooner had she spoken it than Dolores saw from her son's horrified response that, without meaning to, she had stumbled on something like the truth.

'No!' he protested, 'I didn't—'

Suddenly Dolores was serious. 'Harry, don't lie to me.'

'But I haven't . . .' His face was turning an uncomfortable red. 'Only Father said . . . when he went away . . . and I'm the only man of the house . . . so I was to tell Bussell . . . but I never knew what . . .'

'Oh! This is monstrous!' Dolores' rage was all against her husband, but Harry was sure he was to blame.

'That's not fair! I have to be a man now, Father said so. Oh, but I wish he was home again!'

'Harry, wait!'

But he had turned and run from the churchyard, leaving Dolores to walk back to the Priory House alone.

Furley Court in fine weather was a glimpse of Paradise. The rooms were cool and quiet, the grounds offered ample shade. One sultry July afternoon, Major Ripley and Sir Diggory retreated to the library. They had discovered a shared interest in antiquities, with unusual Latin inscriptions a particular passion. Major Ripley had come across several curiosities in the churches he had passed through since the fighting began. Sir Diggory was contentedly adding these to his already copious collection while Major Ripley was poring over an earlier volume. The major was in that state of tense absorption which was the nearest he ever came to happiness.

On the shady terrace to the north of the house, Cornet Trimball was engaged in discussing the relative merits of two greyhounds with a couple of cronies. From the bowling lawn came the gentle click of the wooden balls and a low murmur of voices as the other officers pursued their interminable game. In the stable-yard the Irishmen were smoking and chatting, too sated with the heat even to ask O'Rourke for a tune on his fiddle. All was languor and content.

Only Stephen Sutton was out of humour.

He had escaped his fellow officers and sought out the cool shade of the furthest part of the grounds which bordered a beech wood and was seldom used. He sat down on a low seat, but he was too restless to sit for long and soon began to pace up and down the grassy walk . . . but after a few turns he found that walking without going anywhere was worse than inactivity, so he returned to the seat. For once, thoughts of Dolores did not bring satisfaction. He spread his hands on his knees and examined them with distaste. They were strong and muscular, browned by the weather and leathery from hard use. They were serviceable, but now all he saw was their clumsiness. A soldier's hands, not a lover's. When he touched Dolores, his hands granted her no pleasure.

He was not given to self-deception. When they were together, she offered him her body and asked for nothing in return. Their love-making was her gift to him. At first this had not troubled him unduly. He had been confident that she would change. But his present idleness afforded plenty of time for brooding and he knew he had no grounds for optimism. Her pleasure now was no more and no less than it had been on the very first occasion. The act was by no means repugnant to her, but it was mechanical, so much so that he was beginning to feel an unexpected reticence. Whenever they met he felt the familiar tug of attraction, but as his desire grew it began to seem to him a gross and callous thing, since it made demands of her while offering nothing in return. The previous night he had made love to her only because his abstinence worried her: she saw it as evidence of his cooling affections. But he had found their coupling unsatisfactory. Far from initiating her into the pleasures of intimacy, he seemed to be learning to share her distaste. As always, they were careful not to talk of any subject which might be uncomfortable: besides, he had no language with which to discuss his concerns and was afraid his attempts would only make her feel she was failing him.

If he had believed she was a woman incapable of sensual pleasure, he might have minded less. But on the day she danced for him when the news of Naseby came he had glimpsed in her eyes the first unmistakable sparks of desire. And sparks, as he knew, however small, can lead to a generous fire if handled right.

But not by him. Had he acquired a courtier's smooth charms, he might have known how to entertain her as she deserved. Perhaps he had been too long a soldier, fought in too many campaigns and butchered too many of His Majesty's enemies. Perhaps it was not just the skin of his hands which was battle-hardened and insensitive: perhaps it was his spirit too.

He took a couple of turns up and down the shady walk, then sat and stared at his hands again. His impatience with his own shortcomings increased. Like the rest of his friends among the Cornish gentry, his early experiences had all been with whores or serving girls who were looking to supplement their meagre wages. He had paid court to one or two young ladies of quality: had he married one, their affection would have had time to grow slowly, and to express itself in many ways. Nothing in his experience so far had prepared him for this liaison with Dolores. If it ever became public, their union would be universally condemned or mocked, and yet he knew that this shameful affair was the finest part of his life so far. If they had been married . . . there was a burning sensation at the base of his throat at the impossible prospect . . . but if that had been the case, there would have been a home and children to share, mealtimes together and routine, a network of friends and neighbours. As it was, these few stolen hours in her bedchamber were all they had, most probably all they would ever have. Each occasion might well be their last. They did not have the luxury of time. He had never been a man who found it easy to put his deepest thoughts into words. And if he did not do so soon, the chance was sure to be lost for ever.

His conversation with Donnelly during the hay-making lodged like a reproach in his mind. Learning a new language, Donnelly had called his dalliance with Corinna Rogers. Several times since then he had been tempted to ask the young Irishman just what he had meant, but he knew he never would. Had they been friends merely, then such a discussion might have taken place. But Stephen had been too long armoured behind the reticence of a commanding officer to consider such familiarity with a subordinate ... or, if he was honest, with anyone else.

Perhaps his older brother. Where Stephen had always been more reserved, Nicolas Sutton had been much less inhibited, and had early on won a reputation as an easy-going seducer. As far as Stephen knew, his brother's only romantic problems were caused by the occasional sulks or furies of his wife Alice. But Nicolas had been wounded at Lansdown, and died during the long journey home, and all the many things that brothers mean to talk of together one day, would never now be spoken.

Stephen had no option but to struggle with this problem on his own.

'Captain Sutton, all alone and so downcast. Am I interrupting you?' He glanced up and saw Corinna Rogers standing in front of him. Under her bonnet, her face was pink with the heat and her throat was beaded with sweat.

'Not at all. I'm only too pleased to be distracted.'

'Thank heavens for that. My father and the major are up to their ears in Latin inscriptions, my father even wanted me to copy some for him – can you imagine? – and my brother Frederick grows more stupid by the day. And dear Lieutenant Donnelly is unable to keep me company this evening. It is all extremely tedious.'

'I'm sorry to hear it,' said Stephen with a grin.

She settled herself beside him on the seat and said, 'Captain Sutton, you are my last hope. If you don't find a way to entertain me, I shall probably expire from sheer *ennui*.'

'Heaven forbid, I'll have to see what I can do.'

It was one of the surprises that had awaited Stephen at Furleys, this easy friendship with Corinna Rogers. Since they had long since declared their attraction for each other, and long since chosen to do nothing about it, they enjoyed the kind of undemanding intimacy that is usually reserved for former lovers. Corinna had never been one to bear a grudge; and besides, Lieutenant Donnelly was all very well in his own way but his conversation was apt to be monotonous. Apart from his devotion to her, which was just as it should be, his thoughts revolved almost entirely around the suffering of his native land, and Ireland's woes were not a topic to engage Corinna's attention for long. She saw no reason why she must pretend to Stephen that her affair with Donnelly was over: so far as her father and brother were concerned, her days at Furley Court were passed in cloistered meditation on past wrongs and future improvement. When she thought of the future at all, she hoped merely that her brother would leave for the battlefield soon. Sir Diggory's increasing indisposition and a tendency to assume, despite all evidence to the contrary, that his daughter could do no wrong, offered her the best chance of maintaining her freedom.

She said comfortably, 'I knew I could rely on you, Captain Sutton. Frederick's wretched cronies treat me with odious courtesy, but I know they despise me behind my back. I don't care a farthing for their opinion, but I cannot stand hypocrisy. You are different, I wonder why? I can talk to you as never in a hundred years could I talk to one of those puffed-up popinjays. Are all Cornishmen so straightforward and honest? Now you are put out already. I've never known a man flinch so from a word of praise. It's all right, I promise not to flatter you any more. Still, you have no illusions about me, but you treat me with respect. I cannot think when that has happened before.'

'You are you,' said Stephen simply, 'I can't explain it more than that.'

'Maybe that is enough. Now we are such friends I can tell you I was most put out the night you did not come to my house. All sorts of explanations passed through my head. I even wondered if Doll Taverner had stolen your affection – imagine that! – but then, of course, I learned that boy had murdered your major, and I began to understand. Anything less than a murder and you'd never have been forgiven.'

'I'm glad I was.'

'Hmm. Donnelly is a pretty youth. "The Lord giveth and the Lord taketh away." I suspect, Captain Sutton, that you have a sweetheart in Cornwall. I imagine her a very lovely and simple girl. Am I right?'

Stephen cleared his throat. The conversation was taking an uncomfortable turn and, with his usual regard for honesty he was uncertain how to respond. At length he said, 'There is a woman who has my heart, yes.'

'And does she care for you?'

'I have reason to believe she does.'

'Then you will marry her when this war is done?'

'If only I could.'

'What, Captain, an intrigue? How delightful. The young lady who has your heart is obviously not the free and simple girl I pictured. Is she married, then?'

Stephen did not answer.

'Oh *ho*. Better and better. And of course, you are far too discreet to talk of her. She is a lucky woman then, even if she is not at liberty. But . . . you are frowning. I wonder why. Perhaps the path of true love does not run smooth in Cornwall either?'

She was regarding him speculatively. Stephen stared at his hands and said nothing for a long time.

Finally he said in a low voice, 'It happens sometimes that there are difficulties . . . though the love be ever so strong.'

'If the woman is married then there are always difficulties. But don't you find that, when the object of desire is finally achieved, the taste is all the better simply because of the problems overcome? They say the air is sweeter on the mountain top because of the effort of the ascent. I know that as soon as I found myself legally bound to poor Tom, the whole business became quite tiresome. Love should be an adventure, not a duty, don't you agree?'

'But sometimes . . .'

'Yes?'

Stephen was at a loss for words. Suddenly Corinna remembered a young ostler who had been so overawed by the opportunity presented to him that he had been quite unmanned. Another reason for Stephen's nonappearance on the night of Darbier's murder occurred to her.

'Captain Sutton, it happens on occasion that a man's capacity to perform falls short of his desire. Do you perhaps have difficulties—?'

'No, no,' Stephen interrupted her swiftly, 'Nothing like that.'

She chuckled and settled herself more comfortably on the seat. 'I've never seen you blush before. I must cause you to do so more often.'

'We had better talk of something else.'

'On the contrary, I am thoroughly curious.' Corinna's delight in talking of love was almost as great as practising it. 'How on earth are we to fill these interminable afternoons if not in conversation . . . and I have always found this a topic of endless interest.'

Stephen looked away. 'I'm not accustomed to talk of it.'

'That is perfectly obvious. It is frequently the case, however, that I have experience enough for two.'

'Yes.' Stephen was battling with the urge to flee. He saw suddenly that this was an opportunity that was unlikely to recur. He had no idea how to proceed with this conversation, but no wish to end it either. He said slowly, 'Supposing there was a woman whose previous experiences had not disposed her to find pleasure in . . . in . . .'

'In what, Captain?'

Stephen stared at her briefly, then looked away again without answering.

'In sexual intimacy? As I thought. Please continue, Captain.'

'Well then, such a woman might be loving, but unable to show it in certain ways. And it might be that the man who cared for her did not have the experience, or the skill, or the understanding to show her the way to . . . so that she might . . . and though they both wanted . . .'

'Ah, Captain Sutton, yes. I see we are to talk in riddles, but I think I understand you. There is a woman – who may or may not be your Cornish beauty, I'd not presume to enquire – who for some reason has no delight in love-making, though she is willing. And you wish to know how best to give her that delight?'

'It's getting late. We should go indoors.'

'Nonsense. I can't remember the last time I was so intrigued by a conversation.'

'You talk so easily. I'd sooner have a tooth pulled.'

'But for the sake of your mysterious not-free lady, you will endure even this?'

'Yes. Yes of course I will.'

'Hmm. When I said that I had experience enough for two, I was not thinking that another woman was to benefit. But why not? It will pass the time.'

'I thought you might have some understanding . . .'

'Indeed I do. Though I must say that your lady friend's problem has never been my own. Rather the opposite, in fact. Still, let me see if I can think of anything that might help.' She was silent for a moment, and then the words of a travelling instrument-maker floated into her mind. He had been employed for a few days to mend her father's harpsichord (and for a few nights had entertained her). 'A woman's body is like a musical instrument,' she said sweetly, 'it is necessary to learn the pitch of each, how it is best to be played so that the truest note emerges.'

Stephen was gazing blankly at his hands.

Corinna saw that though to her this was a game, to him it was a matter of grave importance. She said, 'In general I believe a woman's pleasure is slower to grow than that of a man. A lover must learn to restrain his own desire so that the woman has a chance to match it.'

'Slower?'

'Yes. Many times I have found it necessary to teach a lover to take his time. Love is not medicine to be swallowed with all haste, but a banquet to be savoured for as long as possible. It is quite amazing what a little self-control on the man's part may achieve.'

'I see. Yes.'

Stephen's expression was so uncomfortable that Corinna could barely keep herself from laughing. But she wanted to help him, and she wanted to continue the conversation. She recalled the stories told by one lover who had made a habit of seducing virtuous wives. She said soberly, 'A little strong drink is often beneficial where shyness is a barrier.'

'Drink?'

'Not very much. A mouthful of brandy, perhaps, or a little sack. It can assist in easing the most troublesome of consciences.'

'Fine. Yes. That's been most helpful, Mistress Rogers. Now, I think—' Stephen was rising from the seat but Corinna placed her hand on his thigh to restrain him.

'Not so hasty, Captain. The lesson is hardly begun.'

'But—'

'If you wish to help your bashful Cornish mistress, you will need to learn much more. Have you ever studied, for instance, the map of a woman's body? Surely you would like to discover in which regions the deepest pleasure lies, and how best to draw that pleasure out? Some women, so I am told, delight in caresses to the nape of the neck, while others swoon only when their ear lobes are kissed in a certain way. For my own part, there is a place on my inner arm, just above the elbow which affords exquisite delight. Only let a man brush that region with his thumb in a certain circular motion, and I am utterly lost, though he be as ugly as sin and smell like the very devil.'

Stephen opened his mouth to speak, then shut it again. Although he was once more sitting next to her on the seat, Corinna had for some reason omitted to remove her hand from his thigh.

She shifted into a more comfortable position, and the pressure of her palm increased slightly. Her voice had become low and hypnotic. 'I mentioned kissing just now. Of course, that is a study in itself.' She remembered a distinguished Frenchman, one of her father's guests, whom she had considered too old to bother with until he had first kissed her. 'A kiss may be a question or a statement. It can flatter or cajole or tease. Depending on which part of the anatomy the lips entice—'

'Mistress Rogers—'

'Yes, Captain Sutton?'

She held his gaze in hers before continuing, softly, 'Of course, the kiss becomes a weapon of a different kind where the tongue is employed also . . .' The pattern of her breathing had changed. She moistened her lips with the tip of her tongue. 'Captain Sutton, I do believe I shall have to show you.'

He turned away swiftly. 'This is madness.'

'Why so? Whoever learned to ride a horse by listening to someone talk?'

'But . . .'

'Well then. I refuse to offer one more word of advice unless there is to be a practical demonstration to go with it. Selfishness does not become you, Captain. I find it most unsettling to talk and not to do, and my sweet Irishman is not free again until tomorrow. Besides, I can see that you are quite as eager as I.'

'But Donnelly and . . . we are neither of us free.'

'*I* am perfectly free. Donnelly knows that. And you need not fear disloyalty to your sweetheart. For one thing, she will never know. And if I teach you how to give her satisfaction then the dear lady should be for ever in my debt. You could almost say you are doing this for her sake – though I'd much rather you did not.'

Stephen remembered the courtesies in time. 'I hardly need encouragement to do it for my own sake. But . . .'

'Damn your buts. I have always detested buts. You want to learn, Captain, and there is no one can teach you as well as I can.

Consider for example the different species of caress. There is the one that is soft as a feather which may be employed with great effect on the inner thighs.' As she spoke her hand moved towards her lap. 'And then, of great importance, the different caresses for the breasts, the slow touch which draws sensation towards a woman's nipple, the one that mimics the feel of an infant's mouth . . .'

Her hand was resting now against her breast. Stephen's last objections were vanishing. He said, 'But where? When?'

'Why now, of course. As I remember, you are not to be depended on for a rendezvous. There is a little hut in the beech wood, not five minutes walk from here. Some charcoal-burners left it there a couple of years ago. It is never used, except in winter.'

'Is it safe?'

She smiled her quiet satisfaction. 'It has always proved so in the past.'

Corinna caught hold of his hand as soon as they entered the wood, and led him along a narrow shady path. The charcoal-burners' hut lay in a small clearing, but, being all built of sticks and moss and dried mud, it would have been easy to mistake for a mound of fallen earth. Seeing Stephen's surprise, Corinna smiled.

'You can see how private we can be. Even the badgers and foxes will never trouble us here.'

Stephen realised that the very discomfort of the place added to Corinna's sense of adventure. Having never known anything but soft sheets and feather beds, she could afford the fantasy of squalor. And indeed the little clearing had a dream-like quality. Shafts of sunlight touched the higher leaves, but down below all was cool, and still. Not a leaf moved, even the birds were silent.

He said, 'How did you discover this place?'

She shrugged. 'That is not important. Come—' Stretching out her hand, she stooped to enter the doorway.

Stephen felt an unaccustomed confusion. He said awkwardly, 'Maybe, would it not be better if we simply talked?'

'Talked, Captain Sutton?'

'If you merely told me what you know. There is surely no need—'

She frowned, then raised her eyebrows and smiled. 'You think talking is sufficient? I wonder . . . let me see now.' Still smiling, she began to unlace her pale bodice. 'A woman's breasts may afford her great pleasure, if her lover touches them with skill.' As she was speaking she lifted her breasts free of her clothes and cupped them in her hands. 'Shall I demonstrate for you, Captain? Look, like this, see how my thumbs circle the nipples. Are you sure you do not wish to try for yourself?'

Her gaze had become blurred with the pleasure of her own caress. Stephen found his mouth was suddenly dry, and he was unable to answer.

'Here,' she said, taking his hand and placing it over hers, 'Like this.'

'Yes,' he said, drawing back quickly, 'Yes, I see.'

Her expression narrowed. 'Captain Sutton, do you think I am a whore that I must do all the work myself? Are you so lacking in any manly feelings? Shame on you.' As she spoke she let her dress slip from her shoulders and bunch around her waist. 'Well?'

Stephen was lost. As he followed her into the hut it was possible to believe that this afternoon of unusual heat and hazy shadows, this small space in the middle of the wood and the earth-smelling darkness of the hut were nothing to do with everyday life and the normal codes of conduct by which he lived his life.

By the time he had returned her kisses and she had relieved him of his boots and breeches, they were both far too aroused to waste time with lessons of any kind. After a very short while, when their immediate desire had been satisfied and they lay side by side on the soft leafy earth, Stephen was furious with himself.

'Slower, you said. And that was far from slow. What an imbecile I am.'

'Not at all, your eagerness was flattering. Especially since you proved such an unexpected challenge. Two starving people are hardly in a condition to discuss table manners. Now, to business.'

'Now?'

'Why, of course. Why not?'

Stephen considered. He thought of Dolores, and decided he ought to bring this meeting to an end. He reached for his clothes and said, 'It is time I returned to the house.'

'Captain Sutton, you are utterly transparent. Your conscience is troubling you, that is all. But only consider, you have already been unfaithful to your secret mistress, but so far you have not learned much that will be of any value to her.'

'On the contrary, Mistress Rogers, this has been most informative.'

'You delude yourself, Captain, this has been the easy part. You would be letting your mistress down if you were to abandon your studies at this early stage. Can you really deny her the chance to learn of sensual pleasures, just for the sake of your paltry conscience?'

Somewhere high in the leafy canopy above them, a wood-pecker's mocking cry echoed through the branches. Stephen knew that Corinna's teasing argument was nonsensical, but just at present he could think of no logic with which to counter it. Corinna, though never beautiful, was always dignified. Even as she reclined on the soft earth floor, her hair dishevelled, half in and half out of her clothes, she retained her imperious manner. Stephen leaned over and kissed her. She smiled, took his breeches from his hand and folded them into a pillow for her head.

'Now, to business. We must assume there is a woman who, for whatever reason, wishes to eat, but has no appetite. How are we to remedy this? First of all, with your voice. Fine words will open any door. Women like to be told that they are beautiful and beloved above all others. Did you ever know a poet with an empty bed? And if the words are sincere, as I'm sure yours would be, then so much the better.'

'She already knows I love her.'

'You miss the point, Captain. Though you may have said it a thousand times, she will still delight to hear it again. So, we will assume that you have wooed her with honeyed words. Your next weapons are all those of touch, with your hands and finger-tips, your lips and your tongue. If your lady is shy of speaking, you must learn how to listen to her body so you may know what pleases her best. Later I will show you the signs which indicate when she is ready to receive you. But first, you may kiss me, and I will tell you how you do.'

When Stephen had first ridden with her to Furleys, Corinna had marked him down as a handsome fellow with little real experience but a great potential for improvement. And, that afternoon, she was not disappointed. She had enjoyed their first coupling for its raw, animal energy. When they made love for the second time he displayed an enthusiasm for the workings of

307

their bodies, and a delight in the language of lovers that she found intoxicating. By sharing in his voyage she was able to recapture some of the zest of her first girlhood encounters. But the third occasion was different altogether. Stephen was grown more confident and had discovered the little tricks of mastery which she, normally the most domineering of women, was quite unable to resist. His caresses were unhurried, and even when she urged him on he did not comply straight away, waiting until her own desire had risen to such a pitch that she was tempted to regret she had ever taught the lesson so well. But it was a brief regret, and swept away entirely by the pleasure that followed, pleasure of an intensity that Corinna had not felt in a long time, and that Stephen had never known before. Afterwards they lay together for a long time in the little hut, listening to the woodpecker's teasing cry and watching the watery pattern of sunlight dappling the world beyond their earthy burrow. For ever afterwards the smell of sun-warmed woods brought back to Stephen the physical taste of that long afternoon.

They walked slowly back through the wood. Stephen, who felt as though he had left his bones and sinews behind him in the charcoal-burners' hut, did not notice that Corinna, for once, hardly spoke. As they reached the gate that led back into the grounds, they stopped.

'I'll go first,' she said, 'You follow in a little while. We should not be seen returning together.'

Stephen nodded his compliance. He felt the need of some time alone. His shame at betraying Dolores was matched only by amazement at his earlier ignorance. Added to this was an apprehension lest he had embarked on an adventure that might prove difficult to conclude. He said, 'And . . . Mistress Rogers, I don't know how to thank you.'

'Don't mention it, Captain.' She was fiddling with the ribbon of her bonnet and looking towards the house. 'But I think we may consider your course of instruction complete.'

'That is a pity.' Stephen said this only for politeness' sake. Great though the pleasure had been, he felt no urge to repeat the experience.

Corinna was astute enough to know this. Her earlier sentence had been intended to elicit his present feelings, and she sensed his relief. She felt a brief twinge of annoyance, and as well as that, an emotion that was new to her. She resolved to give

Captain Sutton a wide berth for the next little while. Above all, Corinna was a realist. Captain Sutton would always be her friend, and loyal, but he would never feel strongly for her. And she had no intention of losing her heart to anyone, let alone to a man who was obviously in love with someone else.

Chapter 22

❧

The next day the heat intensified, and the air weighed heavy over the valley. In mid afternoon strange towering clouds appeared above the hills, boiled up like smoke and dissipated, then massed again. By evening came thunder and lightening, but it was not until midnight that the storm broke and rain beat down on the hard earth. To Stephen and Dolores the noise of the rain and the crack and roll of thunder were welcome only because it meant they could speak above their usual enforced whisper.

'Stephen, what are you doing?'

'Just this.'

'It feels strange.'

'Do you like it?'

'I don't know. It's hard to tell.'

'How about this?'

'Oh, that is . . . well, yes, I think I like that. But Stephen, we should hurry. Beth might wake again or . . .'

'Ellen is with her.'

'But Ellen is more afraid of thunder than she is.'

'Stop fretting, my love. Your door is locked and we have the whole night to enjoy. We can take our time. Like this . . .'

'Oh.'

'You were beautiful when you danced. Let me kiss you again.'

'If you like. But Stephen, blow out the candle and—'

'I want to watch you. Look, see how lovely you are.'

'Really? I never thought of that. But when you kiss me . . . there, like that, I feel giddy. Perhaps it was the brandy. Do you think we should stop, someone might . . .'

'There's nothing wrong with giddy. Your face says you like it.'

'Does it? I can't really tell. I never felt like this before.'

'Trust me, Dolores.'

'I do trust you. But you're different tonight. What has happened to you, Stephen?'

'Nothing. I just want to show you how much I love you.'

'Yes. I see. Oh, that tickles.'

'But you're smiling. How about this?'

'I think perhaps I do like that.'

'And this?'

'Yes. Especially that. I think I must be drunk. I feel so strange. But it was such a little glass of brandy.'

'We are kissing-drunk, that's all.'

'Oh. But Stephen, I thought . . . I thought . . . I can't remember now what I thought. All the words seem to be going out of my head.'

'Then let them go.'

'Yes . . . I feel I'm floating.'

'But you won't fall, I'm holding you.'

'I wish you could hold me always.'

'Now, and always.'

'Oh yes, kiss me again that way. Yes, just like that. It frightens me, I can't think why, but I want you to do it more. Is that crazy of me?'

'If so, then I am crazy too.'

'Yes, you've changed, Stephen. What has changed you?'

'Loving you, that's all.'

'Is it . . . but . . . I don't see what . . . I . . .'

In the world beyond their window, the heavy rain continued all night long; a discreet and kindly rain, granting them the privacy to explore their love.

It was the middle of July. Dolores had spent all morning in the stillroom, and after the midday meal she escaped to the further corner of the garden. The baby was playing with his nurse nearby. Every now and then Dolores swept him up and took him to view some fresh treasure: a bright damsel fly or a coloured leaf. She was holding him aloft and pointing up to the swallows as they dived and soared above their heads, when Stephen came into the garden. He walked with studied nonchalance.

At once Dolores handed Robert back to his nurse. 'Take him into the house. He has had enough fresh air for one afternoon.'

The girl, who had been enjoying the sunshine, began to protest, but Dolores dismissed her fiercely. She was aware all the time of Stephen standing nearby, his grey eyes fixed on her, his features impassive.

'Mistress Taverner.'

'Captain Sutton, good day. What a pleasant surprise to see you again after so long.'

It was the hardest task in all the world, to stand so stiff and formal when all her senses were burning with his nearness.

They remained immobile while the nurse retreated with her charge towards the house. Dolores looked about her swiftly. The gardener was out of earshot. There was no one else close enough to overhear them.

'Could you not wait until tonight?' she asked him in a low voice. 'Are you so impatient to see me?' But her eyes were warm with pleasure.

'The carrier came to Furleys this morning. He brought me a letter from my father.' Stephen's face remained grave. 'And there was one for you from your husband. I said that I would bring it, since I was coming into Tilsbury. We need to talk privately.'

'Is it bad news? You look so solemn.'

He stared down between his boots at the crack in the paving stone through which a small-leaved plant was struggling to survive. 'It is mixed.'

Dolores felt a twinge of unease, but she nodded briskly and said, 'Wait for me in the winter parlour then. I shall follow in a moment. Do you have Josiah's letter?'

She read it swiftly while Stephen was walking back to the house, then crumpled the page angrily. As usual it was both brief and pompous. It revealed nothing of his own whereabouts or activity; its only purpose was to remind her that he was kept fully informed on all events at the Priory House. '*Now that the soldiers are all transferred to Furleys, I trust you find yourself less burdened . . .*' Rage boiled up inside her. Bad enough that he should employ his steward to spy on his wife, worse, far worse, to set the son to keep watch on his mother. In spite of all her efforts at reassurance since their conversation in the churchyard, Dolores was certain that Josiah had driven a wedge between them which could never entirely be removed. The easy trust that had always existed between them was gone for ever. For that, she would never forgive her husband.

Suddenly Dolores smiled. He was so certain that he knew her every move and thought; oh, if the smug and domineering fool only knew how pitifully ignorant he really was!

She was still smiling when she closed the door of the winter parlour behind her.

'Stephen!' There was no longer any need to disguise her pleasure at seeing him.

He was standing near the empty fireplace and he turned slightly as she approached, but his expression remained solemn. Dolores stopped. He looked to her like a man who has an unpleasant duty to perform.

She said coldly, 'Your news?'

'A battle has been fought near a place called Langport. Our western army has been defeated. Parliament's New Model carries all before it. Only a miracle will stop them now.'

'Is that all?'

'There is good news too. My father has written to say the boy Tully arrived at Rossmere some weeks ago. It sounds as if he has settled in well. They are short of men to work the land, and he has made himself useful.'

'Then that is surely a matter for rejoicing.'

'Yes.'

But Stephen appeared far from rejoicing. Dolores stood very still, examining his profile carefully. She realised it was some time since she had seen him at close quarters in the day time. Candleshine mellows everything: in this light he appeared harsher, but also in some strange way, far more vulnerable.

Stephen was not sure himself just why he had chosen to take this opportunity to visit Dolores during the day. He was beginning to hate the necessary secrecy of their midnight meetings. His great love for her, which he wanted to trumpet from the house-tops, had to be kept hidden away like a crime. But now, as he faced her in the cool space of the winter parlour, he realised that the deception that was troubling him most was his silence over the matter of Corinna Rogers.

At first he had been so happy with the gifts of pleasure he was bringing Dolores that he had not allowed himself to reflect too deeply on the origin of those gifts. Now he was beginning to feel like a man who has lavished jewels on his lover, without pausing to consider that those jewels were stolen. Each time he took the underground route he passed by Josiah's casket, a tangible reminder that things of great beauty can be worthless unless honestly gained.

He had never realised how high the price of his amorous lessons would be. Now, as he faced Dolores in the winter parlour he knew that he, who had always asserted his honesty, was, by his silence, being dishonest.

'Stephen, what is the matter?'

He turned away. 'Nothing.'

'Do you have to leave Tilsbury?'

'Not yet. Nothing is changed.'

'But there is something, I know it.'

Stephen was silent. He hated his silent lie, but there was no alternative. He could not tell her about Corinna; not because she would be angry – that was only what he deserved – but because of the distress it would cause her. And yet the knowledge of his deceit was a kind of slow suffocation.

Dolores watched him. 'What is it, Stephen?'

'There is nothing. Only war worries. I should not have come.' He remained only a little longer, before he took his hat, bid her farewell and left.

Dolores was puzzled, and increasingly uneasy. She had noticed a gradual alteration in Stephen, and traced its origins back to the days following the thunderstorm. Just as her own pleasure was growing, his seemed increasingly coloured by doubts. Sometimes now he seemed almost reluctant to make love to her, as though he was ashamed. Never for one moment did she imagine he had ceased to love her; she knew him too well for that. But she knew also that he was hiding something from her, and that the burden of it was causing a gulf between them. It seemed, she thought with some exasperation, that just as one barrier came down, another appeared to replace it.

Her unease was tempered by the knowledge that the source of Stephen's discomfort was unlikely to remain hidden for long. He was not a man who was at ease with secrets. If this one was of any significance at all, she was sure to unravel it before long.

It was Sunday morning, and Sir Diggory's gout was sufficiently recovered for him to join Major Ripley and those of his officers who were preparing for divine service. Captain Sutton was a regular churchgoer: no one suspected for a moment that it was the desire to see Mistress Taverner in daylight, rather than any great piety, which inspired his devotions. At the last moment, just as the party was about to leave, Corinna descended the main staircase: she was dressed in a blue and grey outfit that was elegant, but hardly sober, and she wore a high-crowned hat.

She took her father's arm. 'I hope there is a place for me in your carriage, Father,' she said sweetly, 'It is so long since I've attended a service, and I miss it terribly.'

'Quite so, my dear, quite so.' Sir Diggory had somehow worked himself round to the belief that his daughter had been the innocent victim of malicious rumour. He patted her hand.

Frederick, who knew his sister rather better, looked startled. 'Are you sure you want to go?' he asked.

'Certainly, Frederick.' Her smile was blameless. 'Private prayer is all very well, but one requires also the comforts of public devotion. One cannot allow village tittle-tattle to undermine the practice of religion. Don't you agree, Captain Sutton? I know I can rely on your opinion.'

Stephen had been observing Corinna's charade with great amusement and found it hard to remain serious as he replied, 'I can only commend your determination, Mistress Rogers.'

Corinna sailed out into the sunshine and took her seat in her father's carriage, the same carriage in which she had been obliged to make her hasty retreat from Tilsbury only two months before.

In fact she was more anxious than she allowed anyone to see. She knew animosity towards her remained strong in the town. Her maid Ann, who had gone to visit a friend only the week before, had been pelted with stones by a group of children whose mothers did nothing to stop them, and she had returned to Furleys in a state of near hysteria. Corinna did not particularly mind if she never set foot in church again, but she could not abide having her activities restricted. She was happy enough to remain at Furleys for ever, if she knew she was free to come and go as she pleased. She had calculated that this was an excellent opportunity to show her face in Tilsbury again. For one thing, if she was in the company of half a dozen officers, as well as her father and brother, not even the boldest of her critics would dare to speak out against her. She knew the value of habit. Only let the people of Tilsbury become accustomed to seeing her in public once more and, though her reputation was beyond rescue, she would at least have retrieved her freedom of movement.

It was a risk – but the alternative was to spend the rest of her life as a virtual prisoner in Furleys. And that was unthinkable.

Her heart sank however as she entered the church beside her father. It was packed and, though she looked neither to right nor left, she was instantly aware of Tom Rogers sitting in his accustomed place to the left and about half way down the nave. If anything her apprehension made her appear more aloof than before.

The congregation was murmuring its disapproval like a hive of bees as Stephen took up his position but he did not even notice. Experimentation had taught him the precise spot from which he could observe Dolores throughout the service while appearing to attend the minister. For her part Dolores made sure she turned aside frequently to talk either with Philip on her right, or with Beth on her left, so that Stephen might see her profile, and not merely the back of her head. It was a kind of game they had developed, this method of creating an invisible tie between them, so that when Dolores heard Stephen's rich voice singing the psalms just a fraction louder than was necessary, she knew he was only doing it so she could hear him. Locked in their own private world, yet to all onlookers merely following the appointed ritual, both Stephen and Dolores were quite ridiculously happy, and oblivious to all the tensions rippling through the church on that sunny Sunday.

Afterwards, however, even they could not avoid the drama. The party from Furleys was, as usual, the first to leave the church, but Tom Rogers had slipped out before the end of the service and stood foursquare in their path. His handsome face was transformed.

Sir Diggory flapped a pale hand towards him. 'Out of the way, fellow,' he said, 'Go on, man, let us pass.'

'I will speak with my wife first.'

'Don't be a nuisance, Rogers. You've had your money.'

If anything was calculated to provoke Tom to violence, then it was a reference to the money he had been given, most of which he had drunk away while planning sweet revenge and even sweeter reconciliation with his wife. When he took up his stance on the church path, Tom Rogers had no very clear plan in mind: he knew that he must make a protest of some sort. But when he saw Corinna, so plain and yet so very desirable, his only thought was to take her home with him again, beat her soundly and then carry on as before.

He said, 'Corinna—'

She stared at him coldly. 'Do not make a public spectacle, Tom. I am going back to Furleys with my father. You and I have nothing to discuss.'

But Tom was rooted to the spot and could not have moved if he had wanted to. Doggedly, he repeated her name. 'Corinna, you cannot simply go. It's not right. I won't have it.'

Sir Diggory once again flapped his pale hand at the obstacle. 'Be gone, fellow. Must I call the constable?'

Another unfortunate remark; the constable was a cousin of Tom's and had slipped away at the first sign of trouble. Corinna realised this and, though she would have died rather than show it, she was beginning to be seriously alarmed. Now she remembered that her brother Frederick was a notorious coward; his fellow officers were observing the scene from a little distance and were clearly in no hurry to spoil their Sunday morning with a domestic brawl.

'Come home, Corinna,' said Tom, 'I'm taking you home with me.'

'Never.'

Tom heard the tremor of anxiety in her refusal, and suddenly he saw his opportunity. His experience as a soldier had taught him the advantages of brute force, and he knew he stood a good chance of recovering his wife at once if he simply removed her bodily from the churchyard.

'You're coming home with me,' he repeated. 'Now.'

Corinna gripped her father's arm. The churchyard was full of spectators and, without once taking her eyes from Tom's face, she knew that support for him was growing by the minute. Her own resources were minimal. Her father was too frail to make a stand, and her brother would not mind in the least if she was made to return to her husband in Distaff Lane. Unless Frederick made a move, none of his fellow officers would bother to intervene. Her gamble had turned out more disastrously than she would have thought possible.

'No,' she said helplessly.

'We've a score to settle, you and I.'

Tom was so confident now that he was almost smiling. Though she knew it would be disastrous, Corinna was on the point of trying to push past him, since she could think of no alternative, when a tall figure appeared at her side and a familiar voice said, 'Tom, don't be a fool. You may have reason to be angry, but you know full well this is neither the time nor the place.'

Tom's reply was an oddly inarticulate rumble of disgust, a sound reminiscent of distant thunder.

Stephen took Corinna's arm and said quietly, 'Mistress Rogers, let me escort you to your carriage.' Corinna could have sobbed with relief.

Stephen had lingered after the others in the church and so had arrived late on the scene. His public reason for delay was to exchange a few words with the sexton: in fact he was waiting to observe Dolores as she left with her three children. As soon as he followed her from the porch, he saw from the expectant crowd that trouble of some kind was brewing. One glance at Tom Rogers told him also that it would take a battery of cannon to shift the wronged husband from his position on the path: all his cuckold's pride depended on how he acquitted himself now. Stephen had a good deal of sympathy with him, but his loyalty at this moment was all for Corinna, and no one would benefit from a violent scene.

The crowd waited. Almost everyone there knew and respected Captain Sutton and, as soon as he placed himself at Corinna's side his fellow officers, a somewhat shame-faced Frederick Page amongst them, formed a protective cluster behind him. In an instant the balance had tipped against Tom Rogers.

Still eager to avoid an unnecessary confrontation, Stephen led Corinna and her father a little way off the path and over a couple of grassy graves to the lych-gate and the steps down into the street where their carriage was waiting.

'Thank you, Captain Sutton,' said Corinna when she was safely settled on the seat beside her father.

'My pleasure, ma'am.'

It was only then that she felt safe enough to survey the scene she had quitted. Tom, stranded like a solitary boulder after the flood has passed, was still standing in the middle of the church path. Corinna looked coolly back at the hostile crowd, determined to stare down the contempt she saw on every face. Even Doll Taverner, whom she would have expected to show some charity, was watching her with black hatred in her fine eyes.

And then Corinna's heart skipped a beat. She was aware that Stephen Sutton had also observed Mistress Taverner's expression. She saw the way Doll's eyes glanced at Stephen and then back to her own face, and she recognised then that the other woman's hatred was very different from that of the rest of the crowd. No disapproval there, but a very private jealousy. The brief flash of understanding must have showed on Corinna's face, because Dolores flushed and looked away, suddenly absorbed in some all-important business with Beth's collar.

Corinna turned to Stephen with genuine amazement. 'Doll Taverner,' she breathed, 'Whoever would have thought it?'

Before Stephen had a chance to reply, the carriage moved away, and Corinna, overcome with relief and surprise, collapsed against her father's side and astonished him by giggling almost the whole way back to Furleys.

Chapter 23

❧

Stephen was weighed down with foreboding as he rode to the Old Priory ruins that night. Dolores, on the contrary, was so angry that she forgot her fear entirely and entered the secret tunnel without a second thought. She was waiting near the foot of the old tower as Stephen approached.

'Dolores, my love, what are you doing here?'

She wasted no time. 'You have knowledge of that woman, Corinna Rogers, that trollop. You have been with her, I know it. I saw it in your eyes today, I saw it on her face. She knew about me. You must have told her, and all the time you pretended there was nothing. You claim to be so honest, but you're a liar like all the rest. Corinna Rogers, of all people! Answer me then, is it not true?'

Dolores' phrases were barely coherent gasps of pain and fury. Stephen took a pace towards her. She had set the lantern on a jutting shelf of stone and her face was in shadow, but what he saw was torment enough. He stopped dead in his tracks. There was a long silence.

At length he said simply, 'Yes.'

'Oh!'

All at once Dolores found that she was shivering with cold. Her teeth were chattering as she pulled her cloak more tightly around her shoulders. Again Stephen took a step towards her, again he stopped.

'Dear God—' she spoke through clenched teeth. 'I cannot believe it!'

'Dolores—'

'All the time – you pretended – but that woman has been

your mistress – and you have lied—'

'No, listen to me, please. It was only once . . .' Stephen corrected himself. 'There was only one occasion. I cannot say why, I think perhaps I was insane. You have good reason to be angry, but I never told her about you. I said there was a woman I loved but she thought she was in Cornwall. It was only when she saw you today, I do not know how . . . she must have guessed . . .'

'Of course she guessed! Do you think we are both fools?'

'No—'

'Yes, yes you must do. You pretend to be so honest and honourable, and all the time . . . oh, you sicken me!'

'Dolores, I am sorry.'

'Sorry!' The word was like a trigger. 'Sorry! You dare to stand there and tell me you are sorry!'

She stooped briefly and picked something from the rough floor of the ruin. As she rushed at him, her face spiky with rage, Stephen saw she held a piece of fallen masonry in her hand. He half-raised his arms to protect himself but, perhaps deliberately, he was not fast enough, and the blow caught him on the side of the face, causing a deep cut. The stone fell from her hand, but Dolores continued to strike him with her fists, only stopping when she realised her rage was about to give way to tears. Never would she grant him the satisfaction of seeing her weep.

'Oh!' she exclaimed as she turned away to hide her despair, 'You are a monster.'

Stephen stood immobile. Blood was running down his cheek but he did not notice it. He said simply, 'Dolores, please listen to me.'

'Yes? What can you possibly have to say?'

'I don't know,' he said helplessly, 'Only that I wish it had not happened. Corinna Rogers means nothing to me. You are the only woman I care for, the only woman I have ever loved. I am sorry . . .' He broke off, appalled to hear himself mouthing the hackneyed excuses of the adulterer, desperate to find a way to convince Dolores that on this occasion at least the words were sincere.

He sat down on a large block of stone. 'I have been a fool, worse than a fool. I will go now, if you wish.'

'That's right,' taunted Dolores, 'run away as soon as there is trouble. You are a coward as well as a liar. I hope to God I never see you again.'

'Very well, you have every reason . . .'

But neither of them moved. Although she was boiling with rage, Dolores was thinking very fast. At that moment she hated Stephen with a passion, but she did not want him to leave. She wanted him to stay so she could hurt him, and punish him . . . and be with him still.

She said, 'No, don't go.'

'If there was any way I could undo what happened with Mistress Rogers . . .'

'Why, was the experience so unpleasant?'

Stephen did not answer.

'Was it? You say there was one occasion only . . . so I take it she did not please you.'

'Dolores, don't . . .'

'Ah, then I must be wrong, she *did* please you . . .' Still Stephen was silent. 'She must have pleased you very much. So why do you bother to come here at all? Would she not have you any more? This morning you rescued her from her poor husband. I'm sure she'll know how to show her gratitude. So go on then, go back to Furleys, so much more convenient after all, you barely need to go to any trouble at all.'

Stephen raised his hands in protest. 'Dolores, stop. This is torture. You know that I love you, no one else.'

'Tst! How can I know anything when you are so faithless?'

Even as she taunted him with her question, Dolores knew Stephen was telling the truth. In spite of everything she did not doubt his love: she did not understand it in the least, but she knew she could attack him all she liked, safe in the certainty he would never turn away from her. If their circumstances had been different, she might have indulged her anger for a month or more, but she did not have that luxury now.

She said, in a different voice altogether, 'Why, Stephen?'

'I do not know.' He was staring at his hands. 'I was much troubled by the fact that I was failing you, I did not know how to please you. I thought perhaps someone with more experience than I . . .'

There was a profound silence. Dolores opened her mouth to speak, but no sound emerged.

Stephen said, 'It was wrong, wrong and stupid, but at the time I thought . . .'

His words trailed away. In the pitchy black silence of the night

323

there was only the scuffling of birds in their roosts among the ivy.

At length Dolores said, 'That night of the storm . . . you were different . . . I did not understand . . . not at the time, but now . . .'

Stephen's head was bowed. He pressed his hands against his skull. There was nothing he could say.

Dolores' voice was so soft it was hard to make out the words. 'It is . . . incredible.' And then, 'Why did you come back, Stephen, when she was so much more—?'

He did not move a muscle. There were so many ways of answering her question: he had come back because he loved her; no other woman could ever replace her in his affections; when he was apart from her he was only half-alive . . . But those statements had been discredited by his action. And so he did not speak.

The moon was rising and the sky above the high walls of the priory was bright. Dolores could not make out Stephen's face, but his wretchedness was evident from the slump of his shoulders. She knew how much he was suffering, and she was glad of it. He deserved to suffer horribly for what he had done.

She said bitterly, 'You are a fool, Stephen.'

He shifted uncomfortably, but remained without speaking.

It is amazing, thought Dolores, he has been unfaithful to me, and I could hurl abuse at him for the rest of the night, but the bond which unites us would hardly even be threatened. He will care for me, she thought, no matter what I say. And then it occurred to her that this certainty had only come about because of his faithlessness.

At that thought she experienced an unfamiliar sensation somewhere just below her ribs, as if feathers had been glued there and were beginning to tickle. Her anger was all spent. She no longer even wanted him to suffer particularly. After all, they did not have so much time together that they could squander it in long-drawn-out recriminations. Besides, when she looked at it another way, the whole situation was quite ridiculous. Comical, almost. The odd feeling that had begun below her ribs was travelling upwards, and a sound that might almost have been a burst of laughter escaped from her mouth.

Stephen thought at first that she was sobbing. He stood up, wondering if he could offer her sympathy, only to stop, amazed,

324

when he realised she was laughing. He had preferred her anger to this mockery.

He said stiffly, 'I do not see what is amusing.'

Hearing his affronted dignity, Dolores exclaimed, 'Oh Stephen, now *you* are offended! It is too much!' And she burst out in fresh laughter.

Stephen felt himself growing hot. It was one thing for him to admit he had been a fool, but quite another for Dolores to be entertained by his folly. And then, as he listened to the sound of her merriment, helpless and free, he realised he had never heard her laugh before. Even when playing with her children, she did no more than smile at their mischief.

He said hesitantly, 'I've never seen you laughing.'

'No . . .' She wiped her eyes and drew breath. 'I think I had forgotten how. Dear God, what a waste . . . am I mad, do you think? *Una loca*? To find such things amusing, but . . .' She was laughing still.

'Then you are no longer angry?'

'I do not know. I don't seem to be. I don't *feel* angry. You deserve to be cut into tiny pieces and boiled in oil, but just now I cannot be bothered.' She chuckled again, a deep and satisfying sound. 'How crazy it all is.'

'Dolores—'

She took a step backwards and drew herself up very straight.

'Beware, Stephen Sutton, I may be crazy enough to forgive you for what you have done, but Corinna Rogers deserves to be pilloried. I'm warning you, if you ever touch her again, even if it is just to hand her into her father's carriage, she'll regret it for the rest of her life. I will mix up a potion in my stillroom that will leave her warty and crippled and probably blind as well. And as for you—'

'Dolores, please—' He did not know if she was serious or teasing – and Dolores was not altogether sure either.

She said, 'Nona had some medicines to make men forget. Be careful of what I put in your spiced wine in future. Your memory will be scrubbed quite clean. You will have thoughts for no woman but me—'

'There is no need of medicines, for that.'

'Or maybe I should simply poison her and be done with it. She would die slowly, and in great pain, and her face would be so hideous with agony that when they came to lay her out—'

'Dolores, stop.' Stephen put his arms around her. 'You know

full well I can never care for anyone but you.'

She did not resist him, but tipped back her face. Her eyes were laughing. 'I know, Stephen, but you are a man, and weak, and I must find ways to protect you from scheming trollops—'

'Enough.' He kissed her. 'I love you.'

'Yes. It is your misfortune. But now I must return to the house.'

'Shall I come with you?'

'No, your punishment is to be banished from my bedchamber at least one night.'

As she turned to leave him and go back to the hidden tunnel, she began to laugh again. 'Oh Stephen, you will have to come with me after all. I am not angry any more, and cannot face that foul place alone.'

Afterwards, Stephen thought it was the laughter that changed Dolores most. Their love-making, following the interlude with Corinna, was much altered, but it was only when she had discovered the pleasures of laughter, that Dolores was able to give herself completely. Paradoxically, now that they shared so much pleasure, they were able to share serious things as well. All the topics that had previously been taboo were now open for discussion: Darbier's death, her life with Josiah, her Spanish family. There was only one subject they still could not bring themselves to talk of, and that was the future.

Too precious to waste in sleep, those August nights were crammed so full they seemed to last a lifetime – but once over, it felt as if they had passed in the blink of an eye. Mistress Taverner, the efficient and chilly Puritan wife, was transformed during the hours of darkness. At times she was all woman, and delighted to explore new stages in their sensual journey. At others it seemed as though she had changed back into the child she had been on the day her world was destroyed by the Würzburg massacre. Especially when Stephen was detained, or had to leave, she became petulant and unreasonable, and Stephen could see in her the spoilt youngest child of a loving family. On other occasions she was tenderly maternal, and cradled him as if he were her child. And Stephen, who was always his same self, and always would be, was enchanted by the endless variety, never knowing what was going to meet him when he pushed open the panel which led from the priest's hole to the candlelit bedroom.

Living for the nights when they could be together again, they existed with hardly any sleep. Their days passed in a contented haze of expectation, each of them thinking only of the time when they would be together again. So much easier, in that state, to ignore the events in the outside world.

Hardly a day went past without news of another parliamentary victory. King Charles had emerged from his Welsh retreat in an attempt to join up with his Scots army. But even the King's personal bravery could not mask the hopelessness of his situation, and one by one the royalist strongholds fell. Relentless and unhurried, the roundhead army was now impossible to halt. 'What will happen if the King is utterly defeated?' asked Dolores on the night they heard that Sherborne had fallen, but Stephen had no answer to that, and she went on, 'It feels as if the end of the world is coming. But so long as you are here, nothing else matters.'

Two days later came the news that both had been dreading. A parliamentary force was less than twenty miles away, and Tilsbury was their next destination.

When Stephen pushed back the priest's hole panel in the almost certain knowledge that he did so for the last time, there was such a weight on his heart that he could barely muster a smile of greeting. But the moment he saw Dolores, so strangely beautiful and so entirely his, he was instantly content. Her eyes were brimming with tears and she was laughing with the pleasure of seeing him again. Each moment of their last hours was infinitely precious. They moved and spoke with careful deliberation; even their love-making was solemn – a kind of valediction.

At last she said, 'Oh Stephen, whatever are we going to do? I think if I don't see you again I shall die.'

He did not answer, only stroked her shoulder. There was nothing he could say. During the long silence, Dolores felt herself withdrawing, and realised she had spoken untruly. She would grieve for Stephen's absence, but it would never destroy her. However freely she had given herself to him, there had always been a part of her that had held back. Perhaps because of the way her childhood had ended, perhaps because her children were closer to her than bone, Dolores would never be able to give all of herself to anyone. Long ago she had learned both the strengths and limitations of the survivor.

After a long pause, Stephen sighed and leaned to kiss her, but she turned away so that his lips brushed the side of her cheek. Suddenly and unreasonably, she was furious with him. Not once in all the time they had spent together had he suggested that she leave Tilsbury and her husband and make her life with him. If he had asked her during those final few days, she would have agreed without hesitation. But already she understood Stephen's character better than he would ever know hers, and she knew that he could never have asked her to make that sacrifice. She could not long be angry with him for being the man she loved, so she turned and touched his cheek with her fingertips and asked, 'Are we prisoners, then?' But before Stephen had a chance to answer, she went on, 'No. Never. I was a prisoner before I learned to love you. I will never be so again.'

She found herself trying to memorise every detail of his body, the pale hairs that grew on the back of his hands, the lines that were drawn beside his mouth, the long tendons on his forearms, the flecks of gold in his grey eyes. It shocked her that she was already trying to preserve his image in her mind, just as when she was a child she had tried to catalogue every detail of her Spanish home, so that it would continue to exist for her to see again one day.

She said at length, 'Does this have to be the last time we see each other?'

'I do not know.' Stephen was frowning.

If only Josiah were to die, thought Dolores, all our troubles would be solved. Her spirits soared at the idea: how simple it would be, and in this dangerous time of war, quite likely. She had not heard from him in over two weeks; there had been outbreaks of plague in London through the summer; the roads were notoriously dangerous at present – surely he was never going to return! She realised suddenly that the same thoughts were going through Stephen's mind, but whereas the prospect of Josiah's likely death filled her with joy, Stephen despised himself for wishing misfortune to a rival.

She said, 'It may be that Josiah has been murdered by cutthroats,' and she smiled slyly when his startled expression proved that her mind-reading had been accurate. 'You see, Stephen, I can read your thoughts as easily as Harry's or Beth's. No, more easily.'

'Am I so transparent, then?'

'Completely.' And she thought suddenly what a luxury it

would be to have time enough with Stephen – a lifetime, at least – so that she might find him, occasionally, just a fraction too predictable.

'It will soon be dawn,' said Stephen, 'I must go. I will come here again in the morning. No one will think anything of it if I visit your home one last time. I cannot say goodbye just yet.'

'As you wish.' Dolores sat up and watched him as he dressed. 'I ask you one thing only: when we have said our farewells, I never want to see you again. I could not bear the pretence that there was nothing between us.'

'Agreed. In fact I never wish to say goodbye at all. Some things are too painful. And I must believe that I will see you again, one day.'

The expression on his face as he said these words was pure agony, and Dolores understood that this separation was worse for him than for her. She must try what she could do to make it easier.

'So be it,' she said, kissing him, 'No goodbyes.'

The following morning she made sure that she was occupied in the most private portion of the garden when Stephen arrived. The day was overcast and a cool breeze was blowing. She could easily have arranged for their meeting to take place in the greater privacy of the winter parlour, but she had her own reasons for choosing to remain out of doors. The process of detachment which she had felt beginning the previous night had continued during the few hours since then; already she was becoming the woman who would make the best of the empty years that stretched ahead. If she were to feel his arms around her, or the touch of his lips on hers, all her work of self-protection must begin again.

But as he approached, his face betrayed such bleak misery, that she almost changed her mind.

'Dolores,' he said at once, having thought of nothing else since they parted, 'I love you. I have loved you almost from the first time I saw you, and you may believe it or not, as you wish, but I know that I can never stop loving you. I shall love you always.'

'Always, Stephen? That is such a long time.'

'I know. Always. As long as I live.'

She was silent for a little while before replying, softly, 'Yes, Stephen, I do believe you will.'

'It may be that in time you will forget me—'

'No, I can never do that.'

'—Or your feelings may change. But if not—' He reached inside his coat and pulled out a small package. 'I brought you this.' And for the first time that morning he smiled slightly, as the little silver chain slid on to the palm of his hand. 'I wish it was an item of great value, one that had been in my family for generations. But alas, I have no such treasure, neither here nor anywhere else. This has only the worth that my love gives it.'

'You wish me to have it?'

'Yes.'

'Then I am glad it has no worldly value. I have been weighed down by plundered wealth far too long.'

'This was bought and paid for – probably rather more than it is worth. The pedlar was a shrewd fellow and saw that I was eager to buy. I am giving it to you on one condition only.' He hesitated, then, 'It may be a day will come when you no longer think of me with love. Someone else may replace me in your affections – no, hear me out first. If it ever comes about that you no longer wish to see me – whatever has occurred – then return this chain. I will know I must stop hoping . . .'

Stephen's face was so earnest, and his words so oblique, that Dolores was unable to resist a half-smile. 'You mean, should Josiah die?'

He glanced away. 'It is wrong even to talk of it.'

'We may talk of it all we wish but our dilemma is unaltered.' She was still smiling as she took the little chain and examined it thoughtfully. 'So, Stephen, you wish to bind me to you with a chain?'

'I did not mean it to signify a chain. It was the best the pedlar had. If you wish, I can exchange it or—'

'No, Stephen, I was teasing you. I will wear your chain gladly, and not feel bound by it in any way.'

He smiled his relief, then all at once was serious again. 'Dolores, the roundhead soldiers are very close. It is thought they may even reach Tilsbury later today. We may not see each other again—'

'Do not even say such words. Maybe I am becoming a witch like Nona, but I know this is not the end for us.'

'Even so, dear God, I never imagined this parting could be so hard—'

'Remember, Stephen, no goodbyes.'

'I was thinking maybe . . . we need not part . . . there must be some way for us to be together . . .'

Dolores held her breath. 'How, Stephen?'

'If we could only—'

His sentence was never completed. There was a loud shriek from the direction of the house. Beth tumbled out through the back door and came hurtling down the path towards her mother. Her cheeks were burning and her face was bright with joy. She was so absorbed in her news that she never even saw Stephen, but burst out, 'Oh Mother, come quickly! Hurry, oh, Father is come back. Will Dower saw him on the bridge, and Harry is getting Pip and the baby so we can all be there to greet him together. Oh Mother, dearest Mother, isn't it wonderful? Father is come home safe!'

She flung her arms around her mother's waist. Dolores raised her hands in a helpless gesture, and seemed on the point of pushing her away. Then she burst into loud tears and hugged her tightly.

Stephen, watching mother and daughter together, experienced a torment he would never have imagined possible.

He turned on his heel and strode away, to leave by the orchard gate. When Dolores looked up again through her tears, he had already vanished from sight.

Chapter 24

❧

Josiah was installed in the Priory House in time to welcome the parliamentary soldiers when they marched into Tilsbury that evening. The detachment consisted of about two hundred men under the command of a fair-haired colonel who had been a bookseller before the war broke out but who had been promoted swiftly to his present high position owing to his diligence and tactical skill. Once again the little town was brim-full of warlike strangers, but almost at once a significant difference was observed: Colonel Firth's roundheads were able to pay in coin for all they required. This single fact, as much as their general good discipline and sober behaviour, swiftly converted most of the inhabitants of Tilsbury to the parliamentary cause.

No one was more fervent in their support than Josiah Taverner. Since the middle of June, when royalist defeat began to seem inevitable, he had been assiduously cultivating his parliamentary contacts; now he was able to present himself as the most loyal of Puritans. After some heart-searching he had grudgingly donated a few gold items to the parliamentary coffers. Now he invited Colonel Firth and some of his men to make their headquarters at the Priory House, and he spared no effort to see they were well provided for. As far as Mabs and Ellen were concerned, one set of officers was much the same as another, and Mabs was delighted to be given money to spend on food. Only Cary, who was pining for O'Rourke and knew these well-behaved strangers to be his sworn enemies, was sullen as she went about her work.

Dolores was relieved that Josiah was too busy toadying to Colonel Firth and his men to pay much attention to her. He had been gratified by Beth and Harry's obvious delight, and not altogether surprised to see signs of hastily hidden tears on his wife's cheeks. He spent an hour or so closeted with Bussell, and then told Dolores to keep guard in their bedchamber while he checked that the casket of valuables was still safely hidden in the priest's hole tunnel. Dolores waited with growing agitation. She did not allow herself to think of Stephen, but his presence was everywhere in the room; she wondered how Josiah had not noticed it already. And then, when the panel swung slightly open, and it was Josiah's portly body, not Stephen's slender one, which emerged, she felt such a crushing weight against her ribs that it was all she could do to draw breath.

'All is in order,' he said complacently, 'but we'll leave well alone until the last of the soldiers has quitted this place for good. No need to tempt fate, eh?'

Dolores did not answer, only stared at him. This then, this barrel-chested monstrosity of a man with his pale cloud of cinnamon-dusted hair and his ponderous jowls, this was the husband with whom she must endure the years ahead. A great tide of rebellion was welling up inside her.

Josiah surveyed her with his small, shrewd eyes. 'Cat got your tongue? Overcome with the joys of seeing me again, I dare say.' He contemplated her in silence for a few moments: she had always been a fine-looking woman, but he sensed a difference in her now. He could not put his finger on it exactly, but she seemed possessed of an elemental energy that had previously been lacking. Suddenly he found he was looking forward to the night.

He took a step towards her and put his hand on her shoulder. 'Never mind, Doll, your husband is home safe.'

For a moment the sheer hatred that he saw in her eyes left him feeling slightly winded. Then she twisted free of his hand and said, 'My name is Dolores.'

'What?'

'I said, my name is Dolores.'

He patted her cheek. 'You have always been my little Doll,' he said comfortably, 'No sense in changing that now.' He was walking to the door. 'We'll save the rest for later, my dear. Now, there is much to be done to make the soldiers welcome. Do nothing to put yourself forward, Doll. In all things follow my lead.'

'I told you—'

'Later, Doll. Later.'

It was not very much later that Dolores had retreated to her stillroom to fetch a jar of rose-water – and remained there longer than was necessary, fearing that her innermost thoughts must surely be visible on her face.

The solution to her torment seemed suddenly so obvious that she almost laughed. There, on the topmost shelves, were the bottles and jars that held the key to her salvation. In the days before she died Nona had passed on to her the secrets of each. Six drops of this one and a man will sleep for six hours . . . a spoonful of this in a warm drink will soothe a racing heart, but beware of administering too much, it could be fatal . . . or this one, for peaceful sleeps when all hope is gone. Who would be surprised – certainly not Josiah himself who was wheezing rather more now than he had done previously – if, after all the strains and exertions of the past few months, his health began to fail? She reached up and took down first one small bottle, and then another: his illness could be slow and painless, or swift and devastating. Either way the result would be the same: after a few months of necessary mourning, his widow would be free to spend the rest of her days with Stephen.

Merely to imagine the happiness that lay within her grasp, was enough to make her giddy with anticipation.

At Furleys, the same manner of thoughts were passing through Stephen's mind, but since he possessed a more scrupulous conscience, his imaginings filled him with self-disgust. Yet even while he organised his men to repulse the inevitable parliamentary assault, he could not resist speculating how Josiah might react to the discovery of his wife's infidelity. The wronged husband must surely wreak some terrible revenge on his wife – to whom could Dolores turn then? Stephen himself could never ask her to leave her children to start a new life with him – but if she were ever banished from her home, how diligently he would try to make up to her for all she had lost. No sooner had he thought of that, than the image of Dolores grieving for her abandoned children jolted him back to despair. Perhaps, then, on discovering the affair, Josiah's wrath would be all directed against his rival. He might attack Stephen, who could then defend himself with honour. Public outrage would inevitably follow Josiah's death in a duel – but Cornwall was far away and the echoes of scandal would never reach them there. A new life with Dolores and her children on one of the little farms on the Rossmere estate ... the picture was so appealing that Stephen paused in his work – he was instructing the men in the digging of a ditch behind which musketeers were to be placed – and beamed at no one in particular. But the next moment he frowned again. How could he, a soldier in the full vigour of his youth, possibly contemplate killing an elderly merchant and presume to call it a fair fight? More like murder than a duel. Perhaps, after all, the best solution was for Stephen to be killed in the coming defence of Furleys. There was no hope for him and Dolores: he loathed himself even for wishing Josiah's death. He threw himself into his work with a passion and energy that surprised even those who knew him well. Alone among the members of the garrison at Furleys, Stephen relished the prospect of the battle ahead.

The day after the parliamentary force arrived in Tilsbury, Colonel Firth marched most of his men down the road to Furleys and sent a trumpeter to the house inviting the royalists' surrender. Major Ripley, who had passed the morning in the library with his host, discussing Virgil's merits as a tool for divination, sent back a contemptuous refusal and carried on their discussion. A few shots were exchanged, one of the Irishmen slightly injured and a roundhead sergeant was killed. The parliamentary force withdrew and life at Furleys continued much as before.

Stephen was in the stable-yard the following morning, examining his mare who had a badly swollen knee, when O'Rourke asked to speak with him privately. Stephen dismissed the groom, and listened to what O'Rourke had to say with growing interest.

It appeared that Cary had overhead one of the roundhead soldiers at the Priory House boasting that Furleys would not last more than a couple of hours once Sweet Sally arrived. Cary's inevitable question, what kind of woman was Sweet Sally, had led to huge merriment. The lady in question was, it turned out, a saker, a kind of cannon, which was being brought from the south of the county. The soldiers assured her Sweet Sally, would raze Sir Diggory's house to the ground in no time at all.

Cary's alarm at this news was offset by the excitement of acting as a royalist spy. She remembered reading an account of a high-born lady who carried important messages into London hidden in her curls, and, though there was no need for that particular subterfuge at present, she immediately saw herself as the heroine of a drama. As soon as her work was done, she hurried to Furleys and passed on what she had learned to O'Rourke. He was even more interested in her information than she had anticipated, and told her to cultivate the soldiers' friendship so she could learn as much as possible.

'But mind you do not get too friendly,' cautioned O'Rourke, emphasising his point with a whiskery kiss. 'I've no plans to share you, and certainly not with a poxy roundhead.'

Cary had gazed at him with her blameless brown eyes, and asked how he could even imagine such a thing.

When O'Rourke had finished speaking, Stephen asked thoughtfully, 'This cannon is coming from the south?'

'Yes, sir. They expect it to arrive in a couple of days.'

'But if we were to intercept it . . .'

O'Rourke grinned. 'That was my thought entirely, sir.'

Stephen wasted no time in reporting this new development to Major Ripley whom he found, as usual, in the library, behind a stack of books. The major's reaction, however, was unexpected.

'Captain Sutton, I forbid you to make any attempt to sabotage the enemy's cannon.'

'But, sir—'

'Orders, Captain, orders. They are to be obeyed, not questioned. For the next three days you and all the Irish are confined to Furleys. I intend to have no false heroics under my command.'

'May I ask why, sir?'

'Certainly not.' Major Ripley was struggling with a headache and his digestion had been causing him trouble all week. 'I do not make a habit of explaining my decisions to subordinates.'

Stephen was persistent. 'The Irish soldiers are at a greater risk than anyone else if Furleys is taken.'

'I am fully aware of that fact, Captain. I do not need you to teach me my business.' Then, seeing the genuine concern on Stephen's face, he relented slightly. 'Believe me, Captain, the garrison's safety is my main concern. That is why I will not permit you to risk more lives in a hopeless cause. Yes, Captain, a hopeless cause. Sooner or later His Majesty must treat with Parliament for the best possible terms. And that is precisely what I intend to do: treat for reasonable terms. That is all,

Captain. And remember, you and all the men are confined to this place until further notice. Good day.'

Thinking over this conversation later, Stephen wondered why he had not found it more reassuring. Superficially at least, Major Ripley's analysis of their situation was realistic. Even King Charles' most loyal supporters were now advising compromise before still more ground was lost to Parliament. What then was the point of throwing men's lives away in a hopeless cause? It occurred to Stephen that his eagerness to intercept the enemy cannon might have had more to do with his own need for distraction than any real strategic goals. If he were only free to ride and fight, then he might be able to shift the weight of grief that had burdened him since that last night with Dolores. Had it come to this, then, that he was willing to forfeit the lives of his men simply to ease the burden of his own heartache?

O'Rourke was outraged. 'Dear God, Captain, do you know how these murdering roundheads treat their Irish prisoners? I'll gladly die in a good fight, but I'll be damned before I'll submit to being butchered by those Puritan fiends!'

'I'm sorry, O'Rourke. I did what I could. And our orders are to remain here. I intend to see they are obeyed.'

O'Rourke looked at him steadily. The expression in the Irishman's eyes left Stephen in no doubt he felt he was being abandoned by the English officer he had learned to trust.

Two days later the parliamentary troops once again marched from Tilsbury to encircle the house, but this time they had the cannon with them. It was drawn by eight horses and positioned on a grassy mound just out of musket range. The trumpeter went to parley with Major Ripley and returned to Colonel Firth with the message that the royalists had vowed to stout it out. Towards evening the first cannon shot was fired, slightly damaging a corner of the porch. The siege of Furleys had begun.

In the Priory House, Dolores was facing a different sort of siege with far greater determination than Major Ripley and his cronies. On the first evening after Josiah's return, she had informed her husband she intended to keep to a separate room until he gave way over this matter of her name.

'Dolores will be a wife to you again, Josiah – but Doll no longer exists.'

Not understanding what lay behind her decision, Josiah

decided at first to make light of it. He was much occupied with his soldier guests and wished to avoid drawing attention to his domestic problems while they were in the house. After a couple of days, however, when he realised how implacable his little Doll had grown, he rather regretted not having humoured her on this subject right away. Now it would be impossible to capitulate without losing face.

When the first cannon shot was fired at Furleys, Josiah began to lose patience with his wife.

'Enough of this foolishness, woman,' he burst out. He had ceased to call her Doll, but could not bring himself to call her Dolores, so had to make do with 'wife' and 'woman'. 'I insist you return to our bedchamber.'

'When you ask Dolores, she will return.'

Josiah was unnerved by the steady way his wife withstood him. She never raised her voice, but looked him straight in the eye and was grown so heart-wrenchingly beautiful that he found it hard to consider the problem rationally.

'What has happened to you, wife? You have changed while I was away.'

Dolores had anticipated this, and her answer was ready. 'Are you surprised, Josiah? You left me to mind your household for nearly half a year while the town and my home were overrun with soldiers. One man died of terrible wounds and another was murdered. Nona died. Your little Doll would never have been able to survive such events. Dolores did.'

'Tst. It is but a name. Doll, Dolores, what does it matter?'

She shrugged. 'It is important to me, that's all.'

Josiah was silent for a few moments, then he attempted a conciliatory smile. 'Well, my dear, perhaps I have been somewhat niggardly in my praise. You coped admirably while I was gone, and I am proud of you. But now the time has come to hand the reins back to me. A house must have but one master.'

'You mistake me, Josiah. I have no wish to usurp your position. All I ask is to be called by the name I was born with.'

'Yes, in Spain. But you are English now.'

'I am Dolores.'

Josiah lost patience. 'What the devil has got into you, woman? What makes you think you can decide whether you'll be a true wife to me or no? Where did you learn such disobedience? If I did not know you better, I'd almost think there'd been another man—'

The expression of shock that flashed across her face was genuine enough. 'How dare you!'

Josiah felt himself close to violence. Afraid of losing control, he said, 'I'll leave you, wife. But you'd best come to your senses before I am driven to desperate measures.'

Afterwards, he wondered precisely what desperate measures he had been thinking of. In the past, fear of the old woman and her dark powers had always held him in check. Now Nona was dead, and, in theory at least, Josiah was free to do as he wished. The trouble was that what he wished, still and for ever, was that his wife might care for him – or at least fear him – and that goal seemed as elusive as ever.

Dolores was more distressed by their conversation than Josiah imagined. She knew she had only strength of purpose on her side: all the weight of law and custom and power was with Josiah. Yet though it seemed trivial enough in itself, she could not afford to give way on this question of her name. As Josiah's Doll her life would be insupportable. Dolores could hold her head up high.

Or Dolores could use her stillroom arts to achieve freedom. Endlessly these thoughts ran through her mind as she went about her daily round. The contrast between her own dark wishes and the little triumphs and excitements of her household was impossible to reconcile. Beth was thrilled because the baby had learned to pull himself to his feet and, if she held him firmly, he could even take a wavering step. Glancing out of the bedchamber window Dolores happened to see Harry sitting with his father on a bench in the garden. The boy was talking eagerly and gesturing with his hands: he seemed to be describing their efforts to put out the fire in Mother Crew's house, something he had never yet discussed with Dolores. One would have to be blind and deaf not to appreciate the change in Harry since his father's return. The previous evening she had heard his high-pitched childish laughter as he and Beth egged Philip on to some new outrage: the sound was startling because she had not heard it in months. Her family was a mesh of sweetest gossamer, and she forever trapped in its folds.

The siege of Furleys was a brief and inglorious episode in royalist annals. Stephen soon realised that Major Ripley's resistance was a form of ritual only: everyone accepted that a long siege was out of the question, but equally too swift a capitulation would be dishonourable. Some show of defiance was necessary to extract favourable terms of surrender. Sir Diggory was frantic to save his home. When he looked out from a high window and saw the many soldiers ranged through the parkland and imagined them rampaging through his rooms in a frenzy of plunder and destruction, he was all for holding out as long as possible. But when he sat at dinner and listened to the windows rattle as Sweet Sally landed another cannon ball against his walls and chunks of plaster fell from the ceiling on to his long table, he longed to surrender before further damage was done.

Unlike Major Ripley's cavaliers, the Irishmen fought with a savagery born of desperation. The previous autumn Parliament had issued an ordinance condemning any captured Irishman to a felon's death, and this brutal order had been frequently obeyed. On the third night Lieutenant Donnelly, unknown to Stephen or any of the English officers, led a small party of men to spike the roundhead cannon, slitting the throats of several gunners at the same time.

When he learned of this, Major Ripley was outraged, but by the time his anger had cooled, he realised he must treat with Colonel Firth before he had a full-scale mutiny on his hands. His negotiations with the parliamentary force were now conducted with all secrecy until reasonable terms were struck.

At three o'clock on the third night parliamentary soldiers were let into the house by a little-used entrance, and they were in full possession by the time either Stephen or the Irish had any idea of the major's capitulation. Donnelly, O'Rourke and their men, penned up in their lodgings in the stable-yard, carried on a bloody resistance well after the parliamentary colours had been hoisted to flutter over the rooftops of Furleys in the dawn light. But by mid-morning their supplies of match and bullets were all spent and Stephen, who had been assured by Major Ripley that under the terms of the surrender none of his men would be executed, prevailed on them to lay down their arms.

O'Rourke was the last to do so. He was bleeding from a cut to the side of his head, and filthy with sweat. 'I trust you, Captain Sutton,' he said as he flung down his sword, 'But I'll never trust your major or those parliament bastards. Pray to heaven this is no trap you're putting us in.'

'The colonel gave his word,' said Stephen.

But he too was filled with a sick misgiving as the Irishmen, many of them wounded, were marched under heavy guard down the road that led back towards Tilsbury. About ten of them had died in the fighting, and the thirty or so who remained looked suddenly pitifully few and vulnerable. Their guards, mindful of their butchered comrades, were not inclined to be overly scrupulous and two or three mysteriously perished during the short march to captivity.

Colonel Firth, having reconnoitred the ruin when he first arrived in the town, had decided to house his Catholic prisoners in the Old Priory. It would be easy to guard and was not too close either to the town or Furleys. He had his own reasons for not wishing to draw attention to the fate of his captives. Like the vast majority of his fellow roundheads, he regarded all Irish Catholics as papist vermin, but he had been in Tilsbury long enough to learn that they had inexplicably won the affection of the local people.

Captain Firth was an erudite man, and the irony of housing them in a ruined religious house appealed to him. 'Let their popish ruin see the ruin of their popery,' he said to one of his officers when he inspected the makeshift gaol that evening. He regretted only that his pithy maxim had not found a more educated audience.

Chapter 25

❧

Sergeant Michael O'Rourke, born in County Sligo and late of His Majesty King Charles's army, laid his shaggy head against the Old Priory wall and wept. He had not eaten even a crust of bread in three days, the wound to his head was festering and his limbs were shaking with fever, but in spite of all this, his tears sprang in part from a bitter happiness. Beyond the heavily-padlocked oak door he could hear Cary chatting with the roundhead soldiers. She had brought a basket of food and drink to be given to the prisoners, as she and several of the townspeople had been doing each day since their captivity began. The guards had told her the gifts would be passed on, but as soon as she had departed they divided it amongst themselves, or gave it to a couple of scavenging dogs, taunting the starving Irishmen as they did so. 'Here's some fine home-baked bread your girl brought for you, Irish, seasoned with love, I'm sure. And some good ale to wash it down.' Followed by much smacking of lips and contented belching.

But Cary, standing outside in the sunshine, knew none of this. The soldiers told her their captives were being well cared for and would soon be released – ('Death's a merciful release,' they joked afterwards as another man went down with camp fever, and for once O'Rourke was inclined to agree with his tormentors) – and as she had no reason to disbelieve them and was mindful of her new importance as a royalist spy, she lingered to talk with the half a dozen Londoners whose job it was to guard the Irish. Being Cary, however, she inevitably talked more than she listened.

'You must be brave men to do this job,' she said earnestly, and

O'Rourke, listening from just inside the door, could picture the expression on her sturdy face as she spoke.

One of the soldiers, their leader in most things, replied, 'Naturally we're as brave as they come. But guarding this bunch of heroes is not hard, not like some of the battles we've been in. We could tell you stories of real bravery, now.'

'Battles?' Cary dismissed the epic encounters of Marston Moor and Naseby as if they had been no more than Whitsun bouts. 'I'm talking of something far more serious. Surely you've heard of the Grey Lady? The spirit who guards this place? She was a Catholic too, you know. She's sure to be watching out for her brothers in religion.'

'The Grey Lady?'

'Haven't you heard the story? She was in charge of the women who lived here in King Harry's time. When he ordered all the convents to close, she refused to leave. So he sent soldiers to destroy the place and turn her out – men like yourselves they might have been. I did hear once they came from London way. But they must have been heartless brutes, not men at all, because they ravished all the poor nuns, all but the Grey Lady herself. She climbed to the top of the highest tower – that one there, but of course it was nearly twice as tall in those days . . .'

And so she continued. Tales of ghoulish horrors and unnatural death, and every word of it was music to O'Rourke's ears. For once he suspected there might be an element of malice in her stories, though no one would have guessed it from her tone. Though she had no idea of the slow death being inflicted on the Irish soldiers, she knew the roundheads were their enemies, and she thought it would be no bad thing if they sweated a little with fear during the silent watches of the night.

Even in the noon sunshine, one or two of them began to sound a little uneasy, as was evident from their too-emphatic denials.

'What a lot of gibberish nonsense! We've seen nothing to fear, only a few bats and an owl or two. You just tell your Grey Lady to show her face, we'd soon send her back to hell!'

'So you say.' Cary remained unruffled. 'Come to think of it, one of the soldiers who were here in the spring said much the same thing. He said anyone who feared a ghost was a superstitious fool, and just to prove it, he did a sentry duty here alone . . .'

'And?'

'When they changed the watch in the morning it took four men to drag him away. He was holding on to the edge of the tower so tight they had to break every one of his fingers with a hammer before he would let go. His tongue was all black and swollen in his mouth and he'd bitten half through it in his fear. He never spoke again, not proper words, anyway. And do you know, the strangest part of all was from that day onwards he couldn't shut his eyes at all, not to blink, not to sleep. Even after he died – and of course he did die a week or so after – they could not close his eyes, but had to bury him, still staring . . . like this . . .' There was an ominous pause, and O'Rourke could easily picture the wide-eyed dying-of-fright face Cary's audience was enduring, before she went on, 'Even in death he dared not take his eyes off the horrible sight so that when they came to lay him out for burial . . .'

And so it went on. Dear God, prayed O'Rourke, smiling through his fever and his pain, only let me hear Cary describing horrors to the end, and in spite of everything, I swear I shall die a happy man.

Major Ripley and Sir Diggory agreed it was lucky Furleys had fallen to an officer who was a gentleman, and civilised, for all his roundhead Puritan sympathies. It might have been so much worse. There had been no shortage of stories to alarm landowners concerning the revolutionary tendencies of some elements in the roundhead army. As it was, Furleys had suffered no plunder, and very little destruction. Sir Diggory deemed it prudent to make a generous contribution to Parliament's cause, and by the time Colonel Firth and his men departed, his cellars were sure to be empty and his parkland cleared of deer. But on the whole Colonel Firth had demonstrated his fairness and sensibility. Major Ripley and his fellow officers were informed that their swords and pistols would be returned to them as soon as they gave a pledge not to take up arms against Parliament again. Some of the royalist troopers, dazzled by the prospect of actually being paid in coin, agreed to change sides and join the victors. After the initial formalities had been cleared up, Colonel Firth and Major Ripley discovered their shared interest in books. Everything was proceeding with laudable efficiency.

Only Stephen was unimpressed. In the present state of affairs his career as a soldier was almost certainly at an end, but he did

345

not, like the other officers, give his word of parole. So long as the fate of his Irishmen remained uncertain, he did not see how he could pledge his neutrality. Colonel Firth, though at some pains to reach an agreement with him, had difficulty in understanding his position.

'Are you by any chance a secret Catholic, Captain?' he asked.

'Far from it, Colonel. I abhor papacy and have always been loyal to His Majesty's Anglican faith.'

'Then why this concern for a handful of heathen Irish?'

'Because those heathen Irish, as you call them, have been my comrades in arms for nearly six months. They have fought loyally for King Charles. I am still his officer, and my first duty is to my men.'

'They are not men, Captain, they are savages. Little more than animals.'

'Even animals care for their own.'

'Murdering barbarians. Count yourself lucky you did not see my gunners after their throats had been cut by your precious Irishmen. Scum like them must be wiped off the face of the earth.'

'Before the surrender was agreed, Colonel, you gave your word that none of the men would be harmed.'

'Not exactly, Captain. If you remember correctly you will recall that I gave my word – and, like you, I am a man of my word – that none would be *executed*.' The malicious smile that accompanied his final emphasis chilled Stephen to the bone. He was silent for a few moments while the implications of the colonel's statement sank in.

Colonel Firth, imagining Stephen's silence to be a sign of acquiescence, went on in a quiet voice, 'Waste no time or energy on a handful of papist vermin. The Irish are a race whose time has passed. There will be no place for them in these islands in future. When our work here is accomplished we will deal with those murdering devils once and for all. Their country will be populated by righteous men. My own brothers and I have pledged our support for this enterprise and in return we shall be rewarded with some acres of good land in the south west. I understand, Captain, that you have no property of your own. May I suggest you consider the benefits of joining us? Only consider how God has favoured our Protestant cause. Do not try to stand in the way of His mighty purpose.'

Busy with his own thoughts, Stephen had only half-listened

to the colonel's speech, but he was aware of the blind fanaticism informing every word.

At length he said, 'Colonel Firth, clearly there is no point in trying to persuade you to leniency. I request simply that I may have permission to visit them. I will remain your prisoner for the time being. You have my weapons, and furthermore, I give you my word that I will not lift a finger against any of your soldiers.'

'Hmm. What can possibly be the point of such a visit?'

Stephen hesitated only for a moment before replying in a steady voice, 'It is my duty as their officer.'

'Very well then, Captain, permission granted. I am a reasonable man, as well you know, and in time I'm sure you'll realise the futility of befriending such savages. However, if it eases your conscience, you may bid your men farewell. I shall detail Captain Sugar to ride with you. I know you to be a man of honour, but at times like this one cannot afford to take risks. Your visit will take place tomorrow morning. That is all.'

Never in his life before had Stephen felt less worthy to be described as a man of honour. He had placed his men in a roundhead trap. No, they were not to be executed, but their death was intended in some other way. Donnelly, O'Rourke and the others had trusted him, and he had betrayed them. The knowledge was a festering anguish.

He had one chance to make good his error, but that would mean a betrayal of a different kind. Until this moment, right dealing had been the compass by which he had steered his life, but in this present dilemma he could find no honourable option. Besides, he was beginning to see that honour can be an impossible luxury when all the world is dedicated to cruelty and vengeance.

Whichever way he turned he must betray someone who had put their faith in him. Time and again during that warm August night, when sleep was impossible and dawn seemed a lifetime away, he wished he had been killed in the assault on Furleys and so been spared the necessity for an action he was sure to regret for the rest of his life.

Dawn came and brought no solution to his problem. Sick with self-loathing, he dressed slowly, and tried to compose himself for the coming ordeal. There was just a chance, a slim chance, that he might be able to bluster it through.

* * *

As he rode with Captain Sugar towards Tilsbury, Stephen realised his escort had been selected to convince Stephen of the merits of the republican cause. It was impossible not to like Captain Sugar. He had been an ostler before the war and had hopes of running his own inn one day; a decent establishment, he told Stephen it would be, fair service for a fair price. Although Stephen was hardly listening, he was impressed by Captain Sugar's enthusiasm: the fellow had not a shadow of doubt that God Himself favoured Parliament. He had numerous stories to tell that clearly demonstrated divine intervention, from trivial occurrences like horses going lame at a crucial moment to the recent great victory at Naseby. Stephen could not help wondering, as he listened to the outpourings of the snub-nosed young Puritan, if he himself had ever seen the issues as so simple. When he had set off to fight with Sir Bevil Grenvile, first against the Scots in 1639 and then again three years ago at the beginning of the Civil War, he had been equally convinced that right was on the King's side. At the beginning, the war had been about loyalty and the need to maintain order. But now? Now it was about trickery and deceit and the betrayal of all he cared for. He did not know whether to envy his young companion, who honestly believed that God favoured the just, or to pity his naïvety.

Of more immediate concern, however, was the problem of how to distract Captain Sugar so that he could have a few words alone with Donnelly and O'Rourke. He had thought of several subterfuges, but in the end he needed none of them: the stench from their makeshift prison was all he needed.

Even Stephen reeled when the huge oak door was pulled open a few inches for the first time in nearly five days and the fetid air struck him full in the face. Captain Sugar choked, and waved Stephen to go on alone.

'You have five minutes, Captain,' he said, 'I'm sure you'll not want longer in that hell hole.'

The scene was far worse than Stephen had ever imagined. Two of the men were already dead, and rotting where they lay, and half a dozen more were too weak to move. The rest crowded round him demanding water in voices blurred by thirst. Stephen felt white hot rage boil up inside him, but quickly suppressed it: there was no time. One glance at O'Rourke told him the man was on the verge of delirium. He therefore took Donnelly by the arm.

'I must talk with you in secret.'

Donnelly was too weak to protest, but he regarded Stephen with thinly-veiled hatred: English gentlemen stood by each other while the Irish were left to die in their own filth.

'Come to gloat, Captain?'

Stephen looked at him. The youth was starving and half-crazed with thirst. It was almost impossible to detect beneath his matted curls and filth, the young man who had sung Corinna's praises in the hay-field.

He said, 'Listen carefully, I do not have much time. My only purpose is to get you and the others out of here.'

Half a dozen men were edging towards them, but Stephen gestured them to keep back.

'Do nothing until after dark, do not even look towards the place I am going to tell you about. At the foot of the tower you will find two large stones – no, I told you not to look there yet, just listen. Roll those away and you will find the start of an underground tunnel. It was built by your fellow Catholics in the reign of Elizabeth. The other entrance is in the Priory House—'

Now the suspicion and hate had vanished from Donnelly's eyes, and in their place was only a desperate hope.

'Make no move until after midnight. I will try to break into the Priory House just before then to make sure your escape is not intercepted at that end. What you do after that is up to you.'

'I'll murder every one of those devils who call themselves sentries,' said Donnelly, 'How did you find this tunnel? Is it safe?'

Stephen glanced down at his boots. 'I came across it by accident one day when I was checking the ammunition. And yes, it is safe enough. Safer than staying here – I have gone through the whole length of it myself.'

'And it comes out in Master Taverner's house?'

'In one of the upstairs rooms, yes.'

Stephen wondered if there was perhaps a glimmer of a smile in Donnelly's face as they bid each other goodbye.

'Not a word to anyone, not even O'Rourke, until after dark. You have a good chance if you keep it secret.'

'Yes, Captain Sutton.'

Stephen shook him by the hand and then crossed over to the door. Behind him, the groans and pleas of the dying men rose up like a swarm of flies from a rotting carcass.

Out in the fresh air again and his anger erupted. Captain

Sugar and the sentries were lounging on the grass, baskets of food and ale lying untouched beside them.

Stephen seldom lost his temper, but when he did it was a formidable sight. Within minutes the guards were fetching water from the river for the prisoners and handing it through the partly-open door. The two corpses were passed out, and a boy sent to Tilsbury for a cart to carry them to the graveyard. Captain Sugar attempted a mild protest, but he was no match for Stephen with the full force of outrage behind him.

'Let them die of their wounds, let them die of disease and hunger, but for mercy's sake, only a fiend would condemn a fellow soldier to die of thirst! The Grand Turk himself shows more mercy to his captives. Do you want all the people of this town to know how you are torturing these helpless men?'

On the way back to Furleys Captain Sugar once again tried to convince the Cornish officer of the justice of the parliamentary cause, but this time Stephen rebuffed him into silence. He was still incensed at the conditions in which his men were being kept: his only solace was the thought that, with a little water to sustain them, most of them should be strong enough to make their midnight escape.

That night Dolores could not sleep. It was nearly a week since she had last seen Stephen, and the strength she had possessed then was ebbing fast. By day it was not too bad: the children and her household duties kept her busy enough, but at night the sense of loss threatened to become unbearable. Sometimes she thought she would gladly forfeit ten years of her life if she might only feel his arms about her just once more, and feel the grazing touch of his cheek on hers, hear his deep voice murmur her name . . .

Stop, she told herself. That way lies madness. She repeated to herself that Stephen had gone, never to return. She told herself firmly that she was not going to see him again and must therefore make the most of the many good things that remained . . . But then she recollected that at this moment he was less than three miles away, perhaps awake like her, and if so then he too was surely nursing a bruised and aching heart: and the fact that he was so near, yet so impossibly beyond her reach, was an added torment. How much easier the task of forgetting would have been had he already returned to Cornwall, that far-off country which existed in her mind only as a wash of grey sky and sea, with a few stunted trees and lowly houses.

The church clock struck eleven. In the wide bed beside her, Beth muttered and flung a chubby arm across the pillow. Her battle to make Josiah call her by her real name had settled into a war of attrition: the single word had assumed such importance that neither was now prepared to back down. There appeared to be no way out of the impasse and, as the days passed, Dolores no longer wanted one. The prospect of returning to their own bedchamber appalled her, not only because of Josiah's attentions, but because every inch of space in the room was filled with memories of Stephen. If she looked at the mantelshelf above the fireplace she saw Stephen standing with his arm resting on it; if she looked towards the window, there was Stephen by the side of the bed, and pulling on his breeches; if she happened to glance at the secret panel, she imagined it moved slightly, and her heart seemed to skip a beat at the thought that he had returned, she would see him, he was come for her again . . .

Enough. She must learn to control her racing thoughts before they killed her. She turned over and closed her eyes and tried to sleep, but it was impossible. She fingered the chain that lay against her throat, the chain that symbolised her continuing love. If she was never to see Stephen again, dear God, at least let her talk of him. She sat up in bed. 'Stephen,' she murmured. Beth slept on undisturbed. 'Stephen, oh Stephen.' The tears rolled down her cheeks.

From time to time during the day she could not resist encouraging the servants to reminisce about the royalist soldiers. Cary was all for talking about Sergeant O'Rourke, but from time to time she or Mabs would begin a sentence with, 'And do you remember when Captain Sutton–' and Dolores felt a great leap of pleasure at the sound.

She wiped away her tears with the back of her hand and climbed out of bed. Downstairs, one of the dogs was barking. The sound grated on her nerves and, restlessly she lit a candle and went out on to the landing. Now the other dog had joined in, and she heard the scullion, who slept in the kitchen, grumble at them to hold their peace. She decided to give herself a few drops of Nona's old sleepy syrup: these days it was seldom effective, but it was better to do something. The dogs had fallen silent. Probably a hungry fox had come too close to the house.

She crossed the landing and reached the top of the stairs. The night was warm and she had no need of a shawl over her pale shift. She paused for a moment. In the wavering light from the candle she imagined a shadowy movement to the side of the screens passage below. A touch of fear flickered through her: a man had crossed to stand at the foot of the stairs.

And then, when she saw who it was, a great tide of joy flooded through her.

'Stephen, oh Stephen!'

She was half way down the stairs already, but he held up his hand in a warning gesture and said in a voice that was strange and unexpected, 'Mistress Taverner, do not come any closer. I must ask you to listen carefully and do exactly as I say.'

Dolores came to a dead halt, but her heart was racing. Stephen was here, and he carried a sword in his right hand and two pistols at his side. It could mean one thing only: he had thought of a scheme to take her from this prison that was her life. Maybe he meant to challenge Josiah and kill him. If so, he had her blessing entirely.

'What?' she breathed, 'What is it you want me to do?'

'Mistress Taverner, please wake your husband. Tell him someone waits below who must speak with him urgently. Do nothing to arouse his suspicions. So long as you do exactly as I command, neither of you will be hurt. Before you leave your bedchamber, light a second candle and leave it burning there. Then come down with your husband. Hurry. And make no noise.'

Dolores was half-faint with excitement. There was a dark light in Stephen's eyes and a harshness to his voice that she had never heard before, but she understood at once that it was all part of the drama they must act out so Stephen's plan might succeed. She had no idea what his plan was, but she trusted him so entirely she would happily act her part for a year and a day if it meant they could be together at the end of it.

Hiding her joy, she said in an icy voice, 'I will do exactly as you say, Captain Sutton. But I beg you, whatever you intend for my husband and me, do not harm my innocent children.' If the scullion were perhaps listening from behind the door that led to the kitchen quarters, she trusted her play-acting had convinced him. For the moment, she was sure no one but Stephen could see her, so she smiled when she had finished her speech, and blew him a silent kiss.

Stephen turned his head, an expression of utter misery covering his face.

Stepping quietly in her bare feet, Dolores pushed open the door of her bedchamber. Josiah's snores wafted from the direction of the large four-poster. She lit a second candle, as Stephen had ordered, and set it on a small table in the centre of the room before crossing to stand beside the bed. She paused for a moment or two, gazing down at her husband's face: a mass of flesh and folds and whiskery protrusions. But in sleep his face lost its brooding pomposity, and she felt a twinge of pity for the man who, she had no doubt, was about to be sacrificed to her great love. And as she did so, the church clock struck midnight.

'Wake up, Josiah, wake up quickly.' She had to shake his massive shoulder before he was roused, but, as he opened his eyes and saw her standing by his bedside, he was awake at once.

'Well, well, my dearest Doll. You've come to your senses at last, have you? Decided to be a proper wife, eh?'

Her pity vanished as she backed away from his outstretched hand. 'There is a man downstairs has come on urgent business. He says we are not to be alarmed, but he wants no one else to know of our meeting.'

'A man? What man?'

'You will see soon enough. Hurry.'

Josiah was not unduly surprised. Although most of his trade was conducted in the full light of day, there was a portion – and that the most profitable part – which had to be kept for the secret night hours.

'Very well, pass me my gown.' He pulled the dark velvet robe around his shoulders, pushed his feet into embroidered slippers and padded to the door. 'Blow out the light, wife. Or do you perhaps mean to wait here for my return?'

Dolores would have humoured the devil himself if it meant she could be downstairs with Stephen the sooner. 'Maybe I will, Josiah . . . Maybe it is time Dolores made her husband happy. But first I will accompany you—'

'Indeed? Very well, then' Still half-fuddled with sleep, Josiah was too delighted by his wife's apparent change of mood to be suspicious. 'Tut, wife, you surely do not mean to present yourself in your shift. Here . . . put this on . . . and some shoes . . .'

'Yes, yes, just as you wish. But hurry.'

'Why so impatient?'

'Hush, Josiah. No one else must wake.'

At the bottom of the stairs, Josiah stopped. 'Where is this gentleman, wife? What is going on? Is this some kind of—?'

Stephen, who had been sheltering in the shadows at the rear of the passageway, seized hold of Josiah from behind, and placed a short knife to his throat.'

'Silence, keep silence both of you. Master Taverner, I mean no harm to you or your wife. Keep quiet, and do exactly as I tell you. For the next little while you must both be my prisoners.'

'What . . . who . . . what . . . ?' Shock and fury had reduced Josiah to a state of temporary incoherence.

Stephen guided him to one of two chairs he had placed against the wall, and pushed him roughly down. 'Pray be seated, Master Taverner. And your wife by your side. I regret this is poor thanks for the hospitality you have shown me, but there is no alternative. No, do not speak—' for Josiah had opened his mouth to summon the servants to help. 'Believe me, Master Taverner, I would not hesitate to kill you, or your wife as well. More than thirty lives depend upon your silence.'

'Thirty lives?' whispered Dolores, 'What are you talking about, Captain Sutton?'

'Silence, Mistress Taverner.'

Josiah, however, was incapable of silence. 'Captain Sutton? Captain Sutton!' he burst out, 'Are you that same royalist fellow who ate with me at my table? And now you dare to—'

There was nothing for it. Another few moments and the entire household would be alerted. As the man's voice rose, Stephen caught him a blow around the head that almost knocked him from the chair and sent him reeling against his wife. He grunted with pain and clutched his skull. Instinctively, Dolores put her arm around his shoulder.

'Animal!' she said dramatically. Stephen turned away from her blazing eyes.

'Only remain silent a little longer,' he begged, 'No harm will come.'

'But why?'

'Wait.'

The trio had waited only a few moments more in uncomfortable silence, broken from time to time by Josiah's low groans, when Stephen heard the sound he had been waiting for: footfalls on the floorboards above them. Lieutenant Donnelly appeared at the top of the stairs. Michael O'Rourke was with

354

him; he could barely stand unaided, and Donnelly was supporting him.

At the sight of Stephen, Donnelly smiled. 'Sweet heavens, Captain, that was a terrible narrow tunnel you sent us through. Now I know how Jonah must have felt in the belly of that great fish.'

'Hush,' whispered Stephen, 'Do you want to wake the whole house?'

Donnelly glanced towards Josiah. 'You have the situation well under control, I'd say.' A couple more figures appeared in the darkness behind him.

'Hurry, then,' said Stephen, as the four men came down the stairs.

'Get as far from here as you can before they raise the alarm. Are you taking O'Rourke with you?'

'Of course. I'll not leave him to those butchers.'

'He'll slow you down.'

'I know. But I'm in no hurry to leave. I've a score to settle with those roundhead sentries back at the ruin before I get on my way.'

'Are you mad? You will waste valuable time.'

'It will be worth it.'

Donnelly and O'Rourke were beside him in the hallway now, and half a dozen men tramped down the stairs behind them.

'Leave by the side door,' commanded Stephen in a low voice. 'Here, it is open. Make for the garrison at Berkeley. You can leave the wounded there and go on to Bristol. Travel in small groups, that's your best chance to escape capture. Now, go—'

'Yes, Captain Sutton.' Donnelly hesitated, adjusting the weight of the sergeant whom he was half carrying. 'And, sir, thank you. God be with you.'

'And with you. Now, go.'

They vanished into the silent August night.

Dolores and Josiah had watched all this in baffled silence.

Josiah was the first to find his voice. 'The tunnel?' he breathed. 'You have led them out by the tunnel?'

'It was the only way to save them,' Stephen replied stonily. Though he answered Josiah's question, his words were for Dolores.

'How did you learn of it?'

'We stored our ammunition in the Old Priory ruins,' said Stephen, in that new, harsh voice he had been using all evening.

'It was my task to make a thorough examination of the site. I chanced to find the entrance to the tunnel and decided to investigate it further. I never imagined my discovery would prove so useful.'

Josiah listened carefully. He was about to accept the captain's statement, but a doubt remained: the explanation had been too precise. Josiah was no fool, and he wondered why the man who had been happy enough to cuff him into silence earlier was suddenly prepared to answer his question in every detail.

The next moment Dolores let out a muffled cry, somewhere between a sob and a moan, and covered her face with her hands.

Stephen's betrayal was all the harder to bear because from the moment she recognised him standing at the foot of the stairs, she had been convinced this night was the beginning of her deliverance. At any other time she would have kept her composure, but just at the moment such a counterfeit was beyond her. She had believed Stephen was come to rescue her, but the cruel fact was that his men's needs came first. Since she had no idea that the Irishmen's lives were at risk, it seemed obvious to her that Stephen had betrayed her great confidence simply to hasten his men's release. And she had trusted him so completely she had never even made him promise to keep her secret – the secret on which her reputation must depend. Now she looked on the face of the soldier she had believed she loved, and saw a coward and a cheat. If the house had come tumbling down about her ears, she could not have been more shocked.

Half a dozen more soldiers, in various stages of exhaustion and disease, were staggering down the stairs. When Stephen had repeated to them the commands he had given Donnelly and O'Rourke and they too had left the house by the side door, he said, more to Dolores than her husband, 'Master Taverner, I wish there had been another way to rescue these poor men, but believe me, on my honour, there was none.'

Josiah did not speak. He looked at the distress on the captain's face. He turned, and saw his wife, her eyes blazing with rage and cheeks wet with tears. As an approximation of the truth sank home, he felt a second blow, far more punishing than the one Stephen had delivered earlier.

Gasping, as though in great pain, and with the sweat running down his forehead, Josiah raised his hand to point at Stephen, and asked his wife in a trembling voice, 'Is he the man called you Dolores?'

His question dropped like a stone into huge silence.

A couple more figures appeared on the landing. As the first one made his way down, he said to Stephen, 'There's a couple of children up there. They look scared out of their wits. Do you want them dealt with before they raise the alarm?'

Before Stephen could answer, Dolores rose from her seat and, without a word, began to climb the stairs.

Stephen said, 'Mistress Taverner, bring them down here and I promise they'll come to no harm.'

She did not answer. Upstairs she found Beth and Harry quaking behind the partly-open door to Harry's chamber. Beth had been awake from the beginning. She had watched her parents go down the stairs together and had been about to return to her bed, when she heard whispered voices coming from the screens passage. Then the door of her parents' bedchamber swung open, and two men who looked like damned souls escaped from hell and who smelled worse than an open drain staggered out. As soon as they and the two men who followed them were out of sight, Beth just had time to scamper into Harry's room next door and shake him awake. The children had watched in growing terror while the ghostly cavalcade trooped across the landing and vanished down the stairs. Philip, as usual, was sleeping through it all.

And now here was their mother, tall and straight, but looking as though she had seen two hundred ghosts and uttering never a sound, come to usher them down the stairs in the wake of yet another group of men who seemed more dead than alive.

Beth gave a squeal of surprise when she saw Stephen. 'Oh, Captain Sutton,' she exclaimed delightedly, 'If I'd known it was you I'd never have been frightened.' And she was only prevented from running across to greet him properly when her mother yanked her arm ferociously and dragged her to join Josiah.

'What is it? What is happening?' she wailed.

According to Stephen's calculations there were only another half a dozen men still unaccounted for, and he feared they had been too sickly to manage the distance from the ruin to the Priory House. He wondered suddenly if one of the weaker men might have collapsed in the tunnel, and the thought of the poor wretch, too feeble to go either forward or back and blocking the escape of his comrades, was so appalling that he realised he had no choice but to search for him.

At that moment there was a shout in the street outside, a

sound of running footsteps, voices raised in alarm.

A figure appeared on the landing. It was a thin, thieving fellow from Kintyre who had caused frequent trouble in the past among the men. He held up a small box.

'Those others should not have been in such a hurry,' he grinned, 'Look what they missed.'

It was Josiah's casket.

'Damn you!' exclaimed Stephen in a rage, 'Put that down at once.'

Stephen raced up the stairs three at a time and knocked the casket from the man's hands.

'Your greed will cost you your life. Hurry, man, the alarm is raised.'

There was no longer any time to waste issuing instructions or advice: the man must trust to luck and his own low cunning. Stephen bundled him out through the side door. Now he must set about saving himself. He had hoped the escape would not be discovered until dawn, but outside the house, the town was swarming with roundhead soldiers and a man was pounding against the front door.

Stephen turned. If he left by the kitchen door and stole a horse he still had a slim chance of escape, since he knew the surrounding lanes and fields better than any of his enemy.

All but one.

Facing him in the shadowy candlelight when he turned stood Josiah, a massive broadsword held between two hands. While Stephen was distracted by the thief, Josiah had dragged his weapon down from the place where it had lived above the fireplace in the winter parlour for nearly fifteen years, and though its weight was greater than he ever remembered, he stood ready now for his final battle.

'Don't be a fool, Master Taverner,' said Stephen, 'I wish you no harm.'

For answer, Josiah rushed at him, and Stephen had no choice but to draw his own, lighter sword and parry the blow. Josiah came at him again. Though he was old and out of practice, Josiah had become a skilled fighter during his long years as a mercenary, and he was inspired by all the force of outrage and wounded pride. After a few moments, Stephen realised he was fighting for his life.

All around them as they battled was pandemonium. The hammering at the front door grew louder, there were shouts and cries from the stable-yard as the slowest of the Irish fought off their attackers. Beth was screaming hysterically, and Mabs and Ellen and Cary had finally awoken and come down from the attics to watch from the safety of the landing as Stephen and Josiah fought.

Josiah was short of breath, and so exhausted by the weight of his great sword that he could barely drag its tip off the ground. Most of his blows were aimed at Stephen's legs. Stephen could have beaten him easily, but was hampered by a wish to disarm his opponent without inflicting serious injury. Then the older man took a swipe which cut Stephen deep in the thigh. As the blood poured down over his boots, Stephen felt no pain, but fought on in earnest. He parried the next blow easily and, as Josiah was struggling to raise his broadsword, Stephen flicked it from his hands. Another moment, and he could have struck the final blow, but Beth's screams were ringing in his ears. He glanced up and saw Dolores staring at him with an expression that was part eagerness, part loathing, and which he could not read at all. In a moment of decision which he knew would haunt him for the rest of his life, he flung down his sword and turned away from his helpless enemy in disgust.

Josiah, seizing his opportunity, snatched up the fallen weapon and thrust it into Stephen's back.

Chapter 26

❧

It was Tom Rogers who had raised the alarm. The bitterness he harboured towards Sir Diggory and his family had extended to all royalists, and his loathing of Lieutenant Donnelly made him hate the Irish indiscriminately. Unlike the other townspeople, he welcomed their imprisonment, and was often to be found carousing with the guards. On the night Stephen helped the Irish to escape, Tom Rogers had been drinking with the sentries until late. As he was walking back towards town, he noticed two suspicious-looking figures making their way towards the Old Priory. Following them, he was able to observe from behind a thicket of scrub willow as Donnelly began to take his revenge on his tormentors. Tom Rogers was not the man to intervene, but he ran all the way to Furleys and reported what he had seen.

Over the next twenty-four hours more than half the men who had escaped were rounded up. Half a dozen were killed on capture, the rest were herded back to the ruined priory to join the few who had been too weak to leave. The tunnel was destroyed by a small explosion. Among the last to be apprehended were Donnelly and O'Rourke. Since O'Rourke was too weak to travel unaided, Donnelly had decided to hide in an outlying farm for a few hours until his friend was sufficiently recovered to ride a horse. It was while attempting to steal a horse than Donnelly was caught.

Colonel Firth was furious at the nine Irish savages who had got away, and the waste of more of his men's lives. He held Donnelly and O'Rourke, as officers, responsible for the whole fiasco. Since they had murdered three of his men, he was no longer bound by his promise of mercy. As he was now in a hurry

361

to leave the area and proceed to the next royalist garrison, he ordered his men to prepare for departure. The remaining prisoners would be loaded on to wagons and left to rot in a prison where the local population were not so bafflingly devoted to the Irish – all but Donnelly and O'Rourke, whom he ordered to be hanged as the parliamentary army pulled out.

Stephen, luckily, knew none of this. The injury to his back was not serious, since his buff coat had taken most of the blow, but the wound to his thigh had cut through to the bone. For three days he was in a high fever. Corinna, when she visited his bedchamber on the morning after the escape, was shocked, not so much by his wounds, which had a good chance of healing, as by the defeat she saw in his face. He had the look of a man who had no reason to recover. As she pieced together the events of the previous night, she began to understand some of his despair. She was afraid that his self-hatred, not his wounds, might destroy him. She guarded his sick-bed jealously, and allowed none of the servants to speak of anything which could add to his distress.

Colonel Firth was well aware of Stephen's role in the Irish escape. But the Cornishman was too ill to be punished immediately. Besides, as Colonel Firth's vindictiveness towards the Irish increased, he felt the need to temper it with some show of charity.

'You see, my dear,' he said to Corinna when he told her that Stephen was free to return to Cornwall once he was well enough to travel, 'I know when to be merciful.'

Corinna knew some, though by no means all, of the horrors inflicted on the prisoners. She answered tartly, 'I'm sure Lieutenant Donnelly and his friends will be delighted to hear it.'

The smile on the colonel's face froze into an expression of disgust. 'Only fools throw their mercy away on vermin.'

'Then we must thank the Lord for fools, Colonel.' Corinna was shaking with helpless rage, and quitted his presence without another word. She had heard of Donnelly's attack on the guards, and guessed his prospects were now hopeless. She thought it would be a fine thing to be a man, a strong one, so she could tear the colonel's smug head from his shoulders.

She focused her energies on Stephen. She had guessed the real reason for Josiah's murderous attack on him, and she wondered how he was going to respond to his wife's adultery. She listened to any scraps of gossip concerning the inhabitants of the Priory House, but was unable to decipher the rumours.

The roundhead soldiers, when they finally forced their way into the Taverners' home, had difficulty at first in establishing precisely who was injured. Obviously Captain Sutton was one, for he had collapsed and was bleeding profusely. But Master Taverner was also slumped against the wall: his eye was swollen and bruised where Stephen had struck him and his recent exertions had left him gasping for breath and unable to stand. His wife appeared to have been reduced to wide-eyed silence by the shock. Two of the maids helped her up the stairs to her room, while the third took care of the older children. At that moment a small, dark-haired child appeared at the top of the stairs and demanded in a shrill voice to know what was going on.

Dolores heard Philip's cry, but it seemed to her to be coming from a great distance. She sat all that day in a chair by the window of her room, and neither ate nor spoke. Mabs, who knew her mistress as well as anyone did, told the others to leave well alone, and she'd be herself again in a day or so. But Josiah had no intention of leaving her alone.

Later that same day, when his head had been bandaged and news of the captured Irishmen had gone a little way towards mollifying him, he entered their bedchamber. Dolores, seated in her chair, made no sign that she had heard him.

Josiah was assaulted by such a tumble of emotions at the sight of her, that all he could utter was, 'Wife—'

He went and stood before her. He had not known such grief was possible as this pain he felt when he looked at her and imagined her loving another man.

It was not what he had intended, but finally he could hold back the question no longer.

He said brokenly, 'Did you dance for him, Dolores?'

The question hung in the silence for a long time. In the road beyond their window two children were chasing a young dog, and laughing. Dolores had closed her eyes. Two tears rolled down her cheeks.

Josiah turned and left the room without another word. Since he saw no way to shift his wife without an uproar, he slept that night in a back bedroom.

It was Nona that Dolores was pining for in the hours of her silence. She could not bring herself to think of Stephen, but she remembered how her grandmother had nursed her before through the bad times. Though Mabs came in frequently, and chatted and brushed her hair and brought her little trays of food and drink, she yearned to hear Nona's toothless chuckle and fragmented English. She longed to hear the songs that had sustained them in their long exile. Now the music had died inside her, and part of her own self had died with it.

On the third day, Josiah returned. His grief was all gone, and in its place was only a resolute anger. Earlier that morning he stopped Mabs when she was taking Beth to visit her mother.

'Do not take the child in there.'

'I thought her company might do the mistress good.'

'No. I forbid it. The children may see her by and by.'

He went alone into the chamber. Dolores was standing in the centre of the room. She glanced at him briefly when he came in, then quickly looked away. This time, Josiah felt no sorrow, only rage.

He said at once, 'Prepare those things you wish to take with you. After what has happened, you are no longer fit to be mother to my children. I have been making arrangements. You are to go.'

She stared at him.

'Well, and if you've lost the power of speech again, so much the better. You'll be less trouble. No one fusses over a crazy woman. I shall see you are looked after, but don't imagine you'll come back here again – you never will.'

With a mounting triumph, Josiah watched his wife's face as the implication of his words sank in. She appeared to be ageing before his eyes. Her strange beauty had vanished: she looked haggard and wild. He was almost able to believe that she had indeed lost her wits, and that the course he had decided on was right and proper.

She swayed slightly, opened her mouth as if to scream, but no sound emerged.

'Go on then, faint if you will,' he was goading her, 'Scream or weep. It will do you no good at all. My mind is made up. You've only yourself to blame, God knows. I've always done everything for you, and how am I repaid? You go whoring with a soldier the moment my back is turned. Worse, you tell him the only secret I've ever seen fit to trust you with. If the truth of this got out, no one would think badly of me if I killed you – but I'll not let a scandal ruin my children's lives. Praise the Lord, I have their

364

welfare at heart, even though you do not. And that's the reason I will not allow you to corrupt them further. Dear Heavens, when I think of the times I have humoured you, it makes my blood boil, I could . . . but no matter. I'll tell people you've lost your wits and been sent to one of those places where they care for your kind of woman. The children will soon see it is for the best.'

At last Josiah knew the sweet taste of triumph. He had never been able to make his wife love him, but now he could make her suffer. She was completely in his power, and he intended to savour his revenge until one or both of them were dead. And how she was suffering. It was etched deep in every shattered nerve on her face.

'My children,' she gasped, 'I cannot leave my children!'

'Oh, so you can speak when you choose, eh? Just been play-acting all along, have you? Well, it's too late for that.'

'Nona—'

'What?'

'Nona . . .' As she repeated her grandmother's name, a brief expression that might almost have been hope hovered on her face.

'That old witch cannot help you now. I should have destroyed you both years ago. She's gone where—'

Josiah broke off. Dolores had tilted back her head slightly and half-closed her eyes. She was muttering in some strange language that he recognised but did not understand. He felt a sudden wave of helpless panic, a twinge of acute pain stabbed his chest. He gasped, but then, struggling to take possession of himself, he exclaimed in a fury, 'No more of those tricks, do you hear me? They don't fool me now, they won't help you! I'm throwing you out of this house, you'll never see your children again, and there's no power on heaven or earth can help you. D'you understand what I'm telling you? Stop that infernal noise before I – in the name of God, stop, do you hear, stop—'

But Dolores seemed to be in some kind of trance. Her sightless eyes were raised to a point just above his head, and her strange incantation gained in strength and power, until Josiah felt the frenzy of it would drive him insane.

'I'll stop your noise if I have to kill you!' he roared, and raised his hand to strike her down. But she side-stepped the blow and moved swiftly over to the panel that covered the priest's hole, pressing the catch so that it sprang back to reveal the darkness that lay within. Her unearthly chanting continued, growing louder all the time, and then suddenly Josiah realised he could understand every word distinctly.

'I see a man,' she was saying, 'He is a good man, a man of God, a man who brings the grace of Our Lord to this house. He is a priest. He must hide his vocation beneath a cloak of ordinariness. But in this house he believes he is safe from persecution. The family in this house honour him, they know he is a holy man. But look, oh, look closely, there is a traitor in this house. That traitor is still a child, that traitor is a young boy. There is evil in the boy's heart. He has betrayed the priest, he has put his own family in great danger. The child has given away the secret. Look, see, armed men are running up the stairs, they are taking the priest away to die a terrible death. Now they have seized the boy's father too, look, look! The boy watches as his father is captured, but he can do nothing—' Josiah let out an anguished cry and collapsed into a chair. Dolores did not show that she had noticed. She appeared to be wholly wrapped up in her terrible vision. 'Look – can you not see? – now the boy's father is in a filthy prison, he is dying, the plague has struck him down. The boy hears the news and cannot even weep. His father's death is on his hands, his father's agony will pierce his heart until his dying day, he is lost, he—'

She stopped. Josiah's face had turned an ugly purple. He was clutching at the neck of his doublet and gasping for breath. Hot tears poured down his cheeks.

Dolores crossed the room and trickled some flower water on to a piece of clean linen, then bent over him to smooth his cheeks and brow. He tried to push her away, but all the strength had gone out of him.

'Who told you?' he gasped, 'How do you know?'

'There are many ways of knowing.'

'Don't touch me! Keep away from me, you witch.'

She drew back slightly, then spoke to him in her normal voice, and gently, 'I am no witch, Josiah. Only Dolores, your wife. You could not help what you did when you were a child, no more than I could help the wrong I did to you.'

'It wasn't the same,' he protested, 'I never wanted anyone to suffer.'

'But two men died, and one of them was your father.'

Josiah turned his face away from her, and hugged himself in pain. 'I did not mean it to happen, oh God, I never understood.'

'I believe you Josiah. You were only a child,' her voice was soothing, 'If you can forgive me, then I will be a wife to you again, and a mother to your children.'

'Never! You are not fit.'

'We are none of us fit, Josiah. We simply do the best we can.' This time, when she placed the damp linen on his forehead, he did not push her away, but looked up at her, as if he were waiting for something. She loosened the doublet at his throat. 'There,' she said, 'You are well again. How quickly the human heart will heal.' She straightened and stepped back a pace, watching him quite calmly. 'Promise me this, Josiah, that you will never again attempt to separate me from my children, and I will give you the thing you most desire.'

'There is nothing on God's earth I want from you now.'

A half-smile touched her face. 'I will dance for you, Josiah.'

He looked up at her. Tall and stately, she towered over him. He ran his tongue over dry lips.

'Then dance.'

'Do I have your promise?'

'Yes.'

'Say it, then.'

He attempted to rise from the chair, so he could face her at her own level, but his body felt like a huge carcass of corruption and he wondered if he would ever be able to hold himself up as a man again. Still he looked at Dolores. It was as if he was a child again, and begging in crippled silence for his mother's forgiveness. Which never never came.

He was weeping. 'I promise,' he said, 'I will never try to take you from your children.'

Dolores smiled. Her beauty was returning. She moved to the centre of the room and began to hum the familiar tune. She was standing very tall and erect. The melody and the rhythm began to flow through her again. And, as she danced, she found she was dancing for a new kind of freedom. Nona had been right, as always. At the moment of Josiah's collapse, she had suddenly seen his fear and self-loathing, and she had pitied him. She could no longer hate him.

So she danced, to celebrate the ending of her fear.

Mabs was delighted by her mistress's sudden improvement. Late that afternoon, Dolores came down to the kitchen and sat at the large table and sipped some clear chicken soup, while

Mabs watched with approval. Mabs was certain that the moment someone began eating her chicken soup, they were as good as recovered. Beth leaned her forearms on the kitchen table and gazed up at her mother, and talked on and on about the fight between her father and Captain Sutton. Dolores would have preferred any topic but that one, but she understood her daughter's need to talk through the pain and shock.

As she understood so much, now. The prospect of being forever separated from her children had jolted her into her desperate gamble. There was no longer a Nona to care for her; there was no one to rely on but her own self, and in that frantic moment she remembered what Nona had told her when she was dying. Dolores had hardly expected Josiah to be taken in by her charade, and indeed, it had taken the extra inspiration of the story the priest had told her. Until she began to speak, she'd not known for sure that it was Josiah who had betrayed his father and the priest – but his horrified response had been all the proof she needed. He had carried that burden of guilt almost all his life.

Poor Josiah. When he first came into her world he had seemed a giant of a man, part monster, part saviour. And so it had remained. Though she had changed into a woman and a mother, with Josiah she had always felt herself to be a helpless child. Now she saw him more clearly for what he was: a man of uncommon ordinariness; a man who despised himself so profoundly that only with his children could he show his humanity. She knew she would never love him, but she thought now she might be able to tolerate the yoke by which they were joined. Her hatred had vanished when she ceased to fear – as Nona had always said it would.

Beth was insisting on her attention. 'But Father couldn't help fighting Captain Sutton, could he? I mean, all those men had been going through our home, hadn't they, and that wasn't right. Father was only defending us?'

'Yes, dear.' Dolores wished she could help her daughter, but there was not much she could say. Beth had watched her father stab an unarmed man in the back – an unarmed man whom Beth had liked and trusted. Whom her mother had loved and trusted . . . More fools, both of them.

Stephen Sutton had betrayed her. She was beginning to see that a woman in love wants to believe only the best of her lover. He was no more to be trusted than anyone else, but she had refused to see the truth. She was without illusions now – but she was learning that it is one thing to see clearly. Falling out of love is another matter altogether. She felt nothing but contempt for Stephen Sutton, yet still it was impossible to think of him without longing and pain.

She touched the chain which she still wore around her neck, hidden by the wide white collar. The sensible course now, she told herself firmly, was to return it to him while he remained at Furleys. That was the signal they had arranged between them to show that her feelings for him had changed. A brief memory of their last meeting in the garden tripped into her mind, but she turned from it bitterly. How pitiful those words seemed when she looked back on it now . . . empty words, worthless words, words without meaning.

Of course she would send the chain back without delay, but tomorrow was quite soon enough for the sensible gesture. The encounter with Josiah had left her with a feeling of great weariness, and now here was her little Beth, still insisting she be heard.

'But Captain Sutton was not really a wicked man, was he? After all, he helped Jinny's mother when her house caught fire, and when Nona was dying he rescued Pip and then—'

'Oh, little Bee, do stop.' Dolores found this catalogue of Stephen's virtues singularly painful. 'Captain Sutton was just an ordinary man—' With difficulty she swallowed the lump that formed in her throat as she spoke these words before continuing, 'He did some good things, and many bad ones.'

'What sort of bad things?' Beth looked at her hopefully.

'I don't know, but I'm sure he must have done.'

'I just wish he and Father could be friends.'

Dolores smiled. 'That is not at all likely, I'm afraid.'

Mabs was in no doubt as to who paid her wages. 'Any man of sense would have done just what your father did, Beth. Fancy Captain Sutton letting all those ruffians tramp through our house in the middle of the night. They were trying to steal your father's treasure, and then where would we all be? No wonder Master Taverner was angry. Heathen scoundrels, all of them.'

Dolores looked at Mabs with some surprise. She had been as well-disposed towards the Irish soldiers as anyone else in Tilsbury. But Mabs, like plenty of others, tended to judge people according to their current status, and she had come to the conclusion that if those men were being treated worse than common criminals, then they must have done something to deserve their fate. For the time being Mabs' distorted view was helpful to Beth, so Dolores let it pass without comment. Besides, Dolores had turned her back on the soldiers and their barbarism. Her four children and her household were all she would care about from now on – if the Irish and the roundheads and the royalists and heaven knows who else decided to tear each other limb from limb, she'd not even blink an eye, so long as her children were safe.

She stood up. 'Come along Beth. Let's find your brothers and go and see if there are any apples ripe yet. We've been in poor Mabs' way long enough, it's high time we—'

The back door swung violently open and Cary stumped in. Her face was hot and furious, and she burst out at once, 'I wish every roundhead soldier was dead and burning in hell! I'd like to kill them all myself! I wish I could – oh!' And she flung herself down on a stool, covered her face with her hands, and burst into loud weeping.

'Mind your language!' roared Mabs.

But Dolores crouched down beside her and took her hands and said, 'What is it, Cary?'

'Oh ma'am, they're going to hang my Michael!'

'What?'

'It's true, he'll be killed tomorrow. Oh!' She wailed more loudly than ever.

'Michael?' Dolores appealed to Mabs, who looked uncomfortable, torn between disapproval and sympathy.

'She means that Sergeant Michael O'Rourke. There's a kind of understanding between the two of them.'

'But why should he be hanged?'

'That was what I said!' howled Cary. 'He didn't do anything to deserve it. Just because he's an officer, it's not fair. It was Lieutenant Donnelly who attacked the sentries, everyone knows that, Michael was too ill and he'd never even hurt a fly. They should leave my Michael alone.'

'Is this true? When did you hear?'

Cary controlled her sobs as best she could and said, 'I was talking to the sentries, like I always do when I take the food for Michael and the others. Michael told me to chat and be friendly, then I could find out useful things. And I did. I knew about the cannon before anyone else, but when Michael told Captain Sutton and then Major Ripley said nothing must be done,

370

Michael said I was more use than ten majors, he was so angry he—'

'The cannon? What does a cannon have to do with it?'

'Nothing, now. Not since Furleys was taken. But I carried on talking to the roundheads just in case . . . and oh, ma'am, today they told me they are moving on tomorrow, but the last thing they do here will be to hang Donnelly and my Michael. It was all a trick, right from the beginning. When Furleys surrendered their colonel promised the Irish would not be executed, but he meant them to die all the same. Those wicked sentries told me I ought to be grateful my Michael would go quickly because all the rest are going to die of disease or hunger. The colonel only said that about them not being executed so Furleys would surrender. And when Captain Sutton found out he went and told Donnelly about the tunnel, but then Tom Rogers ran all the way to Furleys, oh, I hate him, it was all for spite, everyone knows that. And now Michael is going to die and I cannot save him!'

She hugged herself and rocked back and forwards on the little stool.

Silent and appalled, Beth was watching, and listening to every word.

Mabs said gruffly, 'Don't worry, Cary, Captain Sutton got them out once already. He'll not stand by and let his men be murdered.'

'Oh *him!* Captain Sutton is worse than useless. He's in such a fever because of his wounds they think he'll most likely die. Mistress Rogers told her maid Ann she thinks he doesn't even want to live any more, he blames himself so for everything. She says no one is allowed to tell him about all the men being caught again. He'll never be able to help them now.'

Dolores was suddenly very pale.

'Cary, who told you about Captain Sutton?'

'Everyone knows. He's sure to die, and my Michael will die, and oh, I hate this war and all this endless killing. Why do they keep on and on? Why don't they ever stop?'

'Cary, I only wish I knew.'

Dolores had sunk back on her heels. The girl's story was garbled and far from clear, but one fact had stuck in her mind. If Stephen had known his men were to be killed – or left to die slowly of starvation and disease, which amounted to the same thing – then he could not have acted other than he did. Now she remembered what she had been forcing herself to forget from the very instant when it happened: the expression on Stephen's face when he glanced at her just before he flung down the sword and turned his back on Josiah. It was a look of utter despair.

She turned to her daughter who had dissolved into silent tears: the poor child. Was there no end to the horrors she had to endure? Then she looked at Mabs, who was venting her fury at the injustice of the world on a basin full of batter. And then she looked at Cary, stolid Cary, who so relished tales of murder and bloodshed – all but this one, which touched her so deeply she was sobbing like a small child.

Dolores reached forward and touched Cary's cheek.

'Don't weep, Cary. Perhaps it isn't quite hopeless, not yet. Let's see if we can find a way to save your Michael, and the others too. We'll not let them die without a fight.'

Chapter 27

❧

It seemed to Dolores, as she surveyed the contents of her stillroom, that the jars and bottles and gallipots had taken on characters of their own. Some were comforting, some soothed; others were grim-faced but kind – those were the ones that contained bitter but necessary potions. And there were some – the bottles on the topmost shelf which were marked only with a strange symbol – which were secretive and sinister. Six drops, Nona had said, and a man will sleep for six hours . . .

Dolores tried to think clearly, but after her days of silence and self-imposed hunger, she was feverish and light-headed. She heard Nona's voice again: six drops and a man will sleep . . . as her plan began to crystallise she was both frightened and excited. Her confrontation with Josiah had proved how easily a man may be manipulated once his innermost fears are trapped. She had been totally unprepared for her own heady delight in watching him bend to her will. But even so, was it not perhaps a kind of madness to hope for the same success again so soon – and with a group of men, and strangers?

So many possibilities were dizzying through her mind that Dolores grew confused. She had no way of gauging which ideas were practical and which were ridiculous. She wished she could ask someone's help, but reason told her this challenge must be faced alone.

'Nona,' she said in a low voice, 'Tell me what to do.'

Immediately there was a knock on the door which caused her to shiver with apprehension.

'Wife? Are you in there? Are you alone?'

Josiah must have been waiting outside the door all the time.

He had been following her like a shadow since she had danced for him. She felt a throb of vexation: how was she to achieve anything while Josiah refused to budge from her side? Nona's voice whispered in her head once more: six drops, and a man will sleep.

Dolores took the small brown bottle from the top shelf and slipped it into the bag hanging from her waist before going to the door and opening it. 'Here I am, Josiah. I was mixing something for my headache.'

Her husband stood in the passageway, his head slightly lowered. So many contrary emotions were evident on his face: he knew himself to be weakened before his wife, and he resented his loss of power, yet he was hopeful at the same time that now she had allowed him to watch her dance, all was about to change between them. This fragile optimism was tempered by his suspicion, a dread that if he let her out of his sight everything would return to the way it had been before. And clouding all these thoughts was the desire he felt for her, the ache to hold her dancing body in his arms – and the fear that this pleasure might yet be denied him.

So he stood in the passageway and raised his arms and waited for her to evade him, or push him away. When she did neither, only smiled a strange smile and moved towards him, he wrapped his arms around her.

'Oh, my Dolores,' he breathed, 'When I think of you and that man together, I wish I had killed him. Dear God, if I could only squeeze the memory of him out of you.'

'There's no need of that, my dear,' she answered coolly, 'It was a sort of madness, that's all. I've as good as forgotten him already.'

'Oh, my dear—'

'There, now, we must not be late for evening prayers. After all, Josiah, we have so very much to be thankful for.'

She kissed him lightly on the bridge of his nose, and led him towards the hall, where the household was waiting.

'Why are you laughing, wife?'

'Just from happiness, that we are all together again as we were before.'

But so utterly different, she thought, as she took her seat on the high-backed chair in front of Josiah. She remembered suddenly that when she was very young she had watched with amazement while a small boy led a bull through the street outside her home. The bull had won a terrible name for himself, having maimed two men in the previous week. 'Why is he so gentle with the little boy?' she had asked her father. 'See the ring through the bull's nose,' he had explained, 'The skin there is so tender that the least thing will hurt him. The child is safe enough.'

Josiah had been disarmed. Now she must find a way to be free of him for a couple of hours. While he remained in his present state of anxious devotion, that might well be the hardest part of all the tasks that lay ahead.

'Cary, come into the winter parlour. I need to talk with you in private.'

Josiah, still hovering at her side, was instantly suspicious. 'Why? What secrets can you have with the girl?'

'Secrets, Josiah? What an idea!' Dolores laughed easily. 'It is perfectly obvious she is upset for some reason. Probably just some woman's ailment, but you may join us if you wish.'

'No, no, my dear,' Josiah backed away hastily, 'You deal with it. I shall wait for you at table.'

'I'll ask Mabs to make us some spiced wine.'

Dolores closed the door firmly behind her and went to stand by the empty fireplace. The portrait now hung in place of honour above the mantelshelf. Dolores glanced briefly at her painted image: that woman had the veiled eyes of a sleepwalker. She remembered how she had fretted in silence at having to wear the extravagant jewellery. Now she touched the chain at her throat, and almost smiled. Then she became aware of Cary's anxious regard, and was serious at once.

'Sit down, Cary. Pay close attention. We must act quickly if we want to save the prisoners.'

At once Cary began to sob. 'There's nothing we can do, they'll be hanged in the morning. Oh my poor Michael, it's not fair—'

'Stop that noise at once, and listen carefully.' Aware that Josiah almost certainly had his ear to the door, Dolores spoke in a low voice, but with such authority that Cary dried her eyes on the corner of her apron and waited. 'We may well be able to help them, all of them. But you must do your part too. You will have to be very calm, and very cunning too.'

'Like a spy, ma'am?'

'Yes, Cary, exactly like a spy.'

Cary gulped, sniffed and endeavoured to compose herself. 'What must I do?'

'Have you told the roundhead sentries about the Grey Lady?'

'I suppose I may have done. Everyone knows about her, anyway,'

Dolores smiled. 'Your version of the story is probably more colourful than most.'

'I'm not a liar, ma'am. No one can accuse me of being dishonest, I'm—'

'Hush, Cary, keep your voice down. We will both have to tell a few untruths if your Michael is going to be saved. Listen. I want you to take a basket of food and drink to the Old Priory for the prisoners. Those murdering sentries will probably take it all for themselves, but that is not important. We'll put in a couple of blackjacks of special ale for the roundheads – try to make sure they drink that one first. And while you are there, tell them about the Grey Lady. You can make up anything you like, just so long as it's frightening. Add a few details. You could tell them this is the anniversary of her death, that her ghost is always seen at this time of year, you know the kind of thing I mean.'

Cary was staring at her with round eyes. She had never seen Mistress Taverner like this before. She was clearly in a state of high excitement: her cheeks were flushed and her eyes glittered with a wildness that made Cary uneasy.

'I don't understand, ma'am,' she said stubbornly, 'What's the point of it all? I don't want to get into trouble.'

'For pity's sake, girl, have a little courage. I only want you to take some provisions to the sentries and tell them about the spirit that haunts the Old Priory. Surely that's not much to ask when men's lives are at stake.'

'I just don't see how that will help my Michael.'

'Leave that to me.'

Cary's eyes grew rounder still. 'You'll not poison them, will you?'

'No, Cary. I did consider it, but . . . no, I'm trying to save lives, not take them.'

'That's all right then.' The girl looked far from convinced.

Dolores thought for a moment. 'Imagine what will happen tomorrow morning if we decide to do nothing,' she said. 'Imagine your Michael being dragged from the priory and the noose being placed around his neck. You've seen men hanged before now, haven't you? You know how long it takes, how long

376

the body jerks and twitches before it is finally still, how long the corpses are left there for the birds to peck at. Do you want to have to look at Michael's bones hanging from a tree and all the time know that you had the chance to save him, but chose the coward's way instead?'

'Oh no, ma'am!'

'Then stay calm and do exactly as I tell you. No sign of tears, now. And remember, most important of all, you must never breathe a word of this to anyone.'

'I'd never do that.'

A little later Cary set off for the priory ruins with a basket over her arm. Having something to do always calmed her nerves and she was warming to her part in the adventure. She was beginning to see herself as the heroine of a future ballad, or the subject of a penny book: *A True and Precise Relation of the Story of Cary Stubbs, and how she did with Great Bravery save her True Love from a Terrible Death at the hands of the Perfidious Roundheads and* . . .

She was sure it would be a fine thing to be famous. The hardest part of all, she could see that quite plain, was going to be Mistress Taverner's final injunction not to tell anyone about her part in this great drama.

Darkness was coming earlier on these evenings of late August. Dolores, alone in the dining hall with Josiah and watching the shadows deepen, was struggling to suppress her agitation.

'Come, wife, why so restless? Sit beside me on the settle.'

Dolores returned from the window, where she had been watching in vain for Cary. She forced herself to smile as she sat down beside her husband.

'My nerves are uneasy,' she confided, 'I don't believe I shall be myself again until the soldiers are gone.'

'They leave in the morning, so I am told. Here, come closer, my little Doll . . . no, no, my Dolores – see, I am learning. Soon we'll to bed. You need not be anxious any more.' He put his arm around her shoulder and pulled her against his side. His hand was trembling. He placed his lips against the side of her head. 'I will make you forget that other man,' he breathed heavily, 'I will make you my own wife again.'

'Yes, Josiah, but won't you taste your wine? Mabs made it specially.'

'By and by. I am not thirsty.'

'But she took such trouble.' Dolores could not take her eyes off the flagon of wine and the filled glass which had been set on the table before them.

'Tut, stop fussing. It is only wine. I'll have a drop in a while.'

Dolores was fighting down a crazed impulse to open his mouth and pour the wine forcibly down his throat. She had no way of knowing how much of Nona's potion was needed to be effective. She had been similarly perplexed when mixing up the ale for Cary to take to the sentries. Cary had been vague about the precise number of men who were guarding the Old Priory, and there was no certainty they would share the drink equally between them. The temptation was to double the dose, but she was afraid that might be dangerous. As she had told Cary, her aim was to save lives, not to take them. But now here was Josiah, adamantly refusing to touch the spiced wine she had laced with Nona's secret medicine, and unless he drank at least some of it, her plan had not the smallest chance of success. She dared not press him to taste the wine again, however, for fear of arousing his suspicions.

'You will dance for me again, won't you, Dolores?'

'Of course. Dolores will always be a true wife to you.'

'I'm glad, so glad.' He slid his hand under her hair and stroked the back of her neck. 'I never wanted to send you away, you know, it was only because you wronged me so.'

'Yes, Josiah.' All the time, Dolores was staring at the glass of wine. Her hand itched to move it just a fraction closer.

'I want you near me always.'

'Yes, Josiah.'

Josiah sighed and eased himself slightly away. He reached out his hand and fingered the glass. Dolores tensed with expectation. Josiah said, 'The Lord works in mysterious ways, does he not? I truly believe that our recent trials may prove to have been a blessing after all.'

'Yes, Josiah.'

'Let us drink to that.'

'Yes, Josiah.'

He picked up his glass and lifted it to his lips. Dolores watched. He began to drink. There was a commotion in the screens passage. He set down the glass as a mightily flustered Mabs came into the room.

'There's a man calls himself a captain and wanted to speak with you, Master Taverner. I told him to wait outside, but he—'

'But he insisted on seeing you without delay, Master Taverner.' Captain Sugar hurried into the hall, easing Mabs to one side as he did so. Dolores caught her breath; suddenly she was oppressed with a sense of foreboding.

She spoke sharply, 'Could you not wait to be announced?'

'I deeply regret the intrusion, ma'am, but my message is urgent.' In fact, the young captain had borne the brunt of his colonel's ill-humour all day and dared not risk another tongue-lashing over this errand.

'Speak then.' Josiah had stood up. He glanced back at his wife with an anxious frown.

'Colonel Firth requests a few moments of your time, Master Taverner. There are some matters to be discussed before his departure.'

'By all means. Tell him I shall ride out to Furleys first thing in the morning.'

'You misunderstand me, sir. Colonel Firth is leaving before dawn. He absolutely requires you to visit Furleys at once.'

'This is highly inconvenient.'

'My apologies.' Captain Sugar had no intention of allowing Josiah to wriggle out of this meeting. 'I brought a spare horse with me. We can leave at once.'

'Very well, I suppose there is no alternative. Dolores, my dear, I shall return with all speed. Do not wait up, but . . .' He squeezed her hand. Such a mixture of hope and fear, desire and mistrust was on his face that she turned away, unable to meet his eyes.

'Won't you finish your wine before you go?' she asked helplessly. Only about a quarter of the precious wine had been drunk.

'No, no. There is no time.'

'But such a shame to waste it.'

'Quite so. Bussell shall have it. Mabs, take the flagon and give it to Bussell. And have a little yourself.' He attempted some humour. 'With all due respect, Captain Sugar, I think we civilians have good reason to celebrate your departure.' The captain fidgeted. 'Very well then, Captain, I am coming.'

Afterwards, Dolores was furious with herself for not having the wit to upset the tray as Mabs was carrying it out, but at the time she only stood, and stared.

When Cary returned from the Old Priory a few minutes after

the horsemen had ridden away, she was so pleased with her own success that she barely noticed Mistress Taverner's agitation.

'There'll be no peace for those sentries tonight,' she gloated, 'I told them such tales of the Grey Lady their eyes were ready to pop out of their sockets. I know you said we are to go saving lives, not taking them, but I'd not mind if they drop dead of fright, especially that big fellow who thinks he's such a champion. They never give the food I take to the prisoners, they keep it all for themselves. I pretended to leave, but then I crept back to watch and they were pouring the ale on the ground and laughing and shouting at the poor men inside. I wish *they* were going to be hanged in the morning. I wish—'

'You say they poured the ale on the ground. Was that the ale for the prisoners, or the jar you took for them?'

'I can't rightly remember, ma'am.'

'Oh, Cary, it was important.'

'I think Tom Rogers may have drunk a fair bit.'

'Tom?'

'Yes, he was there as usual. Crowing over poor Lieutenant Donnelly. He still hates him because of Sir Diggory's daughter. He kept saying how he'd be there to watch him swing in the morning.'

'Tom Rogers.' Dolores repeated the name under her breath as an idea began to form in her mind. After a few moments she said. 'Cary, how quickly can you reach Furleys?'

'Furleys? Why, ma'am?'

'To take a message. But it must reach Furleys with all speed.'

'I know a short cut. I can be there in no time.'

'Good. Wait there while I write it out.' Dolores sat down at the table, took up pen and paper and scrawled hastily. She folded the letter and prepared to seal it. 'After you have handed this to Mistress Rogers I think you ought to disappear, just for a few days. I'll let you know as soon as it is safe to come back. Do you have any family you can visit?'

'I can always go home to the farm.'

'Too close.'

'There's my cousin lives the other side of Bells Wood. She's a strange old woman, never sees a soul for weeks on end.'

'Perfect.' In fact Dolores' main anxiety was that Cary would ruin her plan by talking too freely. 'Now, here is the letter. You must give it into Mistress Rogers' own hands, don't let anyone else take it for you. Do you understand?'

'Mistress Rogers?'

'She is said to have had an affection for Lieutenant Donnelly; she has good reason to help us. Now, hurry, Cary. And remember, not a word of this to anyone at all.'

In her excitement, Cary had forgotten one significant fact: she was terrified of being alone in the dark. The short cut that she had boasted of lay through a small but densely planted wood, and by the time she had negotiated the bramble-tangled path and saw the lights of Furleys glimmering ahead, she was almost beside herself with fear. A black figure rose up suddenly in her path and ordered her to halt. She screamed and would have run all the way back to Tilsbury if strong hands had not caught her by the arm.

'Stop struggling,' a man's voice commanded roughly. 'What are you doing here? Come into the light where we can have a look at you.'

Cary was so relieved at being apprehended by a trio of extremely human sentries rather than a troop of hobgoblins or phantoms that she barely noticed the manhandling. In the light of a single lantern, three faces examined her with interest.

'It's just a girl,' said one.

'I've seen you before.'

'She brings food to the Irish soldiers.'

'And what are you doing here?'

As her terror subsided, Cary found her voice again. 'I've an important message to take to Furleys,' she said.

'And who might that be for?'

'Mistress Rogers.'

'Indeed? And why does she need a secret message delivered at this time of night, eh?'

'That's none of your business.'

'Give me the message and I'll see she gets it. I'd like to make Mistress Rogers my business.'

'My instructions are to give it directly into her own hands.'

'Oh really? And who is this message from?'

'I won't tell you.'

'Some new lover, I've no doubt. The woman is shameless.'

Cary was stung into denial. 'As a matter of fact it's nothing to do with a man. It's much more important than – ' she began, then stopped herself abruptly.

381

'Yes?'

'Never mind. Just let me through to the house.'

'We've orders to let no one through.'

'Oh, go on, let the girl pass. She'll do no harm.'

Cary was congratulating herself on her success as she crossed the grassy park towards the house. But as she approached she was intercepted by a second group of sentries who demanded to know her business. This time she was more irritated than frightened, especially as she recognised some of these men from her visits to the priory ruins.

'For heaven's sakes,' she exclaimed, 'Whatever do you want with two lots of sentries? I've already told the men over yonder what my business was. Now, let me through.'

'Not so fast. We're the ones have to guard the house, they were just passing the time.'

'What?'

'They're guarding the wagons and carts which are all loaded up for the morning. You Tilsbury folk are a thieving bunch. We don't want any of our supplies walking away from us in the night, do we now?'

'I'm not a thief and I don't care a penny for your supplies. Now, let me pass.'

'On you go, then.'

Cary was about to thank him when he said gently, 'You'll no doubt be in a hurry to get back to Tilsbury in time to see those Irish bastards hang in the morning. As I remember, you had a fondness for one of them, a terrible ugly fellow. What did you want to waste your time on a wretch like that for, eh? You'll learn your lesson when he's swinging from the end of a rope, eh?'

'Laugh, go on,' Cary was outraged, 'You won't be laughing in the morning, just you wait!'

Suddenly terrified she was going to say more than she ought, Cary scampered into the protection of the house.

Corinna Rogers was in a small room adjoining her bedchamber. An embroidered shawl lay across her shoulders. She had been in the middle of discussing with her maid Ann what trimmings would be needed to improve her clothes for the winter. Sir Diggory had made it clear that he was now so impoverished, thanks to heavy taxation and the demands of the soldiers, that there was no question of new purchases. Her maid had left the room to fetch a length of braid, and Corinna was glad there was no one but Cary present to witness her discomfort. She had always prided herself on her ability to maintain a composed and aloof expression even in the most irregular of situations. But as she read Dolores' letter, her face became a picture of disbelief and rage.

Dear Corinna,
I believe my husband is now visiting Colonel Firth. He must not return
home until an hour after midnight, at the earliest. Men's lives depend
on this. Please do all in your power to persuade him to stay at Furleys.
I am sure you can think of an effective means of detaining him.
Dolores Taverner.

'How dare she! Why should I be party to her intrigues? What in heaven's name—?'

'Oh, Mistress Rogers, please don't be angry.' Cary was wishing she had thought of learning the contents of the letter before handing it over. 'She has a plan to save the Irish, but she needs your help.'

'The Irish? What on earth does this letter have to do with the Irish?'

'They are to be killed,' said Cary, her tears beginning to flow the moment she said the words. 'All of them are to die one way or another, but my Michael and Lieutenant Donnelly will be hanged in the morning. Donnelly may be a murderer, but my Michael—'

'Donnelly? Hanged?' Corinna was astonished.

'Yes, ma'am.' Cary had not realised this vital fact was unknown to Mistress Rogers.

'But the colonel gave his word, when Furleys surrendered, that no men were to be executed.'

'That was just a wicked lie. A trick, you see. They won't *kill* the Irish, but they'll let them die of starvation and disease, which is the same thing, I reckon. And they say the officers must be hanged because of the soldiers they killed when they tried to escape. But that's not fair because soldiers are supposed to kill each other, and anyway, my Michael didn't even do it.'

'And now they are to hang?'

'At dawn, ma'am. Tomorrow.'

'Are you sure?'

'Certain, ma'am.'

There was a movement in the passageway, the door began to

open. Corinna said sharply, 'Ann, keep out, I'm busy. Make sure we are not disturbed.' The door closed and footsteps retreated.

Corinna began pacing the room. 'It's outrageous. Why was I never told about this? We must think. We must find some way to save them.'

'Mistress Taverner thinks she has a plan. But first she needs your help.'

'What is she going to do?'

'She didn't say, exactly. She just said I had to give you the message, safe in your own hands. And that it was urgent.'

'But . . .'

Corinna felt a black fog was settling around her brain. She had no reason to trust either Dolores or her maidservant, and no way of knowing how this strange request might help the Irish. But if it was true that Donnelly was to be hanged in the morning . . . the young Irishman had been by no means the best lover she had known though he had been the most pleasing to look at. Her interest in the affair had begun to wane some time before Furleys' surrender and his captivity in the Old Priory, but she cherished the memory of his delicate, feline beauty, a beauty all the more remarkable because it veiled the cold cruelty which lay at the heart of him. She had been shocked, but not surprised, when she heard how he had slit the throats of the gunners surrounding Furleys, and then again when she learned he had sacrificed his own escape to take his revenge on the roundhead guards. A beautiful man, but utterly ruthless . . . and now he was to die like a common criminal.

She told herself that in war these tragedies occur all the time and that Donnelly had known the risks when he became a soldier. Then she told herself that if there was a chance of saving him, she could not pass by and do nothing. Then she told herself that Dolores Taverner was hardly likely to rescue a dozen Irish prisoners single-handedly and she would only make herself ridiculous by interfering. Then she told herself that Stephen Sutton might stand a better chance of recovery if he knew his men had finally escaped. Then she told herself this whole scheme was quite possibly a trap laid by Tom Rogers and his cronies to discredit her even further. Then she told herself that she had never, until now, turned aside from a risk, and that she must be getting old, and dull.

She turned to Cary and said, 'You may go.'

'Will you do as my mistress asked?'

'Maybe. But first I must see Colonel Firth.'

The colonel's temper had been deteriorating throughout the day. He prized efficiency above all things, and the preparations for departure had thrown up the usual catalogue of mishap and disaster. Muskets had gone missing, horses were lame, wheels that should have been repaired a week ago were still in pieces in the wheelwright's store. Worst of all, Colonel Firth felt his reputation as a reliable officer had been seriously undermined by the escape of even some of the Irish prisoners. In what now seemed to have been a weak moment, he had agreed to overlook Captain Sutton's part in the affair; he was gratified to know that the captain showed no signs of recovering from his wounds. But he needed someone on whom to vent his irritation, and, for the past twenty minutes, that someone had been Josiah Taverner.

He knew full well that the Puritan merchant had been ignorant of the Irish plans, but the fact remained that they had attempted their escape through his home. In Colonel Firth's present mood, that was reason in plenty for suspicion. Besides, it was a good excuse to frighten the wretched fellow into extra diligence once the soldiers had gone. Although Tilsbury seemed quiet enough, Colonel Firth did not trust any place where Irish papists were so inexplicably popular.

'When Charles Stuart is finally brought down, Parliament will know how to repay those who have supported her through this great enterprise. There will be a great need for men of proven ability and loyalty to run the affairs of each district. In Tilsbury, for instance, Sir Diggory can no longer be relied on. But anyone who has been tainted with rumours of double-dealing will be crushed, as an absolute nothing . . .' As he said the word 'crushed' Colonel Firth stabbed his finger in the air in a gesture of vague menace.

Josiah was growing seriously alarmed. 'I assure you, Colonel, I was entirely ignorant—'

'But you knew of the tunnel's existence?'

'Yes, Colonel, certainly, but—'

'And who else knew?'

Josiah paused, swallowed hard, then said in a low voice, 'No one. No one else knew.'

'Then how did the Irish criminals discover it unless you told them? The place had been thoroughly searched by my men before it was used. Surely even you must agree that it would have been highly unlikely . . .' And so on. Colonel Firth's stated aim was to frighten Josiah Taverner into being Tilsbury's most loyal and ruthless parliamentary supporter once the soldiers pulled out. But that purpose had been met some time back: he continued now just for the satisfaction of watching the fellow sweat and grovel.

Josiah's discomfort, however, was only partly caused by the colonel's tirade. There was a throbbing at the base of his skull, and from time to time the image of Colonel Firth separated into two figures, so that he felt himself doubly accused. Though anxious to affirm his loyalty to Parliament, his chief preoccupation just at present was the necessity of finding a soft bed somewhere and falling instantly asleep. He assumed he was coming down with a slight fever.

At last Colonel Firth indicated that their interview was at an end. Josiah mopped the sweat from his forehead and left the room. He was startled to see Corinna Rogers waiting in the small chamber beside the colonel's, and more surprised still when she approached him and said in that soft voice she used sometimes to such great effect, 'Master Taverner, I'm so glad I found you. Please wait for me just for a moment while I talk with Colonel Firth. I need your opinion on a matter of great urgency.'

'Really, Mistress Rogers, it is late, and I am not feeling altogether well. Could we not talk some other time?'

'Oh, Master Taverner, and I was depending on you, you cannot let me down now. There is no one else I can turn to.'

The look that accompanied her request suddenly reminded Josiah of all the rumours he had heard concerning Sir Diggory's daughter, and he felt more at sea than ever. His instinctive disapproval was offset by a still more instinctive response to the knowing vulnerability of her gaze.

He mopped his forehead with his handkerchief once again and said, 'I'm sure others can be of more help than I can . . . but yes, yes, I'll wait, but please be quick. I must be home . . . my wife, you know . . . but, of course, I'll try to help . . . one must not disappoint . . .' It had become hard to think clearly, and his sentences were grown jumbled.

Corinna laid a small hand on his arm. 'Oh, Master Taverner,' she breathed, 'I knew I could rely on you. My business with Colonel Firth will not detain me long.'

As it happened, her business with Colonel Firth was very

brief indeed. Hounding Josiah had only fuelled his ill humour, and he was irritated by this further interruption.

'Well?' he demanded brusquely, 'What do you want?'

On first arriving at Furleys, Colonel Firth, like many others, had been intrigued by Corinna Rogers: his leniency towards Captain Sutton had been partly inspired by his wish to win her good opinion. He knew, however, that by his actions he had forfeited any chance of that long ago, and the stories he had heard in the meantime concerning her convinced him that her goodwill was not worth having. Besides, by the next morning he'd be gone.

Sensing his mood, Corinna came straight to the point. 'There is a rumour that the two Irish officers, Lieutenant Donnelly and Sergeant O'Rourke, are to be executed at dawn. Also that the others will be so mistreated they too will surely die.'

'And what of that?'

'Is it true?'

'Certainly. They should have been dealt with long since.'

Corinna caught her breath. 'But you gave your word when Furleys surrendered.'

'Donnelly and O'Rourke are common murderers. Hanging is too good for them. I am being lenient.'

'Is there nothing will make you reconsider?'

He sneered at her, the calculated sneer of the righteous man for the woman whose reputation is in tatters and said, 'I assure you, Mistress Rogers, you are wasting my time. There is no inducement you can offer will make me change my mind.'

Corinna felt the colour flood her face as she said, 'You flatter yourself, Colonel. I draw the line at liars and murderers.'

'You prefer scoundrels like Donnelly, I understand.'

'Indeed I do. Lieutenant Donnelly is worth ten of you.'

His sneer turned into a smile of triumph. 'Not for much longer, I fear,' he gloated. 'This time tomorrow your pretty lieutenant will be carrion for crows.'

Corinna was so shocked that she left the room without another word, and was so boiling with rage that it came as something of a surprise to see Master Taverner seated on a settle in the passageway. Her interview with Colonel Firth had made her more determined than ever to undermine the roundhead plans. She paused for a moment to compose herself, then glided across the floor to stand in front of him.

'You are still here,' she purred, 'I am so glad.'

He looked up at her. His eyes were bloodshot. 'How may I help you? I hope it will not take long. I must get home. My wife expects me.'

'Ah, yes. Your dear wife. How is my good friend Doll?'

'Dolores. She likes to be called Dolores now.'

'Does she really? How intriguing. You must tell me all about it.' Her breathy voice seemed to be curling like smoke through his brain. 'How fortunate to have this chance to talk together as friends. With your great experience of the world, I am sure your opinion is worth more than those boys' who call themselves soldiers these days. But we must talk privately. I know I may rely on you to be discreet, but others are not so honourable. Do come with me, please. This is so good of you. In here, I believe we will not be disturbed. You seem unwell, Master Taverner, let me take your arm. Such a strong arm you have, I feel reassured already. Shall we sit together here, like this?'

The roundhead sentries who were guarding the Old Priory ruins that night were no more and no less superstitious than the majority of their fellows. They believed that God had intervened directly to bring about their recent triumphs, and that future victories depended as much on fasting and prayer as on military strength. They believed men could be possessed by devils and that infants who died before baptism were condemned to everlasting hell. They believed dreams foretold future events and that the position of the stars had an effect on men's actions here below. They believed that witches should be burned and that some restless spirits walked the earth as phantoms and ghosts. And, at this stillest hour of darkness, when the chimes of midnight had faded into silence and Cary's stories were fermenting in their thoughts, they were more than ready to believe in the Grey Lady.

Two men were sitting with their backs against the heavy oak door. They were smoking, as much to mask the stench from the prisoners behind them as for the pleasure of their pipes. Apart from the occasional murmur of discomfort from within, all was peaceful.

The larger of the two, the one whom Cary had singled out for special dislike because the others tended to follow his lead, was called Miller. He drew deeply on his pipe and said, for no particular reason except that talk was companionable, 'I'll be glad to leave in the morning.'

'And I,' said his comrade, a scrawny youth called Armitage. They had repeated this sequence of statement and response countless times already that night.

'Tilsbury is a useless town. And as for this place—'

'Evil is here, you can almost smell it in the air.' Armitage spoke with unaccustomed feeling.

'Not much longer now.'

'Nearly morning.'

'I can't wait to see those Irish bastards strung up, that'll be worth staying awake for.'

'Why only the officers? Why not hang the lot and get it over with?'

'They'll be dead enough soon, one way or the other and . . . what was that?'

'What?'

'I thought I saw a light.'

'Where?'

'Over there. Through the trees. Look, there it is again. Quick, fetch the others.'

'Where are they?'

'I don't know. Round the back, I suppose. They were here just now.'

Not yet unduly alarmed by the sight of the flickering light at the edge of the trees, Armitage scurried round the walls of the ruined priory to alert his fellows. Two of them had nodded off, but staggered groggily to their feet when roused. The fifth, as well as Tom Rogers, was sleeping like the dead and could not be woken.

'Something's up,' Armitage reported anxiously to Miller. 'I don't understand it. They look like they're sleeping, but I'm damned if I can wake them.'

'Drunk, eh? The fools, they know the penalty for that.'

'They don't look drunk. They didn't have that much ale.'

'What, then?'

'I think . . .' Armitage spotted the light in the trees again and his teeth began to chatter with fear. 'I think this is the devil's work.'

'Nonsense man. That's nothing but a traveller lost in the woods, most like. Here, give me the lantern, I'll go and look. Light the match and prepare your muskets. We'll see them off, whoever it is.'

Miller had not gone more than a few paces towards the light

when he stopped. Through the darkness he could just make out a pale-robed figure, which might perhaps have been a woman. It was moving strangely, swaying and seeming almost to float over the uneven ground of the wood. Miller summoned his courage.

'Stop!' he shouted, 'Who's that? Say who you are or I'll shoot.'

The weightless body swung round in a graceful arc and turned to come straight towards him.

Miller raised his musket. 'Who's there? Who is it? Answer, damn you!'

The figure appeared to be speaking.

'What was that you said?' Miller's voice emerged, shakily now. As he heard the sound more distinctly he paused, and a cold sweat of terror began to pour down his back.

A strange, high, chanting voice, musical, but unlike any music he had heard before. He did not understand the words, which may have been Latin – but then again it could just as easily have been some hellish language known only to unquiet spirits. Or the incantation of Lucifer's cohorts. He took a step backwards and his musket wavered so that he could not take proper aim.

'Stop!' he shouted again, but now his voice was squeaking with alarm. 'Stop, there, or I'll fire!'

The mysterious, ghostly figure, a lantern held beside its face which was almost entirely hidden by the hood of its cloak, continued towards him with a buoyant stride. The strange song – more of an enchantment than a song – grew in strength and clarity all the time.

'Stop!' shrieked Miller, pulling the trigger on his musket at the same time. There was a bright flash, the bullet whistled away wide of the mark, and still the ghostly creature came towards him.

'Quick,' he shouted, running back to the priory doors where he had left the others. 'Fire your muskets while I reload.'

For answer, there was only silence. The place was deserted. Armitage and the other two had fled the instant they saw that the figure – surely the Grey Lady herself – had ignored the musket fire and was continuing undaunted in their direction.

Finding himself abandoned, Miller, who was a courageous man, prepared to tackle the Grey Lady alone. He began hastily to babble any prayers he could remember to counteract her devilish otherworldly jabbering. At that moment, however, the sky near Furleys was lit up with red and gold light and the ground appeared to shake with the impact of a tremendous roaring. Miller's instant thought was that the gates of the underworld had burst open and the legions of the Antichrist were rising up to walk the earth. Still the phantom walked, and still she sang.

Gibbering with terror, Miller flung down his useless musket, and fled.

Dolores continued with her song, just in case there were soldiers lurking nearby, as she hastened to the door of the ruined priory. She lifted the heavy iron bar with which it had been barricaded. It took all her strength to swing the huge door open, and when she had done so, the wretched odour from the prison made her briefly cease her song, and step back, retching.

She took a deep breath of outside air before stepping into the prison and saying in Latin, 'The Lord be with you. Go in peace,' and then, in case some of the prisoners knew less of the language of their religion than she did, she added in English, 'You are free to go. Hurry. There is not much time,' taking care all the while to disguise her voice.

There was a stunned silence. Then a man's shape detached itself from the darkness and made a rush for the door.

Suddenly there was a huge press of bodies, all scrambling to escape.

'In the name of all that's holy, who are you?' She recognised Donnelly's voice.

'*Pax vobiscum,*' she chanted, then continued, still in Latin, 'Glory be to the Father, and to the Son, and to the Holy Ghost . . .' Random fragments of the mass were all she could remember from her Catholic childhood, but they appeared to be effective. Donnelly, white-faced, crossed himself as he passed her and hurried after his comrades into the night.

O'Rourke was the last. He lurched to his feet and crashed against the doorpost. His eyes were wild and his chances of covering much ground seemed slight.

Dolores reached beneath the folds of her cloak. She had brought Josiah's pistols with her in case her impersonation of the Grey Lady proved ineffective, and these she now handed to O'Rourke.

'The Lord be with you,' she said, and then, 'Go on, man, for God's sake hurry.'

'Jesus Mary,' he breathed in disbelief, as he pushed a shaggy

391

veil of hair from his eyes, 'It is surely not Mistress Taverner?'

'Go!'

She snuffed out the lantern and almost ran down the path that led from the ruins back through the orchard to her own garden. There she removed her cloak, which had a pale lining, and turned it right side out. She said a silent prayer for the safety of the Irishmen in their second attempt at escape, and began to walk slowly back towards the house.

Cary had stayed at Furleys long enough to beg the use of a lantern from one of her friends who worked in the kitchen. She had no intention of going back by the short cut through the woods, but there was no moon, and besides, now that she had followed Mistress Taverner's instructions, she was overwhelmed by morbid thoughts. O'Rourke was to be hanged in the morning and she wanted to have one last sight of him, perhaps even to comfort him before he died, but now she remembered she had been told not to return to Tilsbury. Mistress Taverner had warned her to disappear for a few days. Cary was suddenly afraid that she was in a great deal of trouble; she no longer saw herself as the heroine of a popular ballad, but as an unfortunate girl who was likely to be punished for something she barely understood, and who could not even run home to her family at their farm. Mistress Rogers had not definitely said she would help them, she had no idea what Mistress Taverner intended to do, and now Cary was certain nothing could possibly save the Irish, Michael was going to be hanged and it was all hopeless.

Blinded by tears of misery and frustration, she stumbled down the track which lay across the parkland, and only stopped when confronted by the group of sentries who had challenged her when she first emerged from the woods.

'Let me pass,' she said miserably, 'It's only me.'

The soldiers were bored, and tormenting Cary was better than bickering among themselves.

'Got another message from her ladyship, have you?'

'Who's the lucky fellow? Is it me?'

'Not her Irish friend anyway. He won't look so pretty with a noose around his neck.'

'A fine sight, though, the pair of them, hanging off a tree.'

'Will you be watching? I'll hold your hand if you like.'

For the first and last time in her life, Cary was filled with an overwhelming hatred. She began to answer them in kind, but they only laughed and teased her more.

'I hope the Grey Lady curses you all to hell!' she stormed, then turned and set off along the edge of the wood towards the road which led back to Tilsbury.

'Hey!' shouted one of the soldiers, starting to follow her, 'You can't go that way!'

'You won't stop me!'

'Watch out, the wagons are loaded with powder and—'

'What?' Cary pretended not to hear, but she broke into a sudden run.

'I said—'

A dark shape, which might have been a cart well loaded, appeared ahead of her.

'I hate you!' Cary screamed, 'You're all murderers!'

And she lobbed her lantern into the air in the general direction of the munitions wagon, then dived into the woods and ran for her life.

Corinna Rogers heard the explosion, a deafening roar which rattled all the glass in the windows and set the dogs howling with alarm, when she was crushed by Josiah's great weight against an oak-panelled wall. One of his hands was clasped around the back of her head, while the other was fumbling under her skirts. He was not rough, far from it, but his gestures were blundering and clumsy: she began to think he really was seriously unwell and thought that if she was not careful he could hurt her.

'Ah, Mistress Rogers,' he grunted, 'Please . . . permit me . . .'

'A moment, Master Taverner.' It was difficult to breathe with his huge chest pressed against her face, 'I am not altogether comfortable.'

'Ah yes . . . you must be . . . this is so . . .' He was endeavouring to free himself from his breeches while Corinna was thinking of some way to be revenged on Dolores. If she herself was making this huge sacrifice, and the Irish were not saved, then murder would be too good for Josiah's wife. And then, suddenly, over Josiah's shoulder, she saw the sky light up in pink and red and glittering gold, and Corinna laughed out loud as the whole house shook.

Josiah staggered backwards. He looked at her with horrified eyes and clutched his chest, before uttering an agonised groan and sinking to the floor. In his confused and fevered state, the noise of the explosion burst upon him like the wrath of God to turn him from his great sin.

'*Buíochas le Dia!*' exclaimed Corinna. It was the only Irish Donnelly had ever taught her, and it meant Praise God.

Colonel Firth heard the explosion and, realising its cause at once, he cursed the day he had ever set foot in Tilsbury. Sir Diggory heard the noise, and was convinced his home was finally being destroyed. At the Priory House, Mabs and Bussell were so drugged with ale they had fallen asleep at the kitchen table and could have slept through Armageddon. Beth and Harry heard the noise of the blast and thought a great battle must be taking place at Furleys. Philip, as usual, slept through it all, and would be furious in the morning.

Chapter 28

❧

Stephen stood by the window of his bedchamber while a manservant packed his few possessions into a canvas bag. In the beech woods beyond the park, the first leaves were beginning to change from their tired late-summer green. He pushed the window open slightly: the early-morning air had the sharp fresh taste of September.

Stephen had said goodbye to Sir Diggory the night before. He was the last of the soldiers to leave, and Sir Diggory had made no secret of his pleasure at the farewell. The royalist officers had gone as soon as their parole was arranged, and the roundheads left, as planned, on the morning after the Irish had escaped for the second time. Various explanations were current for their miraculous deliverance. Most of the local people had no doubt that the Grey Lady herself had come to the aid of her fellow Catholics. Colonel Firth was more sceptical. He assumed the sentries had fallen into a drunken stupor and that the prisoners had been rescued by an outside accomplice. The story of the Grey Lady he considered a convenient fiction concocted to hide their crime. The sentries were placed under arrest to await their punishment at the next destination.

What that punishment was, none in Tilsbury ever knew. The soldiers and their concerns had moved on, and hardly anyone missed them. Local women were able once more to take their washing down to be beaten on the flat stones near the bend in the river: no more marching feet or rattle of drums, no more shouted orders or bursts of musket fire. So long as the war continued, Tilsbury could never entirely return to normal, but this at least was a beginning. The departing soldiers had left empty larders and silent chicken coops in their wake, and a fund of stories that would be remembered for years to come, but nothing else.

Stephen inclined to Colonel Firth's views on the escape of the Irish prisoners. Unlike the colonel, however, he cared not how they had been freed from their hellish incarceration, so long as they were at liberty. A couple of men had the misfortune to stumble on an unguarded barrel of sack and had been recaptured while too drunk to know what was happening. Both were now dead. But the rest, Donnelly and O'Rourke and a dozen others, had not been heard of since: presumably they had been able to reach one of the nearby royalist garrisons. Stephen was glad they were free at last. It was his only cause for rejoicing.

He moved away from the window. It was a sin, he knew, but many times during his slow recovery he had found himself wishing the wounds might have proved fatal. There was a dead weight of misery deep inside him that nothing, now, would ever shift. If he was faced with the same dilemma again, he knew he must act in exactly the same way, but that night when he had fought with Josiah was the bitterest of his life. Dolores had trusted him absolutely, and he had betrayed her. Dolores had trusted him . . . only he knew what that trust had meant to her. She, who had learned early in life to hold herself remote from everyone except her children and her grandmother, had given herself to him without reservation. And he had rewarded her by handing over the secret of their love to her husband. It was only too easy to imagine how Josiah was exacting his revenge.

As soon as his fever subsided, Stephen listened for any scrap of gossip, but the silence from the Priory House had been ominous and complete. Mistress Taverner was frequently seen in public; she walked each morning to the market cross with her daughter as before. Harry was soon to go away to school: it was rumoured his mother had opposed this decision, but the opinion in town was that the boy was long overdue some more rigorous education. No word of a rift between husband and wife.

Sometimes, lying awake in the still hours of the night and remembering with what happiness he had ridden to the Old Priory and made his way through the secret tunnel to her bedchamber, Stephen feared that Josiah was only waiting for him to leave Furleys before taking action against Dolores. Surely that man must know how gladly Stephen would come to her rescue and take her with him back to Cornwall.

But there was only silence. Silence, and that final image of Dolores' face when she realised he had revealed her great secret. Such a world of pain and disbelief was in her eyes – it had cut him deeper than ever Josiah's ancient broadsword could have done. In that instant he had learned that there is no defence against self-loathing for the man who has had to sacrifice the person he loves above all others.

Sometimes he prayed she had learned the necessity for his action: that the Irish were not temporary prisoners, but under sentence of certain death. But mostly he tried to persuade himself it was better if she hated him: her future was in Tilsbury with her children and Josiah. He had nothing to offer her. All he had given her was memories – and those must now be poisoned by his betrayal.

His bag was packed. He had so few possessions that the task had not taken long. He tried to rouse himself from his reverie and think instead of the future. He did not succeed: ahead of him was a succession of days filled with the knowledge that he had forfeited his only love.

Walking stiffly, for he still had difficulty bending his wounded leg, he cast a final glance around the chamber which had been his for nearly three months and, ordering his manservant to bring their horses to the back of the house, he went in search of Corinna. It was a fine morning, and he found her in the garden.

'So, Stephen, you are leaving us at last,' she took both his hands in hers, 'I think I shall probably miss you.'

'Not too much, I hope.' Stephen grinned. 'You'll no doubt find ways to keep busy,' for Corinna was rumoured to be meeting a young man who had been hired to care for her brother's hawks.

'True enough,' she agreed. 'I am not really the missing type of woman. I would advise you to follow my excellent example, but I fear you are a hopeless case. There, now you're looking all solemn and silent. In a moment you'll be telling me how you have no time and must be gone—'

'As a matter of fact . . .'

'Heavens above, Stephen, after three months a few minutes will make no difference. Tell me, have you said farewell to Dolores?'

He looked towards the distant woods. 'You know I have not seen her.'

'Nor I. I must confess I am in no hurry to visit to Tilsbury

397

again. But if you like, I'm sure I could get a message to her.'

'There is no point.'

'No?'

'No.'

Corinna made a small gesture of impatience. 'You kind-hearted honest men are always the most stubborn underneath.' She fell silent for a moment. She had never told Stephen of the extraordinary letter she had received from Dolores on the evening the Irish had made their escape. At the time, he had been too ill, and in the days that followed she endeavoured to stamp out the memory of her few hours with Josiah. She had no idea exactly what had occurred at the Old Priory that night, and she hoped sincerely her distraction of Josiah had been helpful, but she was not inclined to boast of it. On the contrary, Josiah's sense of his own corruption had made her feel unclean as never before. For days afterwards she had felt grubby and uncomfortable. She saw no reason to mention it now.

So all she said was, 'I think maybe you underestimate Dolores.'

'I can never do that,' said Stephen.

Corinna shrugged. 'Very well, then, off you go. Back to your precious Cornwall.'

'Yes.' He hesitated, still frowning. 'But what about you, Corinna? What are your plans?'

She gave him a wry smile. 'A woman in my position cannot afford the luxury of plans. I will remain here. There is no other place I may go. My father says he will arrange a divorce, he thinks I will marry again . . . but I do believe this war has ruined him. Without a dowry, I am hardly a likely bride. Maybe that is just as well. Married life did not suit me. I shall remain here . . . and amuse myself as best I can, and care for my father.'

'I can recommend you as a nurse. I doubt I'd have recovered, but for you.'

'Well . . . maybe so . . . it was no hardship, nursing you.' Stephen had taken her by the shoulders and was looking down at her, and his clear grey eyes were warm with gratitude and affection. For a brief moment Corinna wondered how it might have been if he had looked at her with love. Perhaps for a man like Stephen she would have learned to value fidelity . . . perhaps if her brother had discovered her in naked sport with Stephen rather than with Tom Rogers, and they had been obliged to marry, she might have become good, and fat, after all.

Perhaps . . . but probably not. And anyway, the speculation was oddly painful.

'You'd better be on your way,' she laughed, 'In a moment we'll start on all those ridiculous things people feel obliged to say when they know they won't see each other again.'

'Yes. I'll never come back.' He inclined slightly to kiss her forehead, but she tilted her face up and met his lips with her own.

'Let us at least say goodbye properly,' she said. 'Have I not taught you better than that?'

Stephen kissed her again. 'You were an excellent teacher, Corinna. Goodbye, then, properly goodbye.'

'That's better.'

'And thank you.' He turned away.

'For what? Stephen, wait. If I ever hear that Dolores is in trouble . . . of any kind . . . shall I tell you?'

He stopped abruptly. He was frowning. He chivvied a small pebble with the toe of his boot. 'I cannot say. Yes, of course . . . but then, what's the point?'

Still frowning, he strode away across the lawn to the stable-yard where his horse was waiting.

Corinna spent the rest of that morning alternating between a vague sense of longing and regret, and a feeling that if true love brought such sorrow in its wake, then she was better off without it.

A soft breeze was tumbling a few early leaves across their way as Stephen rode towards Tilsbury for the last time. He was headed for Bristol, so had no need to go through the town itself, only across the ford that lay near the muster ground. As he rode closer, he tried not to notice the ragged outline of the ruined priory, nor the square bulk of the Priory House standing on the very outskirts of town, nor the charred remains of Mother Crew's shack where, already, a few sparse weeds were beginning to grow: here each place held a memory and each memory, now, was painful. It was high time he was gone.

'Captain Sutton! Captain Sutton, sir!' For one bright moment Stephen thought it must surely be Beth racing over the open ground to intercept him. He thought perhaps she brought a message from Dolores. But no. Though this child was perhaps the same age as Beth, she had lanky brown hair and was wearing the sturdy dress of a yeoman's daughter.

He reined his mare to a halt. 'What is it? What's the matter?'

'You must come to the farm, Captain Sutton. There's someone to see you.'

'Someone? Who?' Again, that leap of hope.

'Cary said I must not tell you. Oh – !' The girl clapped her hand over her mouth in horror at having yielded up her precious secret so readily.

Stephen hid his disappointment under a smile. 'Cary, eh? Then you must be her sister. You'd better learn more discretion if she's going to give you important messages. There's no harm done this time, but your Cary's in a deal of trouble. Here, why not ride in front of me to the farm.'

Afraid of opening her mouth again for fear of another indiscretion, the little girl – whose name Stephen never discovered – nodded vigorously, took hold of his outstretched hand and was hauled up to sit before him. As he leaned towards her, Stephen felt a bolt of pain slice through his injured leg, and he almost fainted. It was going to be a long, slow journey back to Cornwall, and he had no wish for further delay at this stage. Especially since the way to the farm led through Tilsbury so that he must, after all, ride past the Priory House. He was tempted to hurry: the pain of his leg would be less than the pain of passing close to the house where the happiest and darkest hours of his life had been spent, but even that was not possible because of the child who sat rigid with importance in front of him. So he rode at a steady pace down the wide main street, and looked neither to right nor left and dared not even hope that Cary, when he saw her, might have a message from Dolores.

Cary had been watching for his arrival and came out of the byre as soon as he rode into the yard.

'Captain Sutton,' she was smiling broadly, 'You had my message.'

He looked at her in horror as he slid off his horse. 'Cary, your face. What happened?'

'It was when I set fire to the munitions wagon,' she said, cheerfully enough, 'I'm sure you've heard the story. I should think everyone has heard of me by now.'

'I never knew you'd been injured.'

'I did not realise myself until the next day. I was in such a fright to get away from Furleys. I believe my cap must have caught fire, my hair was all burned, but it will grow again. Mistress Taverner sent special ointments for me to the place where I was hiding, so it has healed well.'

'Mistress Taverner, that's good.'

'I did not mind about my hair. Those sentries must have been blown to kingdom come. I did hear that one of them was found the next day, still clutching hold of his arm which had been ripped off in the blast and running round in circles screaming to have it put back but he could not see because his eyes were just empty holes full of blood and—'

'Cary, that's enough now.'

It was a man's voice, an Irish voice. Stephen turned swiftly and saw Sergeant Michael O'Rourke emerge from the byre and come across the yard to shake him by the hand.

'O'Rourke, what in God's name are you doing here?'

'This and that, Captain Sutton.' O'Rourke grinned and put his arm around Cary's shoulder.

'I thought you got away. What happened?'

'I did, but I was in such poor shape I knew I couldn't have gone far. So I came here. Cary's family had shown me kindness before, and I knew they'd not betray me. But Cary had gone into hiding herself, and those roundheads were searching for her everywhere, so I could not stay. The next day her brother took me a few miles from here, to an old woman's cottage. We hid up there ever since, we both needed time to get strong again.'

'But you'll not remain here. If anyone knew—'

'They don't know the half of it,' Cary interrupted eagerly. 'Folk think all I did was to blow up a couple of wagons, but I did much more than that.'

Stephen grinned. 'Really, Cary?'

'Yes. I took the ale to the sentries at the Old Priory that made them sleep so soundly. They never guessed what was in it. If I'd had my way they'd have all died then and there, every one of them, and serve them right for laughing about the hanging. Michael and the rest would never have escaped if it hadn't been for me and—'

'That's enough, now Cary.'

Stephen, who did not believe a word of her story, told O'Rourke he should be proud of her. 'But where will you go now?' he asked.

'Anywhere we can be safe and find work and stay together,' said O'Rourke. 'Maybe Bristol first.'

'We'll not stay here,' said Cary. 'As soon as the story of what I've done becomes known, I'll be famous, I should think.

401

Someone might want to put me in a song, or something, after what we did.'

'We?' queried Stephen.

'That's enough, now, Cary,' O'Rourke warned. He alone, having recognised Mistress Taverner and heard Cary's account, had a clear understanding of the events of that night. As he never thought Mistress Taverner had any special affection for the Irish, he assumed she had acted simply from a wish to save life. He guessed that, unlike Cary, she had no desire for her heroism to be made public.

Not to be altogether thwarted, Cary changed tack. 'It was the special drops in their ale, you see, so in a way it is unfair for the sentries to be punished, but still, I'd not waste my pity on them. I have heard they were flogged until the skin came right off their backs and you could see through to—'

'That's enough,' O'Rourke said again, but he was grinning as he spoke. Stephen could imagine O'Rourke repeating his words many times, and always with scant success, while he remained with Cary. Then he added, 'We are to marry in a couple of days.'

Stephen congratulated them both. 'I'm sure you will be happy together,' he said, 'There'll always be work and a bed for you both at my father's home, at least so long as I am there.'

'We might take you up on that, Captain Sutton,' said O'Rourke.

More goodbyes, then Stephen mounted his horse and rode back towards Tilsbury once again. And as he approached the little town, the temporary cheerfulness he had felt for Cary and O'Rourke gave way to the familiar ache. He must ride within a few yards of Mistress Taverner's house, and could not even look up, could not even look to see if she was watching the road from an upstairs window.

Back at the farm, Cary was discovering the bitterness of disbelief. 'It's not fair,' she complained to O'Rourke, 'He thought I was making that up about the ale, but it was all true, every word of it.'

'I know, my love, I believe you. But you must get used to the fact that no one else will, ever.'

If she had not been so happy to have her Michael safe with her for ever more, Cary might have found it an unbearable disappointment: to have blown up two wagons of gunpowder and been responsible practically single-handed for the escape of the Irish prisoners – heavens above, what did a girl have to accomplish to become the subject of a ballad or a penny book? She was convinced there was no justice in this world at all.

Dolores had been tending the baby in one of the front bed-chambers and had seen Stephen riding past her house. She realised he must be heading for Cary's farm. She had been kept informed of Cary's whereabouts, and progress, from her sister Joan who had been little Robert's wet nurse. Though he was long since weaned, Joan still came to the Priory House once or twice a week to help Mabs with some of the heavier kitchen work; messages and medicines could be passed back and forth without risk of discovery.

That morning Dolores had been congratulating herself on the way events had turned out, but at the sight of Stephen riding down the street on his tall cob, she realised she had made one serious miscalculation. She knew him so well. As she stood by the upstairs window, little Robert stumbling over the hem of his shift as he tried to evade Ellen and the hair brush, she had only to glimpse the curve of Stephen's back, the angle of his head, the way he looked so resolutely before him to recognise the magnitude of his present pain.

'Oh Stephen,' she murmured, 'I never imagined . . .' Tears spilled out of her eyes and rolled down her cheeks. She brushed them away.

She had been so absorbed in her own concerns that she had not allowed herself to imagine what his suffering might be. Now she saw. She had known him weary, and she had known him sad, but she knew instinctively that the man she had just watched ride past the market cross and out of sight, had lost hope entirely.

She fingered the chain she wore beneath her shift, and wondered what she could do now.

Acting on an old impulse, she went down to her stillroom. Despite the shortage of sugar she had managed to put away nearly as much flower waters, pickles, jams and vinegars, perfumes and powders as usual. There was not an inch of space left on any of the shelves. She leaned back against the wide slate work top, and pondered.

The night of the Irish prisoners' escape had become a memory strange as dreams. When she overheard people speculating about the Irish prisoners' escape, she almost believed herself that it had been the phantom of the Grey Lady who had frightened the sentries away and unbolted the door. She had a clear picture in her mind of walking towards a man who held a musket in his hand and was threatening to fire at her. She had a clear memory of being without fear. When she looked back, she was unable to decide if her bravery had been a kind of madness born of fever, or whether she had, in that moment, discovered a strength greater than either weapons or magic.

The following day, when she was still weak with delayed shock, her bleeding had started. It was three weeks late, and she realised that she was not, after all, to carry Stephen's child. She told herself she was glad, but could not help weeping for the loss, all the same.

Josiah had returned from Furleys just before dawn in a state of guilty horror. He spent nearly the whole of that day on his knees in prayer and made vague references to Satan's coils and the weakness of the flesh. Dolores never asked him what had happened, and he never mentioned it again. He continued to follow her around with anxious devotion. In the world of business he was more than ever the petty tyrant, but with his wife his despotism was at an end. Very occasionally, she sang to him, or allowed him to watch her while she danced; those moments were the nearest Josiah ever came to real content.

Dolores had so many reasons for satisfaction – but she had overlooked one thing. Suddenly decisive, she took down her recipe book and thumbed through it rapidly. She tore out a page containing a recipe for wound ointment and which had white margins at the top and side. She took the quill pen she used for labelling her bottles and jars, wrote hastily, then folded and sealed the letter with warm wax. When she left her stillroom, she locked the door behind her as usual.

She hurried into the kitchen. Woodsmoke and the aroma of apples filled the air. Mabs, as so often, was flushed with the effort of doing several jobs at once.

'Where are the children?' asked Dolores, 'I thought they were in here with you.'

'I've enough to do without those troublemakers under my feet all day. I sent them out to gather windfalls with Ellen.'

Still holding the letter in her hand, Dolores went out through the back door. The high squeal of voices guided her towards the orchard. Beth and Philip were busy with an apple fight. Little Robert, determined to keep up with them, was stumbling through the long grass. Ellen was trailing round after him: her days were almost entirely devoted to him since he had begun to walk. She was beseeching the older ones to be more careful. Dolores smiled. Ellen was besotted with the baby, but quite unable to control the others.

'Oh Pip, not so fast,' she wailed, 'Beth, mind the baby . . .'

Harry was observing from his seat on a low branch of an apple tree. He would have liked to join in the fun, but was too conscious of his dignity as a young man about to leave for school to demean himself with anything so childish as an apple fight.

Philip picked up a particularly squashy windfall and aimed it at Ellen. He was a bad shot and it caught Robert squarely on the backside. The baby was thrilled at being involved in the game, and Philip and Beth howled with laughter.

Smiling, Dolores went to Harry. 'Harry,' she said, 'I have an errand for you. I believe Captain Sutton is leaving Furleys today to return to Cornwall. I saw him ride past towards Cary's farm a short while ago, but he's sure to leave on the Bristol road. Can you take this for him? It's a recipe for a wound ointment that I promised him, and then forgot about.'

Harry's laughter died abruptly. He looked up at her with round and serious eyes. Dolores felt a twinge of shame.

'Can you not give it him yourself?' he asked.

'No,' she said shortly, 'I cannot. It is only a recipe, but you know what gossips people are. Hurry, it's not so much to ask and Bonnet could use a proper ride. Give it to him by the Oxford turn – you'll be out of sight there.'

'Does Father know?'

'It hardly concerns him. You may tell him if you wish – but not until the errand is done.'

She spoke sharply to hide her unease. She had never paused to consider what her eldest child might have conjectured concerning her relations with Captain Sutton.

'So why must I be out of sight when I give it to him?' persisted Harry.

'Just do as you are told,' she said, and then she added, more gently, 'I trust you, Harry.'

He slid down off the branch, took the paper, and began to walk towards the stable. Dolores smothered her distaste at having to use her son as an intermediary. Dear God, she thought impatiently as she walked back towards the house, her children were her whole life, surely it was permissible to ask a favour like this, just once?

Putting all thoughts of the children from her mind, and thankful that Josiah was busy humiliating a local debtor in his study, she went through the house and took up a position on the front step, so she might see Stephen ride by for the very last time.

Stephen had never expected Dolores to be standing in view of the road. He had not meant to even look towards the house, but glimpsing her from a distance, he could not drag his eyes away. She stood absolutely still, her head held proudly high and her arms hanging loosely by her side. She was wearing her dress of simple grey, a white collar falling from her throat, her hair pulled back beneath her coif. Two spots of colour burned on her cheeks. She was watching him intently, but her face was without expression – or, if there was an expression, Stephen could not read it.

From behind the house came the high-pitched clamour of children's voices, then the sound of Mabs scolding the scullion and the lad's answering protests. Smoke rose in a single plume from the kitchen chimney: smell of fresh rushes, smell of beeswax, smells of the house he would never enter again. He drew in his breath, and his mare, as though sensing his intention, slowed her pace. As they drew level with the Priory House she almost came to a halt, but at the last moment Stephen squeezed his heels against her sides. He dragged his eyes away from Dolores' face as the horse moved on, gathering pace once more. Ahead of him now there was only the empty road.

As the sounds and smells of Tilsbúry faded, Stephen was suddenly reminded of the first time he had seen Dolores. Then, too, she had been standing at the edge of the road, and watching. He remembered how that frosty March morning he had thought of her as a sentinel, laying a curse on the soldiers as they approached her town. Later he had learned how mistaken he had been: she had been watching in fear and dread. As well she might, thought Stephen bitterly: the soldiers – he, in particular – had brought with them nothing but misery, misery and betrayal.

So why, he wondered, had she chosen to stand there and watch him ride away? Was it simply to make sure that the last of the hated soldiers was finally leaving? There had been triumph in the tilt of her chin, and an expression almost of serenity in her dark eyes. Perhaps she had simply wanted him to see that despite all the havoc he had brought into her life, she had survived. Her expression might have been intended to convey contempt. Stephen had betrayed her, yes, but now she was free of him, and glad.

He was so deep in thought he did not notice that for the second time that morning, his efforts to leave were being intercepted by a child. But this child was mounted on a small brown pony... this child, with his solemn, homely face and his red-brown hair, was one Stephen would have recognised anywhere.

'Harry, what are you doing here?'

'I came to say goodbye, Captain Sutton,' said Harry gruffly.

Stephen dismounted at once and, not even noticing the pain in his leg, he walked over to the boy. 'I'm glad, Harry, very glad.'

Harry reached forward and fondled Bonnet's dusty mane. He was looking straight ahead as he said, 'I'm going to school next week. And I'll have a bigger pony then. We'll keep Bonnet, of course, but Beth and Pip will ride him. I'm too grown-up for him now.'

Stephen laid his hand on Bonnet's neck. 'He's been a good pony,' he said. He recognised Harry's conflicting emotions – excitement at the prospect of a larger mount, sadness and a touch of guilt at having outgrown his first, and favourite.

'Yes,' said Harry. 'Captain Sutton, I never really said thank you for what you did. Bonnet might have become a soldier's horse if you had not saved her. I'm glad you did that. I don't think Bonnet would have liked army life.'

'No,' agreed Stephen, 'Probably not.'

'Well . . . so, thank you.' He hesitated, then glanced shyly at Stephen. 'Beth and I still talk about you sometimes . . .' Now he was frowning again and staring hard at Bonnet's ears. 'I think maybe Beth misses you a bit, sometimes. I suppose I might too . . . but of course, I'm going away next week so I'm pretty busy.'

Stephen did not speak.

'Oh yes,' said Harry at length, 'And Mother asked me to give you this. It is something to do with wound ointment, I think. I hope . . .' He had been on the verge of saying he hoped Stephen's injury was better, but he shied away from any reference to his father's treacherous attack. 'Well, goodbye then, Captain Sutton.'

'Goodbye, Harry.'

Stephen wanted to tell him to take care of his mother, but he knew he must not. The boy wheeled his pony round and rode down the narrow track that led back to Tilsbury.

The sealed paper lay in his hand, but it was a moment or two before he could bring himself to open it. Black misery was engulfing him. Now at last he understood why Dolores had chosen to watch him as he left: she was returning the chain he had given her. She was proving to him that her love had died.

Sick with foreboding, Stephen remounted slowly. He broke the seal and opened it. There was no chain. Instead, a recipe for wound ointment. The paper had been torn from some book. A message had been scrawled in Dolores' untidy writing across two margins. He read:

The Grey Lady will never return the chain you gave her unless she herself still wears it. She released the Irish to finish the work you had begun. Trust her, as she will always trust you, and God willing, I know we shall meet again one day.

He sat immobile. He stared at the piece of paper in his hand for so long that his manservant began to think he must have fallen into a trance. She was telling him she had been responsible for the release of the Irish prisoners, that she herself had impersonated a phantom in order to terrify the roundhead guards into abandoning their watch. Cary's words came back to him and he cursed himself for not having listened to her talk more closely: perhaps she had indeed, at her mistress's instruction, taken drugged ale to the Old Priory. While he was feverish and helpless, Dolores had accomplished what he had been unable to do. He wanted to shout out in triumph and admiration, he wanted to gallop down the hill to Tilsbury and tell her she was magnificent.

Now at last he knew why she had watched him as he rode past the house. Her letter told him she understood why he had betrayed the secret of the tunnel, and that she loved him still. She had stood on her front step in order to give him another picture of her, one with which to replace the image of her hatred and grief that had haunted him since the night that he and Josiah had fought.

And she told him of her faith that they would be together again one day. She too longed for their reunion. Whether it was simply optimism, or some gift of second sight inherited from Nona, he did not care. All that mattered was the hope.

He looked around him. The September woods were suddenly more beautiful than he remembered seeing in his life before. He turned for one last look at Tilsbury, church spire and market cross, the muster ground by the bend in the river, the orchards and the gardens and the ruins of the ancient priory. And then he looked at the house where he had known such happiness and such pain, and where the woman he would always love was gathering her children round her and preparing for their midday meal.

Then he turned his face to the south, and began the long ride to Cornwall, and home.